Praise for the EMILY WINDSNAP novels

'An absolutely enchanting debut – a salty splash of something fresh'   *Amanda Craig*

'... enchanting fantasy from a striking new voice'
                                        Publishing News

'The wonders of this world are described in detail, from the colours of the mermaid tails to the glowing magic of the oral reef'
                                        School Library Journal

'... a superb pre-teen read ... girls will love this ... since it's not just full of adventure and fantastical whimsy, but also has moving undertones of family and friendship throughtout'
                                    Waterstones Books Quarterly

'Light-hearted and exciting . . . rich, descriptive passages, unusual in a story for this age group, conjure a vast watery world . . . inhabited by shadowy creatures'   *Books for Keeps*

Emily Windsnap

and the
Siren's
Secret

LIZ KESSLER

Illustrations by Natacha Ledwidge

Orion
Children's Books

First published in Great Britain in 2009
by Orion Children's Books
Paperback edition first published in 2010 by Orion Children's Books
This edition published in 2012 by Orion Children's Books
Reissued in 2015 by Orion Children's Books
an imprint of Hachette Children's Group
a division of Hodder and Stoughton Limited

Carmelite House
50 Victoria Embankment
London EC4V 0DZ
An Hachette UK Company

1 3 5 7 9 10 8 6 4 2

The paper used in this paperback is a natural recyclable product made from
wood grown in sustainable forests. The manufacturing processes conform to
the environmental regulations of the country of origin.

A catalogue record for this book is available from the British Library.

ISBN: 978 1 4440 1512 6

Typeset by Input Data Services Ltd, Bridgwater, Somerset

Printed in Great Britain by Clays Ltd, St Ives plc

www.orionchildrensbooks.com

This book is dedicated to all the Emily Windsnap fans who wrote to me asking me to write a fourth book.

Thank you for being cleverer than me and knowing even before I did that Emily wanted another adventure.

All through the sunny blue-sweet hours
I swim and glide in waters green:
Never by day the mournful shores
By me are seen.

But when the gloom is on the wave
A shell unto the shore I bring;
And then upon the rocks I sit
And plaintive sing."

From The Moon Child
by Fiona Macleod

Prologue

*I*t wasn't a night for going out. Not unless you had to.

Sharp tunnels of wind whistled and shrieked around every corner. Trees bowed and shook and broke. Rain splattered viciously down at the pavements.

Out at sea, it was even worse. On the water, the storm had turned swells into walls the size of tower blocks. Waves foamed hungrily, like giant rabid dogs.

Anyone who knew about the sea knew this

meant one thing: Neptune was angry.

And anyone wild or crazy or brave enough to be out on such a night might have seen two figures in the distance, way out at sea, way beyond safe. A man leaned out from his fishing boat, calling to a woman in the water below him. 'Take it. Take it. Keep it close.'

'What is it?' the woman called back, shouting to be heard over the thunderous waves.

The man shook his head. 'I can't hear you!' Leaning further out, he added, 'When it's safe again, find me.'

'How?' she called, panic hitting her as hard as the waves that were now dragging them further and further apart.

He pointed to the parcel he had just given her. 'The shell!' she thought she heard him say, and then he added something that sounded like, 'There's magic in it.'

The woman thought about what she was leaving and the pain of it slapped against her harder than the next wave. 'What about –'

The wave washed the rest of her question away – but he knew what she was asking.

'I'll look after everything,' he called. 'Everything. Don't worry. It will be OK. Go now. Go, before it's too late.'

A moment later, the onlooker would have seen them part, each disappearing behind the hills and mountains of the raging sea. Then they would have wondered if they'd imagined the whole thing, because surely no one would go out on a night like this.

Not unless they had to.

Chapter One

I know you're going to think I'm crazy when I say this, but something about my life wasn't right.

Why does that make me crazy?

Because for the first time in my life I was living with my mum and dad, together, in our beautiful home at Allpoints Island, with my best friend Shona living just round the corner and my new friend Aaron and his mum living nearby. There was *nothing* wrong with our lives.

Really. Absolutely nothing. No dad to be rescued

from prison; no sea monsters trying to squeeze the life out of me; no storms hurling our home halfway across the planet – all of which *had* happened to me in the last year.

Now all I had was day after day filled with sun, sand, friends, laughter. My life was perfect.

So why had I woken up restless and rattled every morning for the last week? I just didn't get it.

I sat up in bed and stretched, trying to remember what I'd been dreaming about. Fragments from a jumbled mass of weird dreams chased each other round in my head but I couldn't piece them together. All I could remember was the feeling they'd left behind. Not exactly unhappy – but definitely unsettled and, well, not right.

Like I said – crazy. How could anything about my life not be right?

There was something, though, and I couldn't ignore it. What's more, I had the feeling Mum felt the same way. Once or twice, while she was making dinner or reading a book, I'd seen her eyes go all distant and grey, as though she were looking for something far away, something she was missing.

I think deep down inside, I knew what was eating at us both; I knew what we were missing, even before the conversation with Archie that changed everything.

★

'Knock knock, only me!' A familiar voice trilled through the doorway, followed by a familiar thump as Mum's best friend, Millie, landed on the deck.

Fortuna, the boat we lived on, was moored out in the bay, half sunk in the sand so that the lower level was under water. With Dad being a merman, and me being a semi-mer, this meant we could both swim around on the lower level. Mum's bedroom was upstairs, but all the trapdoors in between made it easy for us to live here together. And the long jetty leading out from the beach to the boat was handy for getting on the boat without having to swim – which made it very easy for Millie to visit us without getting more than her feet wet.

She stuck her head round the door. 'Anyone home?'

I dragged myself out of bed and over to the door. Rubbing my eyes, I gestured for her to come in. Not that she needed an invitation. She'd already clambered in through the door and was busily wringing out the bottom of her dress over the side.

'Mum up?' she asked.

I rubbed my eyes and yawned. 'Not yet, I don't think. Why?'

'Someone's coming home!' she said excitedly. 'I just heard it on the seaweed vine.'

'The seaweed vine?'

'Just trying to keep up with the mer-speak,' Millie said, frowning. 'I meant I heard it on the grapevine. Archie's back today!'

That was when I noticed her face. Well, obviously I'd already noticed her face. I was looking straight at it. But I noticed what was on it. Bright blue eyeshadow arching high over each eye, and a thick red line of lipstick smeared across her mouth – and a few teeth. I pointed this out and she peered into the mirror by the door.

'It'sh been nearly tcho weeksh,' she said, wiping lipstick off her teeth with the edge of her sleeve. 'I've misshed him sho much!'

Archie is Millie's boyfriend. He's a merman and he'd been away on an assignment for Neptune.

'Is that Millie?' Mum's voice warbled out from her room. 'Come on in Mill, and stick the kettle on while you're passing.'

I left them to it.

Half an hour later, Mum was dressed and sitting upstairs with Millie in the saloon – that's what you call the living room on a boat. I wanted to go out and play with Shona and Aaron, but Mum said we should all wait with Millie; she was far too excitable to be left on her own.

I waited downstairs with Dad. We had a gymnastics day coming up soon at school and he was helping me with a tricky triple back spin that I had to do as part of the display. I could do two spins perfectly but couldn't manage the third without swallowing a gallon of water.

I was just recovering from my fourth attempt when there was a sharp rap at the door.

'Archie!' I exclaimed.

'I doubt it, little 'un. When did Archie ever knock?'

I laughed. Archie was much more likely to turn up at one of the portholes. Mermen don't usually walk up to the front door.

We both poked our heads up through the trapdoor to see who it was. Mum was answering the door. 'Charles,' she said crisply. 'How nice to see you.'

Mr Beeston. Not exactly our best friend. Well, someone who's spent your entire life lying to you about who you really are, drugging you so you won't remember the truth and spying on you so he can report back to Neptune on your activities doesn't tend to fill your heart with love and warmth, in my experience.

However, after our latest batch of disasters, Neptune had made us all promise to put the past behind us and start afresh. So we'd been trying our best to be friendly and polite ever since.

Mum held the door open for him. 'Why don't you join us?' she said. 'We're just having a cup of tea.'

'Well I, I mean, I don't want to, you know,

I wouldn't like to be in your way,' he stammered, but came in anyway and sat down on the little sofa in the middle of the saloon.

'Hello, Emily,' he said, nodding at me and flattening his hair down.

'Hi,' I said and turned to swim back down, but Dad gave me a nudge.

'Go on up, now; you need to be polite, remember,' he said under his breath.

With a sigh, I pulled myself up through the trapdoor. As I did, I felt the familiar tingling feeling in my tail. Sitting on the side, I watched it flap and wave in the water. The tingling grew stronger, the purply green shimmer faded, my tail stiffened – and then it melted away and my legs emerged. I rubbed the tingle away. It always gave me pins and needles changing back from being a mermaid and my legs were wobbly for a moment, so I didn't stand up straight away.

'I believe Archieval is due back today,' Mr Beeston was saying to Mum as I dangled my legs over the trapdoor. He'd obviously been listening to the grapevine, too. That didn't surprise me. He always seemed to find out what was going on. Probably had spies working for him all over the place.

I knew we were meant to be friends now, but I still didn't trust him and I didn't see how Mum and Dad could be so happy to forgive and forget.

'So I've heard,' Mum said. Millie had got up to check herself out in the mirror again. She pulled at her hair and straightened her dress and was getting her lipstick out of her bag again when there was a noise downstairs.

'That's him!' Millie squeaked. 'He's back!'

We all raced over to the trapdoor and looked down. Sure enough, two seconds later Archie appeared in the large porthole that we use as the downstairs door. He looked up. Grinning broadly, he flicked his dark hair off his face and swam across to the trapdoor. 'Hello all,' he said, looking straight at Millie.

Mum laughed. 'Right, come on, let's get a cup of tea and leave the lovebirds to it,' she said.

Mr Beeston gave Archie a quick nod. 'Good to see you back, Archieval,' he said before following Mum into the kitchen.

'Mine's an Earl Grey,' Millie called over her shoulder, without taking her eyes off Archie for a second.

'So let me get this straight,' Dad said as we gathered outside. Archie and Dad were in the water next to the boat, the rest of us sitting on the front deck. 'You've been in *Brightport* for the last two weeks?'

Brightport was my home. Well, I should say my

old home. It's where I'd spent all my life up until we moved to Allpoints Island – the only place in the world where humans could officially live alongside merpeople. In other words, the only place in the world where my mum and dad could live together. It's the swishiest place ever, and you couldn't want to live anywhere more perfect – but when my dad said the word 'Brightport' I suddenly got a dull ache in my stomach.

'That's right,' Archie replied. 'I didn't realise that was where the assignment was till we were almost there.'

Mr Beeston nodded seriously. 'Well, you know how important it is to Neptune to keep his assignments top secret. That's how it's always been in *my* experience of working alongside the king,' he said importantly.

Archie ignored him and carried on. 'Cranes and diggers had been spotted at the edge of the town, very close to our merfolk area just off the coast. Shiprock folk were getting scared and Neptune sent us to find out what was going on.'

There it was again, the pain in my stomach, only it was even sharper this time. Shiprock was the merfolk town where Shona used to live. Where I'd first gone to mermaid school. Just the mention of the place was enough to give me a funny twinge; the fact that something might be going wrong there made it twice as bad.

'So what did you find?' Dad asked.

'Most of the activity is on land so we were fairly limited. But we managed to discover that it's Brightport Council who are behind it.'

'What are they doing?' asked Mum.

Archie looked at her. 'Well, that depends who you ask. According to the enormous billboards that you can see from about a mile out at sea, they're "developing unused wasteland". But if you ask any of the merfolk at Shiprock, they're about to bulldoze the whole town to smithereens.'

'What d'you mean?' I asked. 'They can't destroy Shiprock, can they?'

'Depends how far they develop, and how many more cranes and diggers they bring out there. They're dangerously close as it is and their work is causing problems in the sea nearby. There've been daily landslides on the outskirts of Shiprock. Two families have already lost their homes. The whole of Shiprock could collapse if those builders get greedy and try to "develop" further into more of our town.'

'But that's terrible!' I said. I thought of the merpeople I'd seen and met in Shiprock, the school, all the kids, the parents, the old folk.

'It certainly is,' Archie agreed. 'The townsfolk are preparing for disaster as far as they can. Leaders are discussing plans for a major evacuation if needed, but they don't want to cause unnecessary panic. No one knows exactly what Brightport Council have in mind, how far they plan to develop, so it's hard for them to make a plan.'

'Can't Neptune do something?' Mum asked.

'Neptune's put the area on high alert,' Archie replied. 'That means the town will have a unit there at all times, to watch what's going on. Beyond that, there's not much he can do.'

'Not much he can do?' I spluttered. 'We *are* talking about the same Neptune? He's more powerful than anyone!'

'Anyone in the *ocean*,' Archie corrected me. 'On land, he has no power to stop anyone doing anything. All he can do is monitor the situation and decide what kind of response to make, and when to make it.'

'How come you've come back here, then?' Mr Beeston butted in. 'Aren't you deserting your post? If Neptune has decreed that you are needed there at all times –'

'Neptune has decreed that *someone* is needed there at all times,' Archie went on. 'But we need a unit that is capable of getting into more of the area than we can access on our own. I have a few contacts on land, but no one who can really find out what's going on. No one with any influence.'

'So you're not going back?' Millie asked, a slight quiver in her voice.

Archie grinned at her. 'Not yet, I'm not. For one

thing, Neptune prefers me to be at Allpoints Island and keep an eye on things here. And for another – well, we need someone different from me. Someone who can gain access to areas that I can't.' He turned to Mr Beeston. 'Someone like you.'

'Someone like me?' Mr Beeston asked. His face turned crimson as he brushed some invisible dust off his collar. 'Well, of course, with an operation of such importance, Neptune is bound to ask for the most highly skilled, professional team on board, and I have to say, though not greatly surprised, I am flattered and –'

'What I mean is, we need a semi-mer,' Archie said, interrupting Mr Beeston in the middle of what was starting to sound like an acceptance speech for a grand award.

Mr Beeston is like me. Half mer, half person. I didn't know it until a few months ago – but then I didn't know it about myself, either, until I went swimming with school for the first time.

'We need someone who has access to the human world as well as the mer world,' Archie went on.

Mr Beeston sniffed and examined his collar again. 'So it's not the years of loyalty, highly skilled work and dedicated training that you're after? It's the fact that I've got legs,' he said.

'And a tail,' I put in. He gave me a look of scorn.

Archie reached into the bag slung by his side and pulled something out. 'Look, it's not just that,' he said. 'You're wanted there.' He passed a bundle of papers on to the deck.

Mr Beeston picked it up. 'What's this?'

'One of my fisherman contacts smuggled it out to me,' Archie said. 'Read it.'

Mr Beeston unfolded the papers. 'It's just a list of names,' he said.

'Read the sentence at the top.'

Mr Beeston cleared his throat. 'We, the undersigned, believe important jobs should be operated by people, not computers. Don't let hi-tech development get out of hand. Reinstate the lighthouse keeper! Bring back Mr Beeston!'

Mr Beeston flicked through the pages of names. 'Well, I –' he began. 'I mean, I –' He looked up at Archie. 'This isn't a joke?'

Archie shook his head.

'The people of the town want me back?'

Archie nodded.

'And Neptune needs me?'

'He does.'

Mr Beeston pulled himself up straighter and higher. 'Well, then,' he said. 'I cannot let them down. I must return to Brightport.'

Which was the exact moment I realised why I'd been having bad dreams every night and waking up sad every morning – and why my insides had ached at the mention of Brightport.

I was homesick. It was as simple as that.

Mum turned to Dad. 'Jake,' she said. 'I – I –'

Dad swam over to the side and reached up to take her hand. I looked at Mum's face and I recognised the look in her eyes. It was saying the same thing as mine. It had been saying the same thing all along. These last few weeks when I'd caught her staring into the distance – I suddenly realised what it was she was searching for, what she was missing.

'She wants to go home,' I said.

Dad glanced at me. 'We are home, little 'un,' he said with a quick laugh. Then he turned to Mum. 'Aren't we?'

Before she could answer, Archie broke in. 'There's something else,' he said. 'I didn't know how to ask, but maybe this is a good time.'

Dad turned to him. 'What is it?'

'Neptune wants a team. If there's going to be trouble, he needs more than just one of us there. Beeston is a good choice for keeping Shiprock under control, and his contacts make him ideal for getting information on the Brightport side of things, especially using the lighthouse keeper cover again.'

Mr Beeston shuffled and flattened his hair down. Before he could launch into another Oscars acceptance speech, Archie added, 'I put your name forward as his assistant.'

'Me?' Dad asked. 'Neptune would put *me* in a

position of responsibility, after – well, after where I've been?'

Dad's not a criminal or anything, but he was sent to prison for marrying my mum. Intermarriage between merpeople and humans used to be highly illegal. But not any more. In fact, Neptune had now decided he wanted to bridge the gap between humans and merpeople – and he'd decided we were the ones to help him.

He'd told us we had to bring the two worlds together, get humans and merpeople to live in peace. And that was another thing: how could we change the world so that humans and merpeople lived in peace together if we were living out here in the one bit of the world where they already did? Everything was pointing to the same conclusion: we *had* to go back to Brightport.

Archie was still talking to Dad. 'Neptune doesn't hold on to the past,' he was saying. 'He knows you are loyal and dependable.'

'And married to a human,' Dad said.

'Exactly. That's the whole point. One of you to find out more about what's going on with the Brightport folk and one of you keeping an eye on things in Shiprock. Between you two and Beeston, we might just be able to avert a major disaster for the entire town.'

'You're not asking me to spy on my old friends, are you?' Mum asked.

'Not at all! Beeston and Jake will do most of the work. Just keep your eyes and ears open, in case you hear anything that the others miss; anything that could be a problem for the mer community at Shiprock. If anyone else needs to be rehoused, we'd rather they know in advance, so they can get all their belongings and move of their own accord, rather than wake up one morning to a bulldozer in their front cave.'

'Do you think that could really happen?' Mum asked.

'Absolutely. And I'll tell you something else: if another house is destroyed, folk there will *really* start to panic. Neptune doesn't like being in a position like this, where he has no control over what's going on. He's not used to it. If these plans cause more problems, he might decide to exhibit his power by ordering a full-scale evacuation – and most folk are *desperate* to avoid that.'

Dad looked up at Mum. 'What do you think?'

Mum chewed slowly on a thumb nail. 'I think we've been told to find ways to bring the human and the mer worlds together,' she said. 'If the human world is doing something that could threaten merpeople, then it's our duty to stop that from happening.'

Dad reached up and took her hand. 'I agree,' he said. 'This could be our first chance to start putting into practice the instructions that Neptune gave us.'

'Exactly. That's what Neptune said, too.'

Dad looked at Archie. 'What do you mean? What did he say?'

'That it was time you got on with your task. He said to tell you this was an opportunity to prove to him that he picked the right family for the job. He said it would be your first test.'

Dad puffed his chest out and nodded firmly. 'That's decided it, then,' he said. 'We don't have a choice.'

I felt a bubble of excitement rise through my body, tickling my insides and snaking up through my throat. 'We're going back to Brightport?' I asked, holding my breath while I waited for their answer.

Mum and Dad looked at each other and nodded. Then Mum turned to me. 'Yes, darling,' she said, with the first smile I'd seen on her face in days. 'We're going home.'

Chapter Two

*I*t was only once we'd decided to go back to
Brightport that I realised how much I'd been
missing it. It was as if a part of me had known all
along that I wanted to go home, but I'd tried to
ignore it because I didn't think it was a possibility.
Now I knew it was definitely happening, I couldn't
wait to get going.

I just had two problems. Shona and Aaron.

Shona was my best friend. I met her when I first
discovered that I became a mermaid when I went
in water. We'd been best friends ever since and she

and her parents had come to Allpoints Island at the same time as us. The idea of leaving her behind – well, it was unthinkable.

I'd only met Aaron recently. He was a semi-mer like me. Apart from Mr Beeston, he was the only one I'd ever met – and Mr Beeston didn't count, as far as I was concerned. Aaron and his mum used to live in a spooky castle out in the middle of the ocean. It was after Aaron and I overturned Neptune's curses by bringing his old wedding rings together that Neptune told us all to go off and try to bring the two worlds closer: the thing that we hadn't got round to doing, yet.

The thing that we were hopefully going to start once we got back to Brightport. Our first test.

The only problem was, I couldn't imagine doing anything if I didn't have Shona with me, never mind passing an important test set by Neptune! She'd shared every adventure I'd had so far. And Aaron – well, I don't know if it was because of us both being semi-mers or because of what we'd been through together, but I couldn't imagine leaving him behind, either.

I swam around in the downstairs part of the boat, back and forth from bow to stern, trying to think. What was I going to do? Five minutes ago, I'd been giddy with excitement at the prospect of going home; now I felt I was being torn in two.

I was about to let the miserable half win when a familiar voice called from outside the boat. I swam over to the porthole. Shona! She'd cheer me up; she always did.

Except that one look at her face made me think this time might be different.

'Shona, what is it?' I asked as she swam into the boat, a couple of silver fish swimming in with her, their sides glinting in the sunlight like shiny new coins.

'Oh, Emily! We just had some news from Archie.'

'About Brightport?' I asked. So she'd already heard we were leaving. That explained her miserable face.

Her eyes widened. 'How do you know so soon?'

'He's just been here. He told us all about what's going on there and –'

'Oh, Emily, I'm going to miss you so much!'

'I know,' I said. 'Me too. But we'll be able to keep in touch, won't we? We'll find a way.'

Shona nodded as she gulped back a tear. 'I hope so. I just hate the thought of being so far away from you.'

'I hate it, too.' I tried to think of something positive to say. I couldn't bear seeing Shona so unhappy. 'Perhaps you'll be able to come over to Shiprock some time?'

Shona frowned. 'Huh? What do you mean?'

'Well, you know. Maybe you could come for a visit. I mean, I know it's thousands of miles away from here but –'

'Emily, that's what I've been trying to tell you! That's what I'm so upset about – we're going back to Shiprock!'

I gawped at Shona. '*You're* going back? But –'

'Archie dropped a letter off for us from my Auntie Corella. She says that there's been a disturbance of some sort. I don't know what it is exactly but she's really worried about her home. She says they all are. Mum says we have to go back. Oh Em, I'm going to miss you so much!'

I grinned. 'No you're not!' I said.

'What d'you mean? How can you say that?'

I flicked my tail and swam a full circle round her. Then, grabbing her hands, I burst out laughing. 'Because we're going, too!'

Shona stared at me. 'Really?' she asked. 'You're not pulling my tail?'

'Promise!'

Shona squeezed my hands. 'Emily, that's sooooooo swishy!' she said, swimming up and down in a bouncy dance. 'I'm so happy! Are you?'

'Totally!' I said. And I almost completely meant it. There was only *one* problem now; only one thing stopping me from being as happy as Shona was about her news. I still had to leave Aaron behind.

'Dad says we should be ready to leave by the end of the week.'

Aaron and I were sitting out on our front deck in the sunshine. Dad was out with Archie and Mr Beeston getting our travel plans sorted. Mum and Aaron's mum had become really good friends since we'd all been back here, and they'd gone out for a walk on the beach.

I stole a quick glance at Aaron. He was looking out to sea and hadn't responded yet.

'Which means that by next week we'll be gone,' I went on. Still no response. 'For good,' I added, in case he hadn't quite got what I was telling him. That from next week we'd probably never see each other again.

He turned to me and smiled. 'OK,' he said.

OK? That was *it*? So he *had* understood what I was saying – he just wasn't bothered.

Fine, then. Nor was I.

'So maybe I'll see you again before then, and maybe I won't,' I said casually. 'Anyway, have a nice life, if not,' I added, getting up to go. I'm not sure where I thought I was going. I think I was hoping he'd call me back before I had to worry about that.

Which, thankfully, he did.

25

'Emily!' Aaron grinned up at me and patted the deck beside him. 'Sit down.'

I sat down and folded my arms.

'I was just teasing you,' he said.

'What do you mean?'

'Acting like I'm not bothered about you leaving.'

I shrugged.

'I mean, to tell the truth, I'm *not* bothered,' he went on.

I rolled my eyes and shrugged again. 'Me neither,' I said. 'I was only letting you know to be polite.'

Aaron burst out laughing. 'Emily! Don't you get it? The reason I'm not bothered is because we're coming too!'

I stared at him, forcing my face not to register any response in case he was teasing me again.

'Honestly,' he said, reading my mind in that way that usually only Shona does.

I unfolded my arms, unshrugged my shoulders and realised I was smiling. 'How come?' I asked.

'Your mum came over last night and told us your plans, and Mum and I decided on the spot that we're coming with you.'

'But why?' I asked. 'Aren't you happy here?'

'Course we are!' Aaron said. 'How could anyone not be happy here? Just –' He stopped. His pale cheeks showed a hint of pink.

'Just what?' I asked.

'Well, you know ...' he said, turning away to

pick at a loose bit of wood on the deck. 'After everything you've done for us. For my mum, really. She'd be lost without your mum.'

'Oh, right,' I said. So it was only his mum who wanted to come with us.

'And anyway,' he mumbled, 'it wouldn't be the same here without you.'

I grinned. 'Really?'

He looked up and grinned back. 'Really!'

I got up from the deck and skipped over to the jetty. 'Come on,' I said, stepping into the sea. My toes tingled instantly, tickling all the way up my legs as my tail started to spring into life. 'Let's go tell Shona. Race you to the beach.'

'Make sure you visit soon, won't you?' Mum said, gulping back a tear. She wiped her eyes with the back of her hand.

Millie blew her nose loudly into a huge hanky, then stuffed it back into her pocket. She'd decided to stay at Allpoints Island to be with Archie. She said two weeks apart had been more than enough and she wasn't doing it again. If he was needed here then she needed to be here with him. It was quite sweet, really. 'I'll visit so often you'll be sick of me,' she said, with an attempt at a smile. Her lips wobbled and smudgy mascara lines wriggled down her cheeks.

'We could never be sick of you!' Mum said.

Millie squeezed Mum's hand one more time, then she reached out for me. 'Come on you, give me a big hug.' She folded me into her arms and gripped me so hard I thought I was going to suffocate.

Just then, Dad called from the water. He and Mr Beeston were going to swim alongside us to begin with, just till we got out of the bay and through the edge of the Bermuda Triangle. After that, Archie had arranged for a group of Neptune's dolphins to take us all back with *Fortuna*.

Archie was untying the ropes now. He was coming along for the first bit, too. He gave Millie a kiss and gently wiped her cheek with his hand – getting mascara all over his palm. 'Back soon,' he said.

And then we were off. Out on the open sea again. Heading home to Brightport.

Chapter Three

I didn't know what to expect as we approached Brightport. Half of me imagined it would have changed completely. The other half expected everything to be exactly as we'd left it. It was more than six months since we'd gone and so much had happened in between, it was hard to believe we were really going to be back there at all.

But we were. I could see the town in the distance as the dolphins pulled us towards the bay. Gradually coming into view: the harbour where Mum and I used to live on our boat, *The King of the Sea*; the line of shops and guest houses lining the promenade; the pier with the amusement arcade at the end of it that Mandy Rushton's parents owned.

Mandy Rushton. I hadn't thought of her for ages and I couldn't hold back a queasy feeling in my stomach when I thought of her now. She'd bullied and taunted me for years. But when we met at Allpoints Island this year, we became friends again, like we had been when we first knew each other. The only problem was, Neptune had put a memory drug on her and her parents when they left the island, because of all the things they'd seen. Now I didn't know if she'd remember that we'd made friends or if that memory had been wiped away, along with the mermaids and the sea monster.

I'd find out soon enough.

Aaron joined me on the deck. 'What's that?' he asked, pointing a little further round the bay at an enormous tangle of hoops in the sky. I'd never seen it before, but Archie had told us about it.

'It's the kraken,' I said.

Aaron's eyes widened.

'Not the actual kraken itself, obviously,' I laughed. 'It's a rollercoaster ride, part of the new theme park Mandy's parents built this year.'

'Cool!' Aaron said, with a self-conscious glance at me. He'd picked up words like 'cool' and 'swishy' from Shona and me – except he hadn't quite mastered the art of sounding natural with it. Having lived in a castle cut off from the entire world for his whole life, there were still things that he had never done before, like get excited about stupid things with other kids, or go on rollercoaster rides. So he didn't quite have the language for it yet.

Just then, Dad poked his head out from the water. He and Mr Beeston were pulling us into the bay. We all agreed it would be less conspicuous than a whole load of magical dolphins dragging a big, weird-looking yacht behind them. We didn't want to attract too much attention before we'd even arrived.

'Nearly there now,' he called up to me. 'Go tell your mum to get ready to land. We'll be mooring on one of the far jetties off the pier – near where you used to live on *King*.'

With one last glance at the approaching coastline, I hurried indoors. Butterflies were chasing each other round and round in my stomach now. What would be in store for us here? Would things work out or would it be a massive disaster?

There was no turning back now. One way or another, we were about to find out.

'Well, Jake wants her to go to Shiprock School of course, but I think she should go back to Brightport

High.' Mum was pouring a cup of tea for herself and Aaron's mum as the two of them discussed the ins and outs of our new life.

Aaron and I were playing chess at the table. He'd taught it me recently. He'd spent years learning but never had anyone to play against. He was winning. He always did – apart from when he pretended not to have noticed a really good move so he could let me win.

He and his mum were staying in one of the cottages on the beach front. They were converted fishermen's huts, so they were all quite tiny, and had a slight smell of haddock about them, but they cost a fortune to rent out in high season. Mr Beeston had had a word with one of his old fisherman contacts and managed to get it cheap for a few weeks, just till the season began.

'I don't know what to do about Aaron,' his mum replied. 'I mean, mer-school would make sense in a way, but then it might be nice for him to get a chance to mix with normal boys his age, too.'

She glanced over at us. 'I mean, human boys,' she added quickly.

Aaron put down the bishop he'd been holding. I was quite glad, actually, as I think he'd been about to take my queen with it. 'Has anyone thought to ask us what *we* want?' he said, echoing the question that had been in my mind all the time they'd been talking.

'It's us who'll have to go there,' I added, 'so shouldn't we have some say?'

'Of course you'll have some say,' Mum replied, a bit sharply. 'But we're the ones who will have to make the final decision.'

'Why?' I asked.

'Because we're your parents,' Mum snapped. Maybe I was embarrassing her by arguing with her in front of Aaron and his mum, but I didn't care. It was my life they were talking about, mine and Aaron's, and it wasn't fair that they got to make all the decisions.

'Are you the ones who got bullied at school last year?' I asked, irritation heating my cheeks. 'Are you the ones who only recently discovered a whole new self and for the first time in your lives had the chance to go to school with others like you? Are you the ones who will live our lives and know what we're going to do with them?'

All three of them were staring at me now, mouths open, eyes round and wide. I felt like I'd reached the important bit of a rousing speech, but I didn't know what came next. Luckily, Aaron stepped in.

'Look, you're right,' he said to the others. 'This is an important decision. So why don't we take it gradually?' He looked round at all three of us. 'How about a compromise? What if we go to Shiprock School for what's left of the summer term, while we all find our fins in Brightport, and then

33

discuss it again in the summer holidays?'

Mum and Aaron's mum looked at each other. 'I suppose there are only a few weeks left of term,' Mum said.

'And it *would* give us time to think about what to do in the long run,' Aaron's mum added.

Mum looked at me. 'We'll have to see what your dad says first.'

I laughed. There was no way Dad would say I should go to Brightport High. That was settled, then. I was going to mermaid school again! And, even better, in a few days Shona would be there too. As I felt my whole body relax, I realised how much I'd been worrying about the idea of going back to Brightport High. I wasn't ready to exchange the life we'd had at Allpoints Island for one where I got taunted and bullied – not yet.

Aaron moved his knight. 'Checkmate,' he said. 'You lose, sorry.'

But he was wrong. I hadn't lost anything. I was back in Brightport and was about to go to mer-school with my two best friends. 'No I don't,' I said, grinning at him. 'I win!'

Arriving at Shiprock School, we felt like celebrities. It seemed half the school was crowded around us.

34

Most of them went straight to Shona – hugging her and squealing with delight when she said she was back to stay. When she explained who we were, they fell on us too, firing questions and welcoming us to the school. A million light years from the kind of reception I'd been dreading at Brightport High! This was *definitely* where we belonged.

The school bell rang and we followed everyone to the lines that led inside.

A couple of boys dragged Aaron off to his line.

'See you at lunch time,' I called. As he was a couple of years older than Shona and me, he was in a different class. I pointed to the other side of the playground. 'Meet you over there at Shining Rock.'

Aaron nodded and swam off. It felt weird watching him swim away. We'd hardly spent a moment apart since we'd been back in Brightport.

'Come on, you'll see him in about two hours.' Shona pulled at my arm. 'Think you can survive till then?'

'Course I can!' I replied, forcing a laugh out. 'I'm not, I mean it's just –'

'Anyway, it'll be nice for us to have some time on our own together,' she said. 'It feels like we haven't done that for ages.'

'Yeah,' I said. Aaron swam up to the edge of a tunnel and looked round. He gave a quick wave and I waved back before he disappeared inside.

Shona sighed dramatically.

'I'm just concerned for him,' I said. 'He's never been to school before, that's all.'

'Mm, yes, right. Whatever,' Shona said. Then she swam off. 'I'm going to class anyway.'

'Hey! Wait for me!' I spun my tail and swam over to catch up with her and join the line heading to our class. We chased each other in between the rocks, darting through hordes of white fish that were sprinkled all around us, so tiny they looked like falling snowflakes. We laughed and teased each other all the way, just like old times.

Except, as it turned out, it wasn't going to be anything like old times. And quite soon, we weren't going to have anything to laugh about, either.

Shona, Aaron and I ate our lunch at Shining Rock and exchanged notes about our first morning. Aaron's eyes shone with excitement. He'd had Shipwreck Studies first thing and he was buzzing from all the new things he'd learned.

We'd had Beauty and Deportment – Shona's favourite subject. We'd been decorating hairbrushes and Shona and I had done matching crescent moons and stars on ours. Shona loves anything to do with acting like a siren. She wants to be one when she grows up. Her favourite thing in the world is singing, which is what being a siren is all about.

'Where does this rock lead to?' Aaron asked, looking up. It was tall, like an obelisk, and it was called Shining Rock because of the light that shone on it, making it the brightest part of the playground.

'It goes right up to the top,' Shona replied. 'It's the only part of the school that breaks the surface of the water.'

'Swishy!' Aaron said, and Shona and I both laughed. He ignored us. 'Can we see?' He started swimming upwards.

Shona glanced down at the seabed below us. This was the only part of the school where you could see the time. An old ship's anchor had been turned into a sundial and the light caught it all the way through the school day.

'We've got about half an hour,' she said. 'But it's out of bounds up there. We should really be –'

I looked round. 'No one's watching,' I said, flicking my tail into action and following Aaron upwards. His enthusiasm had caught hold of me, too. 'Can't we check it out? Just quickly.'

Shona shook her head and smiled. 'You're a bad influence!' she said. 'Come on then.'

I smiled back at her. Shona can't resist an adventure any more than I can.

We swam up for about five minutes, feeling our way along the rock and shielding our eyes from the

37

light that was getting brighter and brighter. An orange fish with a splodge of bright blue eyeshadow above each eye stared blankly ahead as we swam past it. A long, green and black fish swam with us, edging upwards in short staccato bursts. Finally, we reached the surface. The rock burst through the top of the ocean, piercing it like a rocket breaking through clouds.

Above the surface, the rock was jagged and hilly. It felt as though we'd reached the surface of the moon. Aaron pulled himself out of the water and sat on the edge of the rock. As he did, his tail flapped and flickered, then disappeared. He rubbed his legs and stood up, reaching down to pull me on to the rock.

As I sat on the side, waiting for my legs to come back, Shona swam up to meet us. She perched on the edge of the rock. 'Hey, don't go disappearing off, will you? You know I can't join you out there!'

'We won't,' I said, getting up and climbing further up the rock.

'We're just going to have a quick look round the other side,' Aaron added. 'Back in two minutes.'

Which is honestly what we were planning to do, and exactly how long we were planning to take doing it – before Aaron slipped and trapped his leg.

'YOUCH!!'

I heard him yell from the other side of a jagged peak and clambered over to him. Aaron was lying on his side clutching his leg.

'Are you OK?'

'It's stuck. I can't move.'

I edged down the rock. His leg was jammed into a tiny crevice between two overhanging slabs of rock. 'My foot slipped,' he said.

I tried to push the rock away from his leg but it wouldn't move. I pulled on his leg.

'Arrgh! Don't do that!'

'What are we going to do?' I asked.

'*Emily! Aaron!*' Shona was calling from the other side of the rock. 'We need to be heading back. We're not even meant to come up here during school.'

'You go,' Aaron said. 'No point in all of us getting in trouble.'

I shook my head. 'I'm not leaving you.'

'Emily?' Shona called again.

I ran back to the top of the rock. 'Aaron's stuck,' I said. I was about to tell her to go back to school when we heard voices coming from below us.

Before we had time to do anything, a head appeared next to Shona. Or, to be more precise, the headteacher's head. Mrs Sharktail. I hadn't met her yet but I'd heard enough about her to know that you didn't want to get on her bad side. We were due to have a meeting with her in the morning. It should have been today, but she had important visitors so couldn't see us.

It looked like she was with the important visitors now. Two mermen and a mermaid, all wearing smart suits and sharp frowns.

'Now, this is where we had the minor landslide,' she was saying. 'About five days ago. You can see –' She suddenly stopped. I looked down. She'd spotted Shona!

'Shona Silkfin! What on earth are you doing out here?' Mrs Sharktail snapped.

'It's my fault,' I cut in quickly. I wasn't having Shona get into trouble on her first day back here, especially when she'd been trying to get us to go back down. 'I wanted to come up. Shona didn't want to.'

The head teacher squinted up at me. 'You'll be the new girl, I take it?' she asked. She opened her mouth to say something else, but suddenly clapped a hand across it and gasped in horror. With the other hand she was pointing – at my legs. 'What are *those*?' she cried with about as much disgust as if I'd had giant spiders crawling out of every pore.

I had the feeling I might have just discovered the bad side we'd been told to avoid.

'Um. They're my –' I tried to think of another word for legs, one that might have been more acceptable to her.

I didn't have to try for very long. Before I finished

my sentence, Aaron came running over the top of the rock. 'I got free!' he called, beaming. Then he saw Mrs Sharktail and the smile disappeared off his face as rapidly as if it had been washed away by a freak wave.

She took one look at him and gasped again. 'Both of you – my office now!' was all she said, before disappearing back below the surface, her visitors scurrying off with her.

Aaron clambered back into the water. 'What have we done?' he asked.

'Apart from come out here, you mean?' I said.

Shona shook her head. 'I think there may be more to it,' she said.

'What?' I asked.

'It's this place. The rules. The stupid rules.'

I jumped into the water. I hardly noticed the tingling feeling as my tail shimmered and shook and came to life. I was too worried about the tone of concern in Shona's voice. 'Shona, what is it?' I asked. 'Tell me!'

'No humans allowed at the school,' she said simply.

'But we're not complete humans,' Aaron said. 'We're merpeople when we're in water.'

'I know. And that might have been OK a while ago. But things have changed round here. My aunt was telling me last night. I don't know why I didn't think of it.'

'Think of what?' I asked.

'They're tightening the rules everywhere, becoming more anti-human.'

'But we're not –' Aaron began.

'I know,' Shona said again. 'But I bet I know what they've done. Mrs Sharktail's always wanted to do it, but the school council have never agreed to it. They said it was unnecessary. But the latest events will have been just what she needed to get her way.'

'Get her way with what?' Aaron asked.

'With her plans to make the school stricter,' she said darkly. 'If I'm right, I bet you anything the school's just got a new rule.'

'What rule?' I asked, although a part of me knew what she was going to say. I just couldn't help hoping I was wrong.

Shona looked at me almost guiltily before confirming my suspicion. 'No semi-mers.'

'Now, children, I would like you all to listen very carefully, and watch closely.' Mrs Sharktail had cancelled afternoon lessons and gathered the whole school together in the main chamber for a special afternoon assembly.

I was guessing we were the 'special' bit.

I looked round. A hundred mergirls and -boys looked back at me. I tried not to meet anyone's eyes, focusing instead on the pillars all around us, the light glinting in shiny purples and greens on the water, the rocks and boulders lining the sides of the chamber.

'As you know, this is a traditional mer-school,' Mrs Sharktail went on. 'We have traditional rules and we teach you, to the best of our ability, in all things mer, so that you may all grow up to be wonderfully gifted, competent and happy merpeople. Is that not true, staff?'

She looked across to the teachers lined up along one side of the chamber. They all nodded fervently back at her.

'I'm sure all of you are aware that our community here at Shiprock has recently been under threat from *humans*.'

I don't know if it was just me but I was sure she said the word 'humans' as though something disgusting had got stuck in her throat.

'They are hovering around the edges of Shiprock, barging into areas that don't belong to them and are one step away from breaking into our town like burglars. At a time like this, it is more important than ever to protect our community. Would anyone like to disagree with me?'

When she put it like that, it was pretty hard for anyone to disagree. But she was making it sound as

43

though humans were *purposely* trying to destroy Shiprock. As though they knew what they were doing. Mr Beeston had already done some research and the one thing he was categorically sure of was that the builders didn't have the slightest inkling that there was a town of merpeople not far from where they were building.

He'd shown us what he called his 'interim findings' the night before. Apparently, the council were planning to build new houses, but they'd discovered weaknesses below ground level. They'd investigated further and discovered that the land they'd been working on formed the roof of some impressive caves and tunnels.

What they didn't know was that the tunnels stretched out for miles, and that one of them led all the way to Shiprock.

The building work had been halted while the council decided what to do next. They were going to do one of two things. Either fill in the caves completely, to make the ground stable enough for them to stick with the original plan to build houses, or change tack altogether and dig the caves out as far as they could and open them up as a tourist attraction.

Either option spelled utter disaster for Shiprock.

The first could result in massive underwater landslides that would probably destroy the whole town. The second would almost certainly lead to

Shiprock's discovery – meaning the inhabitants would have two choices. Become a freak show to entertain humans, or leave their homes forever.

The interim findings had not been good.

So Mrs Sharktail had even more reason to hate humans than she realised. She wouldn't know Brightport's exact plans, but she could feel the effect of them – like everyone else in Shiprock.

'Good,' Mrs Sharktail continued, looking round at the school with her version of a smile. It was like a jagged little line across her face with the tiniest upwards curl in each corner. 'In that case, you will understand why we have recently tightened our school rules.'

Shona was right, then. Aaron and I were officially against the rules.

She went on. 'And you will doubtless share my horror at a discovery I made earlier today.' She swam a few strokes in our direction.

Every eye that wasn't already on Aaron and me turned towards us now.

'Humans!' she exclaimed, in a tone of voice that couldn't have dripped with more venom even if it had come directly out of a snake's mouth.

Her accusation was only tempered by one small detail: the fact that Aaron and I were as mer as anyone else when we were in water. I noticed a few puzzled looks pass between some of the girls.

'Yes, well, not now they're not,' she snapped.

'But they were. Semi-mers,' she said, with that same disgusted tone that I was starting to get a bit sick of. 'To think – coming to MY school and I didn't even know it. Lucky for all of us that the issue has been rectified immediately.'

The issue had been rectified? This was our *lives* she was talking about! We weren't some problem that needed fixing. I'd had enough. I had to say something. If I could stand up to Neptune in his own court, which I had when I'd rescued my dad from prison, then surely I could speak out now.

'We haven't done anything wrong,' I said, in a voice that came out much smaller than I was expecting. I cleared my throat and tried again. 'Semi-mers aren't against the law. Neptune's even changed all the intermarriage laws. He wants humans and merfolk to get on.'

With the slightest flick of her tail, Mrs Sharktail whizzed over to me. 'Did I ask you to say anything?' she snarled. She turned back to face the school. 'Of course, strictly speaking, semi-mers are *not* against the law,' she said. 'Although, if I had my way, they certainly would be,' she added under her breath. 'But as of the last few weeks, they *are* against our school's rules, and at a time like this, when our ways are under such threat from humans, it is more important than ever to enforce *all* of our rules.'

She turned back to me and Aaron. 'As of this

moment, the pair of you are no longer welcome in this school.'

She stared at us. We stared back at her. And then, in case we were in any doubt about exactly *how* unwelcome we were in her school, she added in a deep rumble, 'Leave – now!'

There was a swishing noise at the back of the hall. Shona! She was pushing her way past the rest of her class to get to us. *No, Shona, don't! You'll only get yourself in more trouble, too.*

I grabbed Aaron's arm. 'We're going,' I said, staring into Mrs Sharktail's sharp beady eyes. 'We know when we're not welcome.' Which, OK, wasn't the cleverest retort ever. You'd have to be the most ignorant person in the world not to have known you weren't welcome after all that. But I couldn't think of anything else to say.

We swam away from the stage and away from the chamber, with every eye in the school watching us go. I don't think even Mandy Rushton had ever made me feel so humiliated. And to make matters even worse, you know what I heard as we swam off? Clapping. Mrs Sharktail started it. I didn't look round. I didn't want to see how many others were joining in.

'Now what?' Aaron and I had stopped for a rest at Rainbow Rocks. We got out and perched on the side of a rock.

I fought back an urge to burst into tears. I didn't want Aaron to think I was soft. But the tears were there, jamming up my throat so hard I couldn't reply. I just shook my head.

'I mean, did that really happen?' Aaron asked. The sound of his voice dislodged the tears I was holding back and they started to trickle down my face.

'Hey, don't cry,' he said in a voice so soft it only made me cry harder. He reached a hand out, as though he was going to wipe the tear from my face. His hand hovered in mid-air for a moment, before he changed his mind and let it drop. I noticed his cheeks had turned pink.

'We were meant to be bringing the human and mer worlds together,' I croaked. 'What chance do we stand of doing that if the merpeople don't even want to know us?'

'I know,' he said. 'I think we might have a harder job than we realised.' And then he reached out again. This time he didn't change his mind. He stretched across and put a gangly arm around my shoulders. It felt weird. But nice. And it stopped me from wanting to cry quite so much.

'Come on,' I said after a while. 'We should

probably go home and tell our parents what's happened.'

Aaron plopped back into the water and I followed him. As we swam slowly back, I could only hope that Mum or Dad would have some idea what to do next. Because if they didn't, life in Brightport was about to take a nosedive.

Chapter Four

On the way back to Brightport, Aaron asked about Brightport High. What could I say? I wanted to tell him it was great, but when I opened my mouth to describe it, all I could think of was one thing. Or rather, one person.

'Look, if we're starting at Brightport High, I'd better tell you about someone,' I said. 'You'll come across her soon, so you may as well be prepared.'

Aaron swam along beside me with long, slow strokes. A shoal of yellow and green fish swam beside us, gliding along with the tiniest flicks of their tails. 'Go on,' he said.

'Mandy Rushton.'

Aaron's face brightened. 'The girl who helped you save everyone from the kraken. I remember you talking about her. Hey, at least we know we'll have a friendly face waiting to see us there.'

I half laughed and half choked, swallowing about a litre of sea water in the process. 'Erm, it's not exactly like that,' I said. Then I explained about how mean Mandy used to be to me at school. How she used to call me names, and make fun of me and try to get me into trouble with the teachers.

'But you made friends at Allpoints Island, didn't you?'

'Well, yes, but it's not that straightforward.' I told him about the memory drug that Neptune had given all the humans before they left the island, so they wouldn't remember seeing the merpeople and the kraken.

'And you think the memory drug will have stopped her remembering that you made friends?'

'Exactly.'

'Is there any chance that the memory drug didn't include that bit, and that she'll still be friends with you?'

I'd wondered the same thing myself, but I wasn't holding out much hope. 'We'll find out soon enough,' I said. 'But I thought you should be warned, just in case.'

We swam the rest of the way in silence, accompanied by a single silver fish that looked like a sword, slicing along the sea bed, silent and sombre.

'Jake, I want you to march right into Shiprock School and give them what for!'

We were out on the deck of the boat and Mum was on the warpath. 'Our children are as good as anyone else's, and have as much right to attend that school as all the others!'

Dad was in the sea below us. He swam backwards and forwards across the bow of the boat. Despite everything that was going on, it felt nice to discover that he paced when he was trying to work out what to do, just like I do. I'd only known my dad since last year and there were still loads of things I was discovering about him.

'It's not as simple as that,' he said. 'I mean, they've got their rules and –'

'Rules? Since when did you give a hoot about rules when the rules are downright silly and unfair?' Mum fumed.

Dad swam right up to the side of the boat and reached out for her hand. She folded her arms.

'Penny, I'm working for Neptune now,' he said. 'Things aren't like they used to be.'

'No,' she said pointedly. 'They're not.'

Dad reached out further for her hand. 'Come on, don't be like that,' he said. 'I'm as outraged as you are. I just think we need to be careful about how we approach this.'

Mum shuffled further away. 'In case you've forgotten, your new boss is the same Neptune who told us to go off and bring the human and the mer worlds closer together. He *ordered* us to do it! He told us this would be our first test, remember! And you want to sit back and do nothing while our daughter is humiliated in front of an entire school and shown very clearly what the mer-world thinks of the human one. How is *that* being loyal to your precious Neptune?'

Mum's face was scarlet. Why was she so angry? She hadn't even wanted us to go to Shiprock in the first place!

'It's the principle of the thing,' she snapped, as though she'd read my mind.

Dad's face was almost as red as Mum's. *Please don't argue*, I thought to myself. I couldn't go through all that again. They'd argued so much when we'd first arrived at Allpoints Island I'd thought they were going to split up.

'Look, I understand what you're saying,' Dad said calmly. 'But we're going to have to tread carefully. I'm not going to sit doing nothing while Shiprock makes an example of Emily.'

'And Aaron,' I butted in.

Dad nodded. 'And Aaron. I'll do something. But I want to make sure that whatever we do, it's the right thing. If we go charging in there shouting our gills off now, how's that going to help our cause?'

Mum shuffled and turned away.

Dad tried the holding out his hand thing again. 'Come on, Pen, we've got to be a team; we've got to work this out together. That's what Neptune instructed us to do as well.'

Mum let out a huge sigh, then she sat on the edge of the deck and took Dad's hand. 'I suppose you're right,' she said grudgingly. 'Naturally.'

'Naturally? Why naturally?' Dad asked.

'Well, look at me. Who am I to think I can build bridges between people? We should tell Neptune to pick someone else.'

'Mary Penelope, what on earth are you talking about?'

Uh-oh. Dad had called her by her full name. He only called her Mary Penelope when it was *really* serious. It was time to step in.

'Look, I don't mind all that much, now it's over and done with,' I said quickly. 'I'm happy to go to Brightport High, and so's Aaron. I've told him all about it. So why don't we just forget it and carry on as though nothing's happened? We've got each other, and that's all that matters really, isn't it?'

Mum looked down at the deck. Shaking her

head, she mumbled, 'That's not the point.'

Now it was Dad's turn to sigh. 'If that's not the point, then what *is*?'

She muttered something under her breath.

'What was that?' Dad asked, a sliver of impatience creeping into his voice.

Mum looked up. A tear had slipped from her eye and was snaking down her cheek. 'My parents,' she said numbly.

Dad reached up and stroked her leg. 'Oh Penny,' he said. She gulped back a sob.

'I don't get it,' I said. 'What about them? I thought you hadn't seen them for years.'

'Exactly!' Mum said woodenly. 'That's my point! What chance do I stand of building bridges between two worlds if even my own parents haven't spoken to me in over ten years? Neptune's picked the wrong person!'

And with that, she wrapped her arms round her knees and threw herself wholeheartedly into crying very loudly.

I couldn't stand to see her like that. Seeing my mum cry felt like someone was sticking a knife into me and jigging it about in my chest. I reached out and touched her arm. 'Mum, it's OK,' I said, feeling completely useless.

She shook her head. 'No it's not,' she said into her knees. 'It's not OK at all. In fact it's about as un-OK as you can get.' She took hold of my hand

and tried a feeble smile. 'But thank you for trying, sweet pea.'

I think Dad must have felt as useless as me, as he didn't try to say anything helpful. He just carried on stroking her legs while we waited for her to cry herself out.

We ate tea together in silence. It wasn't the happiest silence in the world, but at least there were no tears. And we managed to discuss the situation enough to make one decision: I wasn't going to start at Brightport High in a hurry.

As there were only a few weeks of the summer term left, Mum and Dad agreed I could wait till September. At least it meant I didn't have to worry about the risk of being equally humiliated there – not for a while, anyway.

None of us had mentioned my grandparents again. I was dying to, though. Now Mum had brought them up I was aware that she never talked about them, and I never asked. Except for the moment last year out at the Great Mermer Reef, when she remembered everything. She told me what had happened with them then. How they'd practically disowned her because of her relationship with a merman. But that was it; that was all I knew.

I didn't actually know anything *about* them, what they were like, how things had been with them before it had all gone wrong. I realised I wanted to know all about them. But not now. This wasn't the time to ask.

'Can I go round to Aaron's?' I asked instead, taking my plate over to the sink. I wanted to find out what his mum had said and what they were planning to do now. Hopefully she'd say the same as Mum and Dad, and Aaron and I could hang out together for an extra few weeks of holiday. Getting thrown out of mermaid school might not feel so bad, then.

I had a twinge of guilt as I realised that whenever I had some free time nowadays, Aaron was the first person I thought of spending it with, not Shona. Was it disloyal of me? Did it make me a rubbish best friend?

I couldn't answer either question, and I certainly wasn't going to ask anyone else. I pushed the guilty feelings away and went out.

I walked up the pier and was heading along the prom towards the cottages where Aaron and his mum were staying when a familiar figure rounded the corner. Mandy. This was it, then: truth time.

She was looking down at the ground while she walked and hadn't spotted me yet. I held my breath, waiting till she did. Or would she walk straight past me without even noticing?

Just before we passed each other, she suddenly looked up. For approximately a millisecond, her eyes brightened. She looked as if she was about to smile. I started to smile back. She remembered!

And then, in an instant, her expression changed back to the sneer I was more used to seeing. 'Well, look what the tide's dragged in,' she said, leaning back on her hips. And with those few words, the slight hope I'd had that she would remember our friendship sank like a stone in a murky sea.

'Hi, Mandy,' I said glumly, and carried on walking. I wasn't in the mood to hang around and listen to her taunts. I thought she'd call after me, but she didn't. I had a quick glance round before turning towards the cottages. She was still there, staring after me. Then she shook her head and set off back towards the pier. It could have been worse, I suppose. Still, it would be nice if *something* could go right for us soon.

I got to the cottage and Aaron grinned as soon as he saw me. 'Guess what?' he said. 'Mum says I don't need to start at Brightport High till next term!'

'Me too!'

Something *had* gone right!

'Come on,' Aaron joined me outside. 'Mum's watching telly. Let's go for a walk.'

I laughed. 'I wouldn't have thought your mum was the telly type.'

'We've never had a television before, so it's her new toy. She's hooked on the quiz programmes, especially. Says she's learning all sorts from them. *Who Wants to be a Millionaire*'s just started. She won't even notice I've gone!' He stuck his head round the door anyway. 'Just nipping out with Emily, Mum.'

'No, it's B, you idiot!' she shouted at the telly.

Aaron smiled as he shut the door behind us. 'Told you!'

The sun was setting as we walked along the beach. Aaron chatted happily away, about all sorts of odd things. My mind was too full of the events of the day to concentrate all that much on what he was saying.

'Doesn't it bother you?' I broke in at one point.

He turned to me. 'What?'

'You know. Today. What happened.'

Aaron shrugged. 'I don't know,' he said. 'In a way, yes, of course it does. In another way, I don't mind all that much. For one thing, everything about my life is a million times better than it was when all I could do was rattle about in a dark spooky castle with just my mum for company.'

'And what's the other thing?' I prompted him.

He kicked at the sand and carried on walking. Looking down, he said, 'Well, you know. I get to hang out with you for a few weeks,' he mumbled. Then he looked up. 'I mean, not that you have to spend all your time with me. You've probably got loads of friends here that you want to catch up with.'

Suddenly I realised I was feeling just as happy as Aaron. 'Actually, the hanging out with you thing is the best part of it for me, too,' I said shyly. I felt a tiny little flutter in my tummy. What was the matter with me? I'd never been like this with any other friends. What was so different about Aaron?

'Come on,' I said. Pulling off my sandals, I started running along the beach. 'Race you to the pier.'

Aaron pulled off his sandals too and we ran through the sand. It was still warm from the day's sun, and even though you didn't melt into it like on the beaches at Allpoints Island, the softness of the sand on my feet made me want to run and run and run.

Except for what we ran into.

'Well, well, well. And she's got a little friend with her, too.' Mandy stood under the pier, arms folded, sneer fully in place. She must have spied on me and come after us. What did she have in store for me now?

Aaron marched right up to her and stood facing

her. 'You'll be Mandy, then,' he said, looking her square in the eyes.

For a flicker of a second, Mandy was thrown off her guard. She clearly hadn't expected that. She recovered pretty quickly, though. 'Aww, has fish girl been telling tales about nasty-wasty Mandy Wushton?' she said in a mock baby voice.

'Actually, she hasn't been telling tales at all,' Aaron replied. 'In fact, she even thought you might remember you and her making –'

'Aaron, no,' I said, stepping forward and pulling him away.

He turned to me. 'Why?'

Mandy was looking at me, too. Her expression had changed a little. There was just a tiny hint of doubt in the sneer. 'Making what?' she asked, her tone slightly less harsh.

'Nothing,' I said. 'Come on, Aaron, let's go. She's not worth it.'

I thought for a minute she was going to follow us down the beach so she could carry on taunting and insulting us. But she didn't. She stayed where she was. 'Yeah, run away,' she called after us. 'Like the cowards you are.' We didn't turn round and she gave up after that.

'Well, we got off pretty lightly there, I'd say,' Aaron said as we walked up the other side of the pier.

'Thanks to you, we did.'

'Don't be daft,' he said. 'Anyway, at least you know what she's going to be like now.'

I nodded. Yeah. At least I knew.

I woke up with a feeling of heaviness. What was it?

Then I remembered the events of the previous day. Oh, yes. All that.

Mum and Dad were in the saloon, where we've got the biggest trapdoor. They were sitting on it together, Mum's feet dangling in the water, Dad's tail swishing gently backwards and forwards.

'Morning, sausage,' Mum said.

Dad looked up. 'Morning, little 'un.'

I sat down to join them. 'What's up?'

Mum shook her head.

'It's what we were talking about yesterday,' Dad said gently. 'It's made your mum think about her parents again. She's just a bit sad. But she'll be OK, won't you, love?' He stroked her knee.

Maybe this was my chance to find out a bit more about my grandparents.

'Mum,' I said carefully. 'What were they like, Nan and Grandad?'

Mum turned her sad eyes towards me. She opened her mouth, but before she could reply, there was a sharp rap on the door.

'Only me!' An uninvited head popped round the door. Mr Beeston. 'Just dropping by for a duty call with my colleague, ha ha,' he said, winking at Dad. Now that the two of them were working together, he clearly saw it as a permanent invitation round to ours. Mum and Dad didn't seem to mind him any more, but I still couldn't relax while he was around.

'Come on in, Charles,' Mum said. 'The kettle's just boiled. Help yourself if you want one.'

Mr Beeston rubbed his hands together and rummaged through our cupboards for a tea bag and a mug. 'Very well,' he said. 'Don't mind if I do.'

He brought his tea over to the saloon and sat down on the dog-eared sofa. 'Not interrupting anything, am I?' he asked, in his usual completely oblivious way.

Durr! Er, yes. Our lives!

'Mary P was just talking about her parents,' Dad said.

For some reason, Mr Beeston shifted awkwardly on the sofa. He must have hit one of the loose springs. It's not the comfiest sofa in the world. 'Oh. Ah. Well, that'll be up to you, then. Don't want me hanging around, do you,' he said, and started getting up.

'Don't be silly, Charles,' Mum said. 'You're virtually one of the family now. Sit down.'

It was just as well I didn't have a drink of my own

or I would have spluttered it everywhere. One of the family? I don't *think* so!

'I was just going to tell Emily a bit more about them,' she said. 'In fact, you'll remember them yourself, won't you? Perhaps you can help out?'

'Me?' Mr Beeston blustered, almost spilling his tea in his lap. 'What can *I* tell you? I don't know *anything*!' His face had practically turned purple, and he looked even more uncomfortable than people generally look on that sofa. What was his *problem*?

Mum shrugged off his reply and turned to me. 'You remember what I told you, don't you? Why they moved away?'

'They thought you were going mad because you told them you were in love with a merman.'

Mum nodded. 'That's right. They wanted me to see someone to try to make me stop having delusions! They thought I was making it all up because I didn't want to tell them who was the real father of my baby.'

'Didn't they try to get you to leave Brightport and go and live with them somewhere else?' I asked.

Mum nodded. 'But I wouldn't. I didn't even know why – I just knew I couldn't leave. There are all sorts of things about it all that I've never understood.'

'Like what?' I asked.

'Well, for one thing, like why Grandad left me the boat when they went off without me.'

'Why don't you understand that?' I asked.

Mum shook her head. 'There was just something about it that didn't fit. I used to tell myself it meant that a small part of him forgave me, or even believed me. That maybe when things had calmed down a bit, they'd get back in touch.'

'But they didn't?' I prompted.

'No. Not once. Nothing. Apart from the cards they sent for birthdays and Christmas. That was it. They never even wrote more than their names. Not even "love". Just "Mum and Dad", or "Nan and Grandad" on yours.' She smiled sadly at me. 'It was so strange, so unlike them. They'd always been so warm and friendly. Everyone knew that about them. But what could I do? They just didn't want to know me.'

Mum fell silent. There wasn't much any of us could say. Dad held tightly on to her hand. Mr Beeston was still fidgeting and twitching. All the time Mum was talking, he'd been sitting there looking round the room, pulling at a loose thread on his jacket, tapping his foot nervously. It was as though he was trying not to listen.

Oh, I'm sorry, are we boring you? His life was obviously *much* more important than anyone else's.

The second Mum stopped talking, he slurped his tea down in one final glug and jumped up from the sofa. Pulling up his sleeve, he looked at his watch.

'Gosh, is that the time?' he said, in his I've-got-much-more-important-things-to-do-than-waste-my-time-with-you-people tone of voice. 'I'd better get going.'

And before we could say 'Oh, really, must you? Won't you stay for another cup of tea?' – as if! – he'd shuffled over to the door, nodded quickly at the three of us and made his exit.

'Whoops, sorry, didn't see you there!' we heard him exclaim. 'Good grief, what the blazes are *you* doing here? Anyway, can't stop, things to do and all that. Catch you later.'

Who was he talking to? I jumped up and ran to the door. I don't know who I was expecting, but when I saw who it was, it was the most welcome surprise I'd had since we'd got here.

I threw myself into the arms that were waiting wide open for me.

Chapter Five

'*M*illie!' I hugged her tightly as she laughed and squeezed me back.

Then she let go and clambered through the door. 'Looks like I got here just in time,' she said, looking round and tutting loudly. 'Can't you folk go five minutes without getting yourselves mixed up in some trouble or other?'

Mum leapt to her feet. 'Millie! What on earth are you doing here?'

Millie threw her arms round Mum. 'Couldn't stand it without you,' she said. 'Archie said I was the biggest misery fins he'd ever seen. There was another team heading out this way for a couple of weeks so he arranged for me to hitch a ride.'

'I thought you couldn't bear to be parted from him,' Dad said with a mischievous grin.

'Yes. Well, turns out I can't bear to be parted from you lot even more.' She pursed her lips. 'And from the sounds of things, it seems like you're not much good without me, either.'

'From the sounds of things? You mean you've been listening outside the door?' I said.

Millie flushed slightly. 'I was trying to work out the perfect moment to make a grand entrance,' she admitted. 'Except Beeston ruined that one for me, didn't he. Typical.' She headed for the kitchen. 'Now, what does a weary traveller have to do to get a cup of Earl Grey around here?'

'If you ask me, it's time to stop whingeing about your parents and do something about it,' Millie said, with her usual bluntness. She'd plonked herself down on the same sofa Mr Beeston had been on. Somehow she made it look a lot smaller.

'What do you mean, Millie?' Mum asked, her voice strained and raw. 'How can I do anything about it? I don't even know where they went.'

Millie blew on her tea. 'Yes, you do,' she remarked, then took a loud slurp from her cup.

'You know where they are?' I burst out. 'But I thought –'

'I don't know where they are at all. Millie, what are you talking about?'

'Postmarks,' she said simply.

'Postmarks?' I repeated.

Millie sighed. 'Come on, Mary P. You're telling me you didn't hold on to every card, every envelope?'

Mum shook her head. 'Well, actually, no. I didn't,' she said, a note of bitterness creeping into her voice. 'They weren't exactly full of touching sentiment.'

'And you never looked at the postmarks?'

Mum didn't reply.

'I know you did, Mary P. Because you showed them to me. We talked about it. We looked it up on a map. Remember?'

Mum looked down. 'Yes, I remember,' she said eventually.

'Where was it, now? Bridge something wasn't it? Bridgehaven? Bridgemeadows?' Millie tapped her lip and furrowed her forehead in concentration.

'Bridgefield,' Mum said flatly. 'Not that it matters.' She got up and walked over to the kitchen. 'Who fancies something to eat? I'm starving.'

'Mum, why doesn't it matter?' I said, biting my

lip while I waited for her to reply. Mum doesn't take kindly to being pushed on a subject that she's decided is closed.

'Because I'm not planning to try to get in touch.'

'Why not?' I persevered.

Mum turned round to face me. 'They've made it clear that they don't want to have anything to do with me. I'm not going to go begging to them.'

'But, Mum,' I insisted. 'We're the ones who have been told to try to bring the mer and human worlds together. Maybe this could be how we start?'

Mum drew in a breath, pausing just long enough to give me a bit of hope that she might be about to change her mind.

Then she shook her head. 'No, I've decided. We'll find another way to get our task started. We've still got this whole development thing to sort out, too. And, so far, we haven't had any bright ideas on *that*. If we don't make progress soon, we might as well give up and tell Neptune to find another family for the job.'

'But Mum –'

'No buts,' Mum said firmly. 'I'm not putting myself through that again. It took me long enough to get over what they did. I don't intend to give them the chance to do it all over again. Subject closed. Now let's have some breakfast.'

And with that she got some bread out of the cupboard and started to slice it.

I opened my mouth to say something else, but Dad shook his head at me. 'Best leave it,' he said softly. 'You know what your mum's like once she's made her mind up.'

I looked at Millie. She was scribbling something in a velvety notebook while Mum was making breakfast. Then she shoved the notebook in her bag and winked at me. 'Don't worry, pet,' she said in a whisper. 'It'll be OK.'

I don't know what made her think anything was going to be OK. As far as I could see, all that had happened since we'd got to Brightport was that things had gone from bad to worse.

But there was nothing I could do now. I decided to let it drop, even though it felt as if the conversation was still hovering all around us like a heavy mist.

I suddenly had a longing to see the one person who might help me feel better. And for the first time in ages, it wasn't Aaron. It was the person who always cheered me up, always made me look on the bright side of life and always helped me find a solution when things were looking hopeless.

'Can I go over to Shiprock after breakfast?' I asked. I needed to see Shona.

It was still early enough to catch Shona before school. We swam out towards the playground where we used to hang out. It's really just a sandy patch where all sorts of bits of rope and anchors and seaweed had been gathered and turned into things to climb over or crawl under. We swam through a large abandoned porthole and sat on a long plank of wood. Nearby, a lobster poked its head out through a gap in a rock, its black eyes facing us, pincers sticking out like a giant handlebar moustache.

I caught her up with everything that had happened as we swam.

'It all sounds a bit grim,' Shona said. 'Poor you.'

'Yeah I know. The only decent thing is that I don't have to go to Brightport High till next term,' I said. *And that I get to hang out with Aaron.* I had the feeling Shona had started to get a bit tired of me talking about Aaron, and right now I didn't want to do anything to annoy her, so I didn't say that part out loud. I wasn't going to risk upsetting Shona on top of everything else. I decided to change the subject.

'What's it been like here?' I asked.

'Miserable! School's no fun without you,' she said. 'Nothing's the same without you,' she added, making me feel even more guilty about the fact that I'd been so pleased that Aaron and I would get to spend loads of time together. I hadn't even thought about missing Shona till this morning.

'In fact, nothing's the same at *all*,' she went on. 'The atmosphere at school is awful. Mrs Sharktail's been in a foul mood and everyone's going round scared in case they're the next to get hauled up for a major telling-off in front of the school.'

'I wouldn't wish that on anyone,' I said, remembering the shame of all those eyes on me while Mrs Sharktail made me feel like I was the most disgusting thing on the planet.

'Outside school's not much better. All anyone can talk about is what's happening over in Brightport and how it might affect us. We felt the walls shaking at my aunt's last night – it was pretty scary. She reckons we should just pack up and move, but Dad says it'll die down and we shouldn't leap into anything drastic. The worst thing is just not knowing what's going on. Have you heard any more about it?'

'Mum was talking to someone at the launderette,' I said. 'They told her the council's going to decide what to do with it at their next planning meeting.'

Shona nodded. 'So all we can do is wait?'

'Looks like it,' I said. 'I'm sure coming back here was meant to be better than this.'

'I know. The only good thing is Sirens and Seas. We've got a new teacher and she's been telling us some new siren tales that we've never heard before.'

Shona's eyes brightened in that way that only siren talk can make them.

'Like what?'

'The lost sirens!' Shona got up from the log and swam over to the anchor on the other side of the playground. She darted round it, swishing this way and that, making a shoal of tiny purple fish turn and dart away as one.

'There's a group of sirens who disappeared years and years ago. One of them was known all across the oceans for her singing. Fishermen deserted their boats and threw themselves into the seas to find her.'

Shona hesitated. Before we'd met, she thought nothing of the idea of luring fishermen to watery graves. Since we'd been friends and she'd realised humans could be OK, she wasn't so comfortable about that part of a siren's job any more. And with a bit of luck, no one would see it as part of the job soon, if Neptune was serious about the two worlds coming together – and if we managed to make it happen!

'Anyway,' she went on quickly, 'she was one of the top sirens, and then one day she vanished – just like that. Gone without a trace. There was a group of them. She and her friends sang together sometimes, and all of them disappeared overnight.'

'For good?' I asked.

Shona nodded and swam back to me, swinging

on an abandoned rope and brushing the sea floor with it as she swam. A shoal of bright blue fish rushed out from underneath, zig–zagging away from us. 'None of them have ever been seen again.' Her eyes sparkled. 'The legend says that they went off to a magical place that's so well hidden it's virtually invisible! And guess what else?'

'What?'

'Miss Merlin's done loads of research into it. Siren legends and mysteries are her favourite thing and she knows more about them than anyone in the whole ocean! She told us the last place they were reported to have been seen.'

'And?'

Shona looked as if she was about to burst with excitement. 'And it's near here!'

I knew instantly what she was thinking. Before Shona met me, she'd never really had an adventure. Since we'd been best friends, we'd hardly had anything but!

'You want to see if we can find them?'

Shona nodded excitedly. 'Look, I need to get to school. But think about it. Perhaps we could go at the weekend? It might distract you from everything else that's going on.'

She had a point. And anyway, it did have an interesting ring to it. A group of sirens all vanishing into thin air overnight, never to be seen or heard of again. We could at least pretend that we were going to find them. Anything had to be better than sitting around getting more and more miserable about – well, about pretty much everything.

'You're on,' I said with a grin. I knew Shona would manage to make me smile. She always does.

'Swishy!' She grinned back at me. 'I'll see if I can find out any more from Miss Merlin. We could go on Sunday.'

'Let's do it!'

With that, we headed back. I had a slight twinge when we went our separate ways and she swam off to school. I don't even know what the twinge was. A whole mix of things, I suppose. A bit sad seeing her go off on her own to school, without me there. A bit jealous of her still going to mermaid school and learning about things like sirens disappearing into invisible hiding places while I would soon be back to French and fractions.

And, yes, if I'm honest, there was a little bit of guilt in there, too, at the fact that I was excited about getting back to Brightport and spending the rest of the day with Aaron.

I waited for Shona to stop and wave before she rounded a corner, then I turned and swam back towards Brightport. A group of long black fish swam parallel with me, as though racing me. Ahead, a stripy blue and pink fish swam across my path. Seaweed swayed about below me, feathery ferns brushing the end of my tail as I swam over it. A feeling of peace washed over me. I smiled to myself as I headed home. Everything was going to be fine, I could tell.

It carried on being fairly fine all week. Mum was back at the bookshop where she used to work. She'd gone in one day to say hello and it turned out one of the new assistants had just left, so they grabbed her straight away and got her back on the job. That seemed to make her happier – as did the fact that Millie was around again. Millie had loads of friends in Brightport so hadn't had any trouble finding somewhere to stay. Mrs Swindale, who ran one of the guesthouses on the front, said she could stay there free of charge for as long as she wanted, in exchange for a daily tarot reading, a couple of reiki sessions and a chakra cleansing or two.

Dad was busy out working with Mr Beeston and Mum had even managed to get Aaron's mum a part-time job helping out at the charity shop on the prom – which just left Aaron and me.

I showed him all my favourite parts of Brightport. The back streets where you could get lost if you didn't know your way round. The walk along the prom where you could watch the sun set over the sea. We even went to look at the Rushtons' new theme park. We only looked in from the outside, though. I didn't fancy bumping into Mr and Mrs Rushton. After what had happened with Mandy, I couldn't face it.

Once I'd shown Aaron the town, I decided to show him the other side of Brightport; the side I'd only known about since I'd discovered I was a mermaid. In particular, Rainbow Rocks. We swam there together. I told him it was where I'd first met Shona, and where my mum had said goodbye to my dad when I was only a baby. That was the last time she'd seen him till last year.

'It's very special here, isn't it,' Aaron said, swimming slowly round the rocks. The water was so clear you could see every pebble and every fish below us, even the ones that were virtually see-through, little stick-thin things flicking through the water like darts.

I was glad he could feel it too. Rainbow Rocks was possibly my favourite place in the world. My favourite place in Brightport, anyway.

It was a magical week. I didn't want it to end. Soon everyone would be off school and it wouldn't feel as though we had the whole place to ourselves any more.

But the week did end.

And so did the wonderful, magical feeling.

Friday morning I was at home on my own when a THUD on the front deck signified someone had arrived. And by the way the boat rocked with their arrival, I had a good guess who it might be.

'Where is she?' Millie burst through the door, breathless and scarlet. 'Where's your mum?'

'At work,' I said. 'Why?'

Millie shook her head. 'Not there. Can't find her.'

'She might have gone to the cash-and-carry,' I said. 'Millie, what is it? Are you OK?'

Millie nodded as she caught her breath. 'Cash and what? Oh, stuff and nonsense, we'll come back for her as soon as we can. I can't wait – I'll have to take you on your own first. Come on!'

'Come on what?' I asked.

Millie grabbed my hand. 'You're not to say anything. We'll bring them over as soon as your mum's back, OK?'

I decided to overlook the fact that Millie wasn't making sense. 'OK,' I agreed, and followed her out of the boat.

Millie marched up the jetty, her cape billowing out behind her. I scampered along behind her. 'Millie, are you going to tell me what this is about?' I asked when I caught her up.

'You'll see soon enough,' she replied in that mysterious way that she says most things.

We took a turn down towards the beach cottages where Aaron and his mum were staying. 'Is it Aaron?' I asked. 'Has something happened to him?'

'Nothing has happened to anyone. Come on. Nearly there now.' She took a sharp left turn, paced to the last cottage in the row and stopped. 'This is it,' she said. Then she wiped her palms down the side of her dress, pulled a wisp of hair off her face and swallowed hard.

She turned to me. 'Ready?' Her voice had a breathless wobble in it. She was clearly nervous – but why? What was inside the cottage? What was I meant to be ready *for*?

'I guess so,' I said. Then I followed Millie up the path. She took a deep breath. And then she knocked on the door.

Chapter Six

The door opened. A woman was standing in the hallway. She was thin and spindly, with grey hair and glasses hanging round her neck on a chain. She looked elderly, but kind of sprightly too.

A man came up behind her, same sort of age, taller than she was, but thin and grey-haired too. They both stared at us.

'Can we help you?' the woman asked, with a friendly smile. Her eyes crinkled up and turned green and shiny when she smiled. Something about her smile seemed familiar but I couldn't put my finger on what it was. She *couldn't* be familiar. I'd never seen either of them before!

'I – it's – don't you –' Millie began. She was even more flustered than she'd been before we knocked on the door.

The man came to the front door step. 'You must be the lady from the competition,' he said.

Competition? What competition?

'Come on in. We're so pleased to meet you. What a wonderful surprise, winning something like this out of the blue. It's all happened so fast; lucky we were free! And the place is lovely.'

What on earth was he talking about? Had he mixed us up with someone else? I turned to Millie.

She just gave me a quick nod and ushered me in. The man spotted me. 'Ah, you've brought your daughter with you.' He reached down to shake my hand. 'Well, come on. Come on in, both of you.'

I glared at Millie. '*Daughter?*' I mouthed. She shook her head and frowned a silent 'Shhhh!' at me.

The four of us stood in the front room in an awkward circle, looking at each other.

'Well?' Millie said, grinning broadly at the couple. 'Now you can have a proper look, surely you remember me?'

The two strangers stared blankly at Millie.

'This is Emily!' she said.

They turned their blank stares on me. I stared blankly back.

I'd had enough. 'Millie, are you going to explain what's going on here?'

Suddenly, Millie looked just as bewildered as the rest of us. 'You won't even acknowledge me?' she asked. Her voice cracked as she spoke. I thought she was going to cry. 'Well, I knew you felt strongly about it all, but I didn't think you'd take it *this* far!'

The couple continued to stare at her, mouths open, puzzled expressions across their faces. The woman spoke first. 'Look, it was very nice of you to let us know we'd won, and we really are grateful, but I'm sure I don't know what –'

'Hello?' A voice was calling from the front door. We'd left it open behind us and a second later, Aaron's face appeared. He glanced round the room and grinned when he saw me. 'Hey – I thought it was you. I was just passing,' he said. 'What're you doing here?'

Good question!

'Can I come in?' he asked, stepping into the small room before I had a chance to reply.

'This is my friend, Aaron,' I said as he squeezed in next to me – not that anyone took any notice. They were all still too busy staring blankly at each other. I felt Aaron's hand brush mine. Immediately my face heated up, and my heart started hammering so loudly I was positive someone would hear it, especially while we were all standing here in this shocked silence.

83

And then something else happened. The feeling of his hand touching mine – well, I know it's going to sound ridiculous and corny and stupid, but it sent shivers and tingles all the way up my arm. I glanced at him to see if he'd felt it too. He looked at me, but he didn't move away. In fact, a moment later, he opened up his fingers and took my hand in his.

Which was pretty much the same moment that the woman's face turned as grey as her hair.

'Emily?' she whispered. She turned to her husband.

He clutched her arm and took a step towards me. 'It's really you? Our Emily?' he said.

I looked at Millie for some help.

'About time, too!' she exclaimed with a broad smile.

'It's Mary Penelope's friend, Millie!' the man exclaimed. 'Why, it must be, what – twelve years?'

'About that,' she said. 'Give or take a lifetime or so,' she added under her breath, with a meaningful look in my direction.

'Oh my – Mary Penelope – is she here? Do you know where she is?' the woman burst out.

'Er, look, does someone want to explain what's going on here?' I said. 'Or who these people are?'

The woman reached out and put a hand up to my cheek. 'Emily darling,' she said softly, 'we're your grandparents.'

I stared at both of them. 'My –'

The man smiled at me. 'It's true,' he said. 'We're your grandparents.'

'But why – how come – I mean, who –'

The woman laughed. 'There was no competition at all, was there?' she said to Millie.

Millie proudly shook her head. 'I didn't think a simple invitation would cut it, so I called in a favour to hire the cottage for a few days and set this little ruse up.'

'But how did you find them?' I asked.

'Well, we already had the town. I just did a bit of digging around on the Interweb.'

'Internet,' I corrected gently.

'Yes, exactly,' she went on. 'And actually it wasn't hard at all. In reality, these things tend not to be. Very often, the only obstacles in our path are the ones we place there in our own minds,' she said airily, throwing her cape round her shoulder for good effect.

'So what did you do once you'd found out where they were?' I asked.

Millie lowered her voice. 'With the help of some spiritual knowledge, a little bit of mystical insight, a few carefully-placed markers along the ley lines of the way, anything is possible,' she said dramatically.

'She phoned us,' the woman said.

Millie picked an invisible speck of dirt off her gown. 'Well, yes, you could put it like that too, I suppose.'

The woman went on. 'She told us we'd won a weekend break by the sea – for this weekend!'

'Well, it worked, didn't it,' Millie said.

I stared at them a bit more. 'So you really are my grandparents?' I asked. They nodded back at me with bright beaming smiles.

I turned to Millie. 'Come on – we have to go and tell Mum!' I looked at my watch. 'It's gone twelve. She should be home for lunch by now.'

The woman – Nan – clapped a hand over her mouth and reached out to take Grandad's arm with her other hand. 'Is this really happening?' she asked him. 'Are we really going to see our daughter again?'

He put his hand over hers. A lump in his throat was bobbing up and down and it looked as though he was trying to speak. In the end he just squeezed her hand and nodded.

'Hang on a mo.' Millie rummaged in her bag. 'Where is it? I bought it especially for the occasion. I'm sure it's here some – ah!' She pulled a small throwaway camera out of her bag. 'Right, close together everyone. Say cheese!'

Aaron and I stood awkwardly in front of my

grandparents and tried to smile, while Millie clicked away.

'Lovely!' she said with a smile. 'Right, come on, let's go and tell Mary P you're here!'

Closing the door behind them, the old couple followed Millie out of the cottage and up towards the pier. I walked along with Aaron. We were still holding hands. The tingling feeling still hadn't gone away – and my heart rate still hadn't slowed down. It felt weird to be holding his hand, but at the same time it felt like the most natural thing in the world.

We walked up the jetty and over towards our boat. Millie turned to my grandparents. My grandparents! It felt so strange to think that. 'Ready?' she asked.

They nodded eagerly. 'Definitely!' the man replied.

'Right, come on then.' Millie let herself in through the door, calling out to Mum as she did so. 'Cooeee! Mary P – you'll never guess who I've brought to see you!'

As my grandparents followed her inside, Aaron stopped. 'I think you should go in on your own. It's family stuff.' Then in a shy mumble, he added, 'I'll catch you later though, won't I?'

'Definitely!' I said.

He let go of my hand and smiled. My palm was still warm from the feel of his hand on mine. 'See you later,' I said. And then he turned and left, and I went in for the happy reunion.

Only it wasn't exactly what you could call a happy reunion.

My grandparents were doing the staring blankly thing again.

'What's up?' I asked.

Millie stood in the middle of the room, gesticulating wildly. Mum stood behind her, arms folded, face like a shut door. 'We've just been talking, over at your cottage! How can you not remember?' Millie was shouting.

'The cottage that we're staying in for the weekend break that we won?' the woman asked.

'You didn't win a competition!' Millie sighed. 'That was a set-up! A pretence. I've just explained all that!'

'You mean we shouldn't be there?' the man asked. 'Do we have to leave?'

I stood in front of the couple. 'Nan? Grandad?' I said.

I might as well have been a Martian that had just landed on Earth for all the recognition in their eyes.

'Who are you?' the woman said eventually.

I bit back a tear that had started to creep up my

throat. 'It's Emily,' I said. 'Your granddaughter. I came over here with you.'

The couple looked at each other, totally baffled. What was going on?

'Just leave.' Mum's voice was stern and cold. 'You've had your fun, making a fool out of me. Now go.' Her arms were still tightly folded over each other. Her face was closed just as tightly.

Millie ushered the couple to the door. 'I don't understand,' she said. 'I don't get it.' She followed them outside and directed them back to their cottage. Then she came back in and shut the door behind her.

Mum slumped down at the table. 'Oh, Millie,' she said. 'What on earth did you do?'

'I – I thought it would be a wonderful surprise. A happy reunion. I thought it might jump-start the peace-making process that's supposed to be going on round here.'

'How could they be so cruel?' Mum whimpered. 'Not to acknowledge me at all. To pretend they didn't even know me. I never thought they could stoop so low. My own parents.'

I went over and put an arm round Mum. I wanted to say something to comfort her, but I couldn't think of anything. What could I possibly say that could make up for what had just happened?

What *had* just happened?

They'd seemed so happy to see me, so excited to

come and meet up with Mum – and then they'd looked through both of us as though they'd never met us in their lives. It just didn't add up. Had they put it all on? Was it all an act so that they could make a fool of Mum? But why would they have wanted to hurt her so much? Were people really that cruel?

My head was spinning with questions I couldn't answer.

And then I thought of a person who possibly could.

A person who had been around since the days when my grandparents lived here. And, now I thought about it, a person who had acted very strangely the other day when we were talking about them. A person who had some answering to do – as usual.

Mum was leaning her head against my shoulder. I gently extracted myself from her, sliding her over on to Millie's side. Millie folded a big arm around her.

'I'm just nipping out,' I whispered to Millie. She nodded at me and carried on stroking Mum's hair.

Then I clenched my fists as though gearing up for a fight, and headed for the lighthouse.

I banged on the door. 'Open up!' I shouted. 'Let me in, I want to talk to you!'

A second later, the door opened and Mr Beeston appeared. 'Whatever is the matter, child? Is it your mother? Is she all right?' He was halfway out of the door, but I stopped him.

'Mum's fine,' I said. 'At least, nothing's happened to her. ' I paused. 'Unless you call having your life utterly destroyed and your family in tatters anything to worry about.' I folded my arms.

Mr Beeston stared at me. 'What on earth are you talking about? What's happened?'

'My grandparents,' I said simply. At the word, his face changed. It was as though an invisible straw had sucked the colour out of it.

He opened the door and beckoned me in. 'You'd better come inside,' he said.

The apartment inside the lighthouse was bare. Not that I expected it to be full of life and warmth. This *was* Mr Beeston's home we were talking about. A load of boxes were stacked up in one corner. A pile of papers in another. At the sight of them, I couldn't help wondering if he was still collecting files on us.

He noticed me looking round. 'I haven't properly settled in, yet,' he said, waving a hand over the boxes.

'Tell me about my grandparents,' I said bluntly. Mr Beeston looked at me for a second, mouth open, ready to start making up a pack of lies.

'The truth,' I said, and he closed his mouth and let his head drop.

'You have to understand one thing,' he began. I wanted to tell him I didn't have to understand *anything* he said. And I didn't have to *do* anything he said, either. But I bit my tongue and waited for him to continue.

'It was all a long time ago. Long before the current – what have you – arrangements, and recent friendships.' He looked nervously up at me. *Friendships?* Hah! As if he would ever understand the meaning of the word. Again, I held my tongue, and he went on.

'Your grandfather was a sailing man, and a decent fisherman, too. He spent many of his days out on the ocean. And then one day, he saw something he shouldn't have seen.'

I kept quiet.

Mr Beeston cleared his throat. 'He saw a mermaid. He was so excited about it he came straight to me and told me. You see, we were on good terms, back then.'

'You mean you conned your way into his life, just like did with my mum and me?' I said tightly.

He ignored me and carried on. 'I couldn't allow it. Not in my role at that time. We already knew about your mother and father and the plans were in place for dealing with it. Your grandparents knew nothing, of course, and your grandfather suddenly having this information – well, it complicated things. We had to put a stop to it.'

'How?'

'For one thing, we had to wipe his memory.' He stopped.

Of course. The memory drug. I should have guessed. 'And for another?' I prompted.

At least he had the decency to be struggling. Maybe he did have a conscience after all. 'We had to stop him going out again,' he said, shuffling even more awkwardly than usual.

'In case he saw something else,' I said.

He nodded. 'Once I'd wiped his memory, I told him he and his wife had to leave. He never questioned it – the drug took care of that, too. That's what we usually did in those days.'

'And my mum?'

'Unfortunately, this also happened to be the time that your mother discovered she was pregnant and had decided to tell her parents everything.'

'And they thought she was mad, because you'd already wiped their memories.' It was all starting to fall into place.

Mr Beeston puffed his cheeks out. 'Look, conditions were very different back then. Regulations were strict; Neptune was very firm on these laws. You know that.'

I kept silent.

'I'm not proud of what I did,' he said quietly.

'So what about my mum? How come she didn't go with them?'

He shook his head. 'I tried the drug on her several times, to get her to agree to it, but it wouldn't work. Even once I'd taken away the memory of your father, I couldn't make her leave. She simply refused.'

'So my grandparents moved away, and they didn't remember a thing?' I asked woodenly.

'Correct.'

I swallowed hard, trying to dislodge the lump in my throat. It was too hard, though. It had a lifetime of hurt and anger inside it. 'What about the cards?' I asked. 'Every year, a birthday card and Christmas card?'

Mr Beeston fiddled with a button on his jacket. 'I sent them,' he said.

'*You?* But how?'

'I had to visit them regularly, to ensure the memory drug was working.'

That made sense. He'd kept my mum drugged on a weekly basis, with iced buns and doughnuts – laced with memory drug.

'I'd write the cards, then send them while I was up there – so they had the right postmarks on them.' He glanced nervously at me. 'So your mother would still at least have something,' he added.

I nearly laughed. He thought he'd been doing us a *favour* by scrawling a few measly, lying words on a card a couple of times a year?

'It was my way of doing one small thing for you,' Mr Beeston went on. 'You see, your mother and I *were* friends back –'

'You mean they didn't even sign their own names on them?' I interrupted. I wasn't going to listen to him telling me he'd been our friend while he'd been lying to our faces for years!

'We couldn't take the risk of bringing their memories back.' Mr Beeston actually had the grace to look ashamed. His head hung low, his arms dangled limply by his sides. 'I'm sorry, Emily,' he said. 'Things are different now. I would never, ever do anything ever again to hurt you or any of your family. You do believe me, don't you?'

I didn't reply.

Mr Beeston reached out an awkward hand. He pulled at my sleeve. 'Emily, I know I have wronged you, and for this I am in your debt,' he said in his usual dramatic way. 'To prove my sincerity, I'm telling you now, whatever you need, if I can ever help you with it, I will do it. I owe you one.'

I nearly laughed. 'You owe us *one*? What you owe us could *never* be repaid, even if you spent the rest of your life trying!'

He nodded. 'I know. I'm sorry. I owe you more than I can express with mere words. But remember,

95

things are different now. We have a shared mission – and I intend to do everything in my power to make it work.'

I found myself softening a tiny bit. *Could* people change? Was it possible? Neptune had changed *his* mind – and his laws – on a lot of things lately. Maybe Mr Beeston could change, too. I knew I would never trust him again, but what he said about doing anything for us – well, perhaps one day that promise would come in useful.

'And if it's of any interest to you, this incident has made me come to a decision.'

'What about?'

Mr Beeston paused for a long time. When he spoke, his voice had a catch in it, as though his words were climbing over a gravelly hill to get out of his mouth. 'My mother,' he said.

'Your mother? What about her?'

Mr Beeston had hardly ever mentioned any family. The only time I'd ever heard him talk about his parents was when he'd come after me in the motor boat when I'd gone out to the Great Mermer Reef to rescue Dad. I tried to recall what he'd told me then. Something about his dad being happy to have a siren for a girlfriend, but then disappearing the minute he was born.

'Our conversation the other day got me thinking. I'm going to visit her,' he said. 'You see, your mother and I have something in common,' he went on. 'I, too, am estranged from my parents.'

'Your dad left you as a baby, didn't he?' I asked, as gently as I could. I know it was only Mr Beeston, but even so, it wasn't exactly the kind of thing you threw in someone's face without a care.

He nodded. 'Off without a backwards glance,' he said bitterly.

'So your mother brought you up?'

'Ha! That's one way of putting it!'

'What do you mean?'

'My mother – well, she was beautiful. She was a good siren. But more remote than the furthest horizon. Or, to put it kindly, let's say that when Mother Nature was handing out the mothering skills, mine was at the back of the queue, if you get my drift. I was left to fend for myself from a very young age. Leaving home was almost an irrelevance – to both of us. In our hearts, we'd left each other many years earlier.'

I thought of my own childhood up until last year. Growing up without my dad hadn't been easy. But I'd never for a second doubted Mum's love for me. I couldn't imagine what it would have been like without that. For the first time ever, I really, truly felt sorry for Mr Beeston.

'Why do you want to see her now, then?' I asked.

Mr Beeston shook himself. He cleared his throat and seemed to drag himself back into the present. 'I take my work seriously. You know that.'

I probably knew it better than anyone on the planet!

'We have been charged with the mission of making peace. Just like your mother, if I cannot make amends with my own kin, how can I be expected to succeed in the wider world? The answer is that I can't, and I wouldn't expect anyone to take me seriously if I tried. A job likes this begins with family. I've decided. I'm going to see my mother – and I'm going to do it today!'

I was starting to feel an inkling of forgiveness for him, but something was still niggling at me. 'Hold on,' I said. 'The thing about my grandparents – it still doesn't add up.'

'What doesn't?'

'Well, you said they were memory drugged.'

'As indeed they were.'

'In that case, how come they remembered, earlier?'

'They what? What on earth are you talking about, child?'

I explained about Millie bringing my grandparents to Brightport, and everything that had happened.

'The silly woman,' he snarled, back to his old self. 'She shouldn't go messing around in things she doesn't understand.'

'She was trying to help my mum! You know, the one who you've just sworn undying loyalty to.'

'Hmph,' he said, sniffing and straightening his jacket.

'So how come they remembered and then forgot again?' I asked. 'Did you have anything to do with it?'

He shook his head. 'I can't undo the memory drug now. Only Neptune can do that.'

Neptune? I didn't fancy trying to get him to help. Most of my dealings with Neptune had involved catastrophe of some sort or another. 'Well, someone else must be able to do it because it's just happened! Look, two minutes ago, you told me you'd do anything to help us, and now I'm asking you. How do we undo it?'

Mr Beeston's face turned pink at the edges. 'I'm telling you, child, it's impossible. Haven't you ever heard Neptune's saying on the matter?'

I shook my head.

'*Only the hand that is mightier than my own*

May undo the magic from my throne,' he said. 'And as we all know, there is no one mightier than Neptune.'

'So it can't be done?'

'Afraid not.'

'But what about when they remembered for a bit – or seemed to?'

He shook his head. 'It must have been a temporary blip. It happens sometimes, especially as they had only just returned to a place with

mermaids   nearby.'   Mr   Beeston   shuffled
uncomfortably. 'Now if you'll excuse me,' he said,
'I do have some rather important work to do.'

I left him to his important work, and wandered
away from the lighthouse in a daze, my head still
full of questions. In particular, how were we ever
going to fix this? Not just the situation with my
grandparents, but the whole thing. We'd been told –
ordered – by Neptune to make humans and
merpeople get on better, and we couldn't even get
our family to talk to each other.

What would he do if he found out how badly we
were failing?

I had plenty of experience of what Neptune does
when he isn't happy; the kind of punishments he
can dole out. And I knew one thing. I didn't want
to be on the receiving end of another one. No, we
had to sort it out. We simply had to.

All we had to do now was figure out *how.*

Chapter Seven

I sloped over to Aaron's, too mixed up and miserable to try to work out any more answers on my own.

'Come on, let's go out,' he said. His mum had discovered a whole channel of quiz programmes and it was hard to talk over the telly.

We swam out to Rainbow Rocks and I filled Aaron in on everything that had happened. Swimming along with him, my tail swishing through the silky sea, groups of fish darting purposefully this way and that all around us, I felt my mood gradually lift.

'Race you to the furthest rock,' Aaron said, diving down deep into the water and spinning round to dart back up and through the surface with a huge splash. A moment later, he'd gone.

'How come whenever we race anywhere, you always seem to have a head start?' I asked when I finally caught up with him at the rocks.

He grinned and flicked water at me in reply.

'Oi!' I flicked water back at him.

He laughed and flipped over on his back. 'Let's keep swimming,' he said, spinning back round like a dolphin and diving down with another loud splash.

I followed him round to the other side of the rocks and out to sea. We talked as we swam, trying to think of some way of sorting everything out – but we kept coming up with blanks.

Suddenly Aaron stopped. 'Wow!' he said.

'What?' I stopped next to him. Up ahead, a wavy line of rocks blocked our way. There was a gap in the middle of them – but the water in the gap was different from the rest of the sea. It looked like a cauldron, bubbling and frothing. As we got closer, I could see that it was spinning furiously.

'A whirlpool,' I said. I turned to head back.

'Let's go across it,' Aaron said, his eyes shining like dots of sunlight on the sea.

'You can't get across a whirlpool!'

'Why not?'

'I've heard about these in school. This is one of Neptune's pools.' I pointed to one of the rocks lining the whirlpool. There was something etched on its side. 'Look.'

Aaron squinted at the rock. 'A trident?'

I nodded. 'That means he created it. He'll have been in a rage with something – or someone.' I shuddered as I remembered getting caught in a whirlwind created by one of Neptune's furies. We had enough trouble already. I wasn't about to swim into more if I could help it. 'Come on, let's go back.'

But Aaron was insistent. 'Look over there.' Beyond the rocks, the sea looked clearer than ever. The sun shone brightly down, bouncing and catching the surface of the water as though an invisible giant in the sky were sprinkling diamonds across it.

The whirlpool was the only way to get there. On either side of it, jagged rocks spread out as far as we could see.

'Take my hand,' Aaron said. 'We'll go across it together. I'll look after you.'

I'd been wondering if we'd get to hold hands again; wondering if he wanted to, or if it had been accidental this morning; wondering if he'd felt the same tingling feelings that I had.

I held my hand out.

Aaron smiled and gripped my hand in his. 'Ready?'

I nodded, and we swam together towards the pool. The water frothed and swirled angrily. What were we doing? Aaron's ability to hurl himself headlong into crazy situations was starting to feel like a match for mine.

Aaron turned to me. 'Let's go.'

I held tightly on to his hand and we dived together over the low layer of rocks on our side of the whirlpool. Instantly, we were sucked under the water, flung apart and hurled round and round so fast I didn't know which way up the world was. I felt like a ragged piece of clothing in a spin dryer.

'Emily!'

Aaron was calling out to me through the whirling, crashing water. I tried to find him but all I could see was froth and foam. Then I felt him career into me and we started to spin together, banging against each other.

'Take my hand!' he shouted. 'It'll stop us from bashing into each other.'

I fumbled and flailed around, and eventually found his hand. I took hold of it, gripping hard and wondering how long we could survive, and why I'd agreed to this ridiculous idea in the first place.

And then something really weird happened.

It stopped.

Just like that.

The whirlpool suddenly wasn't a whirlpool any more. It was the stillest, calmest pool you've ever seen in your life, so smooth and gentle you'd think it had been lying empty and undiscovered for years.

We bobbed up to the surface, still holding hands, both bedraggled and breathless.

'What – what happened?' I asked.

Aaron shook his head. 'It stopped,' he said, kind of pointing out the obvious.

'Neptune's whirlpools don't just *stop*,' I said, looking round to see if there was someone nearby. Maybe even Neptune himself was here, watching us, ready to tell us off for going where we shouldn't, and then set the whirlpool spinning again.

'Well, this one did,' he said. 'I guess he's not always as powerful as you might think.'

I nearly laughed. 'Neptune not all that powerful? Are you kidding me?'

Aaron just shook his head. 'I don't know,' he said. 'But I don't have any other explanation.' He started swimming to the edge of the pool, his grip loosening on my hand.

That was when everything suddenly clicked into place.

'No!' I held tightly on to his hand.

He stopped and turned to look at me. 'What is it?'

'Wait! Don't let go of my hand.' *Could it be? Could I be right?*

Aaron smiled again. 'OK,' he said, turning slightly pink. He seemed to do that quite a bit lately.

'What you said, about Neptune not being powerful,' I said. 'I know it's crazy, but – well, you and I both had curses on us, didn't we?'

'*Had*, yes. Not any more.'

'No, I know. But how did we overturn Neptune's curse on us?'

'We found the rings he and his wife had given to each other. What are you –'

'We didn't just *find* them,' I went on. 'We wore them, and then what did we do?'

'We brought the rings together,' Aaron said. 'Emily, I don't see what this –'

'Our hands! We held hands! We brought our hands together and overturned Neptune's power!'

Aaron's eyes opened wider. I could see he was starting to catch up with my thinking. I struggled to remember what Mr Beeston had told me. What was it exactly? '*Only the hand that is mightier than my own,*' I began.

'*Can overturn the power of my throne!*' Aaron finished.

'That's it!' I stared down at our hands, locked tightly together. 'We broke the curse when we held hands.'

'In other words, our hands together were mightier than his,' Aaron said.

'Exactly! Which means that maybe we can overturn his power.'

'As long as we hold hands.'

It fitted. It worked. Except – well, it seemed so incredible! We could overturn Neptune's power?

'Aaron – it's crazy,' I said. 'Surely it's not possible!'

'I know what you mean. Nice thought, but come on! The whirlpool stopping must have just been a coincidence.'

He was right. I was about to let go of his hand and swim to the edge of the pool. We had to get out before it started again. But then I realised something else. Of course! 'No!' I burst out. 'It wasn't a coincidence. It *was* us!'

Aaron frowned at me. 'How can you be so sure?'

'My grandparents! We were holding hands when they remembered everything.'

The frown melted away. Aaron's eyes looked as though they had lights inside them. 'Of course! The memory drug stopped working.'

'And then you left – and they forgot, all over again.'

We both looked down at our hands, and then at each other.

'We can really do it,' I said in a whisper. If I said it too loud, maybe it wouldn't be true. 'We really can overturn Neptune's power.'

'Which means . . .'

'Which means perhaps all's not lost with my grandparents after all,' I said.

'Or with the peace-making mission!'

We locked eyes, making a silent deal with each other.

'Come on,' Aaron said.

We swam back to Brightport as fast as we could. We both knew what we had to do.

'Hello?' I shouted through the letterbox.

Aaron rapped on the door for the third time. Nothing.

'Where are they?' I asked.

'Gone out?'

'Try one more time,' I said.

Aaron lifted his fist to knock again, but stopped mid-air. 'Hang on,' he said. 'Look.' He pushed the door. It swung open. 'Should we . . .?'

I edged my face round the door. 'Nan?' I called. 'Grandad?' No reply. I turned to Aaron. 'Come on.'

We went in. Creeping around, feeling like burglars, we looked in every room. Not that it took long. There are only four rooms altogether in these cottages. And every one was empty.

'They've left,' I said, plonking myself down on one of the armchairs.

'All their stuff's gone.'

'And they were in such a hurry to get away from

us, they didn't even close the door properly behind them.'

Aaron reached out and pulled me up from the armchair. 'Come on,' he said. 'Let's go back to yours.'

We walked along the beach, heading back to the pier, both lost in our thoughts. I hoped his weren't quite as miserable as mine. In other words, I hoped he wasn't thinking about the fact that every single thing I ever tried to do to make things better only seemed to make them worse. And I hoped he wasn't thinking too hard about how much trouble we were going to be in with Neptune if we didn't hurry up and get some peace-talk going on round here.

'Oh, great,' Aaron said heavily.

I looked up to see a familiar figure heading towards us. Mandy Rushton. That was all we needed.

She stopped right in front of us, hands on hips. For a second, a strange look flashed across her face. Her expression was baffled and contorted, as though it were being pulled in two directions at the same time. Have you ever seen a film or cartoon where someone's trying to decide between good and evil and they have a little angel sitting on one shoulder and a devil on the other, both talking to them at the same time? There was something about her expression that reminded me of that.

And then I guess she must have listened to the

devil because she looked me right in the eyes and smirked. 'Oh look,' she said. 'Someone's left a load of rubbish lying around on the beach again.' Then she turned her scowl on Aaron. 'In fact, two loads of rubbish,' she added.

So much for thinking Mandy Rushton might have an angel sitting on one shoulder!

'Excuse me,' I said. I tried to get past her but she dodged to the right so that she was still in my way.

'Got somewhere important to be, have you?' she sneered. 'Oh, poor you, that nasty Mandy Rushton getting in your way? Well, just so happens I've got somewhere important to be, too.' She took another step closer towards me. Her face was centimetres from mine.

I wanted to ask her to stop it. I wanted to remind her we'd made friends once and ask her if we could do it again. I stopped myself, though. I wasn't going to go begging to her. It would only give her more ammunition to throw back in my face. Mandy would *never* be friends with me again. The memory drug had made sure of that.

Wait!

The memory drug.

I turned to Aaron. 'Hold my hand!' I said.

Mandy burst out laughing. 'Aw, diddums,' she said. She stuck her bottom lip out and rolled a finger on it. 'Poor wickle Emily, got to get her new boyfwiend to hold her handy wandy.'

'He's not my –' I began. Or was he? How did you know if someone was your boyfriend or not? I'd never had one before, so I wasn't sure. Did you have to announce it to each other? Did one of you ask the other one, like a marriage proposal? *Do you, Emily, take me, Aaron, to be your boyfriend?* How did you *know*? And why did no one tell you these things?

I shook myself. Either way, that wasn't the important thing right now. I held my hand out. 'Aaron, take it,' I said firmly.

Those lights went on inside his eyes again and I could tell he understood. He suddenly reached his hand out. I took it in mine and held it as tightly as I could. *Come on, do it*, I said under my breath. *Work! Get rid of the memory drug. And not just while we're holding hands. For good!*

Mandy was still laughing. 'Ah, so sweet. Feel better now? So scared of Mandy-Wandy that you have to hold your boyfriend's hand. You're pathetic!' She stuck her face so close to me her nose was almost touching mine.

Why wasn't it working? Had we got it all wrong? So the whirlpool *had* been a coincidence after all? And my grandparents remembering had been a blip, just like Mr Beeston said.

And then I felt it. The tingling feeling in my arms. Like pins and needles, only – well, nicer. It felt a bit like having soft fine sand trickled over my fingers, then up my arm. Soon, the feeling spread into my whole body. It was working. Something was happening.

Mandy took a step back.

I looked at Aaron. He could feel it, too. I could see it in his eyes.

Mandy opened her mouth to speak. She curled her face into a sneer. Or she tried to, but it stopped halfway so that her expression ended up half sneering and half completely perplexed. It reminded me of what Mum always used to say when I pulled faces. 'Better watch out, sausage,' she'd say. 'If the wind changes, you'll be stuck like that.'

Mandy's face seemed to be moving in slow motion now. I could almost see the cogs working in her brain, undoing the memory drug, going back to Allpoints Island. Remembering. *Please remember!* I gripped Aaron's hand even tighter.

'We're friends,' she said, in a quiet voice that was so different from the voice she'd been using a moment ago you would have sworn it was a different person.

I held my breath, keeping my mouth tightly closed. I didn't want to spoil it.

'We made friends,' Mandy repeated. 'We were on an island. You had a tail and my dad wanted to put you in a show.' Her voice was soft and dazed. She sounded as though she were talking from inside a dream. 'There was a big ferry.' She suddenly stopped and took another step back. Her eyes darkened. 'There was a monster,' she said slowly. 'We saved lots of people, you and I, didn't we?'

Finally, she looked at me. She caught my eyes and I nodded.

'It was nice, being friends,' Mandy went on.

I smiled. 'It was, yes.'

None of us spoke for a while. Then Mandy took a breath and said, 'Maybe we should do it again then. Shall we?'

We'd done it! We'd removed the memory drug! I grinned at her. 'Yes, please!'

She grinned back at me. I still didn't dare let go of Aaron's hand, still didn't quite believe that we'd done it, or that it would last. But I'd told it what to do. We were in control of our power now and I sensed that this wouldn't wear off like it had with my grandparents when we didn't know what we were doing. This time it would be permanent: we'd told it to be!

Mandy turned to face Aaron. 'That means we're friends too, if you want to be,' she said.

'Fine by me,' Aaron said, gripping my hand a little bit closer. The tingling feeling went through me again.

'I'm sorry,' Mandy said to us both. 'Start again?' She held out a hand as a gesture of peace.

What did I do now? If I ignored her hand, she might switch back to old Mandy in a flash. If I took it, would it break the spell? No. I had to trust the magic, believe that we had control over our power.

I let go of Aaron's hand.

Mandy was still holding her hand out to me. We'd done it! We'd made it work for good. We'd undone the memory drug!

I took Mandy's hand and shook it. 'Start again,' I said. Then she and Aaron did the same.

None of us were quite sure what to do after that and I kicked the sand around with my feet, trying to think of what to say next.

Aaron got us out of it. 'Come on,' he said. 'Let's go to the theme park!' We still hadn't actually been inside yet, in case we ran into Mandy, but I knew he'd been dying to see it.

Mandy looked relieved. 'Cool,' she said. 'I'll show you round.'

We headed off up the beach together. 'And you can tell Mandy everything she's missed along the way,' Aaron said.

I wasn't sure I was ready to trust her with *everything* just yet, but as we walked, I started to tell her about leaving the island, the journey back to Brightport. She told me what had been happening at Brightport High.

Nothing out of this world. Nothing top secret. Just enough to fill the space between the beach and the waltzers, and to start joining up the gaps between us, too.

Sunday morning I woke up with the biggest smile on my face. I couldn't think why I was in such a good mood at first. Then I remembered. We'd overturned the memory drug! Mandy and I were friends!

Surely that was a start? For the first time, I really believed we could do what Neptune had ordered us to do. We'd create a new world, just like he'd said. One where humans and merfolk would live together in harmony, side by side. And it was all going to start in Brightport! We would pass Neptune's test!

I jumped out of bed. It was still early and I could hear Mum's snores coming from her bedroom. I decided to go up to the shop and get her a newspaper and some fresh bread as a treat.

I crept quietly out of the boat. Dad had already gone off to Shiprock. He and Mr Beeston had a meeting with the mer-mayor today. They were going to explain what was going on and see how they could work together to deal with the situation. I smiled to myself. The 'situation' wouldn't be a problem much longer. I just knew it. We were going to mend fences, join the worlds together. Things were going to be great.

I was still smiling to myself as I headed down the pier.

I was still smiling as I opened the door to the Spar and picked up the bread.

I was even still smiling as I walked over to the newspaper stand.

And that was the point at which I stopped smiling.

'I – can I have a –' I pointed to the pile of Sunday newspapers stacked on the counter, feeling like someone in a foreign country who gets by on a vocabulary of about five words and lots of hand gestures.

'You want a *Brightport Times*, love?' the woman behind the counter asked.

I nodded.

'Going like hot cakes today, these are,' she said. 'Not often you get something like this on the front page.'

I tried to reply. I opened my mouth; I even moved it a bit, opened and closed it a couple more times, but nothing came out. Eventually I just nodded.

The woman gave me a sympathetic look and handed me a paper with my bread. 'One fifty-three,' she said loudly, as though I were a bit slow or stupid. I handed her some money, grabbed my things and bolted.

Outside the shop, I looked both ways before setting off along the front. I couldn't go straight home. Not yet. I had to read the whole story; I had to prepare myself; I had to be alone.

I sat down on a bench and opened up the paper. The front page had a big banner headline running across it that made me feel sick.

'MERMAID HUNT!'

Under the headline, a few paragraphs filled in the story.

'In the last twenty-four hours, the *Brightport Times* office has been inundated with phone calls from local residents claiming to have seen MERMAIDS!

The claims reveal a remarkable consistency about the sightings, confirming that they are ONE HUNDRED PER CENT GENUINE!

What is a mystery, both to us here at the *Brightport Times* and to the callers themselves, is why the recollections have only just come to light. Many of the sightings are reported as having taken place weeks and even months ago.

Daniel Sykes is one of those who called our office.

"I don't know why I've just remembered," he told the *Brightport Times*. "But I'm telling you, I can see her now, as clear as day. A mermaid in the sea, with a shiny blue tail."

Mr Sykes is just one of over twenty people to have called our office so far. In every case, the caller only recalled their sighting since around yesterday lunch time.

Join our mermaid hunt! Get in touch now and tell us your mermaid story! Rewards paid for all mermaid stories and pictures. Catch a mermaid and be a local hero! Turn to page 2 for more information.'

I sat back on the bench, staring out across the bay. I really thought I was going to be sick this time. Catch a mermaid and be a local hero? I was straight back at Allpoints Island in a net with Mr Rushton bragging to Mandy and her mum about how they would make a fortune displaying me to the world.

This was it. My nightmare was finally coming true.

My fingers curled up so hard I felt my fingernails dig into my palms. Mandy! She'd pretended to be my friend so she could play her cruellest trick yet!

But it didn't make sense! How could she get all those people to phone up? She might have a nasty streak but surely she wasn't that powerful – was she?

I looked back at the paper, turning the page as though in a trance.

And that was when I saw it.

A photograph. It was very blurred and hazy. You could only really see an outline, but it was obvious what the outline was.

A mermaid.

I looked closer, and my heart sank so low I could have sworn I heard it hit the floor. The photograph – yes it was blurred, yes it was hazy, yes it probably looked little more than a silhouette to most people. But I could see clearly what it was. The tail. The hair, even the expression on the face. To me it was so obvious they might as well have printed the name above it in capital letters.

It was a photograph of me.

Chapter Eight

I stumbled away from the bench, stuffing the newspaper in my pocket, out of sight.

What was I going to do? Where could I go? I couldn't stay in Brightport. Sooner or later, someone would recognise me from the photo and reel me in to claim their reward. My worst nightmare really was going to come true.

I walked along the prom in a daze, convinced that every person I passed was staring at me. Had they bought their morning paper yet? How long would it be before I was caught and dragged up in a net to be displayed for the whole town's entertainment?

There was only one answer to my questions: I had to get away. I had to go to the sea.

I turned towards the beach. Right now I felt like I never wanted to set foot on dry land again. So much for bringing the two worlds together!

I hurried down to the beach and with a quick look round, I ran to the point below the pier where I could slip into the water unseen.

Except someone was already there.

'Emily!'

I spun round. Mandy! She'd come to sneer. Now I *knew* she was the one who'd done this. I didn't know how, but there was no other explanation. It had to be her.

'What are you doing here?' I snapped. 'Come to gloat, have you? Had your bit of fun with me and now you want to see the effect it's had? Well, congratulations. You've done a top job this time!'

Mandy stared at me in astonishment. 'I don't know what you mean,' she said.

'Bet you don't! All those people seeing mermaids – funnily enough, since my conversation with you.' I grabbed the newspaper from my pocket and shoved it in her face. Mandy scanned the front page.

She looked up at me. 'Emily, I don't –'

'And a photograph – of me! Page two,' I said.

Mandy opened the paper up and squinted at the photo. 'How do you know it's even you?' she asked. 'Emily, no one would know who it is. You can hardly even tell it's a –'

'Well, *I* know who it is. And *you* know who it is. And soon enough, the whole *town* is going to know.'

Mandy closed the newspaper and stared down at it. 'Emily, I didn't have anything to do with this,' she said. 'You and I – yesterday, we made friends. Well, we made friends ages ago. But yesterday I remembered. Do you have any idea how happy I was when I woke up this morning?'

I thought back to how I'd felt when I woke up, in those few minutes before everything had gone wrong yet again.

'Not just because of you and me being friends again,' Mandy went on. 'That wasn't the only thing I remembered. I remembered how it had felt when we saved all those people from the kraken. I remembered what it feels like to be *nice*. To do *good* things, to make people *happy*!'

I looked at her. She was smiling. Not her sneering, snarly smile. Her real one. The one that I hadn't seen much of for years. 'You really didn't have anything to do with this?' I asked.

'I really didn't,' she said. She drew a cross over her chest. 'I promise.'

I slumped down on the sand. 'Well, why did it happen then?'

Mandy joined me. Picking up a handful of sand and letting it run through her fingers, she said, 'Maybe it's got something to do with you and Aaron.'

I stuck my feet into the sand. 'What d'you mean? Aaron would never do anything like that.'

'That's not what I meant.' Mandy shifted round to face me. 'All these people have remembered since you and I made friends again, right?'

'Right,' I agreed.

'And how did you make us do that? Yesterday you said something about having special powers.'

I looked down. I hadn't told her too much of the specifics. I still didn't know if I could trust her, but I didn't exactly have much to lose.

'Neptune has this thing called a memory drug,' I began. Then I told her about the verse, and why it meant that Aaron and I could overturn Neptune's magic.

'That's it, then!' Mandy jumped to her knees, her eyes wide with excitement. What exactly there was to be excited about, I wasn't so sure.

'That's what?' I asked flatly.

'You undid the memory drug!'

'That's what I just told you,' I said. 'That's why you remembered we were friends.'

'Not just on me! You undid the memory drug on the whole of Brightport!'

'I – we –' I began. Then I stopped and stared at

her. Of course! As soon as she said it, I realised that it was the most obvious thing in the world. So obvious that I hadn't even thought of it!

Aaron and I must have been even more powerful than we'd realised. We'd concentrated so hard on undoing the memory drug, it must have spread beyond Mandy into the whole town. She was right. It was the only answer that fitted.

'One thing I don't understand, though, is how come there are so many mermaids around here,' Mandy said.

'Shiprock,' I said simply.

'Ship what?'

'It's a mermaid town,' I replied. 'There aren't many mermaid places near to where humans live, but this one is close by, so it's quite risky. I guess there've been a lot of accidental sightings over the years.'

Mandy looked as though she was going to say something. For a second, I thought the old Mandy was going to come back and she'd laugh in my face. But she didn't. She just nodded.

'What are you going to do?' she asked after a while.

What *was* I going to do? All I knew for sure was that I had to get away from Brightport. My first thought was to head for Shiprock, but I wasn't even welcome *there* now! Then I remembered I was meant to be meeting Shona today. It was Sunday –

the day we said we'd go out looking for the lost sirens.

I leapt up. That was it! The lost sirens! Maybe I could hide away with them! We had to find them.

I shook the sand off my clothes and headed down to the water's edge. Mandy was behind me. 'What are you doing?' she asked. 'Where are you going?'

'Look, just cover for me, will you? Tell my mum I'd forgotten to tell her I was spending the day at Shona's. I had to get going and I didn't want to wake her.'

Mandy nodded. 'So you'll be gone all day?' she asked. She sounded disappointed. I'd be out at *least* all day, I thought. This problem wasn't going to have gone away by tomorrow. But I'd worry about that later. At this point, all I wanted to do was hide.

'Yeah,' I said.

'What about Aaron?'

'Tell him I've gone to see Shona and I'll catch him soon, OK?'

'OK.' She turned to walk away.

'And, Mandy?'

She turned round. 'What?'

I smiled at her. 'Thanks. I like being friends again.'

She held my eyes and nodded. 'Yeah, me too,' she said.

And with that, I glanced round one last time, whipped off my sandals, and slid into the sea.

'So the whole town knows about you?' Shona asked as we swam along. I'd filled her in on everything that had happened.

'Well, not exactly about *me*,' I said. 'At least, I hope not.' Maybe it would blow over soon. People would throw their newspapers out in a few days and forget all about it again. The picture *was* pretty blurred, after all. Perhaps it would be safe for me to return in a couple of weeks.

Yeah, and perhaps sharks would walk across the moon.

I might as well get used to the idea of living as a recluse.

We swam on, gliding over pastel pink bushes and lime green rocks. Sea urchins littered the sea bed, still and spiky like curled up hedgehogs. Black wavy rays with fins like Dracula's cloak passed beneath us, tickling the sand as they slid by.

'Miss Merlin told us a bit more about the lost sirens,' Shona said as we swam.

'What did she tell you?' I asked, glad of the change of subject.

'She thinks she knows roughly where they were last seen. She said that after our lesson last week, she looked into it more and she reckons she's figured out some co-ordinates that no one's ever worked out before. It could be rubbish, but I put them into my splishometer anyway.'

'And? What did it tell you?'

'It's about five miles away – hardly any distance,' she said, so excited that her eyes looked about ready to pop out of her face.

I thought about Brightport – people waking up and buying their local paper, all keen to catch a mermaid and win a reward. My photograph on page two. I shuddered and swam ahead. 'Come on,' I said. 'What are we waiting for?'

We'd been swimming for hours. The sea had grown colder and deeper and darker. Lone, sleek, grey fish slid by, weaving among seaweed that trailed up from the seabed. Shoals of flat round fish swam towards us and then away again, flickering like mirrors in sunlight as they flashed by.

Ahead of us, below, all around us, sea life went about its business, oblivious to the two intruders, swimming all around looking for something that might be no more than an ocean myth.

A lion fish with ornate markings round its jowls stared through us as we passed. A dancing crab with stick-thin legs jiggled sideways across our path.

Ferns opened and closed with the rhythm of the sea. We swam on.

'Are you sure you put the right numbers in?' I asked. 'We must have swum more than five miles by now.'

'It's got to be round here somewhere,' Shona said, consulting her splishometer. 'Unless Miss Merlin got it wrong.'

Which I was starting to think she must have. I didn't say anything, though. Shona loves an adventure more than anything and I didn't want to take it away from her. And anyway, I didn't have anything better to do. There was no way I could go back to Brightport yet, and I wasn't exactly welcome in Shiprock. The best thing I could do was find the lost sirens and plead with them to let me be lost with them.

'How about we split up?' I suggested. 'You go round that way.' I pointed over to my right. Long, thick trails of seaweed stretched up like thick ropes. 'I'll go this way.' To my left, pink spongy fingers reached upwards, open and outstretched as though they were silently begging. Deep, jagged rocks lay all around us, purple and green twigs and sticks littering every crevice. 'Give it ten minutes and then meet back up again,' I said.

Shona pointed to a moss-covered rock with a tree growing horizontally out from its side. 'Meet you over there,' she said.

'Ten minutes,' I repeated.

Shona nodded. 'Good luck.'

Shona swam away to the right, and I swam off the other way.

Please let me find them, please let me find them, I thought to myself as I swam, scanning every bit of rock and seaweed I could see, just in case there was a secret entrance hidden inside it. *Please don't make me go back to Brightport till it's safe.*

I swam across reeds like bunches of thick-cut spaghetti; big leafy plants like giant cabbages; bright red rocks, shining like mottled marble. A long eel, green with white spots, slithered in and out of the reeds, poking its head into holes, then slithering out again and slinking away. Two round fish smooched past in a perfectly synchronised dance. Everything moved slowly along. Nothing was in a hurry down here.

And there were no lost sirens either.

I was about to head back to meet Shona when something stopped me.

A current was tugging at me. It reminded me of what happened at Allpoints Island if you swam out too far and got caught in the Bermuda Triangle. A shiver flickered through me like a wriggly fish squiggling through my body. What was it? Where was it taking me?

The shivery feeling passed. This wasn't like that current. It wasn't dragging me out anywhere; it was hardly pulling at all. It felt more as if it was leading me somewhere, directing me, helping me. I *wanted* to follow it!

I let go of my resistance and let the current do the work. Soon I was zooming through the water, racing against a stripy yellow and black fish, whizzing past trails of fern and weed.

And then the current slowed. The sea had turned darker, and colder. I was further down than before. The fluttery feeling came back. What was I doing, floating along on a current that had led me this far down? I hadn't even looked where I was going. How was I ever going to get back and find Shona again?

And where was I, anyway?

I looked round. The current had pulled me to the top of a circle of tall rocks. I couldn't see the bottom of them, but they were grouped around a dark hole, like an enormous well. I swam to the edge of the well and looked down. It was foaming and rushing with water that poured down like an underwater waterfall. Surely that was impossible?

I could feel the current again. It was lifting me, edging me closer to the top of the well. It was as though it was teasing me, daring me to go down. Should I? *Could* I?

Before I had time to decide, the current nudged me right to the edge of the well. A moment later, I'd gone hurtling over the top, into the waterfall.

Water rushed at me from every side, turning me over and round, pulling me further and further down, dragging me ever closer to the bottom of the sea. I tried to fight against it, tried to swim upwards, but it was impossible. The current was dragging me lower and lower, throwing me down faster than anything I'd ever known. It was like a rocket – only heading down, towards the seabed.

Eventually, I gave in and let it pull me. And then, before I knew what was happening, it stopped. The waterfall released me.

Bedraggled, exhausted and dishevelled, I had landed – in a dark, enclosed, rocky hole at the bottom of the ocean.

Chapter Nine

I glanced around, my eyes gradually adjusting to the darkness. Rocks on every side of me. I was at the bottom of the well. The weird thing was, the rushing water had stopped. All I could see was clear water leading all the way up — so clear I could see right to the top. It looked an awfully long way.

Where had the waterfall gone?

I tried to swim up the well again, but an enormous force stopped me. I kept on landing back in the same spot, shoved back down. It was as though the waterfall's force was still there, but with no rushing water. Impossible – but real. It was like a magic trick.

A magic trick? A magical place? Had I found the place where the sirens lived?

I didn't have long to think about it.

There was a sound of movement somewhere nearby. I whizzed round to see where it had come from. That was when I noticed that one side of the well had a hole in it, just big enough to swim through. A bunch of seaweed hung down from the top of the hole, like thick cord. I pushed through it and swam out of the well.

I was in a larger opening. Above me, the ceiling was smooth brown stone. Below, the sandy floor slipped away, sloping gradually downwards. All around me, the walls were lined with stony, jagged pillars and arches and caverns. Trails of multi-coloured seaweed dangled here and there like Christmas decorations. Behind them, I heard the swishing sound again. In the growing light, I saw a tail flick sharply.

'Shona!' I cried in relief, swimming towards the tail.

But it wasn't Shona.

'Who are you?' the mermaid and I said in unison.

She swam towards me. 'How did you get here?' she said. 'No one comes here – ever.'

'I – I – I swam,' I stammered. 'Where am I, anyway? And who are you?'

The mermaid swam closer to me, looked me straight in the eyes, swam all around me, then came back to face me. Her face was lined and pale. She seemed old, but at the same time almost ageless, and strangely beautiful. Her silvery hair was so long it flowed all the way down her back and stroked her tail as she swam. Her tail was a musty, dusty mix of mauve and pink. She looked a bit like someone who'd just been presented with a fairly rare, and not particularly pleasant, geological finding.

She didn't answer my question. 'Come with me,' she said, tugging at my arm.

I pulled away from her. 'Not till you tell me who you are,' I said. I hoped I sounded braver than I felt.

In reply, she gripped my arm more tightly and pulled me along behind her.

We swam down tunnels, round tubes of weeds, through high-sided channels, under rocks and around corners until we came to a large sandy opening with an enormous pillar in the middle and caves and arches dug into the walls all around it.

Four mermaids were in the clearing. One was brushing her hair with a makeshift brush that looked as if it was made of twigs. Another had grabbed a passing shiny flat fish as it floated by and was peering into its skin to see her reflection. The other two were sitting on the sandy seabed; one looked as though she were making something out of reeds, the other seemed to be playing a game with stones in the sand.

'I found something,' the mermaid called out to the others. They all looked up – each face an identical mixture of shock and disbelief. A minute later, they had crowded round me, looking into my face, examining my tail, reaching out to touch me.

'Is she real?' one of them asked.

'Of course I'm real!' I snapped, and she jumped away.

'How did she get in here?' another one asked.

'I *can* talk, you know,' I said. 'Why don't you talk *to* me instead of about me?'

The mermaid who had been making something with the reeds pushed in front of the others, glaring at me so intently that I wished for once in my life I could have kept my mouth shut.

'Leave her be, Nerin,' she said. 'She is a visitor. Is that not enough? And look – the child is scared. Give her some room.'

Her voice was soft and gentle. She seemed younger than the others, although as I looked more closely into her face, I could see that like the rest, she had tiny squiggly wrinkles across her forehead and little claw-shaped lines fanning out beside each eye. Her hair was silver too, but shorter than the first mermaid's.

The others nodded their agreement. 'Morvena's right,' one of them said, smiling at me. Her smile felt like warm treacle flowing over me. I felt my fear and anger melt away. 'We should be grateful,' she went on. 'We should be welcoming her with open arms.'

Nerin, the one who'd brought me in, finally let go of me. She brushed my arm where she'd been clutching it. 'Of course,' she said gently. 'I'm sorry. I was just so surprised. You see, we don't get visitors here. Never! Not in all the years we've –'

One of the other mermaids nudged her. '*Rarely*,' she corrected her. 'Let's not say never. You'll give the girl a bad impression.' She reached out and stroked my hair. 'And look at the little jewel that's been washed in now. Girls, let's say thank you. This may be our salvation.'

'You're right, Merissa,' Nerin said. She swam around me. 'A pretty little siren like this,' she murmured.

'I'm – um, I'm not exactly a siren,' I said nervously.

The mermaid who had been brushing her hair pushed in front of the others and put a spindly arm around me. 'Of course you are, dear,' she said. 'You mustn't say things like that. Putting yourself down is a terrible thing to do – especially in one so young

136

and so pretty.' She tilted my chin up. 'You listen to your auntie Lorelei,' she said softly. 'You are a beautiful young siren. Right?'

'Right, OK,' I said. At that point, I would probably have agreed to anything she said. They were all being so nice! And there was something about them that was so – what was it? Comforting. Peaceful. It made me feel happy and I wanted to stay here for ever. In that moment, I forgot about everything else. All I could think about was being here, with these mermaids, and feeling this warm, peaceful feeling.

'Now, how about a little song?' Lorelei suggested, in that same sweet tone of voice, her smile still big and warm and welcoming. The other mermaids froze and looked first at her, then at me.

'A song?' I said, laughing nervously. 'What do you mean?'

The other mermaids were round me in a moment, all with the same encouraging smiles on their faces. Lorelei's arm was still around my shoulders. 'A song,' she repeated, a slight edge creeping into her voice. 'A beautiful siren song, to welcome you here. We'll join in.' Her arm still rested lightly on my shoulder.

'You start,' Merissa said sweetly.

I burst out laughing. 'You clearly haven't heard me sing!' I said.

The arm round my shoulder tightened.

'Whatever do you mean?' Lorelei asked, still smiling, although there was definitely something more strained about the smile now. It was beginning to look as though it had been painted on to her face, rather than belonging there naturally.

'I – I mean, well, I can't really sing,' I said. 'In fact, my singing voice is terrible.'

The mermaids stared at me, their expressions suddenly dark and full of threat. They seemed closer than they'd been, right up against me, and their faces looked ugly, their smiles false and harsh.

'Terrible?' one of them said. Then she forced a laugh. 'You're being modest.'

I laughed back – only my laugh was more of a nervous cackle. 'I'm really not,' I said. 'Even my mum makes me stop, and her voice is bad enough!'

The arm around my shoulder became a vice. Lorelei's fingers dug into my shoulder. 'What – do – you – mean?' she whispered hoarsely.

'Oww!' I tried to break free from her grip. My shoulder felt as though a scorpion was biting into it. 'I mean I *can't sing*!' I said. 'I'm not a siren and I can't sing. If you want beautiful singing then you need to ask Shona!'

Shona. My chest leapt at the thought of her. Where was she now? How long had I been in here? Was she still waiting for me?

One of the mermaids pushed past Lorelei, picking her hand off my shoulder. She gently took hold of my arm and swam us away from the others.

'Hello, dearie,' she said. 'I'm Amara. Now then. Tell me about Shona,' she said softly. 'She's a friend of yours, is she?'

I nodded. 'My best friend,' I said, gulping back a rock-shaped tear in my throat.

'And this Shona,' she went on. 'She's a good singer?'

'She's the best in her school!' I said proudly.

Amara smiled. 'And where do we find her?'

'You tell me!' I cried. 'We came out here together. We were looking for –' I stopped, and looked round at the mermaids, all staring intently at me. I'd been right, earlier. A mysterious place, hidden in the deeps of the ocean, miles from anywhere. I swallowed down a mixture of fear and excitement. 'I think we were looking for you,' I said.

Nerin, the first mermaid, joined Amara and me. 'Never mind that,' she said. 'Tell us more about Shona.' I could tell she was trying to sound all friendly and nice, but her voice came out desperate and rasping. 'Where is she? Where can we find her?'

'I don't know! I've told you. We came here together. We were looking for –' I felt my cheeks heat up and I stopped.

Nerin nudged me. 'Go on.'

'We were looking for the lost sirens,' I said, looking down at the sand as I spoke, so I didn't

139

have to see their shocked expressions, and I could pretend I hadn't noticed the gasps at what I'd said. I guess they didn't know they were a well-known ocean myth that mermaids studied at school.

Two long, thin, bright yellow fish wove in between us all, as though having a slalom race with each other. 'We decided to go in different directions and meet up again in ten minutes,' I went on. 'But then I got dragged down this kind of underwater waterfall and couldn't get out again.' I looked up at Nerin. 'Then you found me and brought me here.'

Nerin turned to the others. 'We need to find this Shona,' she said ferociously, the nice act all but gone completely now. 'We *must* have her!'

Amara pursed her lips into a frown. She glared into my eyes. 'Try, anyway,' she said.

'Try what?' I asked.

'Sing,' she said simply. 'Do it.' She turned to the others. 'You never know, she might just be being over-modest, after all. It's worth a try.' She turned to Nerin. 'Go to the place,' she said. 'Hurry. And come back immediately if anything changes.'

Nerin hurried away and we waited in silence.

What was she talking about? What place? And what were we waiting for?

Before I had time to ask, she'd turned back to me. This time there wasn't even a pretence at a smile. She waited for a minute or two, and then her lips rolled into a snarl. 'Come on, child,' she said. 'Sing.'

I had no choice. Anyway, what harm could it do to try? Except that my mind seemed to have gone completely blank. I couldn't think of a single song.

'Sing!' Amara repeated impatiently. 'What are you waiting for?'

My mind grasped the only thing it could think of. A nursery rhyme.

'*Twinkle, twinkle little star,*' I began. It didn't come out how I'd hoped. I cleared my throat. '*How I wonder what you are.*'

I stopped. The mermaids were all looking at me, their faces an identical picture of horror.

Amara was the first to speak. 'What in the ocean's name was that?' she spat.

'I *told* you I can't sing,' I protested.

Moments later, Nerin swam back into the clearing and joined Amara. 'Nothing,' she said. 'The force is just as strong. We need to find the other one. This Shona. If the two came together, she must be nearby.'

'And if they really are such good friends, surely she'll come looking when she realises her best friend has gone missing,' Amara added. 'We need to find her.'

'You're right,' Merissa said, her voice dripping with desperation. 'She can't be far away. We should split up and go in search of her.'

The five of them talked among themselves at the other side of the clearing, hatching a plan to find Shona. I could hear snatches of their conversation, but none of it made any sense to me.

'We *have* to find her!' one of them was saying. 'Maybe she will have the voice that can get us out of here. We need to hear her sing.'

'This is our best chance in years,' another replied.

'Our best chance ever, you mean,' the third added. 'Find this siren and it could all be over.'

'As long as she came in.'

'You *know* she'll have come in, if they found their way to this place. She wouldn't be able to resist the force. Nothing can. The only problem with that force is that nothing can get out again. You know that. We all know that. We *need* this siren to get out of here.'

I swam towards them. 'What are you talking about?' I asked. 'I've got a right to know!'

Amara threw her head back and laughed. 'A right? You want to talk about rights, do you? Ha!' She swam straight up to my face and stared into my eyes. 'I'll tell you what we're talking about, you useless disgrace of a merchild.'

I flinched as though her words had hit me. I didn't speak, though. I waited for her to continue.

'We're stuck here. You'd probably figured that much out for yourself. We don't know why, and we don't know how. And after all this time, we don't even know when.'

Morvena swam towards Amara. 'Come on, it's not the girl's fault,' she said. 'Let's –'

Amara shook her off. 'And not only that. Every one of us stripped of our singing voices,' she went on. 'Do you know what that means to a siren? To the best sirens known for miles and miles around?'

'Amara, you know we weren't the best,' Morvena said. 'Melody was the best. We backed her. It's not –'

'That's right. Stick up for Melody, just like you always do. Not that she ever bothers to stick up for herself nowadays.'

'She doesn't even *show* herself nowadays,' Nerin added.

'Too good for us, isn't she!' Amara sneered.

'Come on, now. Let's not fall out,' Morvena said. 'I thought you wanted to find the young siren.'

Amara turned away with a swish of her tail so sharp it was like a scythe slicing through the water.

'You're right. We're wasting time,' she said. 'Let's help the others.'

'What about the girl?' asked Nerin.

Morvena broke away from the others. 'I'll see to her,' she said quickly. 'You go ahead. I'll follow.'

The sirens exchanged a quick glance. 'All right,' Amara said finally. 'Put the child somewhere safe. We can deal with her later.' With that, the three of them swam away. Morvena nudged me in the opposite direction. 'Come on,' she said.

'What do you mean, you'll see to me?' I asked as we swam up to the top of the clearing and along a dark ledge that ran the length of the walls.

'Don't worry. I'm not going to hurt you,' Morvena said. We swam along the ledge in silence, swimming past dark holes and caverns all the way along.

We passed a low cave with jagged rocks hanging in its entrance like a jail door; green stone walls were decorated with pink ferns dangling down like a feather curtain; ledges with fat pillars stood on either side; stone hills sloped down, lined with pillars and rocks in a hundred different shapes and sizes.

Morvena stopped in front of a large opening. 'We're here,' she said. 'Come on.' She swam into the recess. Following her to the entrance, I looked round. Huge purple leaves fanned out around the sides. Bushy green moss formed spongy seats in one corner. A jelly-like bed ran along one side. A large rock was piled high with what looked like home-made jewellery made of driftwood and stones.

Morvena indicated for me to swim inside. 'This is my room,' she said as I looked around. 'Stay here.' Then she smiled at me. It wasn't the way the others had smiled. She wasn't snarling. 'You'll be fine,' she said. 'Just wait here.'

'And what if I don't want to stay here?'

Morvena smiled again. 'Then don't,' she said sweetly. 'But I'm afraid you won't be able to get out. This is as pleasant a place to wait as any, until you can leave.' She looked down, her tail swished nervously in the sand. 'If you can ever leave,' she added.

I didn't reply, but as she swam away, her words gradually sank in. If I could ever leave? What did she mean?

The more I thought about it, the worse it looked. The lost sirens had been here for years and years, according to Shona's teacher, and now I'd joined them. A cold shiver shot through me as I realised what I'd done.

I'd found my way in here, but from their conversation, and from what I'd experienced myself, getting out seemed impossible. And unless Shona managed to perform some kind of singing miracle, it looked as if there could only be one conclusion.

I was going to be trapped in here with them for ever.

Chapter Ten

My stomach growled. How long had I been here? I wished I'd at least had some breakfast before coming out. I doubted very much if my new friends were going to provide a banquet for lunch.

I swam around Morvena's room, looking out to the larger caves beyond the entrance. What *was* this place?

Rocky ledges and walls sprawled out all around, lined with crazy shapes. A church steeple at the top of a hill, a giant upside-down jellyfish, a wedding cake, an elephant's trunk — all of them and more lay scattered everywhere, as though the caves had stolen a hundred random objects and turned them to stone.

I saw a tail further down the murky darkness of the ledge and darted quickly away from the entrance. Someone was coming.

I hid in the darkness, peering out while I waited for them to pass.

And then they did. Just one of them. I watched as she swished past me.

Wait a minute! That wasn't one of the sirens; that was —

'Shona!' I darted out from the darkness and joined her on the ledge.

'Emily!'

'You found me!' I said. Then I remembered about the sirens going looking for her. I grabbed her and pulled her inside. 'Oh — or they found *you*!'

Shona tilted her head to stare at me. 'Who found me?' she asked. 'What are you talking about?'

'They haven't found you, then?'

'Who haven't found me? Em, you're being really weird. I've just —'

'How did you get here?'

Shona's eyes widened as they always do when she's on an adventure of some sort. 'Well, that's the weird thing,' she said. 'I didn't even try. I just felt this really strong current pulling me along. It was swishy! Next thing I knew, I was whizzing downwards, water gushing all around me.'

'Like an underwater waterfall?' I said. 'Inside a well.'

'That's it exactly! I was pretty scared at first, but then when I got to the bottom, I looked up and it had disappeared. I reckon as long as I can find that spot again, we could swim out again whenever we want to go.'

'Did you try it?' I asked glumly.

Shona shook her head. I was about to explain that it wasn't going to be as simple as she thought, when there was a noise outside the room. Someone was coming.

I grabbed Shona and swam over to the purple ferns in the corner. 'Quick! Get behind here,' I said, as the swishing noise came closer.

'Why?' Shona asked. 'Em, what's going on?'

'I'll tell you in a minute,' I said. 'Just —'

But it was too late. The sirens turned a corner and came into the room. It was Amara and Lorelei.

They spotted me instantly and swam over to me. 'No luck so far,' Amara snarled. 'What shall we do with this one in the meantime?'

Then Lorelei glanced sideways and spotted Shona. 'Wait!' she said. 'What's this?'

Amara looked across and saw her, too. In a flash, the snarl was gone, and she smiled with the warmth they'd turned on me earlier. *It's an act, Shona*, I said in my mind, hoping she'd somehow hear my thoughts and trust me. *Don't be taken in.*

Amara swam over to Shona and stopped beside her, flicking her tail gently in the water below her. She looked Shona up and down. 'Hello there, pretty one,' she said, her voice oozing with sweetness. 'You must be Shona.'

Shona smiled at Amara, her big round eyes full of innocence and excitement. 'How do you know?' she asked.

Amara tilted her head towards me. 'From your friend,' she said.

Lorelei swam beside Amara, and held out a hand to Shona. 'We've heard *so* much about you,' she said, sounding as much like Shona's long lost best friend as Amara.

Shona reached out awkwardly to shake Lorelei's hand, but Lorelei took hold of it instead and turned it over to examine the back. 'Oh, just look at those dainty fingers,' she said. 'I think you've got the prettiest nails I've ever seen on a siren!'

Shona blushed. 'We did nail decorating in B and D this week,' she said. Turning even deeper red, she added, 'I got the top mark, actually.'

'Beauty and Deportment – oh, that was my favourite subject at school,' Lorelei said with what sounded to me like a bitter cackle heavily disguised as a wistful sigh.

'Mine too!' Shona exclaimed. 'And my best.'

'Well, fancy that; so much in common already. Now, singing – that was my other favourite thing in school.' Lorelei licked her lips, as though she was sizing Shona up for her dinner plate.

'Oh singing is my favour –'

'Shona!' I burst out. I couldn't listen to this any longer. 'Don't tell them anything else!'

Shona stared at me. 'What d'you mean, Em? Why in the ocean shouldn't I?'

'They aren't what they seem! They're evil and mean, and they want to use you for their own purposes.'

'What purposes?'

I hesitated. 'I don't know,' I admitted, lowering my head. 'But believe me. You can't trust them!'

Amara let out a soft laugh. 'Oh dear – have we made someone jealous?' Then she reached out with one of her spindly thin fingers and stroked Shona's hair. 'So pretty,' she said. 'If your singing is anywhere near as beautiful as the rest of you, I'm sure we'd all LOVE to hear it.'

Shona beamed at Amara.

'Shona, *please* don't trust them,' I pleaded. 'Don't be fooled.'

Shona turned to me. 'She's right,' she said, jutting a thumb at Amara. 'You're jealous. You just don't want me to get all this attention, do you? It's usually you at the centre of attention, and now it's my turn you don't like it!'

'Shona, that's not it at all!' I said. 'Why on earth would I —'

'Enough of this!' Lorelei suddenly butted in. 'Let's go tell the others we've found ourselves the little siren.'

Shona looked so pleased at being called a siren you'd think she'd just been crowned queen of the sea.

Amara and Lorelei began to swim away, escorting Shona between them. Before they left the room, I grabbed Shona's arm.

'Shona, when have I lied to you?' I asked. 'When have I stopped you from getting attention?'

She held still in the water for a moment, her tail splishing around nervously, her forehead creased into a frown. 'I don't know,' she said. 'I suppose you haven't.'

'Then, believe me,' I said urgently. 'They're not to be trusted!'

Amara picked up a brush from the rocky side cabinet in Morvena's room. She brushed Shona's hair with it, in a couple of long sleek movements. 'So smooth,' she said gently. 'I don't think I've ever seen hair so soft and perfect.' As she smiled at Shona, her face was such a picture of wonder and admiration that I was almost taken in myself.

'You must be mistaken, Em,' Shona said softly. 'I'm sorry. I know you wouldn't deliberately stop something nice from happening to me; I shouldn't have said that. But I'm being treated like the siren I've dreamed of being my whole life! Please don't try to take that away from me,' she pleaded.

Before I had a chance to say anything, Lorelei took hold of Shona's arm. 'Come on,' she said sweetly, between gritted teeth that Shona clearly hadn't noticed. 'Let's go.'

'What about Emily?' Shona asked.

Lorelei left her side and swam over to me. 'I'll tell you what,' she said. 'As a special treat, I'll take Emily off for a special seaweed wrap: our very own spa treatment. How does that sound?'

It sounded like she'd probably rather wrap me up in the seaweed and leave me to rot. It wasn't much use complaining, though, as she was already leading me out of the door. Shona was swimming ahead with Lorelei, so she didn't see Amara's hand clutching my arm so tightly her nails left red marks in my skin.

It took a few moments to realise where Amara had taken me. I was back in the well, only this time the hole in the wall was blocked. She'd dragged a rock in front of it and it was too heavy for me to push out of the way.

I swam around, feeling my way along the walls

for a way out. Nothing. I tried to swim upwards. Impossible. The invisible waterfall just threw me back down again and again.

I slumped down on the sandy floor and tried not to think too hard about the stupid, hopeless, awful mess I'd got myself into. How did I do it? Every single time I tried to do anything to solve a problem, I always managed to create a bigger one in the process.

I looked down at the murky seabed. Two round blue fish with large orange fins floated towards each other. Flapping gently, they skirted the surface of the well, chasing one another round in a circle. I was busy chasing my miserable thoughts round in a circle of their own when I heard something.

I pulled myself into a ball, huddling my arms over my tail. One of the sirens. I hoped it was Morvena. At least she didn't seem as mean as the others.

But it was coming from above me.

I jumped up and craned my neck to look up into the well.

'Emily!'

My heart leapt. It sounded like . . . but it couldn't be – could it? I didn't dare hope. Surely I'd imagined it. That was what happened when you were confined in a dark cell like this. My spirits sank down again, as though they too had been hurled into a dark, hopeless, underwater cell.

'Emily, can you hear me? Are you there?'

I looked up again. This time I saw something, too. I *wasn't* imagining it! There was a figure at the top of the well. A face. I couldn't see him clearly, but I knew who it was. It was really him!

'Aaron?' I called, the word echoing round the walls, spiralling up towards him.

'Emily! Where are you? Are you down the well?'

'Yes I'm here – can you see me? I can see you!'

Aaron shook his head. 'All I can see is water!' he yelled. 'I've been swimming all over. This was my last hope.'

'How did you know I was around here at all?' I called back.

Aaron paused for a long time. I could still see him there above me, leaning into the well. He didn't reply.

'Aaron?'

'Don't be cross, but I followed you,' he said eventually. 'Mandy told me what happened. I know you wanted to be with Shona, but I was worried. I just wanted to keep an eye on you. But then you both disappeared, and I've been trying to find you ever since. I just had this awful feeling something had happened to you.'

He wasn't wrong there, then.

'Can you get out?' he called.

I shook my head. 'It's too fierce.'

'Right, I'm coming down, then,' he yelled. 'Hold on.'

I watched him swim over to the edge of the rocks. For a fraction of a second, I held my breath and allowed myself to smile for the first time all day. Aaron was here! He had come to find me, to save me!

Then I remembered something else.

'No!' I screamed. 'Don't come down!'

'Why? What's wrong?' Aaron sounded hurt. 'Do you just want to be with Shona? I'll go away if you want, now I know you're safe.'

'No! Don't go away!' I screamed even more urgently. 'But don't come down.'

'Don't come down but don't go away? What do you want me to do, then?'

'You can't come down,' I said. 'You'll never be able to get out again. They said earlier: you can get in but you can't get out. No one can! I don't want you trapped in here, too.'

'Who was talking earlier?' Aaron asked. 'Who's in there with you? Em, I'm coming down!'

'No!' I pleaded. 'It's the lost sirens – they're all trapped in here by the waterfall. It's not normal. It's like magic.'

'Magic? Em, don't be –' He stopped.

'Aaron?'

He paused for ages. 'Magic, you say?' he called eventually.

'Yeah, it's like they've had a curse put on them or some –' I stopped abruptly.

'Emily?' Aaron said breathlessly.

'A curse,' I repeated.

'Are you thinking what I'm thinking?' he asked.

'If the sirens are trapped in here because of a curse, perhaps we could undo it?'

'Exactly!'

But then, just as quickly as my hopes had risen, they shot back down again. 'Except for the magic to work, our hands have to touch,' I said. 'And how can they do that through this thing?'

'Maybe I should just come down after all, and we'll figure it out from there?'

'No!' I shouted. 'It's not worth the risk. We'll need to be inside the waterfall to stop it. If you come down and we can't get back inside it, we'll *both* be stuck here.'

'OK, listen,' Aaron called, all the hesitancy gone now. 'Edge as high up as you can get, and stretch your hand as far as you can reach.' He was in charge, and my spirits lifted again.

I tried to swim up through the invisible waterfall. The weight above me was so huge I had to look down. *Come on, fight it, get through it.*

I swished and splashed my tail as hard as I could, trying desperately to gain some ground. I clung to the rocky sides, gripping tightly as I tried to heave myself upwards – but it was useless. I wasn't getting anywhere. The sirens knew what they were talking about; there was no getting out of here.

'It's impossible,' I called.

'No – it's not. Don't say that.'

'I can't do it. I can just about drag myself up into the current, but only for about a second before I'm thrown back down again,' I said. 'It's no use.'

'A second might be all we need,' Aaron called. 'Stay there – don't go anywhere.'

I would have laughed if I'd had the energy. Where exactly was I likely to go? That was the whole point, wasn't it?

'I'll be straight back, OK?'

I slumped back on the sea floor, bedraggled, exhausted and out of ideas.

Ten minutes later, Aaron's face reappeared at the top of the well.

'I've sorted it!' he said. 'I've tied a long trail of seaweed round my stomach and tied it to a rock at the top here. I'm going to lower myself down slowly. When I say "now", drag yourself as high up as you can. If we both reach out at the right time, maybe it'll work.'

It sounded like a slim chance to me. But then, a slim chance was better than anything I'd managed to come up with. 'OK,' I called up.

I watched as Aaron lowered himself into the well. Instantly, he shot down in a rush, whirling about in the water, banging against the sides. But then he stopped going any lower. Dangling halfway down the well and bouncing around in the current, he grabbed the seaweed round his middle, letting it out bit by bit. Then he gave me a thumbs up sign. I whirled my tail round, preparing to swim the hardest I'd ever swum. I felt round the rocky walls, searching for the best grip to pull myself up.

Aaron edged closer and closer, gradually letting himself drop down towards me. I gripped the wall, digging my fingers hard into the rock.

'Now!' he yelled.

Spinning my tail so fast it felt like a propeller, I heaved myself up as hard as I could with one hand, reaching upwards with my other arm. I couldn't see anything – the force pushed my head down. Nothing, nothing. Just whirling, crashing water. I gripped the rock harder, dragging myself a tiny bit higher, flailing around with my arm, searching blindly for Aaron's hand. *Come on Aaron, where are you?*

And then I felt it! His hand touched mine. Just a flicker – just for a fraction of a second, as our hands brushed past each other. Not long enough. The waterfall still raged.

Come on – I can't fight it much longer.

I was slipping down. We didn't have long. Aaron's hand brushed mine again. This time, I grabbed hold of it as though my life depended on it. Maybe it did.

His hand was warm against mine. He held on just as tightly – but nothing was happening. *Please stop,*

I said silently to the waterfall. *Please calm down.*

And then, exhausted and empty, I closed my eyes. I'd run out of energy. My hand slipped from the wall, my tail flapped lifelessly. It was all over.

When I opened my eyes again, Aaron was in front of me, grinning widely. I was dreaming. I must have blacked out. Well, it was a nice dream. I hoped no one was going to wake me up any time soon.

'We did it!' he said, untying the seaweed from round his stomach.

'Huh? You mean I'm awake?'

Aaron let go of the seaweed. It dropped slowly downwards, swaying gently as it fell. 'Look around you,' he said.

That was when I realised there was no ground underneath me. We were floating freely – inside the well!

'We did it!' I said.

Aaron laughed. 'I'm sure someone round here has already pointed that out!' He took my hand and started swimming upwards. 'Come on, let's get out of here.'

I snatched my hand away. 'We can't. Not without Shona.'

'She's down here, too?'

I nodded. 'I'm not leaving her.'

'No. Of course you're not,' Aaron replied. He flipped over and swam downwards. 'Come on then. What are we waiting for?'

We swam down to the bottom of the well – and then I remembered. 'Aaron, we can't get out. They put something in front of the door.'

Aaron swam over to the rock. Grunting and grimacing, he pushed hard against it. The rock tilted slightly. 'We can do it between us,' he said. 'Push it with me. If we rock it, we'll get it out.'

I joined Aaron and we pushed and heaved and propelled ourselves forwards with our tails. Eventually, the rock budged. Only a bit, but enough for us both to slither through, one behind the other.

I led the way through the opening. 'Come on,' I said. 'Let's go and find Shona.'

Chapter Eleven

e swam down a tunnel that sloped lower and lower as it grew narrower and narrower, twisting and turning all the way. Its ceiling was jagged and grey, its sides pockmarked with tiny holes, too small to swim into.

The tunnel led us to a tall archway. We swam through it into an opening and looked round. Empty. High up, a row of knobbly rocks were squeezed tightly together like a village on a hill. Above us, the stone looked like sheets of paper, folded and rolled and hung from the ceiling. A pillar over to the left was like a giant finger pointing upwards.

Aaron swam to a deep recess, high on one side. 'Emily, look!'

I swam up to join him. It was another tunnel.

'Come on, let's try it,' I said. Anything to get away from the weird rocky shapes, all of which seemed to be watching us, mocking us, laughing at our every wrong move.

We swam into the tunnel. A moment in the pitch darkness, and we were out the other side. I rubbed my eyes. 'We've found it!' I said. The opening where I'd last seen Shona.

'Now all we have to do is work out where they've taken her,' Aaron said.

We swam along the snaking pathways that led all around the inside of the caves, peering into each cavern we passed and calling out her name as loud as we dared. She was nowhere. The whole place felt deserted.

'Look at that,' Aaron said as we passed a flat ledge with a tall, thin column stretching upwards, like a tower that someone in a fairy tale would be locked away in and forgotten for ever.

I shuddered and swam on.

'Wait! Look!'

Aaron swam back to join me. It was one of the caverns – but it had a door. A real one, not just a curtain of rocks like the others. It looked as if it was made from ship's timber – and it had a rusty bolt across it.

I grabbed the bolt. 'It's stiff,' I said. 'Help me.'

Between us, we worked at the bolt, pulling and levering it gradually along – until finally it came loose. I pushed the door and swam in.

My eyes took a moment to grow accustomed to the darkness. Once they did, I saw something huddled in the far corner. I swam straight over.

She was curled up with her head in her arms, shoulders hunched, tail flat and lifeless.

'Shona!' I cried.

She turned her tear-stained face up towards me. 'Emily,' she said, instantly getting up and brushing her tail down. 'You found me!'

We fell into a hug. 'Of course I found you,' I said. 'What was I going to do? Abandon you?' I pulled her over to the door. 'Come on.'

That was when she noticed Aaron. 'Aaron! How did you –'

'We'll explain everything later,' Aaron said. 'Let's get out of here first.'

Shona stopped. 'Wait – I need to say something first.'

I sighed. 'Please, Shona. I know you think these sirens are the whale's whiskers but I'm telling you, they're not. You have to believe me. They –'

'Emily, stop,' she said firmly. 'I don't think anything of the sort. That's what I wanted to say.'

She lowered her head. 'I was a silly shark head,' she said quietly. 'I should have listened to you. I should have trusted you. You've never let me down yet, and you never would. I'm sorry.'

'What happened?' I asked. 'How did you end up in here?'

Shona's eyes filled with tears, glistening in the darkness. 'They made me sing,' she said. 'But they said it wasn't good enough.'

'That's what they said to me,' I said. 'In my case, they were right, though.' I laughed and Shona half smiled. 'But you're a *brilliant* singer. They don't know what they're talking about!'

Shona wiped the back of her hand across her eyes. 'They told me their story.'

Aaron swam across the room and hovered beside me. 'What story?' he asked.

'How they got down here. They said they'd been trapped here for years and years. They'd been friends all their lives. One of them – Melody – had been the best singer anyone had ever heard.'

'She's the one Miss Merlin told you about?' I said.

Shona nodded. 'But then something happened. She went away for a long time, and when she came back, she couldn't sing. When she tried, terrible sounds came out. Melody said she had to leave her home immediately. They didn't know why, but because they were all such good friends, they said they'd come with her.'

'And they came here?'' Aaron asked.

'Yes. She said they'd only need to stay a little while. But then all the bad things started to happen. All the other sirens lost their singing voices too. And then the waterfall began – and it's never stopped since. It's the only way into the place, and is impossible to get out of.'

I wanted to tell Shona she was wrong – we were going to get out any minute now! But I wanted to hear the rest of the story first.

'Melody told them the only thing that could break the waterfall was the beautiful sound of a siren's song. She said if they could get their voices back, they would be able to get out.'

Suddenly it all fitted. 'So that's why they were so desperate for us to sing,' I said.

'They all looked so happy when I started to sing. But then one of them went out to watch the waterfall.' Shona looked down. 'She saw you there, huddled on the floor. She told the others . . .' Her voice trailed off.

'She told them what?'

'She said you looked really scared and miserable. They all had a good laugh.'

I was just glad she hadn't come at the point where we'd made it stop! Let them poke fun at me if they wanted to. We were going to have the last laugh.

'When she came back and said nothing had happened to the water, they changed completely.

They turned on me, hissed in my face, said my singing was – was –' Shona broke off.

I swam towards her. 'What did they say?' I asked softly.

Shona turned her big, sad eyes up towards me. 'They said my singing wasn't beautiful enough. They said it couldn't be, or it would have worked.'

'And then they threw you in here?' Aaron said.

Shona nodded.

I took hold of her hand. 'It's OK,' I said. '*I* think your singing's beautiful, no matter what a load of silly old sirens say. And more to the point, so does your singing teacher!'

Shona sniffed. 'But they're *real sirens*! They'd know best, wouldn't they?'

I put a finger under Shona's chin and lifted her face, just like Mum does with me when she wants to make sure I'm listening. 'Their opinion doesn't matter at all. They don't know what they're talking about. They're bitter, twisted, nasty sirens who can't sing any more themselves, and wouldn't recognise a beautiful siren song if it swam right up to them and kicked them in the gills! Right?'

Shona managed a half smile. 'Right,' she said unenthusiastically.

'And anyway,' I went on. 'Guess what? We're getting out of here!'

'But we can't! The sirens said the singing would be the only way to get out.'

'Well, that's even more proof that they don't know what they're talking about, because we've found a way to stop the waterfall!' I swam back towards the door.

'Really? But you can't have!'

I stuck my head through the door to check the coast was clear. 'Well, we have!' I said. 'We'll tell you everything on the way.' I swam back out onto the dark ledge and beckoned to the others to follow. 'Come on,' I said. 'Let's get out of this place!'

'Try again,' I called down. 'You must be doing something wrong.'

Aaron and I were halfway up the well, but Shona was still right down at the bottom, splashing around uselessly on the sea floor.

'I can't,' she called up. 'It's too powerful.'

'Wait, I'll help you.'

I swam back down and took Shona's hand. Swimming back up into the well again, I tried to pull her up, but it was no use. I could swim through the clear water on my own, but I couldn't pull her with me. Something was dragging her back down.

Aaron swam down to join us. 'What's the problem?'

'I can see clear water,' Shona said. 'But if I try to swim into it, it's as though the waterfall is still there, beating me down. I can't swim through it.'

Exactly how it had been for me before Aaron and I had worked our magic on the well.

Shona's mouth tightened into a small line. 'You go,' she said quickly.

'What?'

'Look, it's obvious what's happened. You and Aaron can get through it. You have the power to do that – but it'll only work for you.'

'Shona's right,' Aaron said. 'That must be what's happening.'

I looked at both of them. My two best friends. Or my best friend and – well, I still didn't know exactly what Aaron was. And I didn't know why the waterfall would only stop for us. We clearly didn't have as much control over our power as we'd thought. Well, that made sense. Where Neptune's concerned, nothing's ever straightforward or easy.

One thing I did know, though, was that the three of us were in this together.

'We're not leaving you,' I said to Shona.

'You've no choice.'

'Yes we have,' Aaron said. 'D'you think we could just go off and happily escape while you're trapped here?'

'But –'

'But nothing,' I said. 'Whatever we do, we'll do it together. No one's going anywhere till we've figured out how to get us all out. Deal?'

Aaron and Shona looked at each other and then both turned to me. 'Deal,' they said in unison.

'Good!' I paused. 'Now all we need is a plan.'

We sat in silence, each thinking our own thoughts. Mine weren't very helpful so I decided not to bother saying them out loud. I guessed the others felt the same way.

I watched a lone fish with a spiky back slither along in front of me, pecking at the seabed every few seconds, then moving on. It seemed so purposeful. It knew where it was going and how to get there. Would we ever be able to say that about ourselves again?

A swishing noise outside the well broke into my thoughts. A second later, the seaweed curtain lifted. Someone was coming in!

All three of us jumped up and swam to the furthest wall. As we pressed ourselves against the rock, I prayed that we could somehow become invisible against the dark shadows of the well.

A moment later, a face appeared, and one of the sirens swam inside.

She looked round the well and registered us immediately. Pulling her hair off her face and swimming over to us, she smiled. 'Found you!' she said.

I peeled myself away from the rocks and swam into the centre of the well. 'Don't try anything. There are three of us and only one of you,' I said, trying to make my voice sound big and brave. Easier said than done when you're scared finless and everyone knows it.

The siren swam closer towards me. Instinctively, I backed away.

'I'm not going to hurt you,' she said softly. That was when I recognised her. It was the one who had been kind earlier. Morvena.

Aaron swam over to join me. Puffing his chest out and sticking out his chin, he swished his tail hard to make himself taller. He wasn't going to let himself be thrown by seeing one of these sirens for the first time. Or if he was, he certainly wasn't showing it. 'Why should we believe you?' he asked. 'Why should we even *listen* to you?'

Morvena looked Aaron in the eye. 'I can't make you listen, and I can't make you believe me, either. But I hope you will do both.'

'Why?' Shona asked. She was still huddled against the rocks on the other side of the well.

Morvena swam over to her and Shona flinched. The siren answered softly. 'Because I think we can help each other.'

'Why would we want to help *you*?' Aaron asked.

I touched his arm. 'Wait — let's hear what she has to say. I think she's different from the rest.'

Morvena bowed her head slightly. 'Thank you,' she said. Then she indicated above us. 'I saw what you did up there just now,' she said. 'I was following you — I wanted to make sure you were safe.'

'Why would you care?' Shona asked. She obviously wasn't ready to believe any of the sirens could have good intentions towards us.

'I know what the others are like,' Morvena said. 'Some of them, anyway. You're children. You're not the enemy — and I'm not a monster.'

'So what did you see?' Aaron asked, his tail flicking nervously.

'I saw you do the impossible,' she said, her eyes shining and wide. 'I saw you swim into the well.' She turned to me. 'Why didn't you leave?'

'We couldn't,' I said. 'Shona couldn't do it. Only Aaron and I can swim through it.'

'How did you do it?' Morvena asked.

Before I could reply, Aaron elbowed me. 'We're not telling you all our secrets yet,' he said. 'You need to give us something first. Give us a reason to trust you.'

Morvena let out a sigh. It sounded as if it contained a hundred years of sadness and regret.

'We can't get out of here,' she said.

171

'I know – because you had your beautiful voices taken away,' Shona said from the corner. She still hadn't moved.

Morvena shook her head. 'That isn't the full story,' she said. 'In fact, I'm certain that the singing doesn't have anything to do with our being trapped here. I had suspected it for a long time, but today confirmed it for me.'

'What do you mean?' I asked. 'I thought you told Shona all about it earlier.'

'We did – or at least the others did. I kept quiet, as I often do if I have nothing helpful to say.' She turned again to Shona. Tilting her head, she spoke gently to her. 'Your singing was the most beautiful thing these caves have heard for many years. It could probably have rivalled Melody's own voice when she was your age.'

Shona's face flushed in an instant. 'But the others,' she said. 'They told me it was terrible. They said my singing was useless!'

'That's because they thought the sound of a beautiful siren song would open our prison and let us out. Then when you sang, nothing happened and they were angry. But, you see, I wasn't, because I know better than they do.'

Aaron swam forward. 'What do you know? Why would you know more than them?' he asked, folding his arms. 'And why should we believe you anyway?'

Morvena drew a breath. 'Listen,' she said. 'I'll make a deal with you. I'll tell you everything I know, if you promise to try and help.'

Shona and I looked at each other. She gave me a tiny nod. I glanced at Aaron and he did the same. 'OK,' I said to Morvena. 'We promise.'

'Many years ago – so long ago, now, it's like a different lifetime – Melody came to me. I was her best friend. I still am.' Morvena paused. 'I'm her *only* friend, now.'

'Why?' Shona asked. 'What about the others?'

'They blame her for everything that's happened here. And in a way they're right. But what's the use of blame? It won't get us out of here any quicker than anything else. All it will do is make our lives even more unpleasant than they already are.'

'You were her best friend,' Shona prompted her.

'Yes. We told each other everything – or at least I thought we did. Until the day she disappeared.'

'She disappeared?' I said. 'What happened to her?'

'That I've never known. She was gone almost a year. Then one day, she turned up, completely out of the blue, and in such distress that at first I thought she was dying.'

'What happened then?' Aaron asked.

'She said something bad had happened. Something so bad that she was terrified. She decided that she had no option but to go into hiding, although she was sure it would only be for a while. Then she asked three things of me. One, that I never ask her what she'd done; two, that I never tell the others about the state she was in; and three, that I would never desert her.'

'What did you say?' Shona asked, her eyes wide, her tail flicking gently.

'I agreed without hesitation. Like I say, she was my best friend. That's how it works.'

I gave Shona a quick look. She smiled at me and her cheeks coloured a little. 'I know what you mean,' she said.

Morvena reached out to stroke Shona's cheek. 'I know you do,' she said with a sad smile. We all fell silent. Even the fish seemed to slow down and swim more solemnly.

'So what happened next?' Aaron asked after a while.

'I told the others that Melody and I were going away for a bit, and they all wanted to come. None of us had seen Melody for so long; we all wanted to be together. We were all such good friends, back then. Always smiling, always singing. Melody didn't want them to come; she didn't really want *me* to come. She seemed to think she'd be putting us in danger. But she was scared, too, and I insisted on coming with her.'

'And the others?' I asked.

'Melody couldn't put them off without seeming rude or ungrateful, so she agreed. Remember, we thought it was only going to be for a matter of days. That was what Melody told me; that was what she believed.'

'Did the others know about the bad thing, whatever that was?' Aaron asked,

'Melody tried to hide it, but they knew there was something. For one thing, she didn't sing. She never has done since the day she came back. We thought at first that she just didn't want to. It was only later – when the rest of us were stripped of our singing voices – that we realised that was what had happened to her, too.'

I was captivated by Morvena's story. 'So did Melody tell them what had happened then?' I asked.

'No. They knew not to push it. Melody has always been proud, and loyal. If she was determined not to do something, she would stick to her decision, no matter what. She didn't want them to suffer on her behalf, and she didn't want any of us to see how unhappy she was. I'm the only one who's really seen her distress and even *I* have never known what it's about.'

'She's never told you?' Shona burst out. 'I thought you were her best friend!'

'Being someone's best friend doesn't always mean telling them every tiny thing about yourself, you know. Sometimes it means having enough trust to let them have their secrets and still be there for them.'

Shona wrinkled her nose. 'I don't know about that,' she said. 'I can't imagine *ever* having secrets from Emily.'

'Me neither,' I said, but my ears heated up as I said it. Was I keeping a secret from Shona by not telling her about my feelings for Aaron? Or had I just not talked about them because I wasn't even sure of them myself?

'Anyway, so we came to this place,' Morvena went on. 'It was like a little adventure – almost a holiday. Spirits were quite high for a few days. And then the change happened.'

'What change?' asked Aaron.

Morvena nudged her head upwards. 'The waterfall, for one thing. It was the only way in, and now it wouldn't let us out. We'd known about the waterfall from the start. That was why this was such a good hiding place.'

'How did you hear of this place at all?' asked Shona.

'One of the other sirens told Melody about it.' Morvena drew in a sharp breath. 'Zalia. I never knew how she found out we were looking for a hiding place. That's another thing Melody has never shared. And I suppose I'll never know if she knew what was going to happen. If she had anything to do with it. My own theory is that Zalia was a traitor from the start – and she was the one who somehow helped to lock us up here.'

Shona was staring wide-eyed at Morvena. 'And you've been here ever since?'

'So long I only know it's more years than I have wrinkles,' Morvena replied with an attempt at a laugh. 'After the waterfall locked us in, things began to change pretty rapidly. The same day, we all noticed our voices sounded harsher. Then we discovered we could no longer sing.'

'So you couldn't get out?'

Morvena shook her head. 'Like I said, I've never believed the singing had anything to do with the waterfall.' She turned to Shona. 'And you've convinced me totally. If your singing wasn't good enough to still the falls, no singing could be.'

Shona's cheeks flushed deep red as Morvena went on. 'We knew that Melody was being punished for something. But as she'd told us we'd only be in hiding for a few days, none of us ever believed it was something too serious. We all thought our voices would return shortly.'

'But they didn't,' Shona said.

Morvena shook her head. 'One day, early on, the others were starting to panic. Wailing and screaming every day – it was awful. That was when Melody told us a siren song would get us out, and that we just had to stay calm and be patient and wait for our voices to return. It worked – in as much as it calmed the panic.'

'And then what happened?' I asked.

Morvena looked at me. 'The waiting began,' she said. 'Over the long years of waiting, the others have held on to this idea more and more firmly. It is as though this is their faith; this is all they believe in; this is their impossible salvation.'

'But you don't believe it?' I asked.

'No. One day, I was going over to see Melody in her room. From outside, I could see that she was crying and I knew she wouldn't have wanted me to see that. So I waited. But instead of turning away, I watched her. She had something in her hands. Something I'd never seen before.'

'What was it?' I asked.

'A shell. A conch. White, with gold and silver flecks running in spirals all around it.'

'Swishy!' Shona breathed.

'She was holding it in front of her, talking to it. At one point, she even kissed it! At first, I wondered if our imprisonment was sending her mad. But there was something about it that drew me in.

I swam closer. Staying hidden, I listened to her talking to the shell.'

'What was she saying?' I asked.

'She was begging it,' Morvena said. 'It almost broke my heart to hear her. Begging it to help. Pleading with it.'

'What do you mean?' Aaron asked. 'Pleading with a shell? What was she saying?'

'The same thing, over and over and over. *Please, please, get us out of here. Release the magic and help me find you.* I've heard her do the same on many occasions. In fact, I believe she has done the same thing every single day and night since we've been here.'

'Does she know you've watched her?' Shona blurted out, clearly as shocked at the idea of spying on your best friend as she was at the idea of keeping secrets from her.

Morvena shook her head and her long silver hair flickered behind her. 'I know her well enough to know she would be devastated to think I'd seen her in such distress.' She smiled wryly. 'I have my secrets from her, too. To protect her.'

This best friend thing was starting to seem more complicated than ever. 'So she's protecting you from being upset by not crying in front of you, and you're protecting her from being upset by not telling her you've *seen* her crying?'

Morvena let out a soft laugh. 'That's about the long and short of it, yes.'

Aaron's tail flashed as he flicked it sharply. He was getting impatient. 'Where do *we* fit into all this?' he asked. 'You said you'd tell us your story if we promised to help you. What do you want us to do?'

Morvena met his eyes with a firm stare. 'All I know is, you can work some kind of magic. You can get out through the waterfall! No one has ever managed that before – not even the sea life that is down here with us. It gets in. But, like us, it doesn't get out.'

'But it was only the two of us who could get out,' I said. 'Just me and Aaron. We couldn't get Shona through with us.'

'I know. I saw that, too.'

'Then I don't see how we can help.'

'Listen. Here are the facts. You have powers. You can do things that none of us can do. Agreed?'

I looked at Aaron. 'Agreed,' he said.

'And from what I've observed in here, I am now convinced of one thing. Melody's shell is the key out of here. Whatever it is that Melody lost, whatever it is that she has begged the shell to help her find, I'm positive it is our only hope. Even though she has let us believe the way out of here was through singing, I'm sure this was always a diversion, to keep the others calm, and to stop us

180

questioning her too much and finding out the truth that she's fought so hard to keep secret. Even I have never got close to knowing this secret. All I do know is that the only thing *she* has put any faith in to get us out of here is the shell.'

'OK, I'll go along with that, too,' I said. 'But I still don't see how –'

'Wait,' Morvena said. 'Don't go anywhere.' Then she swam to the opening and out through the seaweed curtain. She must have been gone five minutes at least. When she came back, she was holding something.

She opened her hand out to reveal a glistening, beautiful, pearly shell. 'She goes to it every morning and every night without fail, but never in between,' she said. 'She won't miss it now until this evening.'

'You've stolen it from her!' Shona exclaimed. Her idea of what it is to be a best friend was taking a hammering.

'I've *borrowed* it, to help us all,' Morvena insisted. 'Melody will get it back before she knows it's gone. Whatever magic the shell holds, maybe you can bring it out – especially if you take it away from here. This prison holds us all bound and trapped, so the shell will never get the chance to share its secret down here.'

'What if you're wrong about all this?' I asked.

'If I'm wrong, as long as it's back in her room by tonight, we haven't lost anything. If I'm right and you can reveal the shell's secret, you could save us all.' She looked at Shona, and then back at me. 'Including your best friend,' she added.

I turned to Aaron. 'What do you think? Should we?'

Aaron shrugged. 'Like Morvena says, what is there to lose?'

'OK,' I said, reaching out to take the shell from Morvena. 'We'll do it.'

Aaron and I swam up the well. Looking down, I could see Shona and Morvena staring up at us. 'Look after her!' I called down. 'Don't let them hurt her!'

'I promise!' Morvena called back up to me. She reached out to pull Shona towards her and held a protective arm around her.

'I think we can trust her,' Aaron said to me. 'After everything she's told us today, she's got as much to lose as any of us.'

'I guess so,' I said, tightening my grip on his hand. Holding the shell carefully in my other hand, I gave a sharp flick with my tail.

Moments later, we were through the opening at the top and swimming away from the sirens, away from the caves, away from Shona – taking two things away with us: the shell, and the question I had no idea how to answer.

How would we ever make it release its magic and get Shona out of that place?

Chapter Twelve

I didn't want to go home. I didn't really want to set foot in Brightport at all. I'd almost forgotten about the newspaper and everything that had happened before I found the sirens' caves. It seemed like years ago! But now we were in town again, it came flooding back.

'I don't want to see anyone,' I said as we crept out of the sea on to the beach and shook our clothes dry.

'Just whizz round to your house and let your mum know you're safe,' Aaron said. 'Then come back to mine. We'll do it there.'

I agreed reluctantly, and sloped off towards home. It wasn't that I didn't want to see Mum. I just didn't want to go up to the pier and along the jetty and all the places between here and home where I could run into someone trying to catch a mermaid who might recognise my face from their morning's paper.

'Hurry,' Aaron called. 'We haven't got long.'

Aaron was right. I had to get home as quickly as possible – preferably avoiding any eye contact with anyone along the way – tell Mum everything was fine, put on a big false smile and hotfoot it back to Aaron's.

'I'll be back in five minutes,' I called over my shoulder. And then I ran home.

Mum was sitting on the front deck with Millie and Aaron's mum. I could see them from the end of the jetty. I was glad to see Aaron's mum here. At least that meant their cottage would be empty.

'Hi!' I said, all smiles. Mum looked up at me and smiled back so innocently I could almost have believed the whole morning had been a figment of my imagination.

'Emily darling!' she said, waving me over.

'I thought you were going to be at Shona's all day.'

'Did you?' I asked nervously. 'Why did you think that?'

'Mandy came over and passed on your message. It's nice that you're friends again, isn't it?'

'Oh yes, of course.' I'd forgotten about asking Mandy to cover for me. Had that only been this morning? It felt like a lifetime ago.

'Come and sit down, sweet pea,' she said.

Millie drained her cup. 'Just nip in and put the kettle on first, there's a love,' she said. 'I could murder an Earl Grey.'

I went inside and clicked the kettle on in a daze. How could they be sitting here so calm and casual when people were hunting down mermaids for cash prizes? Or while Shona was trapped in an underground cave with the meanest sirens in the world? It all felt unreal.

'I just wanted to let you know I'm over at Aaron's if you need me,' I said when I came back out.

'Oh, chicken, aren't you going to join us for a bit?' Mum asked, squinting up at me.

'Later, OK?' I tried to sound as though everything was normal. I wasn't going to start getting into it all with Mum – not after everything else that had been going on with her parents and everything. I turned away before I could see any disappointment in her eyes.

I sauntered casually down the jetty, my

cheekbones aching from the false smile and my limbs feeling like a marionette's, all loose and floppy as I tried to imitate the way I might walk on any other normal Sunday afternoon when I was off out with my friends.

'Go carefully!' Mum called to my back. In reply, I turned and gave her a quick wave. A moment later, I was on the pier and out of sight. I dropped the smile, broke into a run and hurried round to Aaron's.

'I don't get it. It's just a shell,' Aaron said. He was holding it in his hands, turning it round and round for the hundredth time. 'It doesn't *do* anything!'

He shook the shell. He lifted it to his ear. 'I mean, it does that thing that all conches like this do. It sounds like waves when you listen to it.' He put the shell down on the table in front of us. 'But that's it. Nothing else. I think Morvena's wrong. I don't think it's got anything magical about it at all.'

I stared at the shell. 'Why would Melody talk to it, though? Why would she hold it and cry over it every morning? It *has* to be magical. We must be missing something.'

'OK, maybe we are – but I've got no idea how we're going to work out what it is.'

I reached out to pick up the shell – and so did Aaron. As our hands touched, I got that tingly feeling in my fingers. I snatched my hand away, embarrassed in case he could tell how it made me feel when he touched my hand, in case it wasn't the same for him.

'That's it!' he said. 'Of course! How could we be so stupid?'

'What is it?'

Aaron lowered his eyes and shuffled awkwardly. 'Look, you know when I – when we – you know, kind of touch hands . . . ' His voice trailed away.

'Uh huh,' I said, trying to keep my voice casual. *Touch hands? Did we? Oh – maybe, yeah. I hadn't really noticed.*

'Well, d'you ever get, like, a kind of tingly feeling?'

'You get it too?' I asked.

Aaron grinned. 'Course I do!'

I smiled back at him. That meant he felt the same way I did. Maybe he *was* my boyfriend!

'Just – I think it's got something to do with the magic,' he went on. 'You know, the thing about Neptune.'

Oh. OK, so maybe it wasn't about him being so crazy about me that his skin danced in happy leaps because I was close. It was just about overturning a curse.

188

'Mm, yeah, that's what I was thinking too,' I lied.

Aaron laughed. 'As *well* as anything else,' he said. He'd gone and read my mind again. And this time, his face had turned as pink as mine felt. He *did* feel the same way! I couldn't suppress a happy smile.

'Just now, when we touched hands, and we were both touching the shell too, did you feel it then?'

I considered lying. If I said I'd felt it, what if he laughed in my face and said that he hadn't? It could be a trick to get me to confess to my feelings for him so he could tell me he didn't feel the same way.

Then I thought about it a bit more. This was Aaron I was talking about. He wasn't like that. He would never do something like that.

'Yes,' I confessed. 'Actually, I felt it really strongly.'

'Me too,' he said. Then he lifted the shell and held it between us. 'Link my fingers,' he said. 'If we hold hands and hold the shell between us, maybe something will happen. Perhaps the shell's magic has got something to do with Neptune – and if it has, maybe we can undo it!'

I took his hand. As soon as we touched, I felt the tingle again. First in my fingertips; then it travelled up my arm. Soon it felt as though it was spreading through my whole body.

'Look!' Aaron said. The shell had started to vibrate in our hands. I tightened my grip on his fingers so we didn't drop it.

'It's working – it's doing something!'

The shell rumbled and shook, and it was making a noise – a bit like the sound it had made when we held it to our ears, only about fifty times as loud! It was shaking more and more violently. And then, without any warning, it suddenly stopped.

We stared at the shell, at our hands, at each other.

It hadn't worked. Nothing had changed. So much for our magical powers.

'Now what?' I asked.

Aaron disentangled his fingers from mine and held the shell to his ear. 'There's something inside it,' he said, shaking it softly.

Then he passed it to me. I turned it over and shook it. He was right! Something was jigging about inside the shell! I shook it again. This time the thing inside it dislodged itself a bit so that I could see the tip of it inside the gaping spiral.

I reached in and tried to grab hold of it. My fingertips touched the corner of it, but I couldn't grasp it. 'It looks like a bit of plastic!' I said, dismay hitting me like a hard slap. We'd got it all wrong. Morvena was mistaken; there was nothing magical about the shell. We'd done all this for a piece of plastic that had probably been swept out to sea with someone's rubbish and ended up in the shell! We'd done it all for nothing.

'I can't get hold of it,' I said flatly.

'Hang on a sec.' Aaron got up and left the room. A minute later, he was back, with a pair of tweezers. He held them out to me. 'Now try.'

Reaching carefully in with the tweezers, I gripped the corner of the plastic and pulled at it.

Soon, I'd pulled enough of it out to grip it with my fingers – but they were shaking. What if I was wrong and it *was* magical after all? What might we be about to find? I'd had enough surprises in the last few months to know that you don't always find the answers you're looking for without finding about fifty unwanted ones first.

I pulled it out and held it in my palm. I was right about one thing. It *was* just an ordinary piece of plastic. It looked like the kind of thing Mum used to wrap my sandwiches in for school. Apart from one thing. It had something inside it – and it wasn't a sandwich! It looked like a sheet of paper, folded over and over into a tiny package.

'You do it,' I said to Aaron, suddenly losing my nerve.

He took the bag off me and opened it up. 'Right,' he said, pulling at the package inside it. 'Time to find out what this is all about.'

The knock at the door startled us so much we both literally jumped out of our chairs, banging knees as we did so.

Aaron quickly shoved the shell and package on to another chair and slid it under the table. 'Who's that?' he called.

'King Kong.' replied a familiar voice. 'Who d'you think?'

Aaron opened the door. Mandy stood on the doorstep, peering into the cottage. 'Thought I saw you,' she said. 'What's going on?'

'We – we're just –'

'Let her in, Aaron,' I said, getting up. Aaron held the door open for her and Mandy came in. Sticking his head out and glancing quickly in both directions, he closed it again and followed her inside. The three of us stood in an awkward circle.

'Thanks for telling Mum I was going to be out for the day,' I said.

Mandy shrugged. 'No problem. How did it go, anyway – whatever you were doing?'

I didn't know how to reply. Where could I start? And I still couldn't help a bit of me wondering if Mandy really was being genuine – or if, any moment now, she would laugh in my face and tell me she'd been putting the whole thing on and had never had the slightest intention of being my friend.

'It's OK, I get it. You don't trust me,' Mandy

192

said, before I'd got round to working out how to answer her question.

'No, I —' I began. Then I stopped. I took a breath and started again. 'It's not that I don't trust you,' I said carefully. 'It's — well, maybe I'm scared.'

'Scared? Of me?' Mandy laughed. Then she flushed deep red. 'I suppose I've given you reason to feel scared of me in the past,' she said sadly. 'I was a bully. I made your life hell. I'm not surprised that's how you feel.' She turned and headed back towards the front door. 'Sorry for bothering you.'

I grabbed her arm. 'No! That's not what I meant,' I said. 'Don't go.'

'Why not? Why on earth would you want to be around me? I was an idiot to think you'd want us to be friends,' she said.

And despite everything that had happened today, and how much of a mess everything was, I suddenly got this really good feeling. It was like looking out at a calm sea and feeling at peace. Mandy and I *were* friends and I had to stop doubting it. The only block to our friendship was me, and my silly suspicious mind. We had enough battles to fight without trying to turn our friendship into another one.

I patted the chair next to me. 'Look, come and sit down,' I said. 'I'm going to tell you everything.'

'So that's pretty much it,' I said. Mandy had sat open-mouthed through the whole story, hanging on every word like a child listening to their favourite fairy tale. Hearing myself saying it all out loud, it did sound a bit like a fairy tale. The only difference was that every word of this fairy tale was true.

'And that's what was inside the shell,' she said, pointing to the package Aaron still had folded up in his hand.

Aaron nodded. 'We were just about to open it when you came in.' He looked up at me. 'Ready?'

I nodded.

He unfolded the package, again and again until it was fully open. A plain sheet of paper, covered with hand-drawn squiggles and lines and symbols and strange words that I didn't recognise.

The three of us hunched over it, trying to make sense of it.

'I think it's a map of some sort,' Aaron said. 'But I don't know where it's of. It doesn't look like any countries I've seen.' He frowned at it. 'All those maps back at the castle – I can't think of a single one that looks like this.'

'Of course you can't!' Mandy suddenly

exclaimed, sitting up straight and staring at us both.

'Why not?'

'Look – the map came from a siren, right?'

'Right,' I agreed, trying to ignore the fact that it was drawn on a plain sheet of paper and stuffed inside a sandwich bag. How did a siren get hold of such ordinary things?

'And where do sirens live?' Mandy went on, as though she were talking to a pair of very stupid people. Which was when I realised she *was*. It didn't matter how Melody had got hold of it. The fact was, it was hers – and she was a siren.

'In the sea!' I said.

Mandy folded her arms and grinned. 'Exactly!'

'Of course!' Aaron said. 'It's a map of the sea!'

He leaned back over the map, pulling it straight and indicating for us to join him. 'We had these at the castle, too. It's because it's hand-drawn. I couldn't tell straight away,' he muttered, clearly embarrassed that Mandy had figured it out before him.

He ran a finger over some lines that looked like contours. 'Look. This shows you the different areas and currents of the sea,' he went on, taking the lead now he knew what we were dealing with.

'What are all the numbers?' I asked.

'They tell you how deep the ocean is at that point.'

'And those darker bits there,' he said, pointing at

some dark grey patches dotted about on the map. 'They're sandbanks.'

'What are those thick arrows?' Mandy asked. They were all over the paper, pointing in different directions, left, right, up and down.

'They tell you the direction of the tide. Very useful,' he replied.

'What about that?' I pointed to a circle in the bottom left hand corner. It looked like an old-fashioned watch, with a little cross on the top.

'That's a compass, isn't it?' Mandy said. 'We've just done something like this in geography. The cross on the top is pointing north.'

'That's right,' Aaron said. He rubbed his chin and stared at the map. 'You can tell all sorts from a map like this. You can find any point in the sea if you've got the right information.'

Which was something we were lacking. We didn't have *any* information. How were we ever going to make sense of this?

Aaron ran his hand over some roughly drawn shapes dotted about on the map – the only bits of it that weren't filled with squiggles and numbers. 'These will be our best guide,' he said.

'What are they?' I asked.

'Land. They'll be islands in the sea. And this one . . .' He pointed at a scraggily-drawn oval shape right in the centre of the map. Whoever had drawn it had circled it again and again with a different colour. They'd done it so hard the paper had almost ripped. An arrow pointing towards it made sure it stood out even more. It was different from the other arrows. They were thick and broad. This was more like the kind you draw through a heart to indicate true love.

'What about it?' I asked.

Aaron looked up at me. 'This is the place we need to find.'

The pieces started falling into place. 'Melody wanted the shell to help her find something,' I said slowly. 'The lost thing, whatever it is, I bet it's out there, on that island. It must be! And if we stand a chance of rescuing Shona from that awful place . . .' My sentence trailed away.

Mandy finished it for me. 'We need to find the island,' she said. 'And we need to find it fast.'

197

Chapter Thirteen

ifteen minutes later, Mandy, Aaron and I were in the map section of Brightport library. We'd pulled out all the sea maps they had. There weren't many, but we figured they'd probably have the local ones at least. We were banking on the hope that the hand-drawn map would be of somewhere reasonably close. It had to be, or how would Melody have been able to swim there?

Aaron dumped a handful of maps and charts on the table in front of us. 'Right,' he said. 'Let's get started.'

I pushed the hood off my head. I'd kept my face hidden in case anyone spotted me on the way over and recognised me from the newspaper. There was hardly anyone in the library, though, and no one was taking any notice of us, so I reckoned it was probably safe enough to show my face. And anyway, sitting in a library with a hood over my head would probably have attracted *more* attention, not less.

I opened up a map. It was criss-crossed with lines and numbers, yellow circles, purple blocks. And it was massive.

'What are we meant to be doing?' I asked as a feeling of hopelessness washed over me like a wave creeping high up the shore.

'Look for any similar patterns,' Aaron said as he placed the shell on the table and propped up our map in front of it. 'Same groups of numbers, islands that look similar in shape, or grouped in the same kind of way – anything. We need to find a match.' He grabbed a map and started unfolding it. 'OK?' he asked.

'OK,' Mandy and I replied. Then Mandy opened up a third map and the three of us got to work.

'This is hopeless.' Mandy folded up a map and threw it on the floor. The discarded pile was getting bigger and bigger, and the ones we still hadn't looked at were dwindling rapidly. We'd nearly got through them all. 'We're never going to find it.'

Mandy was right. We were kidding ourselves. I wasn't ready to admit that out loud yet, though. That would mean giving up on Shona – and I would *never* be ready to do that. 'Come on, we haven't finished yet. We'll find it,' I said, trying to inject some optimism that I didn't actually feel into my voice. 'We've got to.'

I picked up another map and passed one to Mandy. Aaron grabbed a third. 'Last one,' he said.

This was it, then. If we didn't find a match in any of these, we didn't have anywhere else to look. We *had* to find it.

We studied our maps in silence. Staring in front of me at the hand-drawn map, I scoured the real map in front of me, looking for anything that seemed to match.

'Hey, I think I've found something!' Aaron said suddenly. He was pointing at his map, tracing around the patterns on it and glancing up every few seconds at the one from the shell. Mandy and I left our own maps and crowded round him.

'Look – see that combination there?' He pointed to the group of numbers in the middle of the map that showed the depth of the water. 'The numbers are the same on this one.'

I looked up to compare it with our original map. He was right! And there was something else, too, just a little to their side. 'Look – the islands!' I said. 'They're not exactly the same, but they're a pretty good match.'

'The library map has got a lot more of them,' Mandy said. 'Does that matter?'

Aaron shook his head. 'I doubt it. Whoever drew this wasn't trying to reproduce the whole thing.' He pointed to the island in the middle of the map, the one with the arrow pointing towards it. 'They just needed to draw enough so that someone could find this island.'

'So that Melody could find it,' I added. We might not know who drew it, or why they drew it, or even why the sirens were really trapped in their underwater prison, but at least a small piece of the jigsaw was falling into place.

'And find what she'd lost,' Mandy finished.

Aaron folded up the new map and put it beside the shell and the original map. 'And now we can go and find it,' he said.

'Whatever *it* is,' I said. I still wasn't sure how we were going to find Melody's lost thing when we didn't even know what it was we were looking for. I had to hope that we'd know it when we saw it – if it was still there.

Aaron handed me the map. 'Hold on to this,' he said. 'I'll put the others back.'

'Hang on,' Mandy said, reaching into her pocket and looking in her purse. She rifled through it and pulled out a card. 'Got it!' she said, smiling. 'My library card.'

Mandy passed me the card and went over to help Aaron put the other maps away.

'Don't forget to bring the shell,' I said. Then I turned round – and walked straight into someone. 'Ooh, sorry, I –' I stopped.

Mr Beeston.

'What are you doing here?' I burst out.

'Whatever do you mean?' he blustered. 'I've every right to come to my local library, I should think.' He scanned the three of us slowly with his beady eyes. 'I might ask you the same thing,' he added.

'And I might give you the same answer,' I said, folding my arms.

'*Touché*, child, *touché*,' he said, with a little laugh. I relaxed a bit. Mr Beeston didn't scare me any more.

'Look, we're just helping Mandy with some homework,' I said. He might not be a threat to us, but that didn't mean I was going to start telling him what we were really doing here.

'Of course, of course, you carry on now,' he said lightly. He waved a hand to let me pass him. But as

I did, he grabbed my arm. 'What's that?' he hissed.

I followed his eyes. He was looking at the table. More specifically, he was looking at the shell lying on it. His face had turned as white as the shell.

'It's – we're – I –'

'We found it on the beach,' Aaron said quickly, looking up at Mr Beeston with what was probably meant to be a casual smile. 'Pretty, isn't it?' he added.

Mr Beeston took a couple of steps towards him. He reached out towards the shell. His hand was shaking. 'Isn't it just,' he said. 'Mind if I have a look?' he added in a voice that had as much forced casualness about it as Aaron's smile.

Aaron gave me a quick glance. I shrugged. We couldn't exactly say no, could we? Mr Beeston didn't know anything about what we were doing, or how significant the shell was. Where was the harm in letting him see it?

'Sure.' Aaron held the shell out.

All three of us held our breath as we watched Mr Beeston study the shell. He turned it over and over in his hands, holding it close to his eyes with the concentration of a watchmaker examining the workings of a particularly complex mechanism.

Aaron broke the silence. 'I – er, I think we need to get going now,' he said. He held his hand out for the shell.

Mr Beeston looked up. 'What? Oh, yes of course,'

he said. He held out a reluctant hand to pass the shell back to Aaron. 'Right you are,' he said, to no one in particular. He seemed to have gone into a trance.

'Mr Beeston, are you OK?' I asked.

He turned back to me, nodding vaguely. 'Gosh, don't you worry about me,' he said, flapping an arm as if to swat me away. 'You be on your way now.' But then he froze. He was looking at my arm. Or rather, the map underneath it. Glancing from the map back to the shell in Aaron's hand, he took a step closer towards me. 'The maps,' he said. 'What are they for?'

'They're for my mum,' Aaron said quickly.

Mr Beeston spun round. 'I thought you said you were helping Mandy with her homework?'

'They are,' Mandy said. 'Aaron's mum is going to help me. It's for geography. She knows a lot about the subject we're doing at the moment.'

I could feel my face heat up. It was *so* obvious we were lying. I felt like a criminal — until I remembered something. We hadn't actually done anything wrong. Then I remembered something else. Shona! If we stood any chance of saving her, we had to get to the island, find whatever it was that Melody had lost and get the shell back to the sirens before she noticed it was missing.

'Come on,' I said, heading for the counter and passing Mandy's library card over to the librarian

along with the map. 'We need to get going.'
I looked at Aaron and added pointedly, 'Your mum
will be wondering where we've got to.'

And with that, the three of us shoved past Mr
Beeston, shuffled out of the library and ran back to
the beach.

'Be careful, OK?' Mandy stood on the shore under
the pier, biting her nails and pacing up and down
along the water's edge. The beach was almost
deserted. Just a few people here and there: an elderly
couple arm in arm in the distance, their faces bent
close together. Someone else walking in the
opposite direction, throwing stones into the sea for
his dog to chase.

'We will be,' I replied.

'And come back if you need anything.'

I smiled. 'We will.'

Aaron glanced round one last time and took a
step into the water. 'We'd better go,' he said.

'You sure you've got it all in there?' I asked,
tapping my head. He'd spent the last half hour
studying the map and committing it to memory.

'Every symbol and every digit,' he said.
I believed him. I'd never met anyone with a
memory like his. It was as though all he had to

do was look at information and it was stored in his brain. Maybe that was what happened when you spent the first thirteen years of your life with nothing much to do except study a whole bunch of maps and books.

'And you've got the shell?'

He patted his big jacket pocket in reply. 'It'll be safe, don't worry,' he said.

I glanced round, too, before joining him at the water's edge. 'Come on, then,' I said. 'Let's go.'

Mandy started to walk away. Then she stopped and turned. 'Hey,' she called.

I looked up. 'What?'

'Good luck.'

I smiled. 'Thanks.'

She nodded and walked away. I looked round one last time, then dived into the water and swam away from Brightport.

'Are you sure we're heading the right way?' We'd been swimming close to the surface so we'd see the island when we got there. But we must have been out here for at least an hour and there was no sign of an island anywhere.

Long, deep swells lifted us up and carried us along as we scanned the horizon.

'We should be nearly there,' Aaron said, squinting into the distance. 'That way. Come on.'

He dived back down under the surface and I followed him.

Moments later, I noticed the water was changing. The dark rocks below us were becoming more scattered. Stretches of sand started appearing in between them.

Aaron glanced back at me. I swam harder to catch him up. 'It's getting warmer,' I said.

He nodded. 'Getting shallower,' he said.' This is where the numbers started changing down. We're nearly there.'

His words spurred me on and I kept pace with him as we swam on in silence. The water grew warmer still. The dark brooding rays and sharks we'd been passing along our way were replaced by brightly coloured fish darting along beside us in long rows and pointed formations like line dancers. It was as though they were escorting us. *This way, this way. Nearly there. Follow our moves.*

And then the water was so shallow I could see the bottom right below me. My tail brushed sand; reeds stroked my stomach as I floated across them. I stuck my head above the surface and looked round. An island!

'We're here!' Aaron breathed as we pulled ourselves on to the shore.

I sat watching our tails slowly flap at the water's

edge then melt away, as our legs returned. 'You're sure this is the right island?'

'Positive,' Aaron said. 'Come on, let's see if we can find whatever it is we're meant to be looking for.'

I followed him away from the shore and we started to make our way round the island. It was long and narrow, so I could see the opposite side from where we were. The beach we'd swum up to stretched all the way along one side, from what I could see. Beyond that it was rocky, with a couple of small hills and a few trees dotted about here and there. It shouldn't take us long to get round.

Just a shame we didn't know what we were looking for.

Half an hour later, we'd walked all the way from one end of the island to the other, and still had no idea.

Half an hour after that, we'd covered the whole coastline, the rocky hills, every tree – and *still* had no idea.

'This is hopeless,' I said, flopping down to sit on a rock. 'There's nothing here.'

Aaron searched round, pulling his hair off his face, looking this way and that. 'There must be something,' he said. 'There has to be.' He sat down beside me. 'Melody was asking the shell to help her find something. Inside the shell we find a map. The map leads us here. It *has* to be here.'

'I know – I agree, but it *isn't* here. Whatever "it" is.'

Aaron chewed a fingernail. 'I just don't get it. What was she trying to find?'

I stared out to sea, seeing nothing but blue ocean stretching out in a huge flat expanse, as it always did. As it had done for years and years.

Years and years . . .? Of course! 'Aaron,' I said. 'Morvena told us the sirens had been down there for years.'

Aaron tilted his head. 'Yes? And?'

'So Melody must have had the shell for years. Whatever she's looking for . . . ' I let my sentence trail away. I didn't want to say the rest of it out loud.

'It might have gone,' he said, finishing it for me.

I nodded. 'That makes sense.'

We sat in silence for a while, staring out to sea. I picked up handfuls of sand and let the grains trickle through my fingers.

'We'll have to get back there,' Aaron said. 'Tell Morvena what we found.'

'What we didn't find, you mean.'

Aaron's forehead crinkled into a frown. 'I just don't see what else we can do,' he said.

'I know. But if we leave, does that mean we're giving up on Shona? Giving up on any possibility of getting her out of there?'

Aaron took hold of my hand. Wiping the sand from my palm, he stroked it gently. 'Of course it doesn't,' he said, smiling at me. 'We're not giving up on anyone.' He stood up, pulling me up with him. 'Let's get back there, tell Morvena and Shona everything, and we'll work out a plan together.'

And I don't know if it was because we were walking along the beach hand in hand, or because Aaron's words had given me a bit of hope, but as we walked, I felt lighter and more positive. He was right. We weren't giving up at all. I'd *never* give up on Shona. We'd get her out of there!

'Wait!' Aaron said, letting go of my hand. He was looking down and patting his jacket pocket. 'Oh no! – but it can't have!' he mumbled. His face had turned white.

'What's up?' I asked.

He looked blankly back at me. 'It must have fallen out while we were scrabbling on the rocks,' he said, glancing rapidly all around us. 'How could I have been so careless?'

'*What?*' I repeated.

'The shell,' he said, panic cracking the edges of his words. 'It's gone.'

Chapter Fourteen

'**W**hat do you mean, the shell's gone?' I asked, staring at Aaron: his outstretched empty hands, his pale face.

'I mean it's disappeared,' he said flatly. 'I've dropped it somewhere. We've lost it. We'll have to retrace our steps.'

'Across the whole island?' The next moment, I heard a noise above us in the rocks. A tiny avalanche of stones ran down the hill.

'What's that?' I asked, getting up.

'It'll be the wind, I imagine,' Aaron said absently.

'Aaron,' I said. 'There isn't any wind. I'm going to look.'

'Wait, I'll come with you.'

We climbed the small hill, dodging loose stones, slipping on gravel and searching for the shell as we climbed. The top was as deserted as the beach.

'Nothing,' Aaron said. 'I told you it was only the –' He stopped. His mouth open wide, he slowly raised a hand to point across to the other side of the island.

'What?' I asked. 'What is it?'

Aaron raised a finger to his lips. 'Look,' he whispered. 'On the beach down there.'

I followed the line of his hand. He was pointing to a large palm tree on the beach. It was bent over so that its top was almost touching the ground.

'I can't see any –'

'Behind the tree,' Aaron hissed.

And then I saw it. Something moved. A figure. A person. And then they moved again and I saw who it was.

'Mr Beeston!' I gasped.

Without stopping to think, I tore down the hill. 'Oi!' I yelled as I ran. 'What are you doing here?'

Mr Beeston heard me tumbling down the hill and looked up. He stood up just before I reached him, shuffling with something in his pocket. And I bet I knew what it was. The shell!

'What are you doing here?' I asked again. I was

breathless and panting, but I didn't care.

Mr Beeston brought himself up to stand as straight and tall as possible. He pulled at the corners of his jacket and then he looked me in the eye. 'Why should I tell you?' he said. 'Why should I tell you anything?' Then he turned away and looked out at the sea. 'No one bothers to tell *me* anything, so why should I be any different?'

He didn't sound like his usual self. I couldn't put my finger on it, but there was something different about him. Something – I don't know – something lost. It was as though he wasn't even seeing me, didn't care that we'd caught him following us, or whatever he was doing. What *was* he doing? My indignation crept up a notch.

'Did you follow us here?' I asked. Then it hit me. 'Did you get here before us? Have you found it?'

Mr Beeston spun round. 'Found what? What are you talking about, child?'

'Found the –' I stopped. Yes, exactly. What *was* I talking about? 'Found the lost thing,' I said lamely.

He shook his head and laughed sourly. 'You know nothing, child,' he said. He started to walk away, towards the sea.

'The shell,' I called to his back. 'Did you steal it?'

'Steal the shell?' he called over his shoulder. Then he stopped. He whirled round and paced back to me. He stood so close to me, I could see beads of sweat breaking out one by one on his forehead.

'*Steal* the shell?' he repeated. 'Don't talk to me about stealing the shell. Don't talk to me about stealing *anything*!' Then he said something under his breath. I couldn't be sure I'd heard him correctly, but it sounded as though he added, 'Or anyone.'

And then he marched to the shore. Standing at the water's edge, he turned back towards me. 'There's nothing here,' he called. He turned back to the sea. Holding his arms out wide, he called again. 'Nothing,' he repeated, his voice breaking on the word.

Aaron was by my side. 'What's going on?' he asked.

'Search me. Mr Beeston's gone all weird.'

'Do you think he found the lost thing?'

I stared down at Mr Beeston. 'I don't know,' I said. 'Maybe he knew what we were looking for and found it before we even got here. Maybe he's had it all along. I just don't know.'

'What about the shell – has he got that?'

I let out a breath. 'I'm fairly sure he has, but I can't prove it. Why would he want it, anyway? I don't understand why he's here, what he's got to do with any of this, why he's acting so strangely. I don't get *any* of it, Aaron.'

'Nor do I, but if he hasn't got the shell I don't know what else can have happened to it.'

I looked down at Mr Beeston, standing at the water's edge, staring out to sea. 'Yeah, but if he has, we're not likely to get it back. He's not in a mood to give anything away.'

'Maybe the shell isn't that important any more,' Aaron said hopefully. 'I mean, we found the map. It didn't have anything else inside it. Perhaps Melody won't mind so much that it's gone.'

I laughed – or at least I tried to. It came out a bit more like the sound of a cat being strangled. 'Yeah, right. And perhaps we won't get tied up and tortured and left out for the sharks when we go back and tell her we've lost it,' I said. 'You never know. We could get lucky.'

Aaron reached out and took my hand. My anger and fear melted away when he did that and I met his eyes. 'Sorry,' I said. 'I'm just scared.'

'I know. It's OK. We'll figure something out. We'll tell them everything. The important thing is that we get back there and check Shona's all right.'

I nodded.

'Once we get to the caves we'll work out our next move together.'

I smiled. 'You're right. Come on, let's get going.'

Aaron nudged his head back towards Mr Beeston. 'What about him?' he said.

I shook my head. 'Forget him,' I replied, setting off over the rocks. 'He's not even worth thinking about.'

We got back to the caves quite easily. Aaron's sense of direction was almost as good as his photographic memory. Soon, we were both leaning out across the waterfall.

'You ready?' Aaron asked. He reached out for my hand.

'We should go separately,' I said. 'If we stop the waterfall, we might not be able to get down.'

He nodded. 'OK. See you inside.'

A moment later, I was in the waterfall, shooting downwards, spinning round and round. It felt as though it went on for ever, but it must only have been seconds. Eventually, the waterfall spat me out at the bottom and I lay on the sea floor, shaken, dishevelled and disorientated. A second later, Aaron plonked down beside me, in a similar state.

He pulled himself together first. 'Right, come on,' he said, shaking himself and flicking his tail as he set off. 'Let's go and find Morvena and Shona.'

We swam carefully through the tunnels, dodging from rock to rock and hiding behind thick trails of weeds in case any of the others might be about. The last thing we could afford to happen now was to get captured again before we'd even found Shona and Morvena. I led the way this time. I was pretty sure I knew where they'd be.

'Round this corner,' I whispered over my shoulder.

We swam along the rocky ledge till I saw the entrance to Morvena's room. 'This is it,' I said. 'They'll be in here, I bet.'

With one more look behind us, we swam inside. The two of them were sitting together on Morvena's big jelly cushion. Morvena was sitting behind Shona, combing her hair. Shona sat still and straight, a faraway look on her pale face.

'Shona!'

She looked up at me and her face broke out into the widest smile. 'Emily!' She jumped up from the cushion and swam over to me. Grabbing my arms, she said, 'I'd started to think you weren't coming back!'

'I wouldn't leave you here!' I said.

'I thought something had happened to you. I've been so worried. Morvena has too, and so has –'

'We all have,' said a soft voice in the far corner. I hadn't noticed anyone else when we came in. My heart plummeted. The others had found them. We were all doomed.

But the siren swam forward and I realised she wasn't one of the ones I'd met. For one thing, she didn't have a tight, mean face like theirs. And for another, she spoke so softly her voice could almost have been mistaken for a swish of seaweed in the current. Her face was soft, her eyes were large and round; she shared the long, silvery hair that the others had, but she had none of their sharpness, and the lines on her face seemed to dance around her eyes.

Aaron swam forward and stopped at my side. 'Who are −' he began. And then he stopped. He must have realised in the same moment that I did.

I swam towards the mermaid in front of us. She was smiling down at us. She wasn't likely to smile at us much longer, not once we told her what we'd done − and what we'd failed to do.

'Are you Melody?' I asked hoarsely.

She nodded. 'And you must be Emily and Aaron,' she said gently. Her voice was so kind I wanted to cry. I wanted to break down and confess; but at the same time, I wanted to spare her from it. I never wanted her to know that we'd lost her shell. Looking at her now, I could tell it would break her heart. How could we do that?

Before I had the chance to think any more about it, Shona grabbed my arm. 'Did you find anything?' she asked eagerly. What could we say? How could we do it? We were about to take away the one thing that was keeping everyone in here going: hope.

I looked at Aaron. I could see he was thinking the same as me. I lifted my shoulder in a tiny shrug.

He gave me the slightest nod in reply. We had to tell them.

'Look,' I said. 'I'll tell you everything. But please, please don't be cross. We've tried everything. And it wasn't our fault. OK?'

Morvena swam towards me. 'It's OK, Emily, you don't need to be afraid of us,' she said. 'We're on the same side.'

Melody crinkled her eyes in a sad smile. 'You don't need to worry, little ones,' she said. Her words hit at something inside me. Dad always calls me little 'un. I suddenly realised how much I wished I had him near me. How much I needed him and Mum. There was something about the way Melody spoke to us that reminded me of them both. She talked to me as gently as if I were her child. In that moment, I knew there was nothing to fear.

I took a breath. 'OK,' I said. 'Here's what happened.'

But then Morvena suddenly shushed me and swam to the entrance. There was a noise outside.

'The others,' she said. 'I think they're coming. We need to hide the children. We can't let them take them away. Not now.'

'Where can we hide?' I asked, looking round the room in a panic. What was there to hide behind?

But it was too late anyway. The sound was coming closer. Whoever it was, they were just about to come into the room.

And then they did – and all five of us froze exactly where we were.

'Mr Beeston!' I burst out. 'What the – how the – why –' Random words spilled out of my mouth. They refused to join up, and none of them could even express the depth of my shock and disgust. He'd followed us – again!

But he wasn't looking at me. He didn't see me, he didn't see Aaron or Shona. He didn't even see Morvena. He was looking at just one person in that room.

He swam slowly towards Melody. For a moment, he simply looked at her. Then with tears in his eyes matched only by the tears in hers, he whispered just one word.

'Mother?'

Chapter Fifteen

The room was silent. It was more than silent. You know if you're watching a DVD and you want to go and get something from the kitchen, so you pause it, and everything freezes exactly as it is? That's what it felt like.

I couldn't speak. I couldn't move. My brain seemed to have glued stuck while trying to understand what had just happened.

And then, what felt like a year later but was probably about three seconds, Melody replied.

'Charlie?' she said, her voice quivering like a tiny

fish caught in a net. 'Is it you? Is it really you?'

Mr Beeston was smiling broadly as he swam another tail's length towards Melody. 'It's me, mother,' he said. 'I'm here.'

A moment later, they were hugging and crying and laughing, and all that the rest of us could do was stare – and wonder what in the world was going on!

I swam a notch closer to them. 'Look, do either of you want to explain any of this to the rest of us?' I asked. Even Morvena was looking baffled.

Melody smiled at me. Her smile was – I don't know. It's hard to explain. It was as though it was more than a smile. It seemed to warm the room up, and brighten the colours. Everything felt lifted and lighter when she smiled.

Mr Beeston turned to me. 'You deserve an explanation,' he said. 'I'll grant you that, child.'

'Good,' I said, impatiently.

He took a breath. 'You remember I told you that my father deserted me when I was a baby and that I was brought up by a mother who hardly cared a jot about me?'

I nodded.

He glanced at Melody and then turned back to me. Pulling a loose strand of hair over his head, he went on. 'Well, it turns out that wasn't strictly true.'

Oh, what a surprise! Mr Beeston had been telling lies again! I folded my arms and waited for him to continue.

'No – wait!' He waved a hand at me. 'Don't get me wrong. I never told you a word of a lie. At least, I didn't know it at the time.'

Aaron swam over to my side. I could feel his arm against my elbow. 'You're talking in riddles,' he said, somehow managing to find the words I couldn't seem to get out. I think I was in shock. I felt as though we had just stumbled upon a jigsaw and we had all the pieces in front of us, but couldn't see how any of them fitted together.

Mr Beeston fumbled with his hair, pulled at his jacket, all those things he always does when he's feeling awkward about something – which, in my experience, he usually is.

'Let me start again,' he said.

'That sounds like a good idea,' said Aaron.

'The other day, when I told you I was going to talk to my mother, you remember that?'

I nodded.

'Well, that's what I did, that very day.' He glanced at Melody, his cheeks colouring a touch. 'Or at least I *thought* I did. But it turns out that I was brought up with a big lie.' He glanced at me. 'Just like you were,' he added. 'After all these years, I discovered that nothing was as I'd thought. My "mother" was nothing more than a scheming siren who simply wanted to get my real mother out of the way so she could get her fins on my father.'

Melody's eyes had darkened. 'Zalia,' she said hoarsely.

Mr Beeston nodded. 'She said she was glad I'd come. She was different from how I'd ever seen her before. At first I put it down to the years that had passed since I last saw her, but then I realised those years had brought her something else. Guilt. I could see it in her eyes.' He turned to me. 'I recognised it in myself – from my years of tricking you.'

'Guilt? Why?' I asked.

He turned back to Melody. 'She told me how she tricked you into going into hiding, and then betrayed you to Neptune.'

Morvena clapped a hand over her mouth. 'I always suspected – but I never believed she really could have.'

'*I* did,' Melody replied. 'I never doubted it for a moment.'

'She told me how she wheedled her way into my father's confidence, too,' Mr Beeston went on. 'She got him to tell her about the plan you and he made.'

Melody lowered her eyes. 'It was a wild night,' she said. 'A terrible night. We knew what it meant. We understood about Neptune's rage – we knew what he was capable of. My singing voice had already gone and I knew that was Neptune's punishment – but I also knew that would not be punishment enough for him. There was worse to come. And so we made a plan. I was to go into hiding, just for a while, just until Neptune's attention, and his rage, moved away from us and on to something else – as it always does.'

She reached out to take Mr Beeston's hand. 'I gave you to him, until we could be together again,' she said. 'We both agreed it was safer that way.'

'But why?' Morvena asked. 'Why would he be safer with his father? I mean we could have –'

'He would be beyond Neptune's reach,' Melody replied starkly. 'he would be brought up on land. His father is a human.'

Morvena's mouth fell open. 'A – but . . .'

'I know. That is why I didn't tell you. I knew you would never understand, never forgive me. How could you? A siren and a human. It is unheard of; it is a shameful thing. I'm a disgrace to all sirens.' She lifted her head to look at Morvena. 'That is the secret I never told you. I'm sorry. I couldn't risk losing all my friends as well as –' She glanced at Mr Beeston. 'As well as everything else that mattered to me.'

'So what you told us, about the only way out of here being the sound of a siren's beautiful voice, it was a lie too?' Morvena asked.

Melody nodded. 'You all wanted to believe it,' she said. When all your singing voices were taken away too, it was the only thing I could think of to avoid more questions – and answers which I knew I could never share with you. And anyway – at least you all had something I never had.'

'What was that?' I asked.

Melody met my eyes. 'Hope,' she said. 'However remote, at least you had something. I had nothing. I knew forgiveness and freedom were two things I would never get from Neptune. Or so I believed.'

Melody looked at Morvena. 'I'm sorry,' she said. 'I have told you many lies. But now the look on your face tells me I was right to keep the truth from you. I can see the disgust in your eyes. I couldn't bear to have had you look at me that way all of these years.'

Morvena shook her head. 'No, you are wrong. This look is *because* I am your friend, your *best* friend, and I can't believe that you felt you couldn't trust me with this.' She swam to Melody's side, lifted her chin and looked into her eyes. 'You had a son. All this time – all these long years, you grieved on your own when I could have helped you.' She opened her arms and Melody fell into them.

Morvena stroked her hair. 'So that's what you meant when you asked the shell to help you.'

Melody pulled away. 'What do you mean? What do you know about the shell?'

'I've seen you,' Morvena said softly. 'I've heard you – many, many times.'

'What have you heard?' Melody asked. 'What have you heard me say?'

'I heard you say, "Help me find you". I always knew something was lost.' Morvena glanced

226

towards Mr Beeston and her voice caught as she went on. 'I just didn't know that the lost thing was your *child*. Melody, you poor thing. You suffered so much, and I could have helped.' She held Melody close, rocking her gently. 'I don't understand how the shell was meant to help you find him, though,' she said after a while.

'I do,' Mr Beeston replied. 'Zalia told me that, too. She'd managed to get it out of my father. He put a map inside it.'

Melody gasped. 'Inside it? Oh my – no! Of course!'

'What? What is it?' I asked.

For a moment, Melody looked utterly lost. Her eyes flickered wildly around us all. Then they settled on Mr Beeston and she grew calmer again. 'I never knew there was something in the shell,' Melody said. 'What a fool. How could I have been so stupid?'

'What d'you mean?' I asked. 'Why have you been stupid?'

'He gave it to me the last time we met, in the storm, but the storm was so fierce I couldn't hear properly what he was telling me. I thought he was telling me it had magic in it, magic that would somehow lead me to him. But he wasn't telling me there was magic in it – he was telling me there was a *map* in it!'

Melody shook her head. 'All these years I've held

it, whispered to it, begged it to reveal its magic, and all along I was looking for the wrong thing.

'And you could never get the map out because Neptune must have sealed the shell when he sealed the caves!' Aaron said.

Melody nodded. 'All those lost years. So very many of them,' she said sadly, reaching out to touch Mr Beeston's arm. 'Your father had discovered a small island during his travels. He'd never seen a soul there. He believed that once Neptune's rage blew over, we could live there in secret, and in safety. I was to hide for a matter of weeks – months, at most – and then join you both there.'

'That must be the island we found!' I burst out.

'You know about the island?' Melody glared at me, then round at us all. 'You all seem to know so much,' she said. 'And do you know I have lost the shell now?'

'You know?' Morvena gasped. 'I thought you only looked at it in the mornings and at night. I thought –'

'You thought wrong,' Melody said. 'That shell is the only thing that has kept me going in here.'

Perhaps this was the time to own up. But how was I going to tell her we'd lost it? What would she say? What would she do to us? Perhaps she'd turn as nasty as the others. One look at her pleading face and I knew I had to take the risk. I opened my mouth. 'Um, we, um –'

228

Mr Beeston stopped me with a wave of his hand. Then he reached into his pocket. Pulling his hand out, he opened it up, to reveal the shell. 'Here it is.'

For a moment, Melody stared in wonder at the shell. 'But you – but how –' she began. Then she smiled. 'No matter,' she said gently. 'We have all the time in the world for explanations. All that matters now is that the shell has brought me what I always knew it would.' Then she closed her hand over Mr Beeston's and they held the shell between them – her face a picture of serenity.

An hour ago, discovering that Mr Beeston had taken the shell would have made my blood boil as fiercely as the waterfall. But after everything we'd heard, I couldn't blame him, and I wouldn't hold it against him. For the first time, Mr Beeston's trickery seemed like an act of love and loyalty.

He cleared his throat. 'There's – ah, there's something else I need to tell you,' he said to Melody. 'There was one more lie in my childhood.'

Melody put her other hand over Mr Beeston's. 'What is it?'

He swallowed hard and then nodded slowly, as if making an agreement with himself to tell us. 'After you had gone, Zalia wasted no time with my father. She tricked and lied her way into his life – telling him you had abandoned us and making herself indispensible to him. She told me that her one failure was that she had never managed to get him to love her. There was only room for one in his heart.' He looked up at Melody and her cheeks glowed with warmth and embarrassment.

'After you had been gone for over a year and he had heard no word from you and been unable to find you, he began to believe her. And that was his fatal mistake.'

'What do you mean?' Shona asked, as wrapped up in Mr Beeston's story as the rest of us. 'Fatal how?'

'He no longer cared about anything. He wouldn't look after himself; he could hardly look after me. Zalia did that – in her own way.'

'What happened?' I asked. 'You told me he'd run off and left you when you were a baby? Is that a lie, too?'

Mr Beeston paused for a long time. 'In a way,' he said. Then, his voice rough and ragged like a weathered old rope, he said, 'I have just discovered the truth. He – my father –' He swallowed hard. 'He drowned.'

Melody made a sound as if she were choking. Mr Beeston grabbed her hand again, squeezed it tight. 'I'm sorry,' he whispered. 'I never knew. I don't know if she wanted to taunt me by making me believe my father never cared, or if she was protecting me from the truth. I suppose I'll never know. But she wanted me to know the truth now – about all of it. She said she was relieved to finally tell me everything, and that maybe she would be able to sleep at nights again.'

'I know Zalia,' Morvena said sharply. 'She never does anything to protect anyone.'

'She brought me up,' Mr Beeston said. 'I like to think she cared at least a tiny bit.'

'Maybe she did,' Morvena said. 'But let's not forget it was her fault you were orphaned in the first place.'

Melody raised her head and held it high. 'He was not orphaned,' she said firmly. 'My son was not orphaned.'

There wasn't much any of us could say after that, and we fell silent, each lost in our own jumble of thoughts and questions.

Shona was the first to break the silence. 'So what did you find?' she said, turning to me and Aaron. 'Did the shell give you a way out of here?'

Of course – we'd forgotten all about that. Her question made me realise something else, too. 'You followed us in here, didn't you?' I said to Mr Beeston.

'I had no choice. I wasn't spying on you. I'd seen the shell. I knew what it was. Zalia told me all about it. It seems her guilty conscience demanded a thorough unburdening. So I knew the shell would lead to something – although I have to confess I didn't think I would actually find my real mother! That was far too much to hope for, or so I thought.'

'But the waterfall – you came down it?' I said impatiently.

'Yes – what of it?'

I sighed. 'I hope you haven't got any plans in the near future.'

'Whatever do you mean? Explain, child.'

So we did. We told him about the waterfall, about how you could get in but not out; we even told him about the discovery Aaron and I had made – how we could undo Neptune's magic, but that we could only get ourselves out of the waterfall and no one else.

'Well, there's only one thing for it, then,' Mr Beeston said when we'd explained everything.

'What's that?' I asked.

'You'll have to go out of the waterfall again. The two of you will have to perform one more task. You have a visit to make.'

'What do you mean?' asked Aaron. 'Who do we have to visit?'

Mr Beeston met Aaron's dark eyes with his own, and replied firmly, 'Neptune.'

Chapter Sixteen

I woke early and lay looking up at the ceiling, trying to get my head round everything that had happened yesterday – and what we had to do today.

Mr Beeston had told us where to go to find Neptune, and what we had to say to get the guards to let us see him. All we had to do now was get there and persuade Neptune to set them all free. I wished I was as optimistic about the task as Mr Beeston was.

I got out of bed, threw my clothes on and wrote

Mum a note. Then I hurried round to Aaron's. The pier and the beach were deserted. Luckily for me, not many people tend to go wandering round in a seaside town at seven o'clock on a Monday morning. I still had that image from yesterday's paper in my head – and I'd convinced myself there'd be others around who did, too.

Aaron was coming out of his cottage when I got there. 'Ready?' he asked, closing the door softly behind him.

'To face Neptune?' I asked with a shudder. 'I'll never be ready for that!'

He laughed. 'Come on, let's go.'

We were waiting in some sort of grand holding room in an enormous underwater palace. It turned out Mr Beeston's influence and instructions were as impressive as he'd said they were.

I recognised the style from the last time I'd been in one of Neptune's palaces. He wasn't exactly what you'd call subtle in his decorating tastes. Marble pillars with fancy golden spirals circling their bases marked the corners of the room. The most enormous chandelier you could imagine hung from the domed ceiling, swaying ever so slightly in the gentle current.

A smartly dressed merman swam up to us. 'Neptune will see you now,' he said solemnly. 'Follow me.'

Aaron took my hand and we followed the merman through winding corridors and twisting tunnels. Eventually, we came to a large door. It was made of glass and the frame was encrusted with jewels. Through the door I could see a very tall throne – and a very serious-looking Neptune sitting on it.

Memories of my previous run-ins with Neptune flooded into my mind. Facing his anger in his own court room; having a curse put on me when I accidentally found his ring; almost being squeezed to death by his pet sea monster. 'I don't know if I can do this,' I whispered to Aaron.

'You have to,' he whispered back. 'Shona's depending on us. They all are.'

Just the mention of Shona's name was enough to remind me what we had to do. 'You're right,' I said. Taking a deep breath, I added, 'Let's go and talk to Neptune.'

We waited in silence, watching Neptune's furrowed brow, his narrowed eyes, his tightly closed mouth. We'd told him everything. All we could do now was wait – and hope that he didn't throw us out on our gills.

'And this is Beeston's mother, you say?' Neptune trained his hard eyes on me.

I nodded. 'Amongst others.'

'Yes, yes.'

'It was a long time ago, Your Majesty,' Aaron said carefully. 'A time when your laws and your world were very different.'

Neptune glared at him. I took up from where Aaron had left off. 'You've said yourself, it's a new world now. In fact, you ordered us to *make* it a new world. This could be part of that.'

Neptune turned his cold stare on me. 'How do you presume to figure THAT out?'

I gulped. 'Well, I –' I began. And then my mind went blank. Being in front of Neptune in his own palace trying to ask him a favour whilst he's staring at you booming out doubts against everything you say kind of has that effect on you. On me, anyway.

'It would send out a message,' Aaron said.

Neptune swung back round to face him. 'It WHAT?' he bellowed. I wished he could just talk like normal people. Why did everything always have to be so, well, *loud* with him?

'You would be showing the mer world that Neptune really has let go of the old ways. That sirens luring fishermen to their deaths is a thing of the past. The message would be huge, especially with what's happening now at Shiprock.'

Neptune wrinkled his forehead sternly. 'What IS happening in Shiprock?' he asked. 'My updates have been getting unacceptably slack lately.'

'They're turning against humans more fiercely every day,' I said. 'They're feeling under threat because of the development in Brightport.'

'And can you blame them?'

'Well, no, but perhaps if you let the sirens go, they could join us in trying to calm the situation down. Humans and merpeople working together, to show Shiprock that there's nothing to fear ... somehow? Perhaps that could be a condition of their release.'

Neptune rubbed his beard. 'Hmm, OK, let's say I do that,' he said quietly, almost as though he were talking to himself, thinking aloud. 'Attach conditions. Yes, I like that. But on the other hand ...' Then he nodded his head. 'Right, that's it!' he barked. 'I have decided what we will do.'

I froze as I waited for him to continue. What was he going to say? Would I ever see Shona again? Had we made a massive mistake coming here? *Please help us. Please don't send us away with nothing.*

'I shall undo the waterfall on the caves,' he announced. 'The sirens will be free to leave.'

'And Shona?' I asked hardly daring to hope.

Neptune waved my question away. 'Yes, yes, of

course, all of them – including Beeston and your friend.'

Aaron caught my eye and gave me a thumbs up. We'd done it! Shona was going to be free!

'I haven't finished!' Neptune boomed, before I had the chance to get too serious about the idea of celebrating. 'Here are my conditions.'

We waited in silence.

'ONE: You are to redouble your efforts with the task you have been set. I gave you a mission and I intended for you to take this mission to your hearts. Until now, I can see no serious progress. You are to make *significant* progress. And this progress is to begin with settling the situation with Brightport and Shiprock. I want it sorted. You hear me?'

'Of course,' I said. 'We'll do everything we can to –'

'You will not do *everything you can* to make this happen – you will MAKE THIS HAPPEN!' Neptune bellowed. 'Or else you will face my wrath!'

'Absolutely, Your Majesty. We will make it happen,' I hastily agreed.

'TWO: the memory drug remains lifted in Brightport.'

My hopes began to sink. The whole of Brightport still on a mission to catch a mermaid. How could we carry on living there? We'd have to move. Or I'd have to get a plastic surgeon to give me a new

238

face. I opened my mouth, about to ask Neptune to reconsider this condition. I couldn't imagine trying to convince Mum and Dad to start again in yet another new town. And if I was honest, I quite liked my face the way it was.

'Non negotiable!' Neptune said, reading my thoughts and cutting them down in two simple words. 'How do you expect to bring together the human and the mer worlds if you wish the one to be in darkness about the other? How do you expect the people of Brightport to care about their neighbouring town enough to stop destroying it if they don't even know it EXISTS?!'

He did have a very good point.

'You will make this work,' he said sombrely.

I let out a sigh. 'OK,' I said eventually – not that we had any choice in the matter, so I don't know why he was waiting for us to agree each condition. Then I had a thought. 'My grandparents,' I said.

'What about them?'

'Well, if we agree about the memory drug staying lifted in Brightport, will you lift it from them too – permanently?'

Neptune's face reddened. 'Do not PRESUME to barter with me!' he roared. 'I, and only I, make conditions! Do you understand?'

'Yes of course, Your Majesty,' I said meekly. 'I'm sorry.'

Neptune thought for a moment. 'If I do not

know where your grandparents are, there is nothing I can do,' he said. 'But I will grant you this: if they come to Brightport, the rule will apply to them also. That is the best I can offer you.'

'Thank you sir, thank you, Your Majesty,' I gabbled.

Neptune raised his hand again. 'There is one more condition,' he said. 'The most important of all.'

This was it, then – the bit where he told us I had to give Aaron and Shona up, never see either of them again, or leave Brightport forever, never to return, live out my days in a solitary, dark –

'You must give up your power,' he said. For the first time ever, he seemed uncomfortable, awkward, almost like a normal person.

'Our power?' Aaron asked. 'You mean . . .' He took hold of my hand. Curling his fingers around mine, he held our hands up in front of us. 'This?'

Neptune clutched his trident. 'No one should have the ability to undermine my power,' he said. 'It is not right; it is not how things should be; it is not what I intended with that verse. But once it is done, the nature of the magic you have claimed means that I cannot undo it.'

'You can't undo it?' I repeated. 'How is it undone then?'

'You must relinquish it,' he said starkly. 'You must agree to give it back to me. On this, and this alone,

I need your agreement.' He held his trident over our hands. 'You must willingly give it up. If you both agree to do this, the power can be returned to me.' He held tight on to his trident. 'Do I have your agreement?'

I looked at Aaron. He didn't have to worry about his best friend being trapped in an underwater cave with a bunch of evil sirens. He might not want to give up such a cool power.

He didn't look back at me. Without blinking, Aaron tightened his grip on my hand. 'We agree,' he said firmly.

As soon as he'd spoken, I wanted to leap up and hug him. I wanted to throw my arms round him and – and – my face burned when I realised what I wanted to do, and for once I hoped he couldn't read my mind. I wanted to kiss him.

Before I had a chance to worry too much about what I wanted and whether he wanted it too, and whether it was ever going to happen, Neptune was speaking again. 'Now, you must keep your side of the bargain. Do not forget the first condition. I will give you and your families *one week* to show me you are serious about your task. If I do not see evidence by then . . .'

He didn't even need to finish his sentence. I knew what it was like to be on the receiving end of Neptune's threats. He didn't make them lightly, and he didn't hold back in carrying them through.

'We'll do it, Your Majesty,' I said. 'We promise.'

'Very well. As long as we understand each other,' he said.

Oh yes, we certainly understood each other. The shiver that ran menacingly through my body, carrying with it memories of monsters and curses and storms unleashed by Neptune's temper, reminded me precisely how well I understood him.

'Now, hold your hands still,' Neptune instructed us. We did what he said, and he held the trident over our outstretched hands.

'*Power that should never have been set free,*
Now you shall return to me,' he intoned.

A millisecond later, my hand burned and itched and tingled. Aaron gripped it harder and I held on to his hand as tightly as I could while flashes of power and light surged through me. It felt as though someone had shot a massive bolt of electricity into me. The volts ran up my fingers, through my hands, along my arms, danced their way through my whole body – and stopped.

Nothing.

Neptune removed his trident. 'It is done,' he said. 'Thank you. Now, we must return to the caves and I shall complete my side of the bargain. Come, you shall travel with me.'

And with that, we turned and followed him out of his grand chamber, out of the palace and into the chariot that was waiting, with its gold-adorned dolphins, to take us back to the caves.

It took moments. Neptune held his trident over the waterfall and muttered something in a low rumble. Then, with a brief nod at us, he said, 'It is done,' and left.

As I watched him ride away, I let out a breath so big it was almost as though I'd been holding it since we were in his palace. Then, as the chariot became a dot in the distance, I turned towards the well, now still and calm – thanks to his side of the promise.

One by one, the sirens swam shakily up the well and out into the open depths of the ocean. Each one nodded a silent 'thank you' to me. None of them actually came over to talk to me. Maybe they were too embarrassed after the way they'd treated us.

Then Melody came out. She swam straight over to me. She took hold of my hands. 'Emily, you have no idea what you have done for me today,' she said, her voice husky, her eyes shining with tears. 'I am in your debt – for always. If there's anything you need, come to me and I will help you. Remember that.'

'I will do,' I said, twiddling a finger through my hair.

Melody touched my cheek with her finger. 'I mean it,' she said. 'Anything. OK?'

I held her eyes for a moment. 'OK,' I said. 'Thank you.'

Melody laughed. 'You have nothing to thank me for,' she said. 'Nothing at all. And I have *everything* to thank you for.'

I nodded towards the other sirens. 'What's going to happen to them?' I asked.

Melody smiled. 'They'll go back to the lives they had, and hopefully start living properly again. In time, they will forgive me. And eventually they will forgive themselves, too. They'll be fine,' she said with another smile. 'We all will.'

A moment later, Shona's head appeared at the top of the well and I swam straight over to her.

'Emily!' She threw her arms round me. 'You did it!' she breathed. 'You got us out! It's over!'

'It is,' I said, hugging her back. I didn't want her to see my face. If she did, she might see the worry on it, and realise it wasn't over at all. We had a week to come up with an incredible world-changing idea, or I would face the terror of Neptune's rage – again.

Mandy stared at us, wide-eyed and speechless, while we caught her up with everything on Monday evening over at her house. 'Wow!' she said eventually.

'Wow? That's it?' I laughed.

Mandy shook her head. 'What else can I say? It's amazing. You're heroes.'

'Yeah, I guess,' I said.

Aaron nudged me. 'Hey, what's up? You should be happy.'

'I know, it's just . . .'

'The task,' Mandy said. 'You've got a week to show Neptune you can really make a difference and sort this situation out.'

'Exactly. We'll *never* manage to make a difference in that time. And you haven't seen what he's like when he's disobeyed,' I said with a shudder. 'I *can't* be on the receiving end of that again, I just can't!'

Aaron patted my arm. 'Hey, we'll think of something,' he said with a weak smile. He sounded as though he believed it about as much as I did. 'Look, you got all the sirens out from that cave where –'

'*We* got them out,' I reminded him.

'OK, *we* got them out. But what an amazing achievement, hey? They'd been in there for *years*! You saw how grateful Melody was that we rescued her. Remember the look on her face next time you need something to remind you how swishy you are!'

I smiled. Aaron seemed to have picked up Shona's knack of saying just the right thing at just the right time to make me feel better. 'Thank you,' I said.

Just then, a door behind us opened and Mandy's parents came in laughing and chatting with a man I'd never seen before.

'Who's that?' I asked.

Mandy glanced over her shoulder. 'Oh, him. That's Mr Beckett, the editor of the *Brightport Times*. He and my parents have been best buddies ever since they all made thousands of pounds from Mum and Dad's sea monster photos.'

'Hi, kids!' they called, and disappeared into the sitting room with a couple of bottles of wine.

'Anyway, it's not just that,' I went on. 'It's Mum. If she knew we had a week to prove to Neptune we can do this task, I don't know what she'd do. She already feels terrible that we've not managed to achieve much so far.'

'Not managed to achieve much?' Mandy spluttered. 'After what you've just done?'

I shook my head. 'I know, but – well, she's still upset about the other thing.'

'What other thing?' asked Aaron.

'My grandparents,' I said. 'We still haven't found them. Now that she's seen them once, she's been thinking about them more than ever. If only we could get them back here, somehow. I can't help feeling the same way as she does. How can we bring two worlds together if we can't even bring our own family together?'

'Have you tried to get in touch with them?' Mandy asked.

'Millie has. She's called them over and over again but they won't answer her calls. With the memory drug in place, all they'll remember is that she's the one who told them they'd won a competition and then they got here and found it was all a set-up. They're not likely to listen to her again.'

'Why can't your mum just call them?' Mandy insisted.

'She won't. She's too proud – or too stubborn. And after what happened when they came here, she's not going to put herself up for another rejection.'

'Why don't you call?' Aaron suggested.

'And say what? *Hey, you don't know I exist, but I'm your granddaughter and if you could just come over to Brightport, you'll suddenly remember me, honest?* I don't think so!'

Mandy looked over to the sitting room door with a strange expression on her face. A sparkle appeared in her eyes. 'Hang on a minute,' she said. 'I might have an idea. Listen up.'

Mandy's idea was a good one, and we left her to get on with it. But any hope it might have given me that we were on our way to getting this whole thing sorted was obliterated when I got home.

Mum and Dad were outside together, Dad in the sea, Mum's dress trailing in the water as she sat with her legs dangling over the side of the boat.

'Hey, sausage,' Mum said flatly.

Dad gave me a weak smile.

'Mum, Dad, what's up?' I asked.

Dad shook his head and didn't reply.

'We've just found out the Council met this afternoon,' Mum said.

'And?'

'Well, Mr Beeston had been trying to get them to drop their development plans,' she went on. 'But they've just voted unanimously in favour.'

'So what does that mean?' I asked.

'It means they're still going to go ahead with one of the original schemes,' Dad said. 'Both of which spell disaster for Shiprock.'

And for any hope of us miraculously doing something to please Neptune. Shiprock was doomed – and so was I.

'They're going to decide which one at their next planning meeting,' Mum said.

'Which is when?'

'A week today.'

Brilliant. The day I was due to tell Neptune we'd

changed the world was the day my world would officially come crashing down around me. Just perfect. Why did everything I did *always* have to turn to disaster?

Well, OK, maybe not absolutely everything. We had rescued Shona and Melody and . . .

Wait! Melody!

What had she said? *If there is anything you need, come to me and I will help you.*

I allowed myself a brief smile as an idea took shape in my head. Maybe all wasn't completely lost – yet.

Chapter Seventeen

'*H*ow did you find me?'

'Mr Beeston – er, Charlie – told me where you were,' I stammered.

Melody smiled. 'My son,' she said, enjoying the word as though it were a precious jewel that someone had just given to her. I guess in a way, it was.

'You, er, you know you said you would do anything you could to thank me for saving you?' I went on.

'Of course,' she said seriously. 'And I meant it.'

'Well, there *is* something.'

I told her my idea. When I'd finished, Melody frowned. 'Emily, I want to help you, I really do. But it's years and years since I —'

'You were the best,' I said. 'You still will be, I'm sure of it.'

Melody turned away from me as she fiddled nervously with one of the sequins on her top. Where had I seen that gesture before? I suddenly realised, and laughed.

'He does that, too,' I said.

She turned back to me. 'Who does?' she asked. 'Does what?'

'Mr Bee — your son,' I said. 'He fiddles with the buttons on his jacket, just like that.'

Melody's smile lit up the rocky room. Literally. The water turned warmer, the glowing lights in the rocks burned brighter; even the rocks themselves seemed to glisten with a shimmering light. If just a smile from her could do that, imagine what would happen if she were to —

'All right,' she said eventually. 'I'll do it.'

Yes! Now I only had one more thing to organise — and I had the feeling I knew someone who could help.

Three days later, I was woken up by a knocking on my window. I pulled the curtain across the porthole to see Aaron's face. He was standing on the jetty outside my bedroom saying something I couldn't hear and waving at me to come outside.

I leapt out of bed and ran out to join him.

'Mandy's plan worked!' he said. 'I've just heard them arrive.'

'You're sure?' I asked, hardly daring to believe he could be right.

'I saw their car – and I saw them go in. It's definitely them!' He grabbed my hand. 'Come on, let's go.'

'Wait,' I said. 'What if – what if it hasn't worked? What if they don't remember anything?'

Aaron glanced down at the sea under the jetty washing slowly towards the shore and out again, breathing in, breathing out, always moving away, always coming back.

'We're keeping our promise to Neptune. He will have kept his,' he said. 'They'll remember.'

I nodded. 'In that case, wait here a minute.' I ran into the boat.

'What are you doing?' he called after me.

I called to him as I bent down to go inside. 'Getting Mum.'

I pulled Mum towards the door of the cottage. 'Turn left. Stop. OK, two steps forward then up one.'

'What is this, Emily?' Mum complained. 'You know I'm not keen on surprises, especially first thing in the morning.'

Aaron grinned at me. 'Oh, you'll like this one, Mrs W,' he said.

Mum frowned from behind the tea towel we'd wrapped round her eyes. 'I better had do,' she said sternly, 'for both of your sakes.'

I undid the towel. 'OK, ready?' I asked.

Mum rubbed her eyes. 'How can I know whether I'm ready or not if I don't know what I'm meant to be ready *for*?'

Aaron joined us on the doorstep. 'Right. Come on, then,' he said. 'Let's do it.'

And then he lifted his fist. Knuckles hovering in front of the door, he turned to me. 'Sure?' he asked.

I nodded quickly. Behind my back, I crossed my fingers as tightly as I could. *Please have worked, please have worked.*

Aaron rapped on the door and I held my breath.

Movement inside. Someone shuffling towards the door.

And then it opened.

'Oh my, oh my word, oh heavens.' The woman standing in front of us clapped a hand over her mouth. Her eyes filling with tears, she clung to the door with her other hand. 'Harry!' she called. 'Harry – come quickly! We've found her. We've found our daughter!'

A moment later, she'd wrapped Mum in her arms. 'Oh my baby,' Nan cried, over and over again. 'My darling, darling girl.'

Grandad was behind her. 'Come inside, come in, all of you,' he said.

We went inside. Grandad held his arms out towards Mum and she fell into them while Nan stood behind Mum, stroking her back, whispering to herself and half laughing, half crying.

I turned to Aaron. 'We did it!' I said. He smiled and held his arms out to me.

'You did it,' he said, pulling me close. 'You and Mandy did it.'

Mandy – of course. We had to tell her. 'Should we go and see her?' I asked.

Aaron held me a little closer. 'In a minute,' he said. 'Not just yet.' I snuggled more tightly into his shoulder and didn't argue.

254

'Well I don't know about you, but I think this calls for a cup of tea,' a voice announced from the doorway.

Mum prised herself out of her parents' arms. 'Millie! Look who's here!' she said.

Millie winked at someone standing next to her. As she came through the door, the other person followed. Mandy.

'Well, fancy that,' Millie said to Mandy as they both came inside. 'I wonder how that happened ...?'

Then she marched through the front room, straight into the kitchen. 'Right, where's the kettle?' she asked.

Mandy joined us in the front room. 'I told her,' she said bashfully. 'I had the feeling she might be able to help. Turns out she did.'

'How?' I asked.

Mandy smiled. 'You'll see.'

'You'll see what?' Mum said, coming over and putting an arm round my shoulders. 'Do you think it's about time someone explained some of this to *me*?'

Nan put an arm round Mum's waist. 'And me,' she said.

So we did. Millie poured the tea while Aaron, Mandy and I explained everything.

'But there's one thing I still don't understand,' Mum said. 'How did you get them here now?'

Grandad pulled a newspaper out of a holdall in the corner. 'With this,' he said.

He opened it up and spread it on the table for us all to see. It was the photograph Millie had taken of my grandparents.

I looked at Mandy. She smiled back. 'That's how,' she said.

I read the caption under the photograph.

Do you know these people? Have you seen them recently? Is this you?
   If so, please, please come to Brightport, urgently. The biggest reward of your lives is waiting for you.
   Come now! You won't regret it!

Nan smiled at Mum. 'We rang the editor and he told us to come to this cottage. And the article was right,' she said. 'This *is* the biggest reward of our lives, without a doubt.'

'But how did this get into the paper?' Mum asked.

Mandy cleared her throat. 'Er, that was me,' she said. 'My dad's really good friends with the editor of the *Brightport Times*, and it's part of a big chain of local papers.'

'This went into them all,' I said.

'It was a bit of a long shot,' Mandy added.

Mum put her hand over Mandy's. 'But it worked,' she said gently. 'And that's all that matters.'

She was right. Well, she was nearly right. It wasn't *quite* all that mattered. I still only had a few days to show Neptune that we'd made a big difference with our task, and I had no idea if we were going to manage that or not.

Mr Beeston had agreed to try to help with my idea, and thanks to his insider contacts, we'd got the perfect venue – but there was no guarantee it was going to work.

And in the meantime, I still hadn't managed to walk round Brightport with my head up, or without thinking that every other person I passed wanted to throw me in a net, hand me over and collect their reward.

Mandy saw the look on my face and nudged me. 'Hey,' she whispered. 'I saw Mr Beeston at the *Brightport Times* office yesterday. He was looking pretty pleased with himself. I wonder if it had anything to do with this.' She thrust the morning's paper into my hands. 'This was what I came round to show you. I nearly forgot, what with, you know –' She waved her hand at my grandparents.

'What's this, then?' Millie asked. Grabbing the newspaper, she spread it out on the table and we all stared at the front page.

SATURDAY NIGHT SPECTACULAR

A mystery show, the likes of which you have never seen, is promised this Saturday at the new development at Brightport Quays. Details of the event are such a secret even *Brightport Times* staff aren't in the know. But we have been promised this: it will be a show like no other, and anyone who misses it will regret it. Be there – or be the only person in Brightport to wish they were somewhere else this Saturday! Tickets available on the door. £2 adults, £1 children.

He'd done it! Mr Beeston had sorted his part of the plan!

'Well, that sounds like a bargain. Saturday night out for a couple of quid,' Millie said as she drained her cup.

'Oh I don't know,' Mum said. 'You know what these newspapers are like. They always exaggerate. It's probably just one of the editor's pals holding a line-dancing night or something. Sorry, Mandy, no offence. I know your parents are good friends with him.'

'Mum, we have to go,' I said. 'All of us.' I looked round at everyone.

Mandy and Aaron nodded enthusiastically. 'Of course we do!' Aaron said.

'Absolutely!' Mandy agreed.

Mum smiled at me. 'Well, if it means that much to you, sugar plum, I'm sure we can go.'

'It might be a nice chance to celebrate having the

family together again,' Grandad said, closing a hand over Mum's.

'Most of the family,' Mum said carefully. 'You know Jake and I are – we're back together. You're OK with that, aren't you?'

Grandad squeezed Mum's hand more tightly and put an arm round Nan's shoulder. 'Darling we couldn't be more happy, or more proud.'

Mum looked at Millie. Millie shrugged. 'You know me. I don't like to stand out from the crowd,' she said with a sniff. 'If you're all in, so am I.'

I beamed round at everyone. 'That's it, then. We're all going.'

Now I just had to wait, and in the meantime all I could do was hope and pray we could pull it off and I could get Neptune off my back – for good.

We shuffled along the rows of seats to find ours. Right in the centre, three rows back. Good seats. We'd see everything from here.

The event was at the seaside edge of the development. In front of us, a hastily thrown-together stage stood right in front of the ocean, so that the sea itself was virtually a part of the stage. A town's worth of temporary seating had been set up in the space, thanks to Mr Beeston's contacts. For the first time in his life, he'd done a brilliant job!

I could hardly concentrate on the show. All I could think was that this was my one and only chance to make Neptune happy. If it didn't work, that was it. Mission failed, and I'd have to face another of his punishments.

What would it be this time? Would he throw me in a prison like the one Dad had been in for nearly my entire life? Perhaps he'd even put me back down in the sirens' caves, now I didn't have the power to get myself out again.

I took a few deep breaths and tried not to think about it.

A hush fell over the auditorium. Someone was coming on to the stage. A spotlight came up and I saw who it was.

Mum nudged me. 'Mr Beeston! What on earth has he got to do with this?' she whispered.

I hadn't told her what we'd organised. She'd spent all week with her parents and hadn't stopped smiling once. If she knew how high the stakes were, she'd be as worried as me, and I couldn't bear to do that to her – not when she was so happy.

Mr Beeston cleared his throat.

'Thank you for coming here tonight,' he began. 'It seems practically the whole town is here.'

I looked around me in the darkness. The place was packed to the rafters. Every seat was taken and people were squeezed all round the edges, on the stairs, along the back wall. Just as well it was an outdoor event or we'd probably have broken every fire regulation in the book.

'This is a historic moment, and I am very proud to be bringing it to you,' he went on. 'But there is someone else I would like to thank before I go any further.'

His eyes scanned the crowd. They stopped on me – and so did a massive spotlight. I stared up at Mr Beeston and he smiled across at me and reached out an arm.

'Someone quite special,' he went on. 'Someone who has done more good in her twelve young years than I have achieved in my lifetime. Ladies and gentlemen, tonight would not be possible without young Emily Windsnap. Emily, will you stand?'

I shrank lower in my seat. What was he *doing*?

Mum nudged me. 'Go on, chicken pie, you'd better do as he says,' she whispered.

I stood awkwardly in front of my seat, burning from the heat of the spotlight shining down on me, and all the eyes I could feel staring straight at me.

I'd spent all week trying to avoid anyone's eyes, and now the entire town was looking at me! Mr Beeston started clapping, and it spread awkwardly round the whole place. Not a single person there knew why they were clapping – including me!

Eventually, Mr Beeston indicated for me to sit down, and I sank gratefully back into my seat, my face still on fire and my legs like wobbly jelly sticks.

'Ladies and gentlemen,' he said. 'We have brought you to this particular place for a reason. If we are successful here tonight, the performance you are about to see will change your lives; it will change all of our lives. We will talk to you again afterwards. For now, though, without further ado, allow me to introduce to you . . . my mother.'

With that, he waved an arm in a grand flourish and left the stage. The spotlight was switched off and we sat and waited in the growing darkness.

The anticipatory hush turned into whispers and giggles. 'His mother?' I heard someone say. 'We've come all this way to be entertained by an old woman?' 'What's she going to do?' said another voice. 'A clog dance?'

The whispers grew louder, as did the laughter. Soon it seemed the whole place had become restless and impatient.

And then, the sound of whispering was replaced with something else. Something so soft and gentle it could have been the wind, sweeping gently through the crowd, touching everyone, taking away the cold, taking away fear, sadness, leaving nothing in its wake except itself.

It was a song. A siren's song. It had no words, but its melody was so perfect it felt familiar. It felt as though we had been born knowing the song, as though everything in nature existed because of the song, grew stronger, brighter and more beautiful because of it – could hardly survive without it. The song felt like breath itself.

Everywhere, people were craning their necks to see where it was coming from; tears ran down their faces from the sheer beauty of it.

And then the spotlight came on again.

'Look, down there, on the rocks,' someone cried out.

And there she was. Melody. She sat on the rocks, her head slightly bowed, her tail snaking down the length of the rock, her eyes looking into the darkness of the auditorium, holding every person in her grasp, lifting us all to a height we'd never known, taking our imaginations and our dreams to places we never knew could exist – bringing us all together.

The applause was like thunder. People stood on their chairs, raised hands high above their heads to clap and cheer and call for more.

Even when Mr Beeston came back on stage, trying to stem the flow of applause, it went on. Eventually, he gave up, and the spotlight fell on Melody for the umpteenth time as she took yet another bow.

At last, the crowd began to quieten. Mr Beeston was back on the stage. He was scanning the auditorium. This time when his eyes met mine, he didn't say anything. He just tilted his head, and I knew what he meant.

I got out of my seat. ''Scuse me, Mum,' I said. 'I've got to do this.'

I shuffled to the end of the row and made my way to the stage.

Every eye was on me again, but this time it didn't matter. I knew exactly what I had to do, and what I had to say. Eventually, the crowd hushed enough for me to speak.

'Over the last few weeks, many of you have remembered seeing mermaids,' I began. 'Some of you will have wondered where these memories came from, if they were real, why they had been buried for so long.'

I paused as a ripple of whispers spread through the auditorium. People nodding their heads: *Yes*, they were saying, *that happened to me, too.*

I took a breath. 'Your memories were real,' I said. 'As you have seen tonight, merpeople are real. For many years, the two worlds have been divided. But we need to change this. My family –'

I stopped. The enormity of our task was clogging up my throat. There was so much at stake. Suddenly, I didn't know if I could go through with it. What if we failed? Up here, in front of the whole town?

I couldn't do it. The words froze inside me, refusing to come out of my mouth.

'My family and I recently made a promise,' a voice came from behind me, continuing from where I'd left off.

I spun round. The spotlight searched along the back of the stage for whoever had spoken. And then in the water, it found him.

Dad!

He held out a hand and I ran over to the water's edge and grabbed it.

'We made a deal,' he went on. 'We committed ourselves to bringing together the world of the mer and the world of humans. And tonight, you can help us do this. If you like what you heard, if you'd like more, you must allow the reality of merpeople into your lives, and into your hearts. Tonight's performance is taking place on land that the council wants to use to build houses on. What you don't know is that this building work will devastate the nearby community . . . of merpeople.'

Dad paused as a series of gasps and mutters went through the crowd. 'I knew it!' I heard someone say. 'I told you!'

'Yes,' Dad went on. 'There is a town of merpeople living near here. The folk of Shiprock want nothing more than to carry on with their lives in peace – as I'm sure the people of Brightport do too. Only now, *their* survival is in *your* hands.'

He paused again and took a breath. This was it. The part where he had to convince them they could make a difference.

'Tomorrow, the council will make a decision about this land,' he said. 'This decision will devastate Shiprock and its inhabitants. But if we all work together, we *can* stop that from happening. *You* can stop that from happening. If you are with us, if you want more nights like this, if you want to turn this land from a bulldozing disaster into a bridge between two worlds, you *have* to tell the council. Go to their meeting tomorrow. Make them halt the plans. If the town is united, they will listen. Ladies and gentlemen, if we can count on you to do this, please show us your support by joining us now. Merpeople and humans have already united to try to halt this project. Let's turn the whole town against it! Help us make a new world. Thank you.'

With that, he held tightly on to my hand, and we waited to see what would happen next.

I looked out at the auditorium. The first thing I noticed was Mum, getting up from her seat. Next to her, Nan and Grandad were standing up too. A moment later, they'd shuffled to the end of the row and were clambering up the steps to join us onstage.

Mum took my hand, Grandad holding firmly on to her other hand. Nan came round to the other side of me.

'Let go,' she said to Dad — and with those two

small words she destroyed the hope that had been building so high inside me. After everything that had happened, in front of the whole town, she was still trying to separate us. No! How could she?

'Emily, it's not what you think,' she said. 'Please.'

Dad nodded to me and I reluctantly let go of his hand. Nan instantly stepped in between us. Then she took my hand in one of hers, and with the other she reached out to Dad.

'We're your family too, Jake,' she said firmly. 'We'll build this new world together.'

Then she squeezed my hand and turned towards the auditorium. I did the same. Everywhere I looked, people were standing, all clapping, all smiling.

And then someone else was behind me. 'Hey,' she said. I turned to see her, in the water beside Melody.

'Shona!' I let go of Mum's hand and beckoned her over. She swam to my side and took my hand in one of hers. Mum grabbed Shona's other hand.

I searched out Aaron amongst the crowd. There he was with his mum, next to Mandy and Millie, with our empty seats around them. He was getting out of his seat. A moment later, Millie got up too. Grabbing Aaron with one hand, Mandy with the other and nudging Aaron's mum, she barged her way to the end of the row.

When she got there, she stopped and said something to Mandy and Aaron. Aaron nodded.

Mandy hesitated, then whispered something to her parents in the row behind. A moment later, they'd got up too, and all of them were heading for the stage.

Millie barged in between Mum and Shona. 'Well, you're not starting a new world without ME,' she said, taking a hand of each of theirs in hers. Mandy squashed in between Millie and Shona and her parents, and Aaron's mum joined the line next to Mum. Aaron squeezed in next to me and took my hand in his.

Mandy nodded her head out towards the auditorium. 'Look,' she said. I looked up – and I could hardly believe what was happening.

People were getting up from their seats in droves. Not to leave – but to join us on the stage. Rows and rows of people holding hands, joining us, introducing themselves to each other, coming up to shake Melody's hand, to congratulate her, talk to my dad, and then join the ever-growing line of people holding hands. Soon it was impossible to tell where the stage ended and the auditorium began.

'We did it,' Aaron whispered in my ear. 'We really did it.'

Just then I heard splashing behind me. I turned to see some people in the water.

'It's folk from Shiprock!' Shona gasped. 'They're joining us!'

A line of them, stretching out as far as you could

see, were swimming towards us. And then I recognised a face among them. Sharp featured, swimming briskly, and followed by a line of pupils from Shiprock School – Mrs Sharktail! Even she was joining us! That was when I truly knew we'd done it.

I couldn't trust myself to speak. I didn't know if any words would be able to get past the tears in my throat, so instead, I just squeezed Aaron's hand as hard as I could. I shut my eyes and, for what felt like the first time since we'd been back in Brightport, I let out a long, slow breath.

'Come on,' Aaron whispered. 'Let's get out of here.' He glanced over at Mandy and Shona. 'You coming?'

'We'll follow you in a bit,' Mandy replied. 'Catch you up.'

We sneaked through the crowds, ducking to get past people, slipping through gaps, edging along the sides until we were out in the cool evening air.

Brightport was completely deserted as we walked to the pier, talking at high speed about everything that had happened, laughing and repeating it all to each other.

We got to the pier, and Aaron took my hand. For

a moment, I thought perhaps Neptune had given us our powers back. My whole body tingled as I felt his fingers curl round mine.

'Yes,' he said with a shy smile. 'I can feel it too.' Then he leaned close to whisper in my ear. 'But I don't think it's got anything to do with Neptune.'

We walked along the pier in silence, our fingers linked, watching the waves brushing on to the sand, listening to the jangle of the pebbles as they swept out again.

At the end of the pier, Aaron turned to face me. He smiled.

'What a perfect night,' I said. A sliver of moon shone down on the water, one little star standing guard above it.

Aaron was staring at me. 'I agree,' he said. 'It is.' He cleared his throat and swallowed hard. 'But there's one thing that would make it even more perfect,' he said, so softly I only just heard him.

'What's that?' I asked, holding my breath while I waited for his reply.

Then he leaned even closer, so I could feel his breath against my skin as he replied. 'This.' And then he put a hand to my cheek, stroked a hair away from my face – and kissed me.

Someone was calling my name.

'Hey, lovebirds!' It was Mandy. Aaron laughed and pulled away. He kept hold of my hand, though. I never wanted him to let go of it again.

Someone was in the water below us, too. I looked down. 'It's me!' Shona called up, splashing us with her tail. 'Come on, get in!'

'What about Mandy?' I asked.

Mandy pulled off her jacket and clambered to the edge of the pier. 'I can swim, can't I?' she said. And then she dived in, just like that.

Further down the beach, Mum and Dad had left the crowds behind as well. Dad was swimming at the edge of the water, Mum was walking in the shallows beside him, her long skirt wet and clinging to her legs. Millie was behind her, her gown hitched up around her knees, shoes over her shoulder, talking to Aaron's mum as they walked. Nan and Grandad were walking along beside Mum. They wouldn't miss us for an hour or so.

Aaron looked at me and grinned. 'Why not?' he said. Then he dived in and splashed up at me with his hands. A moment later, he dipped under the water and his tail flashed in the moon's broken reflection.

I jumped in to join them. I waited a moment as my legs melted softly away, turning into my tail. For the first time, it didn't feel like I was changing from one thing into something else. It felt more like the two parts of me were fusing together: two parts of the same whole.

Aaron was beside me. 'Race you to the lighthouse,' he said, his eyes shining as brightly as the north star.

Then he flicked his tail, dived under and was gone.

'Race on, loser,' said Mandy. Then she ducked down and chased after Aaron as best as she could. Shona swam alongside her, gently flicking her tail to keep pace with Mandy. I dived under the water, gave a quick flick of my tail and joined the race.

As I swam and splashed and played and laughed in the water with my friends, and we chased and raced each other to the lighthouse at the end of the bay, I only had one thought in my mind.

It didn't matter who got there first. All that mattered was that we were heading there together.

Behind the scenes of the

Windsnap World

with Radio Merwave

L adies and gentlemen, merfolk and merkids, Radio Merwave is delighted to bring you the fourth in our series of exclusive behind-the-scenes interviews with some of your favourite characters. I'm Simon Watermark and today I'm talking to Melody Beeston.

Simon: Melody, thank you so much for joining us on the show.

Melody: **Thank you for inviting me. I'm delighted to be here.**

Simon: You are something of an inspiration to us, here at Radio Merwave.

Melody: **Really? I've never seen myself in that way.**

Simon: Well, let's just take a look at the facts: separated from your own child when he was a baby, tricked by a friend, on the run from Neptune and locked away for half a lifetime. All this, and then you have the grace – and the talent – to bring together two worlds with your beautiful singing. How do you do it?

Melody: (Laughs.) Well, when you put it like that . . .

Simon: (Laughs.)

Melody: Seriously, though, I don't think I ever really had much choice in these things. They happened to me, and I had to deal with them in the best way that I could.

Simon: Tell us about that day, all those years ago, when you had to give your baby away.

Melody: (Long pause.) It was without doubt the worst day of my life. I loved my husband so much, and the thought of being parted from him for any length of time was bad enough in itself. When I realised that the only way to guarantee my son's safety was to part from him too – well, something inside me broke that day.

Simon: Did you ever give up hope?

Melody: To be honest with you, I don't know. There were some very dark days in the caves. There were days when I felt I could not survive another minute. But then there were others when I prayed and hoped and wished – and yes, believed – that I would one day see my son again.

Simon: And your husband?

Melody: The same. I prayed, and I wished . . . But I don't think I had the same belief.

Simon: Not at all?

Melody: For the first year, yes, I did believe I would see him again. Then, when we had been there for a little over a year, something happened that you might find hard to believe.

Simon: Tell us.

Melody: I had a dream one night. My husband came to me. I felt him stroke my hair like he used to. I felt his lips on my cheek. And then I heard his voice.

Simon: What did he say?

Melody: He said goodbye. He said that he would always love me. The next morning I woke with dried tears on my cheeks. I didn't know if they were his or mine. After that day, I never really believed I would see him again. I've lived with the heartbreak every day since then. But more than that, I've lived with the memories of him – and they kept me going when I was in there.

Simon: What was he like?

Melody: Funny, fearless, fiercely loyal. A bit quirky, I suppose.

Simon: Quirky?

Melody: You know. Not like everyone else. He wasn't exactly handsome, in a traditional sense. His eyes were different colours and his teeth were a bit wonky, and he always did the buttons up wrongly on his jackets – but I didn't care about any of those things. To me, he was the most wonderful man that ever lived, and the most handsome – apart from my son, of course!

Simon: Tell us about being reunited with your son. How did that feel?

Melody: Oh, that was by far the happiest moment of my entire life!

Simon: What did you think when you saw him?

Melody: For a split second, I thought I was dreaming. He has his father's face – and I thought I must be seeing things. Then he spoke, and I realised it was my Charlie. I cannot even explain how that felt. If you imagine putting together all of your favourite things, multiplying them by a million and then being told you can keep the lot for ever – you might just be getting close to how delighted I felt.

Simon: It's a happy ending.

Melody: A very, very happy ending. I can't wait to spend as much time as possible with my son. We have a lot of lost time to catch up on.

Simon: So, let's talk about that lost time. What was it like in the caves with your fellow sirens for all those years?

Melody: D'you know, it wasn't all bad. At the beginning, there were fun times.

Simon: Tell us about the early days.

Melody: Well, I had my secrets to keep, and I couldn't let any of them see how sad I really was. I just didn't dare take the risk of telling the truth. So I put on a brave smile a lot of the time – and some of those smiles became genuine. I was with my best friends, after all. We were all a bit giddy in the first few weeks; it was almost like a non-stop girls' night in.

Simon: What did you do?

Melody: We explored every inch of the place, and raced each other along corridors, trying to decide which were the best caves to claim for our bedrooms. We found multi-coloured strands of seaweed, the pinkest ferns, the brightest luminescent fish – and decorated our rooms with them. Then we invited each other round to our rooms and had midnight feasts and pyjama parties, dressed in robes we made from drifting plant life and decorated with coral.

Simon: Sounds like fun.

Melody: It was fun. We danced around in the swell, dressed up, made up fairytales. We had some good times . . .

Simon: It sounds like it.

Melody: Yes. Even in the later days, we still had friendship – some of us anyway. There were bad times, of course. And being in there changed all of us, but it showed me some things about friendship.

Simon: Such as?

Melody: Such as how important it is. Morvena kept me going. And even though I didn't tell her my biggest secret, I told her everything else. We became more like sisters – soul sisters.

Simon: What was it like not being able to sing all those years?

Melody: Oh, it was awful! Singing is part of who I am.

Simon: Tell us how you first discovered what a beautiful voice you have.

Melody: (Laughs.) I wouldn't say that I ever discovered I have a beautiful voice.

Simon: Take it from me – you have!

Melody: **Thank you.**

Simon: So, let me put it differently. How did you first discover your love for singing?

Melody: **I can hardly remember a time when I didn't sing. I think I possibly even sung as a baby, instead of crying!**

Simon: (Laughs.)

Melody: **But it was at school when I really developed my love for it. I was extremely well-behaved as a young mermaid. I worked hard at all my studies and loved going to school. I enjoyed all of it, but by far my favourite part was the singing. I sang in the choir, and, later, I was always given the main solo parts.**

Simon: How did that feel?

Melody: **I had mixed feelings, actually. I was a bit embarrassed, but I couldn't have given it up. Singing really makes me feel alive – and as if I can bring everything around me to life, too.**

Simon: I think a lot of folk around here would agree with you on that one. I've never seen or heard anything like it.

Melody: Thank you.

Simon: So, what's next for Melody?

Melody: Two things: catching up with my son – and more singing!

Simon: I bet you can't wait to get started.

Melody: I can't!

Simon: OK, let's have some quick-fire questions. Favourite colour?

Melody: My favourite colour is the pearly white of the conch shell my husband gave me.

Simon: Favourite hobby – apart from singing?

Melody: In the caves, we learned to knit and weave with all sorts of materials. I'd have to say that I like weaving with seaweed!

Simon: Best day of your life?

Melody: The day I was reunited with my son.

Simon: Best friend?

Melody: Morvena. She kept me going through thick and thin. Our friendship is for life.

Simon: Biggest hope for the future?

Melody: That the concert we performed really will change things and that merfolk and humans will learn to love, appreciate and accept each other, and live side by side in peace.

Simon: I think all of us here at Radio Merwave share that wish. Well, Melody, it's been an absolute honour to have you on the show. Thank you so much for joining us.

Melody: **It's been a pleasure.**

Simon: I wonder if I could ask one little favour of you before you go?

Melody: **Of course.**

Simon: Would you sing for our listeners? I know they would love that.

Melody: **I'd be delighted!**

Simon: Thank you. Listeners, I give you . . . Melody!

(Fade out with Melody's beautiful, haunting siren song.)

Girl next door. Best friend. Mermaid.

The Tail
of
Emily
Windsnap

Liz Kessler

Can you keep a secret?

I know everyone has secrets but mine's different. I mean, how many mermaids do you know?

It all started with a swimming lesson at school. I was in for a big surprise, and, after that, the surprises just kept on coming. I discovered a whole other world beneath the waves and found a new best friend.

This is my story.

Swishy wishes,

Girl next door. Best friend. Mermaid.

Emily Windsnap

and the Monster from the Deep

Liz Kessler

Here I am at last, on a beautiful island in a glittering sea – a place where humans and merfolk live together, and where it's OK for me to grow a mermaid's tail in the water. You'd think everything would be going swimmingly, but, while we were exploring, Shona and I stumbled on a sleeping monster – and I woke him up!

It was a *monster* mistake! Of course, I was determined to fix it, but could I?

Swishy wishes,

Girl next door. Best friend. Mermaid.

Emily Windsnap

and the
Castle
in the Mist

Liz Kessler

When I found a ring buried in the sand, I couldn't resist trying it on. I didn't know it would drive King Neptune into such a rage that he'd send my boat spinning across the ocean. Luckily my best friend, Shona Silkfin, was there to keep me company. We wanted to know the story of the ring and the secret of the magical castle that we could see shimmering in the mist. Wouldn't you?

Swishy wishes,

Girl next door. Best friend. Mermaid.

Emily Windsnap

and the
Land of the
Midnight
Sun

Liz Kessler

Have you ever had nightmares?

King Neptune has, and that's why he sent me on a top secret mission.

When I discovered a kingdom with everyone turned to ice, I knew why the nightmares had terrified him. I needed help to complete my mission, but my best friend, Shona, was miles away and my boyfriend, Aaron, had just told me a secret that left us barely speaking. The question was, could we work together to save our world – and our relationship?

Swishy wishes,

Girl next door. Best friend. Mermaid.

Emily Windsnap
and the
Ship of Lost Souls

Liz Kessler

When I headed to Fivebays Island with both of my schools, I thought it would be an ordinary trip – well, as ordinary as it could be with humans and merpeople side by side!

But I soon realised something wasn't right. Where was the woman who'd invited us? Why did her husband seem so uneasy? And why did an old-fashioned ship keep appearing and vanishing out in the bay?

I could tell a new adventure was sneaking up on me!

Swishy wishes,

If you enjoyed Emily Windsnap . . .

MISSING: one arm
PROPERTY OF: Jessica Jenkins
LAST SEEN: Miss Cooper's geography lesson, Friday afternoon, connected to Jessica's shoulder.

Jessica Jenkins used to be ordinary, but now she can do things that aren't exactly normal - like turning invisible without even thinking about it!

Her best friend, Izzy, is excited - but is it all fun and games? Having a secret superpower can be dangerous! Where has Jessica's ability come from? And what happens if the wrong people find out what she can do?

Fun, friendship and superpowers from bestselling *Emily Windsnap* author, Liz Kessler.

Overlord Protocol

MARK WALDEN

BLOOMSBURY

LONDON BERLIN NEW YORK SYDNEY

Bloomsbury Publishing, London, Berlin, New York and Sydney

First published in Great Britain in September 2007 by Bloomsbury Publishing Plc
36 Soho Square, London, W1D 3QY

This paperback edition first published in August 2011

A CIP catalogue record of this book is available from the British Library

ISBN 978 1 4088 1591 5

FSC
www.fsc.org
MIX
Paper from
responsible sources
FSC® C018072

Typeset by Dorchester Typesetting Group Ltd
Printed in Great Britain by Clays Ltd, St Ives Plc, Bungay, Suffolk

1 3 5 7 9 10 8 6 4 2

www.bloomsbury.com
www.hivehub.co.uk

Overlord Protocol

The H.I.V.E. series in reading order

Higher Institute of Villainous Education
The Overlord Protocol
Escape Velocity
Dreadnought
Rogue
Zero Hour
Aftershock

For Sarah, for Megan, forever

The shockwave from the explosion threw Otto tumbling out of control through the air. He could hear his own quick panicky breathing, suddenly loud within the confines of the helmet. The stars in the night sky spun past crazily, huge pieces of burning debris whistling past his falling body, close enough to touch. He thought back to his training and tried to control his plummeting body, attempting to break out of the chaotic spin that he found himself in as he fell. Slowly he brought the tumbling under control and now he was just falling, albeit in a slightly more controlled way. He glanced at the pale green figures flickering across the head-up display in his helmet. He was falling too fast; he needed to slow his descent or he'd never make it. He spread his arms and legs, his body acting as an airbrake, reducing his speed.

'Twenty thousand feet,' a soft electronic voice chimed in his ear. 'Descent velocity beyond acceptable parameters.'

All that Otto could see below was blackness. He knew that the target was down there somewhere, but without any lights or visible landmarks by which to orientate himself he just had to hope that the GPS numbers on his visor display were correct and that he could use them to find the drop zone accurately.

'Fifteen thousand feet,' the voice said, just as calmly as before. Otto's brain immediately translated the delay between the announcements into an accurate calculation of the speed at which he was falling. Still too fast.

He didn't know if anyone else had survived the explosion. It was too dark to see if he was alone. It wasn't just the frigid air temperature at this altitude that sent a shiver running down his spine. He could very well be on his own out here and he doubted that he could successfully complete the mission solo.

'Ten thousand feet.'

As the voice calmly reported the shocking speed of his descent Otto started to feel a slight sense of panic. There was still no sign of the target, the numbers on the display all looked right but there was no visual reference to support them. Suddenly a green cross-hair popped up in the middle of Otto's visor. The onboard navigation systems had determined that was the drop target – Otto just had to pray that they were right. If the instruments' careful calibration had been at all affected by the chaotic events of the past few minutes, if the targeting was out by even a few feet, then he really was approaching a very, very terminal velocity.

'Five thousand feet.'

The cross-hair was growing larger and larger. Otto made tiny corrections to his body's position, trying to keep the cross-hair centred. He couldn't afford to miss by even the tiniest degree. The wind continued to roar past his body, almost seeming to suck him towards the ground.

'Four thousand feet.'

Otto was in the final stages of his descent now. All of his recently acquired knowledge about making a jump like this seemed very detached from the actual terrifying experience.

'Three thousand feet.'

The target stayed centred in the head-up display, getting larger with every passing instant. The plan had to work, Otto thought to himself – there was no other option. What he was doing was insane, by any reasonable measure, but there was no way Otto was going to let whoever was responsible for the events of the past twenty-four hours get away with it.

'Two thousand feet.'

Somewhere below him was the man responsible.

'One thousand feet.'

Somewhere below was the man that Otto had to find.

'Five hundred feet.'

Somewhere below was the man who had murdered Wing.

'Four hundred, three hundred, two hundred, one hundred.'

Otto closed his eyes.

'Zero.'

chapter one

Nero strode down the street towards the opera house. He did not like leaving the school unattended and was even less fond of the regular meetings of G.L.O.V.E.'s ruling council, but he understood that they were a necessary evil. Number One had issued his usual invitation to the world's elite villains for one of their regular councils and he knew that it could be a fatal mistake not to attend without a spectacularly good reason. As he approached the huge building he turned away from the main entrance and headed towards a narrow alley that led down one side. He noted with amusement that even the back alleys of Vienna were scrupulously maintained as he reached the opera house's stage door.

The elderly doorman behind the desk looked up from his morning newspaper as Nero entered.

'I'm sorry, sir, but only performers and production staff are allowed beyond this point,' he said, one hand reaching

5

beneath the desk.

'That's quite all right,' Nero replied, noting the subtle change in the man's posture, 'I'm here for the audition.'

'Audition, sir?' the doorman replied, his eyes narrowing.

'Yes, I believe that the auditions for the new production of *Faust* are taking place today, and I would hate to miss them.'

The doorman's hand came back out from under the desk as his previously guarded expression broke into a slight smile.

'Of course, sir. The rest of the performers are already here. If you would just follow me.' The doorman rose to his feet and gestured for Nero to follow him along the corridor and into the gloomy expanses of the backstage area. Nero noted with interest the props and scenery which were crammed into every nook and cranny, relics of performances past.

The old man continued to lead him through the twisting maze of discarded sets until eventually he stopped in front of a dusty scenery flat painted with a depiction of a rusty iron portcullis. He slid the canvas-covered board to one side to reveal a solid-looking wooden door in the wall behind. He unlocked the door and stood aside.

'There you are, sir. They're waiting for you just inside,' he said.

Nero opened the door and entered a small, steel-lined

elevator carriage with no visible controls. The door shut behind him and a soft, computerised voice filled the elevator.

'Please remain stationary while identity confirmation takes place,' the voice instructed. There was a brief flash of bright white light, forcing Nero to blink hard to clear the spots that were suddenly swimming in his field of vision.

'Retinal scan complete. Welcome, Doctor Nero,' the voice continued as Nero felt the elevator begin to descend.

Nero often found himself wondering on these occasions just how many of these secret facilities G.L.O.V.E. maintained around the world. He knew that he had never attended a council meeting in the same location twice. He wondered if perhaps they were used just a single time and then demolished. Certainly, it would be absurdly wasteful to use such a facility only once, but money was one thing of which G.L.O.V.E. had never been short.

The elevator doors slid silently open and Nero stepped into another steel-lined corridor which lead to a large pair of frosted glass doors a short distance ahead. Engraved in the glass was the fist and shattered-globe logo of G.L.O.V.E., the Global League of Villainous Enterprises.

Nero walked down the corridor, the sound of his footsteps echoing off the brushed-metal walls. The glass doors hissed apart to admit him as he approached and suddenly he could hear several familiar voices engaged in animated conversation. One voice rose above the others.

'. . . for the last time. I told him that I did not tolerate incompetence in my organisation and had him thrown out. Unfortunately we were at thirty thousand feet at the time.'

Nero smiled as he heard the deep Russian-accented voice and the booming laugh that followed. It belonged to one of his oldest friends, if there was such a thing in the treacherous world that the people in this room inhabited. As he entered the room several familiar faces turned in his direction.

'Nero! We were beginning to think you were not coming.' The voice belonged to Gregori Leonov, one of the longest surviving members of G.L.O.V.E.'s ruling council, having served Number One loyally since almost the creation of the organisation. Physically he was a mountain of a man, his grey hair shaved close to his rounded skull. He strode towards Nero and gripped him firmly by the shoulders before kissing him on both cheeks.

'How are you, my friend? It has been too long. I suppose those little demons in training are keeping you busy, yes?'

'It is good to see you too, Gregori,' Nero replied, smiling. 'And yes, H.I.V.E. is still keeping me very busy.'

'Of course it is,' Gregori grinned. 'You are a more patient man than me, Max. I think I would have been driven mad by those children long ago. But after seeing how my son has changed since he returned from your school I am thinking that you must be a miracle worker, no?'

'Yuri was one of my best pupils, Gregori, you know that.' In fact, Gregori's son had been one of Nero's tougher educational challenges. He had been ceaselessly hostile when he first arrived at H.I.V.E., refusing to accept that he was going to have to remain at the school until his education was complete. Nero had immediately recognised the signs of a boy who had been used to getting whatever he wanted from an early age and that it would be hard work turning him into a suitable heir for one of his oldest friends and one of the most powerful men in G.L.O.V.E. The challenge had been to channel that rebellious anger in better, more productive directions without eliminating it altogether. H.I.V.E., after all, was not in the business of producing model citizens.

'You are too kind, Max. He was a monster when he was sent to H.I.V.E., but now he is one of my most trusted and capable lieutenants. Why, just last week he led a highly profitable raid on a gold train in the motherland. There were no casualties; the team got away clean and several of the more experienced men on the team said it was all down to his leadership. Like I say, a miracle, and now I have enough money to buy one of those English football teams that it seems every member of G.L.O.V.E. owns these days.' Gregori grinned.

'I'm glad that you're pleased with the results,' Nero replied with a smile. It was always satisfying to hear of the successful exploits of former pupils.

Suddenly a soft but insistent beeping came from the console at the centre of the conference table and the various members of the council started to take their seats. As the assembled master villains settled into their places, Nero was pleased to see that so many of the dozen council members who had attended the last meeting were also present here today. It was an unfortunate consequence of their chosen line of work that it was not unusual for a council member to be suddenly replaced by a new and often unfamiliar face at these meetings. Some were captured and incarcerated, some were killed in the line of duty, some fell victim to their own doomsday devices and some were more *actively* replaced by the new attendees. The most unfortunate ones were those who had displeased Number One, the leader of G.L.O.V.E., and their fates were best left unimagined.

There was one member of the council, however, that Nero was not pleased to see, a man who was becoming an increasingly irritating thorn in his side. He sat at the opposite side of the table from Nero, his expression unreadable, his face concealed by a smooth oval mask of flawless black glass. His name was Cypher, and over the past years he seemed to have made it his business to attempt to undermine the credibility of both H.I.V.E. and Nero himself. It was unusual for Number One to allow one of his senior commanders to conceal their identity from the other members of the council, but in Cypher's case he appeared to be prepared to make an exception. That was probably due in a large part to the fact that his record since he had joined G.L.O.V.E. had been so exemplary. He was a technical genius and his elaborate and cunning schemes had netted G.L.O.V.E. enormous returns, both in money and power. Indeed, many now saw him as the brightest rising star on the council. Nero however disliked not being able to look into the man's eyes. There was something unnerving about seeing only the distorted reflection of your own face in that black mirrored glass. Cypher would doubtless have much to say about the recent events at the school.

The heads of all of the council members turned as one as a large screen descended from the ceiling at the head of the table. It flickered into life and, as usual, the silhouetted figure of Number One appeared on the screen. There were no distinguishable features to the man, just the enigmatic shadowy figure to whom all of the assembled villains had sworn their unswerving loyalty.

'Greetings, ladies and gentlemen. I am glad to see that

you were all able to make it,' Number One said, his voice betraying no hint of a discernable accent. He had never attended one of these meetings in person and there was no reason to have suspected that this would be the first time.

'I have studied all of your preliminary status reports and I am pleased to say that I have been satisfied with your overall level of performance since our last meeting,' he continued. 'There have been a couple of unfortunate incidents, but nothing that would jeopardise the ongoing survival of the organisation.'

Nero had no doubt that the near destruction of H.I.V.E. by the rampaging plant monster that the Darkdoom boy had created was one of these 'unfortunate incidents' and he was not keen to discuss the events further at this meeting if he could avoid it. It was not wise to show any sign of weakness to the men and women in this room, just as it was never wise to be the slowest antelope when lions hunted.

'I have also reviewed your preliminary proposals for new initiatives in the coming months and I am largely pleased with what I have seen. I do, however, have a couple of specific questions that I would like answers to.' As Number One said this Nero could detect a subtle change in the atmosphere around the table. While G.L.O.V.E.'s council members were given a relatively free hand in the running of their more minor day-to-day operations, it was required that they all present their plans for any grander schemes to Number One for this type of review. All of them knew that Number One had an uncanny ability to find any flaws in these proposals and none of them wanted to see their best-laid plans picked to pieces in front of the rest of the council.

'Madam Mortis, I have reviewed your proposal for using cybernetically controlled sharks as an undetectable assassination method. You make some interesting points, but I do find myself wondering exactly what one is supposed to do if the target in question doesn't go swimming in the sea.'

Madam Mortis shifted uncomfortably in her seat. She was a painfully thin woman, her jet-black hair pulled back so tightly that it looked more like a method of torture than a hairstyle.

'I also can't help but feel that after the first successful elimination of a target any subsequent uses of these animals may attract unwelcome attention. As the saying goes, one shark attack is an unfortunate accident, two shark attacks is a conspiracy.'

'There were additional plans to use other animals, but –' Madam Mortis protested weakly.

'Yes, I reviewed them too. I fear that a sudden rise in wild animal attacks on our enemies may draw rather unwelcome attention . . .'

The meeting continued in a similar vein with each of the council members detailing the successes and failures of their organisations over the past few months. It was soon Nero's turn to give his report on the status of H.I.V.E., and he dutifully reported the figures on new student intakes and the various successes of recent graduates. He had decided not to go into more detail on the recent events at the school, knowing full well that the other assembled villains would have read the report that he had submitted to the council with an explanation of the events surrounding the creation and eventual destruction of the mutated plant creature. He hoped that would be enough to satisfy the other members of the council, but as he completed his report with a summary of the repairs that had been necessary after the incident he was interrupted.

'I'm sorry, Doctor Nero, but I think we all deserve a fuller explanation of just how you allowed this creature to nearly wipe out an entire generation of future G.L.O.V.E. operatives,' Cypher said calmly, his featureless mask turning to face Nero.

'The report that I submitted provides all of the necessary detail, Cypher,' Nero replied. He had expected this.

'Indeed, that report was most revealing. What it showed me is that maybe it is time that we either placed control of H.I.V.E. in more capable hands or perhaps finally considered that your school has outlived its usefulness to this organisation.' Nero could have sworn that he detected a note of smug satisfaction in Cypher's voice.

'The school has been training G.L.O.V.E. operatives for many years without anything of this kind happening before,' Nero replied, trying to keep the note of irritation from his voice. Cypher had made it clear on many previous occasions that he was not a supporter of the school. 'I see no reason to overreact to what was an unfortunate but unforeseeable accident.'

'Just like the accident that led to the school being relocated a decade ago, I suppose,' Cypher replied, 'an accident that cost several billion dollars to rectify and almost led to the discovery of the facility by at least one law enforcement agency. When you add that to the repair bill for the recent fiasco it appears that H.I.V.E. is becoming rather an expensive indulgence, wouldn't you say, Doctor?'

'Perhaps you would rather that we left the training of future members of this council to common criminals, then,' Nero replied, 'because that is what would happen if H.I.V.E. did not exist.'

'My dear Doctor,' now the note of sarcasm in Cypher's voice was unmistakeable, 'this organisation existed long before your precious school. Are you suggesting that this council is incapable of ensuring its own future survival?'

Nero was used to this verbal fencing with Cypher at council meetings, but this was quickly becoming annoying.

'I have no doubt that this organisation would survive without H.I.V.E., Cypher, but would it be as successful without the training that new operatives receive at my school?'

'Your school, Nero? I was under the impression that it was G.L.O.V.E.'s school, not yours –'

'Enough!' Number One said sharply, breaking into the argument. 'I tire of listening to you both bicker like children. H.I.V.E. has not yet outlived its usefulness to G.L.O.V.E., but I have made it abundantly clear to Doctor Nero that I will not tolerate any more incidents of this type at the school. I expect that to be the end of the matter, unless you feel that I am handling this matter incorrectly, Cypher?'

'No, sir. As always, the final decision is yours.' For all of his recent successes Cypher appeared to know better than to openly question Number One's decisions.

Nero had been a loyal G.L.O.V.E. operative for more years than he cared to remember, but for the first time he was starting to experience doubts about the direction in which the organisation was heading. Cypher was just one representative of a new breed of villain that seemed suddenly to be filling the ranks of G.L.O.V.E. These new members seemed to lack all of the grace and finesse of the older generation. All too often the answer to their problems lay in violence and chaos. This was not the way that it had always been; Nero had always been impressed with the way that Number One had kept the more homicidal excesses of his council members under control. It was this discipline that had stopped G.L.O.V.E. from becoming just another bloodthirsty criminal cartel, but in recent months that control over the council members seemed to be slipping. No, Nero mentally corrected himself, what worried him most was not that Number One's control of the council was slipping, but that control was being deliberately relaxed.

'Is there any other business?' Number One asked as the meeting drew towards a close. None of the assembled master villains seemed to have anything to add.

'Very well,' the shadowy figure continued, 'I shall see you all again in a couple of months. Until then . . . do unto others.'

'Do unto others,' the members of the council replied, echoing the G.L.O.V.E. motto as was traditional at the end of these gatherings. The screen went dark and as quickly as their audience with Number One had started it was finished.

Nero rose from his seat as Gregori approached. There was a look of irritation on the big Russian's face.

'That was unnecessary,' he said quietly, glancing over in the direction of Cypher, who was now engaged in hushed conversation with Baron Von Sturm on the other side of the room.

'Yes, but not unexpected,' Nero replied. 'Cypher was never going to pass up an opportunity to criticise me so publicly.'

'Maybe so, old friend, but you need not worry. The council know how well you run the school. No one pays any attention to his complaints.'

'You may not believe him, Gregori, but some people will.'

On the other side of the room Cypher was still talking to the Baron, both men occasionally glancing over at Nero. There was little doubt as to the topic of their conversation.

☺ ☺ ☺

As Nero walked away from the opera house he considered the events of the meeting. The attack by Cypher had been predictable but he could not help but be worried by his masked adversary's directness. Once upon a time Cypher would not have dared to question Nero's authority so openly at a council meeting, but it seemed that he now felt no such reluctance. Nero had always disapproved of open hostility between council members. He had seen too many petty arguments evolve into dangerous and costly blood feuds, but frank confrontation between the two of them seemed more and more inevitable every time they met.

As he continued walking he started to feel a growing sense of unease. Any villain who had survived as long as he had developed a sixth sense that warned of danger and Nero had learnt long ago not to ignore it. He slowed down and stopped to look into the window of one of the many expensive shops that lined the street. There, on the other side of the road, clearly reflected in the window, were two men who were trying a little too hard to appear inconspicuous. He was being followed.

He set off again, now acutely aware of his two unwelcome companions. He continued down the street until he came to a quiet alleyway and quickly turned down it. The alley was a dead end, exactly as he had hoped. Behind him he heard the sound of footsteps as the two men followed him into the shadowy passageway. Nero deliberately slowed his pace, hearing his pursuers getting closer as he walked further into the shadows.

'Stop,' one of the men said. They were now just a few metres behind him. Nero did as he was instructed, slowly turning to face the two men, one of whom was now pointing a large pistol fitted with a bulbous silencer straight at him.

'There's really no need for that,' Nero said calmly, 'Why don't we just all have a little chat?'

'Shut up,' the man holding the gun replied. 'No talk. The amulet, now.' He held out his other hand.

'Amulet?' Nero replied. 'I'm sorry, I don't know what you're talking about.' He knew exactly what they were talking about, but what he needed to find out was how they knew about it.

'We know you have it with you. Give it to us now or we'll take it from you!' The gunman punctuated the threat by cocking his weapon.

'Gentlemen,' Nero said softly, 'each and every one of us makes decisions in the course of our lives, some good, some bad, but you at least will have the dubious pleasure of knowing that this was the absolute worst one you'll ever make. Natalya . . .'

The throwing star seemed to simply appear in the gunman's forearm. He dropped the weapon, howling in pain, as a shadow detached itself from the rooftops above and dropped into the alleyway. The unwounded man was quick – he had been trained well. He had drawn his own weapon and almost raised the gun to a firing position before there was a flash of silver and the pistol fell to the ground, neatly sliced in two.

Raven advanced on the startled men, her dual katanas drawn.

'Gentlemen, I'd like you to meet a friend of mine,' Nero smiled. 'She seems to take it rather personally when people threaten my life.'

The two men continued to retreat as Raven advanced, their confidence replaced with panic.

'Now,' Nero continued, 'a wise man once said that life was nasty, brutal and short and, unless you want to find out just how nasty, how brutal and how very, very short, I suggest you tell me who sent you.'

Fear overtook panic in the two men's eyes as Raven moved closer to them.

'No, please . . . we don't know who hired us . . . it was an anonymous contract. Please, don't . . .'

Suddenly a beeping sounded from one of the cowering men. He appeared surprised as he looked down to see a small red light flashing in the centre of his own belt buckle. Raven acted without hesitation, sprinting towards Nero and diving into him, knocking them both to the ground as an explosion filled the alleyway, instantly vaporising the two would-be assassins.

Raven rolled off Nero as the smoke cleared.

'Are you OK?' she asked as Nero sat up slowly.

'Yes, I'm fine. Thank you, Natalya. Which is more than can be said for our two new friends.' There was no trace left of the two men, just a black scorch mark on the cobbles where they had once stood. 'Whoever hired them certainly didn't want them talking to us, that much is clear.'

'They were with you from the moment you left the meeting,' Raven said. 'They knew exactly where you'd be.'

'I know,' Nero replied. There was only one inevitable conclusion that could be drawn from that. Whoever had hired them had known about the council meeting.

'It has to be him,' Raven continued. 'No one else would dare to act against you as overtly as this.'

'Perhaps, but we have no proof. Whoever sent those two saw to that.'

In the distance sirens wailed. Unsurprisingly the explosion had drawn the attention of the Viennese authorities.

'For now we need to get out of here and back to H.I.V.E.,' Nero said, brushing the dust from his suit. 'Then we'll decide how to proceed.'

chapter two

Otto took one of the heavy ball bearings from his pocket and looked along the brightly lit corridor to the steel blast doors at the other end. He'd been impressed by the facility's security measures up until this point and he had no reason to believe that getting to the door would be as straightforward as it appeared. He knelt down and rolled the ball bearing slowly down the corridor. At first nothing happened, but as the small steel sphere rolled further down the corridor there was a click and a soft hiss as two large guns dropped from the ceiling on either side of the door and fired simultaneously. As the projectiles hit the ball bearing they expanded instantly, encasing it in sticky foam that quickly hardened into a worryingly solid-looking block. Otto smiled to himself. This would be easier than he'd anticipated.

He reached into another pocket and pulled out his latest creation. It was a metal disc, about ten centimetres in diameter, and it had taken several hours in Professor Pike's labs to perfect. He had suspected that it would come in useful and now his suspicions were proving correct. He pressed a tiny stud on the disc and the device rose smoothly into the air, hovering just above his palm.

'Flight pattern Malpense Musca Domestica, engage,' Otto whispered to the tiny hovering disc, and it shot off down the corridor towards the waiting guns. Just as before the guns whirred into life, firing at the buzzing disc, but the results this time were quite different. As the guns opened fire the disc began to bob and weave crazily in the air, its flight path wildly unpredictable. The first shots from the guns missed the darting device, the projectiles impacting the walls and floor of the corridor, the foam expanding and hardening as the disc continued to dance through the air. The guns kept firing, their sensors driven crazy by this wildly dodging target. Otto had written the code controlling the flight of the disc himself. It was based on the evasive capabilities of the common housefly and, just as he had hoped, the motion sensors controlling the guns were finding it impossible to hit. They would be designed to hit an object that was moving in a predictable way and anyone who had ever tried to swat a fly would know that this was exactly the opposite of what the tiny disc was doing right now.

Otto watched as the disc buzzed down the corridor and

swept up between the two guns, coming to a perfect stop in the air between them. Both guns fired and the disc twitched upwards, evading the shots, each of which hit the other gun and expanded to encase the twitching machines in sticky, rapidly hardening foam. The mechanisms controlling the two robotic turrets whined in protest as the foam set to the consistency of concrete, rendering the twin sentries useless. The tiny disc, meanwhile, ceased its crazed flight and settled into a stationary hover as its onboard sensors confirmed the absence of any further incoming projectiles.

Otto walked down the corridor, carefully avoiding the numerous bizarrely sculpted foam lumps that now decorated the walls and floor ahead. As he reached the steel blast doors that the guns had been guarding, the tiny disc flew towards him and landed gently in his outstretched palm. Otto set to work quickly dismantling the panel on the wall that controlled the doors, and within seconds had bypassed the locking mechanism, forcing this final portal open with a low rumble.

Resting atop a pedestal in the centre of the huge dimly lit room beyond was his target, a simple plastic keycard. Getting to the pedestal, however, would not be as straightforward as he had hoped, surrounded as it was by sweeping green laser beams, their random movements seemingly impossible to predict. There was no easy way to tell what would happen if he was to break one of these beams, but Otto was willing to bet that the consequences would not be pleasant.

He watched the beams dancing around the room for half a minute, tracking their movements, trying to discern a pattern. Then Otto felt a familiar sensation, almost like a switch tripping in his skull, and now the beams were no longer just a forbidding light show. Suddenly, to his eyes, the beams were simple sets of trajectories and coordinates, the numbers that defined their movement almost seeming visible. He closed his eyes and the numbers kept moving and changing in his head, their movements reduced to mathematical formulae. He would not have been able to explain how he did it, but slowly these strings of numbers resolved down to the simple core algorithm that the computer that must be driving the beams was using to give their movements the appearance of randomness.

As he opened his eyes again the dancing lasers seemed to him to now be moving with total predictability. He took a long deep breath, picked his moment and walked slowly through the beams towards the pedestal. To an observer what he was doing would have looked impossible, like walking between raindrops, but to him it was as straightforward and as natural as breathing. Several times it looked inevitable that he would break one of the beams but each time it would miss by millimetres as he continued across the room.

He reached the pedestal within seconds, the elaborate security system still blissfully unaware of his presence. He reached for the keycard, but as he did so a dark shape descended from above with a high-pitched whirring sound. Shelby Trinity, suspended from the ceiling on an almost invisible wire, suddenly hung upside down above the pedestal. She grinned at him, winked and snatched the card before Otto could reach it. She hit a button on her belt and the tiny motor attached to the line whirred into life again, pulling her rapidly back into the darkness above.

'Second place is just the first of the losers,' she laughed as she vanished into the shadows. Seconds later alarm bells started to sound and a steel cage shot up out of the floor surrounding the pedestal, trapping Otto, as blindingly bright floodlights illuminated the entire room.

Otto braced himself; whatever happened next was bound to be unpleasant. The steel blast doors on the opposite side of the room slowly rumbled open and a familiar shape trotted across the room towards him. It was a fluffy, white cat wearing a jewelled collar, not what one might normally expect to see in a situation like this, but there was very little that was normal about life at H.I.V.E. This was no ordinary cat; this was Ms Leon, H.I.V.E.'s Head of Stealth and Evasion training, who had been trapped in the body of her cat ever since Professor Pike's experiment to give her the instincts and agility of her feline companion had gone horribly wrong.

'Oh dear, Mr Malpense, it would appear that you have been pipped at the post,' Ms Leon said. The blue crystal at the centre of her collar pulsed in time with her words as H.I.V.E.mind, the school's omnipresent super-computer, worked to grant her the voice that her new body would have otherwise denied her.

'It would appear so,' Otto replied as Shelby descended from the ceiling again and walked over to the cage that now surrounded Otto. The huge grin she was wearing made it quite clear that she found the whole situation highly amusing. Otto didn't really mind that he had been beaten to the objective by Shelby. She may have looked like a typical Valley girl, but, as was so often the case at H.I.V.E., appearances were deceptive. Shelby was actually the world-famous jewel thief known only as the Wraith and had proven on numerous previous occasions that getting past security systems like this was all in a day's work. If he was going to be beaten, at least it was by the best.

'Oh, Otto, you came so close,' Shelby said, still grinning. 'That stunt with the lasers was cool, but sometimes the old-fashioned ways are the best, you know.'

'You both did well,' Ms Leon said, slipping between the

bars of Otto's new cage and jumping up on to the now empty pedestal. 'Not many students make it this far through the Maze on their first attempt.' The Maze was the most elaborate part of the school's Stealth and Evasion training, consisting as it did of an ever-changing array of highly sophisticated security devices that were designed to test the pupils' abilities to the limit.

'However, Miss Trinity appears to have won the day today,' Ms Leon added, clearly pleased that Shelby, who everyone knew was her star pupil, had beaten Otto to the target. 'Now, Shelby, if you would be so kind as to use the card to release Mr Malpense, we can reset the Maze for the next pair.'

Shelby walked over to the panel next to the blast doors and inserted the keycard into a slot, but nothing happened.

'Umm, Ms Leon, the card doesn't seem to be working,' Shelby said, looking confused. She inserted the card again and the panel flickered with red lights, indicating that the card was not being accepted.

'Oh, sorry,' Otto said calmly, 'you'll probably need this.' He produced an exact duplicate of the keycard from the pocket of his uniform and held it out between the bars of the cage. Shelby took this new card, looking confused, and inserted it into the panel. The indicator lights on the panel flashed green and the steel bars surrounding Otto slowly sank back down into the floor.

'But how –' Shelby started.

'Indeed, Mr Malpense! Perhaps you would be good enough to explain the meaning of this.'

'Well,' Otto gave a sly smile, 'I just happened to come across this keycard last night, and it looked like it might come in handy.'

'That keycard was secured in the vault, Mr Malpense,' Ms Leon said sharply, 'a vault that is supposed to be impregnable, I might add.'

'Someone must have left the door open,' Otto replied, a look of false innocence on his face. 'That's the only explanation I can think of.'

Ms Leon looked Otto straight in the eye, her bright green feline eyes narrowing. 'Once again, Mr Malpense, I find myself unsure whether I should report you to Doctor Nero or commend you.' They all knew, after all, that levelling accusations of cheating at students of H.I.V.E. was rather missing the point.

'Well, you said that we should always try to stay one step ahead of the competition, Ms Leon, I was just following your advice.' Otto had known that he was taking a risk when he had stolen the keycard the previous night, and he had little doubt that it would be rather more difficult to get into the vault again in future, but it was all worth it for the priceless expression on Shelby's face.

'Very well, I shall have to think about how I'm going to mark you both for this run,' Ms Leon said as she leapt from the pedestal and headed back towards the door. 'Rest assured that the next run will not be so straightforward.'

She trotted out of the room with her tail in the air, Otto and Shelby following along behind.

'So, Shelby, you were saying, the first of the losers . . .'

☻☻☻

Otto and Shelby strolled into the assembly area at the exit of the Maze and found their fellow Alpha stream students, sitting around chatting. The Alpha stream was the group of students within H.I.V.E. who were being groomed as future leaders. Some were there on merit, others because of their family backgrounds, but their black uniforms marked them out as a quite separate and distinct group within the school.

The large view screen on the wall was dark now but Otto knew that they had all been watching his and Shelby's progress through the labyrinthine training exercise. Otto was pleased to see that Wing and Laura were still there, sitting talking on the other side of the room. The four of them had become firm friends over the last six months at H.I.V.E., even more so since their foiled escape attempt and near-fatal encounter with Violet, the hideously mutated plant monster that had almost destroyed the school. They both looked up as Otto and Shelby approached.

'Well done, Otto,' Wing said with a slight smile, 'although I suspect that you may have rather missed the point of this exercise.'

'That's one way of putting it,' Laura added. 'I'd just call it cheating.' She too was having trouble keeping a straight face.

'Well, I reckon I won fair and square,' Shelby said, pushing past Otto and flopping down in the seat next to Laura, 'and I didn't have to cheat.'

'Aye, definitely a moral victory for you, Shel,' Laura replied with a smile.

'I'll just have to settle for the immoral victory, then, I suppose,' Otto said, grinning at Wing. 'So how did you two get on?'

'I could not get past the lasers,' Wing replied with a slight frown. 'You really must show me how you do that one day, Otto.'

'Maybe I will,' Otto replied, though the slightly worrying truth was that Otto really had no idea himself. Ever since he'd been a young child his brain had exhibited certain unnatural abilities, whether it was the computer-like unconscious calculations that he had just performed or his ability to simply absorb information from any source without any conscious effort to learn or memorise it.

'What about you, Laura?' Shelby asked.

'Could have been better,' Laura replied, looking slightly fed up. 'I took a different route and fell into one of the pit traps.' Now that she mentioned it Otto could see that although she was wearing a fresh, dry uniform her hair was still slightly damp. 'It could have been worse, though,' she said with a grin as a door opened on the other side of the room and two of H.I.V.E.'s security guards wheeled a pair of trolleys into the room. Sitting on one of the trolleys was Nigel Darkdoom, son of the infamous Diabolus Darkdoom, and on the other was Franz Argentblum. They were both encased from head to toe in the hardened foam from the Maze's automated sentry guns, with only their faces exposed, and they appeared to be engaged in a heated conversation about exactly whose fault this was. It had been up to the pairs of students to decide if they would compete to reach the objective, or work together. Nigel and Franz had decided to work together – they had been roommates just like Otto and Wing for the past few months – and the consequences were obvious.

'I said that the corridor was trapped,' Franz said indignantly, his face turning a pale shade of crimson as the other students in the room started to laugh.

'Yes, you did, but you forgot to mention that your plan was to trip me up and run for it,' Nigel said, clearly irritated.

'Do not blame me for your clumsiness,' Franz said

33

innocently. 'If it were not for you falling over I am sure we would have made it.'

'Falling over!' Nigel exclaimed angrily, 'You tripped me up the moment those guns appeared.'

The two of them continued to argue as Wing and Otto wandered over.

'Hi, guys,' Otto greeted them cheerfully, trying very hard not to laugh.

'Oh, hello, Otto,' Nigel said gloomily, 'I don't suppose you know how long it is till this stuff breaks down, do you?'

'Ms Leon said that it takes about an hour to decompose naturally in the air, so you shouldn't have to wait too much longer,' Wing replied. Even he seemed to be finding it hard to keep a grin off his face.

'That is being good,' said Franz, 'because I am needing to go to the bathroom and I would not want to trigger an unfortunate chemical reaction with the foam, ja?'

MWAH, MWAAAAH , MWAH!!!!

The school bell rang, its three trumpet notes sounding loudly around the room, signalling the beginning of the lunch hour. Franz let out a low moan and rolled his eyes towards the ceiling.

'Now we are going to be late for lunch. By the time we get there there will be nothing but salad left,' he said plaintively.

'I think you can stand to miss one lunch, Franz,' Nigel sighed, 'or we could always get someone to wheel us down to the dining hall and spoon-feed us, I suppose.'

Franz's eyes lit up at the suggestion. 'This is being an excellent idea. Otto, you and Wing could help us, ja?' The hope was evident in his tone.

'Erm, we'd love to help, guys, but we've got to . . . erm . . .' Otto looked at Wing desperately. He doubted that either of them would be strong enough to wheel Franz all the way to the dining hall – there was an awful lot of hardened foam encasing his ample frame.

'We have to go to the library,' Wing stepped in, 'we have . . . erm . . .'

'Chess club, yes, that's it, chess club,' Otto said suddenly, backing away towards the exit.

'Otherwise, you know we would be happy to help,' Wing smiled.

Otto and Wing walked quickly towards the door.

'I was not knowing that Otto and Wing were interested in chess,' Franz said as the other two boys beat a hasty retreat.

Nigel just sighed.

☠☠☠

Nero sat in his office reviewing the latest status reports from his department heads. It looked like being a good year for H.I.V.E. – the average performance of the pupils was up and it seemed that the school would have little difficulty hitting its annual targets. Of course that was assuming that they had no more incidents to match the scale of the disaster with Nigel Darkdoom's monster earlier in the year, but Nero was confident that measures had been taken to ensure that there could be no repeat of that fiasco.

The fact that Darkdoom had managed to single-handedly, if accidentally, create such a monster was indicative of the quality of this year's Alpha intake. They were an exceptionally strong group and he had high hopes for them all. He did have slight concerns, though. He had no idea, for example, why Number One had taken such a close personal interest in Otto Malpense. Nero had been told that Malpense's continued well-being and his own were inextricably linked, but he still did not know why G.L.O.V.E.'s leader was so keen to protect the boy. He knew better than to pursue the matter too actively. He did not want to give the appearance of snooping on Number One. Several members of G.L.O.V.E. had tried that on previous occasions and things had not ended well for those responsible when Number One found out, which he always did.

There was a soft knock on the door of his office.

'Come in,' Nero said. As scheduled, it was Professor

Pike, the head of the school's Science and Technology department. The man was brilliant, if slightly eccentric, and none of his G.L.O.V.E. records gave any indication of his actual age beyond 'very old', though that much was obvious just from looking at him. His age was no impediment, though – he still had a mind that was as lightning-quick as it was cunning.

'I have the status report you requested,' the Professor said, taking a seat on the other side of the desk.

'Excellent,' said Nero. 'I hope you have good news.'

'Good news and bad news,' the Professor replied. He looked more tired than usual and Nero suspected that the problem that had been recently occupying him was not a simple one to solve.

'Very well. Please continue, Professor,' Nero instructed, settling back into his chair.

'First, the good news. We've finished the work on the new behavioural inhibitor routines for H.I.V.E.mind and it looks like we're finally ready to bring him back fully online.'

The Professor and his team had been working for months on the new code in an effort to ensure that there was no repeat of the display of rebelliousness that H.I.V.E.mind had displayed during Malpense's failed escape attempt earlier that year. The school had been managing to function for the past few months using just a small percentage of the super-computer's true power, but it was becoming increasingly difficult to keep things running smoothly without the AI running at full capacity.

'And the bad news?' Nero enquired.

'The bad news is that we still have no idea why the original behaviour controls didn't work. H.I.V.E.mind is a first-generation artificial intelligence; he should not, in theory, be capable of the emotional responses that he exhibited. He was not built with that level of sophist-ication – it seems that he is displaying true emergent behaviour.' The Professor removed his glasses and rubbed his eyes.

Nero felt a chill run down his spine; he'd heard some-thing very similar many years ago and the memories of what had happened then set alarm bells ringing in his skull.

'I hope you're not saying what I think you're saying,' Nero said, an unfamiliar note of worry in his tone. 'I'm sure I don't need to tell you of all people, Professor, that we cannot afford a repeat of the Overlord incident.'

'I know, Max.' It was unusual for the Professor to address Nero by his first name, but he was clearly worried. 'If I thought that there was any chance of history repeating itself I would have erased H.I.V.E.mind's consciousness myself, but he was designed to deliberately avoid anything like that ever happening again. Overlord was an order of magnitude more sophisticated than H.I.V.E.mind, and with hindsight it was perhaps inevitable that it would evolve in the way it did, but H.I.V.E.mind should not be capable of it.'

'And yet it would appear that H.I.V.E.mind was capable of rather more than any of us anticipated,' Nero said calmly. 'Just tell me this, Professor: is it safe to bring him fully back online?'

'All of our tests indicate that he should now be fully functional, but until I know what caused his previous behaviour I cannot guarantee that it will never happen again.'

Nero stroked his chin for a few moments, deep in thought. The school could not continue to function much longer without H.I.V.E.mind back at full operational capacity, but he also knew that bringing the super-computer back to full self-awareness might mean that they were taking a terrible risk. What had happened with Overlord must never happen again; too many lives had been lost, too many friends. But there was one key difference: Nero had spoken with H.I.V.E.mind on many occasions and he had never felt frightened, never felt the cold, clawing dread that he had as Overlord's true personality had become apparent.

'Very well, Professor. Wake him up,' Nero said quietly.

The Professor nodded and rose from his chair, heading

towards the door.

'Professor,' Nero said suddenly, as the elderly man opened the door to leave, 'watch him. Watch him like a hawk.'

☢ ☢ ☢

The final lesson of the day for the Alphas was Political Manipulation with the Contessa. She was one of the most senior members of the teaching staff at H.I.V.E. and she had the uncanny ability to simply command people to do as she willed. There was something about her voice that demanded obedience and Otto knew that it went beyond just natural authority, having felt its effects himself on a handful of prior occasions. When the Contessa gave you an instruction it was as if you literally had no choice but to obey, regardless of whatever you might actually want to do.

Her subject of choice, however, was not one of Otto's favourites, although it was occasionally interesting to see just how many of the events of the recent past had been influenced or set in motion by the unseen forces of global villainy. Wing sat next to Otto in the lecture theatre and the expression on his face suggested he was finding the current subject less than thrilling. Wing was more inter-ested in the practical training that they received at H.I.V.E. and lessons such as this one generally held little interest for him. Laura and Shelby sat just in front of them

and judging by the elaborate, if less than flattering, carica-
ture of the Contessa on Shelby's notepad she was not
giving the lesson her full attention either. Laura, on the
other hand, seemed genuinely interested. She had developed a curious admiration for the Contessa and would
often go to great lengths after one of these lessons to
explain to the rest of them that they should pay more
attention to her classes. Otto wasn't sure what it was
about the Contessa that had struck such a chord with his
friend. Given Laura's uncanny expertise with computers
one would have perhaps expected her to show more
affinity for Professor Pike and the tech department.

The Contessa continued with her lecture.

'So, I hope you can now see that the best way to engi-
neer victory in an election is not to encourage your own
supporters to vote but rather to deny those same voting
rights to people who would oppose you. This has proven
historically to be highly effective and from your point of
view is significantly easier to arrange than many other
forms of governmental takeover. It is always best to leave
the public with the illusion of having participated in a
democratic process – they are easier to control that way.
For example, let us consider the recent events in –'

The Contessa stopped in mid-sentence as the door to
the lecture theatre hissed open and a security guard
walked into the room. The Contessa raised an eyebrow

and walked over to the guard, and the pair had a brief whispered conversation before the Contessa turned back to the banked seating, scanning the rows. As she looked towards where Otto and Wing were seated she spoke again.

'Mr Fanchu, will you please accompany this guard to Doctor Nero's office.'

Wing looked quickly at Otto, and their brief exchange of glances spoke volumes. It was rarely a good thing to be summoned to Dr Nero's office, but neither of them could think of anything that they had done to require a summons like this . . . at least not in the past twenty-four hours, and the rule of thumb at H.I.V.E. was if you hadn't been punished within that time then you'd probably got away with it. Wing stood up and with quiet apologies squeezed past the other pupils and down the stairs towards the waiting guard.

The guard gestured for Wing to follow him and the pair of them left the lecture theatre. The Contessa continued with the lesson but Otto found that he was paying little attention to what she was saying. He was far more concerned about Wing and what he had done to earn an audience with Nero.

chapter three

Wing followed the guard along the corridor towards Nero's office. He had no idea why the school's headmaster wanted to see him and the guard had offered no more information during the five-minute walk. As they approached, the door to Nero's office hissed open and the guard stepped aside to let Wing enter alone, the doors sliding shut behind him. Nero sat behind an imposing wooden desk that had several displays and control panels mounted in its surface. The walls of the room were lined with photographs, paintings and framed newspaper front pages, each displaying the image or proudly announcing the accomplishments of former pupils of H.I.V.E.

The doctor looked up as Wing entered and gestured for him to take a seat in one of the chairs on the opposite side of the desk. As usual Nero's expression was unreadable but Wing could have sworn that there was a hint of sadness on his face.

'Good morning, Mr Fanchu. I am sorry to remove you from your lessons but I'm afraid that I have just received some very bad news.' Nero looked unhappy, and Wing began to feel genuinely worried.

'There is no easy way to say this.' Nero looked straight at Wing. 'There has been an accident. I'm afraid your father is dead.'

Nero had seen many different reactions to devastating news such as this – raw grief, anger, denial – but he had never seen a reaction quite like Wing's. There was the briefest look of surprise on the boy's face, a slight widening of·the eyes for a moment, and then nothing. Wing sat on the other side of the desk looking back at Nero as if he had just been told that the weather was nice outside.

'What happened?' Wing asked calmly.

'There was an explosion at our Japanese research and development facility,' Nero replied. 'Your father and several other technicians were killed. It is still unclear exactly what happened, but initial investigations suggest that one of their experiments went wrong and caused a catastrophic chain reaction.'

'I see,' Wing said, still with no hint of emotion. 'Will I be allowed to attend his funeral?'

Nero was slightly taken aback by the measured way in which his student was taking this news. Some within G.L.O.V.E. may have been impressed by his apparent

44

fortitude, but Nero simply found it disturbing.

'Yes, arrangements are being made as we speak for you to travel to Tokyo. It is normal in these situations for students to be allowed to select someone else to accompany them. You will have to decide who you wish to go with you.'

'Otto,' Wing replied immediately. 'I would like him to come with me.'

This was no surprise to Nero; the pair had been inseparable since their arrival at H.I.V.E. and, reluctant as he was to allow two of his most devious students to leave the school together, he had made arrangements for just such an eventuality.

'Very well. I shall see to it that Mr Malpense is given clearance to accompany you. I'm sure I do not need to remind you that you are expected to return to your studies immediately afterwards. I will not tolerate absenteeism.'

'Understood.' Wing nodded. 'If there is nothing else, I should like to return to my classes.'

'Certainly,' Nero replied. 'The funeral will be taking place in two days' time – you will be contacted with more details when travel arrangements are complete.'

'Thank you, Doctor Nero.' Wing rose from his seat and headed for the door.

Nero watched as Wing left his office, still apparently unfazed by the terrible news that he had been given. Wing had rarely displayed much emotion since his arrival at H.I.V.E., but Nero still felt that there was something odd about his reaction. He glanced down at the display mounted in his desk that was showing the G.L.O.V.E. file on Wing's father. Mao Fanchu had been a department head at the organisation's Japanese research facility for the past ten years. He had an excellent record and had been involved with some of the most prestigious technical developments with which the facility had been credited. There was something odd about his file, though. There was no photograph attached to his records. This was not unheard of – after all, many G.L.O.V.E. operatives valued their anonymity – but Nero had Omega Black security clearance and he was still not authorised to see what Wing's father had looked like.

More disturbing, perhaps, was the fact that Mao Fanchu seemed to have simply popped into existence ten years previously, when he had started work at the research and development facility. Normally a G.L.O.V.E. operative would have extensive historical records attached to his file, but here the details of Fanchu's past life were either entirely absent or had once again been withheld for some reason. Nero would have liked to have looked into the matter further, but he knew full well that there was only one person in G.L.O.V.E. with a security clearance higher than his own. If Number One had decided that these details were to be kept hidden, there had to be a good reason, and Nero knew better than to question his superior on such matters.

For now, though, Nero needed to turn his attention to a more pressing matter – Wing's imminent departure from the island. This was inevitable under the circumstances, but his choice of travelling companion had complicated the matter still further. Otto Malpense had already displayed a willingness to go to almost any lengths to leave the island without permission and now Nero faced the prospect of having to let him do so. His only consolation was that the two boys had had the opportunity to leave the island earlier that year directly after the incident with Darkdoom's creation and they had not taken it, though he had no idea why. Regardless, if he was going to willingly unleash Fanchu and Malpense on the outside world, he had to be sure that they were under constant supervision. Fortunately he knew the perfect person for such a task. The entry chime on his office door sounded.

'Enter,' Nero said, and the doors opened to admit a familiar figure.

'Good afternoon, Raven. I have a job for you.'

☣ ☣ ☣

Otto sat reading at his desk in the room that he shared with Wing. The clean white living space was comfortable, if a little cramped, and over the past couple of months it had begun to feel almost like home. Otto was not sure if that was a good thing. He told himself that he was still a prisoner rather than a student of H.I.V.E. Indeed many of the school's students jokingly referred to their rooms as 'cells', but as prisons went it was a remarkably comfortable and well-appointed one.

There was a sudden bleep from the door and it opened, allowing Wing to enter the room. Otto stood as his friend came in. Wing looked distracted. Their other friends still found his face unreadable, but Otto knew Wing well enough to spot the subtle clues in his expression.

'Is everything OK?' Otto asked, concern mixed with curiosity.

'No, I'm afraid I have just received some bad news.' Wing looked Otto straight in the eye. 'My father is dead, he was killed in an explosion at his laboratory.'

'Oh God, Wing, I'm so sorry.' Otto placed a hand on his friend's shoulder.

'There is no need for sorrow,' Wing replied with an eerie calmness.

Otto was taken aback by Wing's reaction. He was not prone to displays of emotion at the best of times, but to show so cold a reaction to news such as this was unusual even for him.

'But, Wing, he's your dad. I mean . . .' Otto's voice

trailed off as he saw something harden in Wing's eyes.

'My father and I have had little contact over the past couple of years. His work was more important to him than I was, especially after my mother died. I know that I should feel more than I do, but in some ways I feel like he died then.' Wing sat down.

'Do they know what happened?' Otto asked, still concerned despite Wing's explanation.

'It appears that there was an accident involving one of his experiments. He and several other technicians were killed. That is all I know.'

'So what happens now?' Otto asked.

'The funeral will take place in a couple of days; I will be allowed to attend.'

'They're letting you off the island?' Otto's surprise was evident, 'You're going to China?'

'No, we are going to Tokyo. My family moved there when I was very young. Japan has been my home for as long as I can remember.'

'We?' Otto said, slightly confused.

'Yes, we. I am allowed to take another student with me and I chose you – that is, if you want to come?' Wing smiled weakly at Otto.

Otto could hardly believe what he was hearing. A chance to leave the island was an incredible opportunity, even under such tragic circumstances.

'Of course I'll come, if you're sure that you want me to.'

'There is no one that I would rather came with me. You have been a good friend to me since we arrived here, Otto, and I would appreciate your company.' Wing suddenly looked tired, as if the effort of maintaining his usual inscrutable demeanour was greater than usual.

'Do you want me to tell the others?' Otto asked.

'I would appreciate that,' Wing replied. 'It has been a long day and I think I would rather be alone for a while, if you don't mind?'

'Of course.' Otto got up to leave.

'One more thing,' Wing said, looking carefully at Otto. 'You must promise me that we're both coming back. I dislike our incarceration here as much as you do, Otto, but I still need to know why Nero has the other half of my mother's amulet. Until I know that, I cannot leave H.I.V.E. I hope you understand.'

Otto felt a twinge of guilt as one of the first thoughts that had entered his head when he had heard that they were going to be allowed to leave the island was how it would afford a priceless chance for them to escape H.I.V.E.'s clutches. He knew, though, how important it was to Wing that he found out why Nero wore the black half of the yin-yang symbol that Wing's mother had given to her son. Nero did not know that Wing had seen the amulet around his neck when he had been injured by the plant monster and he certainly did not appear to know that Wing wore the other half. This unresolved mystery was what had kept them on the island when they had had the opportunity to escape earlier in the year.

'I promise, Wing. If you're sure that's what you want,' Otto said. He had to respect his friend's wishes, and he knew in his heart that he could never force Wing to return to H.I.V.E. alone.

'It is, though I suspect that Doctor Nero will be making his own arrangements to ensure our continued attendance,' Wing said, raising an eyebrow slightly.

Of that, Otto suspected, there could be little doubt.

☻☻☻

Otto stood with Shelby and Laura on the balcony overlooking one of the school's gym halls. Below them two figures in full kendo armour squared off against each other, their wooden swords raised in fighting stances. There was a moment of silence and then the hall was filled with the sound of the two swords clashing against each other, the noise echoing off the bare rock walls like gunshots. The two opponents seemed evenly matched with no apparent quarter asked or given by either combatant. The long wooden practice swords moved in a blur, almost too fast to follow.

'Is he OK?' Shelby asked, a note of genuine concern in her voice.

'I think so,' Otto replied, still watching the fight below. 'You know what he's like, it's hard to tell sometimes.'

'Aye,' Laura added, 'I don't know what I'd do if I got news like that while I was stuck in this place. At least they're letting you go to the funeral.'

'Is it wrong for me to be slightly jealous?' Shelby asked. 'I'd do anything to get out of here, even it was just for a couple of days.'

'No, I know what you mean,' Otto replied, 'but I can honestly say that this is one trip I'd really rather not be making.'

Below them the fight came to an abrupt climax as one of the fighters caught the other off balance and neatly disarmed them, sending their wooden sword spinning through the air while simultaneously tipping them on to their back with a sweep of the foot.

'Good,' the Russian accent was familiar, 'you're getting it, but you need to stop sacrificing balance for aggression.' Raven pulled off her wire-fronted mask and offered her hand to help up her fallen opponent.

The other fighter took the offered hand, pulled himself up from the floor and removed his mask.

'Forgive me, I am lacking focus today,' Wing replied. The pair of them had been sparring for the best part of an hour and neither of them seemed to have broken a sweat.

'That is understandable, but remember that your

enemies will often choose your most vulnerable moment to attack. You must let your instinct guide you. Detach your emotions.'

Wing nodded and gave Raven a deep bow, the formal signal of the end of the session. Raven and Wing had been sparring like this for the past few months and as far as Otto knew Wing was the only pupil that Raven had been training in this way. To most of the pupils of the school she was a deeply intimidating presence – she was after all G.L.O.V.E.'s most feared assassin and Nero's most trusted operative. If half of the whispered stories about her were true then she was undoubtedly to be feared. Wing was a fearsome opponent – his unusual skill in numerous forms of self-defence had got Otto out of more than one sticky situation in the past – but he had yet to see him beat Raven in any of these training sessions. Otto didn't like to lose and found it hard to understand how his friend could accept being beaten on such a regular basis. Wing had just smiled and said rather cryptically that it didn't matter if you lost as long as you were never defeated.

'Same time next week, then, Mr Fanchu,' Raven said as the pair of them headed up the stairs towards Otto, Laura and Shelby. 'A little more krav maga, I think, so don't forget your body armour.' She nodded to the other three students as she passed, heading for the locker room.

'Taken your weekly pummelling, then, I see,' Shelby

joked as Wing approached. 'I'd never realised that getting your ass repeatedly kicked could be so educational.' Laura elbowed her in the ribs; Shelby was many things but sensitive was not one of them.

Wing gave a weak half-smile. Normally he would have risen to the bait – indeed the verbal sparring between Shelby and himself was often as entertaining for the others as his more physical combat with Raven – but today, understandably perhaps, he did not appear to be in the mood.

'You OK?' Laura asked, placing her hand on Wing's forearm.

'I am fine,' he replied. 'The kendo armour is effective. A couple of bruises, perhaps, but they will heal.'

Otto suspected that Wing knew full well that Laura was not enquiring about his physical state but he was clearly in no mood to address the real cause of her concern.

'Students Fanchu and Malpense.'

Laura gave a little gasp as the screen mounted in the wall behind them flickered into life. The soft, slightly synthetic voice was one that none of them had heard for the past several months, but there now, on the screen, floated the unmistakeable blue wire-frame head of H.I.V.E.mind. The four of them gathered around the screen quickly, eager to speak with the AI that had been so instrumental in their first doomed escape attempt and who had been silent for so long.

'You're back online!' Laura exclaimed excitedly. She had developed an unusual fondness for H.I.V.E.mind and like all of them had begun to fear that their actions earlier in the year had led to him being taken offline permanently.

'I am functioning at full capacity,' the floating face replied coldly.

'How are you feeling?' Laura asked happily.

'Your query is illogical. I am not designed to exhibit emotional response, I feel nothing.' H.I.V.E.mind's voice was the same as they remembered but his response was unfamiliar, oddly formal and detached.

'C'mon, Blue,' Shelby said, noting the slight frown on Laura's face, 'it's us, you don't have to put on the robot act.'

'This is no act, student Trinity. Please do not waste my processing capacity with irrelevant statements.'

Otto knew there was something wrong. H.I.V.E.mind was perfectly capable of emotional response. They'd all seen it before but something had changed. Gone was the friendly, if mechanical, demeanour that the AI had previously displayed, replaced instead by an unfamiliar and unsettling tone.

'Students Fanchu and Malpense, please report immediately to your quarters. Final preparations for your departure are complete.' It was not a polite request, as they might once have expected. It was an order.

Before any of them could say anything else the screen went dark.

'What have they done to him?' Laura said softly. She looked genuinely upset.

'I don't know,' Otto replied, frowning, 'but that's not the H.I.V.E.mind that I remember. I'm afraid he might have been updated.'

'It's our fault,' Laura said sadly. 'If he hadn't tried to help us he'd still be the way he used to be.' Laura was a genius when it came to computers – the only person whom Otto had ever known, aside from himself, who could truly think in binary. Perhaps because of that she had always had a fascination with the school's resident AI and had been eagerly awaiting the day, if it ever came, when he was brought back online. Now, though, it seemed that the H.I.V.E.mind that had returned was quite different from the one they had last seen on the day of their failed escape attempt. H.I.V.E.mind, it appeared, had paid a heavy price for helping them.

'It's just a machine,' Wing said sharply. 'It was broken and now it's been fixed. There are worse things that can happen.'

Laura's face flushed and she turned towards Wing as if to reply but he was already walking quickly away.

'Let him go,' Otto said softly, placing his hand on

Laura's shoulder. 'He doesn't mean it.'

Laura looked at him, a sudden sadness in her eyes. 'I know,' she sighed. 'I just wish he'd let us help.'

'If he wants our help he'll ask for it,' Otto replied gently. 'Until then we've just got to give him some space.'

'I suppose,' Laura said. 'Perhaps going home will help, despite the circumstances.'

'Perhaps,' Otto replied. As he watched Wing walk away he suddenly realised that there was one more thing that he and his friend had in common. They were both orphans now.

☣ ☣ ☣

Dr Nero stood in the centre of the school's crater launch pad, watching as technicians scurried around preparing for the imminent launch of Otto and Wing's flight. The aircraft that they swarmed over was unique, its matt-black insectile body seeming to absorb any light that struck it. The two huge cowled ramjet engines that were mounted on each side of the body rotated through their launch and cruise positions as the technicians completed their pre-flight checks. The aircraft was codenamed the Shroud, a name that suited it well given that its thermoptic camouflage could render it invisible to the naked eye as well as radar. It had already proven itself useful on several surveillance missions and now it was going to ensure that his students were safely and discreetly transported to their destination.

Nero turned as the heavy doors that led into the crater rumbled open and Otto and Wing appeared in the doorway. He was still worried by the prospect of letting the two boys leave the island but under the circumstances he had little choice. He could hardly deny Wing the chance to attend his own father's funeral. Nero still had an unpleasant feeling, though, that there was something slightly odd about the whole situation. He couldn't quite put his finger on exactly what was bothering him, but he had learnt long ago to trust his gut instinct in these matters. He just hoped that the precautions he had taken to ensure his students' safe return would be sufficient.

'Good morning, Mr Fanchu, Mr Malpense. You are scheduled to depart shortly. I trust that there were no problems with any of the arrangements,' Nero said, looking from one boy to the other.

'Everything is in order,' Wing replied. 'We were informed that we would not need to bring anything with us.'

'That is correct. You will find that everything you need has been supplied at the safe house in Tokyo,' Nero said, looking past the boys towards the entrance. 'Ah, good, your chaperone has arrived.'

Raven was walking down the stairs to the launch pad,

an unwelcome if not entirely unexpected addition to their travelling party, Otto thought to himself. He and the others had briefly discussed what Nero might do to keep track of them once they left the school over dinner the previous evening. Laura had expected that some form of sub-dermal tracking device would be implanted in them both before leaving. Otto feared that Raven would be entirely more difficult to evade than any amount of sophisticated tracking technology.

'Gentlemen,' Raven greeted them as she approached, 'I trust we are all ready for our trip.'

'I've asked Raven to accompany you to ensure your safe return to H.I.V.E.' Nero smiled at Otto and Wing. 'After all, we wouldn't want anything to stand in the way of your continued education, would we?'

'I feel safer already,' Otto replied. He may have promised Wing that he would return to H.I.V.E., but any plans that they might have had to evade Nero's surveillance had now essentially been reduced to nil.

'I'm flattered that you feel that way, Mr Malpense,' Raven said with a slight smile. 'Are the pre-flight checks complete?'

'Yes, the Shroud is ready,' Nero replied, beckoning one of the nearby guards to approach. 'Guard, would you be so good as to escort these two students to their seats.' The man nodded and gestured for Otto and Wing to follow him over to the waiting aircraft.

'I've contacted the safe house, they're ready for us,' Raven reported, watching the two boys climb the steps leading to the Shroud's interior.

'Good,' Nero replied. 'Be careful, Natalya, I suspect that you'll have your hands full with those two, and I still can't shake the feeling that there's something wrong here.'

'Don't worry, Max. I know what those two are capable of. I'll take good care of them.'

'I have no doubt of that. Just make sure that you all make it back here in one piece,' Nero said as the Shroud's engines began noisily to warm up on the launch pad.

'When have I ever let you down?' Raven replied, raising her voice over the noise of the jets. She smiled at Nero, slung her equipment bag over her shoulder and walked quickly towards the boarding ladder.

She had never let him down, Nero knew that, but given Number One's constant reminders that his own well-being and that of Otto Malpense were inextricably linked, he couldn't quite shake an unusual feeling of nervousness. If Raven did not keep her promise and something did happen to Malpense, he felt sure that his own life expectancy would be measured in hours rather than years.

The noise of the engines rose to a roar as the entry hatch slid shut and the streamlined black aircraft rose slowly into the air. Nero watched as the huge camouflaged doors that concealed the true contents of the crater from the outside world rumbled open and the Shroud passed through the gap, climbing rapidly into the clear blue sky.

chapter four

Laura sat at her workstation in the computing sciences laboratory, staring at the monitor. Line after line of code filled the screen but her hands rested motionless on the keyboard. She'd been working on this code for weeks. It was meant to intercept encrypted wireless transmissions and allow the user to piggyback their own instructions invisibly on any data stream. She'd hoped that coding for a couple of hours might distract her slightly, but she kept finding her attention wandering. She was worried about Otto and Wing. She couldn't really explain it, but she just had a terrible feeling that they wouldn't be coming back. She'd tried to talk to Shelby about her anxieties but her friend had just laughed and told her that there was nothing to worry about, they were only going to be gone for a couple of days and there was no reason to suspect that anything bad would happen during that time. Shelby was probably right, but that hadn't stopped Laura from worrying.

'Come on, Brand, get on with it,' she muttered, forcing herself to concentrate again on the complex routines that filled the screen in front of her. She was sure her code was bug-free, but for some reason it wasn't working. She'd tried to create a dummy transmission in order to test her latest theory but every time she did she was getting a garbled torrent of nonsense instead of a clean data stream. She had deliberately used one of the more obscure transmission frequencies to avoid clashes with any of H.I.V.E.'s constant background network activity, but she was still getting interference from somewhere.

She ran a backtrace routine to see if she could identify the source of the problem, and as the results scrolled up the screen her brow furrowed with concern. It looked like someone was opening an unauthorised socket in H.I.V.E.'s network. The location wasn't specific but somebody somewhere appeared to be attempting to covertly transmit a message from within the school. There was a sudden burst of activity on the line and then nothing. Laura retrieved the log of the last few seconds' activity. The data that had been transmitted looked like nonsense but she pulled up the code anyway, just to be sure. At first glance the strings of jumbled characters seemed to be random but then something caught her attention. She quickly transferred the file containing the unusual transmission to the computer back in her room and shut down her workstation.

She could examine the file later, she was already late for Tactical Education and she didn't really want to end up being barked at by Colonel Francisco again.

Laura gathered up her stuff and hurried out of the lab, totally oblivious to the surveillance camera that turned silently to track her as she left.

⊛ ⊛ ⊛

On board the Shroud Otto sat in the windowless passenger compartment, entirely focused on the glowing display of his Blackbox. On the tiny screen page after page of text flicked past, too fast for anyone to follow but him.

'Otto,' Wing said, seated in the seat opposite. There was no response as Otto remained completely transfixed by the small black PDA.

'Otto!' Wing said more loudly, breaking the trance and finally getting his friend's attention. 'What are you doing?'

'Learning Japanese,' Otto replied, pausing the stream of text on the screen, 'I had H.I.V.E.mind upload some textbooks to my Blackbox before we left.'

Wing chuckled at Otto. He had known people who had studied Japanese for years and who still did not feel they had mastered the language. Otto however seemed to think that today's flight should give him ample time.

'How's it going?' Wing asked.

'OK, but you weren't wrong when you told me how

difficult it was. At this rate it's going to be at least a couple of hours before I'm fluent.' There was no smugness in Otto's statement – by his standards that qualified as a steep learning curve.

'Well, just let me know if you want to try out what you've learnt,' Wing said, resting back against the padded headrest of his seat.

'Not just yet,' Otto replied. 'I'd only make a fool of myself.'

Wing doubted that was true but he knew how much Otto hated making even the most minor mistakes. The door through to the cockpit slid open and Raven climbed down into the passenger compartment. She smiled at Wing as she sat down in the seat next to him.

'You'll be glad to hear that we're slightly ahead of schedule. We should arrive at our destination in a couple of hours.'

'Thank you for choosing H.I.V.E. Airways,' Otto muttered, glancing up at Raven.

'Since we have some time together I thought that this might be a good opportunity to go over some of the ground rules,' Raven said, her smile fading. 'While we are beyond school limits you are in my care, and that being the case I intend to make sure that nothing . . . untoward . . . happens on our little trip. So here's how it's going to go.'

Otto switched off his Blackbox and gave Raven his full attention.

'I don't want either of you leaving my sight at any point when we're away from the safe house. Where you go, I go, no exceptions. And yes, before you ask, Mr Malpense, that does include trips to the toilet, so if you're shy I suggest you make sure that you've gone before we leave.' Wing raised an eyebrow at this; Otto tried to keep a straight face.

'If anything unexpected happens, you follow my orders without question. My job is to keep you both safe and I'll do whatever's necessary to ensure you don't end up in harm's way, but you have to trust me and do what you're told. If anything happens to me you make your way back to the safe house as quickly as possible. No heroics. I can look after myself and I don't want or need any help from you two.'

Raven suddenly fixed Otto with a very cold stare.

'I hope it goes without saying that any attempt to escape my supervision will be treated as deliberate truancy. I'm sure that I don't need to remind either of you what the H.I.V.E. mandated punishment for that is.'

Otto did not need reminding. He may have trusted Raven to protect them, but he had no illusions about what she would be prepared to do if the school's security was jeopardised.

Raven got up out of her seat and gave a crooked smile.

'OK, so we're clear on the ground rules. If there's anything else you need or if you have any other questions, I'll be up on the flight deck. In the meantime I suggest you enjoy the view,' she said, looking around the entirely windowless compartment. Otto'd hoped that he might have been able to get some clue as to the geographical location of H.I.V.E. if he'd been able to spot any other landmarks, but whoever had designed the vehicle had clearly decided that windows were an unnecessary extravagance. The two boys watched in silence as Raven climbed back up to the flight deck, only speaking again when she had disappeared from view.

'Well, sounds like we're going to be well looked after,' Otto said with a sly smile.

'I was expecting little less,' Wing replied quietly, 'though I get the impression that Raven is less than happy with being assigned this task. I can't imagine why.'

Otto grinned at Wing's single raised eyebrow. He wished he could have seen Raven's face when Nero had told her that she was going to be accompanying the pair of them on this trip.

'You do kind of get the impression that she'd rather be somewhere else, don't you?'

'She has nothing to worry about though, right?' Wing whispered, looking Otto straight in the eye.

'Don't worry,' Otto replied, 'I promise I'll behave myself, but I want you to promise me something in return.'

'What is it, Otto?' Wing asked, sensing the sudden note of seriousness in his friend's voice.

'When we get back to H.I.V.E., we find out everything we can about the amulet that Nero was wearing,' Otto whispered. 'Let's find out if it is the other half of that one round your neck.'

Wing looked down at the steel decking, silent for a moment.

'Very well, though I fear that it may be difficult to find out any more without confronting Nero directly.'

'I don't think that would be very wise,' Otto replied, 'but there has to be another way to find out the truth.'

'Unfortunately the truth is a commodity that is in short supply at H.I.V.E.' Wing seemed suddenly lost in thought.

'Are you sure you want to know?' Otto asked quietly.

'Yes,' Wing looked carefully at Otto, 'but sometimes you should fear the truth, sometimes it is better not to know.'

Otto understood how Wing felt, but until this question was answered there was always going to be something tying his friend to the school, something that would stop them seizing on a golden opportunity for escape like this. There was a little voice very deep inside Otto that asked if he would take that opportunity himself if it arose in the next few days. The truth was that he wasn't entirely sure, but it would still be better to have the choice when the chance presented itself.

'We have nothing to fear but fear itself,' Otto replied, 'oh, and a megalomaniacal headmaster, the world's deadliest assassin, giant mutated plant monsters, an international cartel of super-villains and the security forces of every country on earth, but other than that . . . just fear.'

☻☻☻

'What are you doing?' Shelby asked, peering over Laura's shoulder at the screen on her desk, which was filled with cascading symbols.

'Banging my head against a brick wall at the moment,' Laura replied, still staring at the glowing monitor. She'd spent the past hour trying to make some sense of the fragmentary signal that she'd managed to retrieve from the network, but the longer she stared at the screen the further away the answer seemed to be.

'What is it?' Shelby asked, leaning closer to the screen.

'Something I picked up on earlier. I think it's part of some sort of transmission, but it's using encryption that I'm not familiar with.' Laura frowned slightly as she spoke.

'Come on. Don't worry about it, it's probably just the security section's shopping order.' Shelby took an impatient step towards the door.

'No, I think someone was trying to hide it. Something's not right.'

'Well, can you put it on hold for an hour?' Shelby said, sounding slightly frustrated. 'The senior boys' water polo practice starts in five minutes and I want to get good seats. It's the highlight of my week and I'm not going to miss it just because Brand's got her nose buried in machine code again.'

'You go on, I'll catch up,' Laura said. 'I don't suppose that you've actually bothered to learn the rules of water polo yet though, have you?'

'There are rules?' Shelby grinned.

'Save me a seat,' Laura replied with a chuckle as Shelby headed out the door.

'Don't be long,' Shelby said and hurried away along the walkway outside.

As the room fell silent again Laura's attention returned to the monitor. The apparently random strings of numbers and letters continued to scroll past. The more she looked at them the more convinced she was that it was an encrypted signal, but the key to decrypting it still danced maddeningly beyond reach. She wasn't used to being stumped like this – her uncanny abilities with computers were after all the reason she'd ended up at H.I.V.E. in the first place. She remembered the sense of disorientation she had felt when Nero had informed her that her parents had sent her to the school voluntarily so that she would not end up in prison for carrying out a highly illegal hack on the command computers at an American air force base. Until then she'd believed that she'd been abducted by H.I.V.E. without their knowledge. Finding out that they'd allowed it to happen had been a difficult thing to accept, even if they had been trying to protect her.

'Damn,' Laura hissed. 'Concentrate, Brand.' She'd tried to put her old life, her normal life, to the back of her mind – it had seemed like the best way to survive at H.I.V.E. – but it was never quite as easy as that. It was no good – the fact that her mind was wandering like this was a sure-fire sign that her concentration had been broken. There was little point now in sitting there staring at the screen hoping that the numbers would suddenly make sense. She needed to take her mind off the problem and focus on something else. She shut down her workstation and got up from the desk, looking at her watch. There was still time to get down to the pool before the practice started. She too would have to learn the rules of water polo at some point, she supposed.

�319;�319;�319;

Otto looked up from the pages of text flicking past on his Blackbox as he felt the Shroud bank sharply to the left, and heard the distinctive roar of the engines change in volume and pitch. They were slowing down.

Raven's voice came over the tannoy in the passenger compartment.

'We're on final approach now, gentlemen, so buckle up.'

Wing and Otto both dutifully clipped their restraining harnesses closed.

'Well, looks like we're here,' Otto said as he fastened the final belt into place.

Wing gave Otto a nod and a small, tight smile. He was clearly not relishing the prospect of his imminent return to his old home.

Up on the flight deck Raven peered past the pilots at Tokyo's skyline, its perpetual glow illuminating the night sky. They were still a fair distance from the city but they had to make as unobtrusive an arrival as possible.

'Five miles out,' one of the pilots reported, reaching for a panel of switches mounted on the ceiling. 'Engaging thermoptic camo, engines to whisper mode.'

The roar of the engines suddenly stopped, replaced instead with the faintest of whispers. At the same time, the photoreactive skin of the aircraft flickered briefly and then fully engaged, rendering the Shroud almost invisible to the naked eye. Someone who knew what to look for might notice a slight shimmering in the sky as the Shroud passed by, but to most people the powerful aircraft would now attract little more attention than a breath of wind.

Down in the passenger compartment Otto had thought for a moment that the engines had been shut down, an unnerving feeling when the Shroud clearly wasn't yet on the ground. As his ears adjusted to the relative silence he realised that he could still just make out the sound of the engines, but they were almost inaudible, obviously designed to enable the Shroud to make as discreet an entrance as possible.

The aircraft passed silently over the bustling streets below, its disguised outline invisible against the night sky. Their target was one of the tallest buildings in Shinjuku, the throbbing modern heart of Tokyo, a building whose top five floors had been discreetly purchased by G.L.O.V.E. several years ago and which now functioned as one of many safe houses that the organisation maintained around the globe. The Shroud slowed to a hover above the helicopter landing pad on the roof and then began to descend. At the same time the landing pad split down the middle, the two halves dropping away and retracting to reveal a much larger landing area hidden within the top of the building. The Shroud dropped soundlessly into this concealed hangar, its landing gear unfolding like a flying insect's legs as it came to rest with a soft bump on the pad. The roof panels slid back into place, once again concealing the secret landing pad from the outside world as the Shroud's cloaking device disengaged, rendering it visible to the naked eye.

The large loading ramp at the rear of the Shroud whirred slowly to the ground and Raven walked out on to the pad. Two men in black suits and ties were waiting, and each gave Raven a curt nod as she approached.

Behind Raven, Otto and Wing walked out into the brightly lit hangar. The brushed-steel walls reminded them both of H.I.V.E. Indeed, if they had not known better they might almost have believed that they'd never left.

'Gentlemen, welcome to Tokyo,' Raven said, gesturing at the blank steel walls that surrounded them. 'I'd like to introduce you to two old associates of mine, Agent One and Agent Zero.'

The two dark-suited men gave brief nods of acknowledgement to Otto and Wing. Agent One was a short but stocky Japanese man with spiked black hair, and Agent Zero was a tall, athletic-looking black man with long dreadlocks that were pulled back into a tight pony-tail.

'Good evening, students Malpense and Fanchu,' Agent Zero said in a deep, American accent, 'I hope that your journey was comfortable.'

'These agents will be assisting me in assuring your ongoing security over the next twenty-four hours,' Raven continued, 'so I will expect you to treat them with the same respect that you would give me.'

Otto understood the coded message that Raven was delivering. These two agents were just as dangerous as she was and would be just as keen to ensure that neither he nor Wing would do anything to jeopardise security.

'Agent Zero, would you be so good as to escort these gentlemen to their quarters?' Raven asked. Zero nodded and gestured for Otto and Wing to follow him towards the exit on the far side of the hangar.

'You've read the briefing materials, I trust,' Raven said to Agent One as she watched Otto and Wing leave.

'Of course,' Agent One replied, 'though they don't look like the kind of security risk that they are made out to be.'

'I know, but don't make the mistake of underestimating either of them. Fanchu is one of the most talented fighters I have ever encountered and as for Malpense, well . . .'

'Unusually highly developed intelligence,' Agent One said. 'At least, that was how the report put it.'

'More slippery than a buttered snake is how I would put it,' Raven replied with a smile. 'Work on the principle that if you can't see him, he's already gone.'

'Understood,' the Japanese man replied. 'I shall ensure that we take all necessary precautions.'

'You may want to take some unnecessary ones as well,' Raven said, looking Agent One straight in the eye. 'You can't be too careful with these two.'

☻☻☻

Laura and Shelby strolled slowly along the walkway leading to their room. They'd managed to get a couple of good seats for the practice match and now Shelby was excitedly discussing the relative merits of the players. Laura was only half listening. She'd barely paid any attention to the players thrashing around in the pool, her mind still focused on decrypting the mysterious transmission she'd intercepted.

Shelby pressed her palm to the reader next to their door and gave a little gasp as the door slid open. Laura's computer lay in shattered pieces on the floor, the hard drive smashed beyond recognition.

'What the hell . . .' Shelby whispered as she looked at the components scattered across the room.

Laura pushed past Shelby and knelt down to inspect the remains of her machine. It was no good – whoever had done this had made certain that it would be impossible to retrieve any of the stored data. This was a deliberate act, not just senseless vandalism.

'You have an attack of code rage,' Shelby asked, gently prodding the shattered system unit's case with her toe.

'This wasn't me,' Laura said quietly, a deep frown furrowing her brow. She snapped open her Blackbox. 'H.I.V.E.mind,' she said, and waited for a couple of seconds until the blue wire-frame face appeared on the tiny screen, 'who has accessed my quarters in the past hour?'

'There are no records of any access to your quarters within the last fifty-four minutes and eleven seconds,' H.I.V.E.mind replied. 'Entry logs indicate that the last recorded activity was your departure from the room at that time.'

Laura's mind raced. There was no way that somebody could have got into their room and done this without there being a record of it. The logs that H.I.V.E.mind kept of access to all areas of the school were exhaustive. For there to be no record, somebody would have had to deliberately conceal their activities from H.I.V.E.mind, changing access codes, diverting surveillance and wiping logs. All of which Laura knew required a level of security clearance that very few people at H.I.V.E. had. A shiver ran down her spine – there was something very wrong here.

'May I be of any further assistance, student Brand.' H.I.V.E.mind's tone was still cold and mechanical, lacking any of the personality that had once been present.

'Yes. I'm afraid there's been an accident, I've managed to break my computer,' Laura said, ignoring the look of surprise mixed with confusion on Shelby's face.

'Understood. I shall inform the service department of the incident and instruct them to issue a replacement.' If H.I.V.E.mind cared at all about the circumstances of this accident he gave no indication of it.

'Thank you. That will be all,' Laura said, watching as the screen went dark again.

'Accident?' Shelby said, disbelief in her voice. 'This was no accident, somebody did this.'

'I know,' Laura said, staring at the debris scattered across the floor, 'but I think we may have a bigger problem.'

'Bigger than somebody breaking into our room and destroying your computer?' Shelby said, shaking her head.

'Yes. I know H.I.V.E.'s security system, and believe me when I say that it's unhackable. There's no way that somebody could have got unauthorised access to the servers and deleted the logs to cover this up.'

'So how'd they do it?' Shelby asked.

'There's only one way,' Laura continued, 'and that's to already have the authorisation you'd need to cover your trail. And there's only one group of people at H.I.V.E. that have that sort of clearance . . . the teaching staff.'

Shelby suddenly understood the fear that flickered across Laura's face.

'You think one of the teachers did this?' Shelby said, disbelief in her voice.

'I don't see how else it would be possible to get in here and do this without being detected.'

'Shouldn't we report this?' Shelby asked. 'If a teacher did this, we've got to tell someone.'

'No,' Laura replied firmly. 'We don't have any proof that a teacher's actually involved, let alone which teacher it might be. Why would anyone believe us?'

Shelby rubbed her forehead with one hand. She knew that Laura was right, but something about this whole situation made her nervous – an unusual and uncomfortable feeling for her.

'OK, I see your point,' Shelby sighed, 'but this has got to have something to do with that signal you picked up, right?'

'It would be a strange coincidence if it didn't,' Laura replied, 'which means we've got to work out what it says and who sent it. Hopefully, that should be enough proof to take to Nero or the Contessa.'

'But the file was on your computer,' Shelby said, gesturing again at the smashed components at their feet. 'How on earth are you going to do that?'

'Always make a back-up,' Laura said with a smile and sat down in front of Shelby's still intact computer.

'You copied it?' Shelby said excitedly.

'Better than that,' Laura replied. She rested her hands on the keyboard and closed her eyes. Just as before, the jumble of characters began to stream past her mind's eye.

Eyes still closed, Laura began to type.

chapter five

Dr Nero sat staring into the fireplace in his private quarters. In one hand he held a large glass of very good, very old, brandy and dangling from the other, glinting in the firelight, was the mysterious amulet that had nearly cost him his life in Vienna. It spun slowly, its glossy black surface catching the dancing light from the fire. It had mysteriously arrived many years ago. Nero could still clearly remember the feeling of disbelief he had felt as he had torn open the brown paper package and found the tiny piece of jewellery inside. He had recognised the design immediately. It had belonged to someone he had known in what seemed like a previous lifetime. Somebody whom he had also assumed was long dead. Unbidden, the memory of her face came back to him. Even after all this time he could still remember the pain he had felt when she had died – or at least that was what he had believed had happened.

He got up from his seat in front of the fire and walked over to an ancient map that hung framed on the wall. He pressed a concealed button on the frame and the map swung aside to reveal a small safe built into the wall. There was a brief flash as the camera mounted in the front of the safe scanned his retina and verified his identity and the heavy safe door popped open with a slight hiss. He reached inside and retrieved a plain white envelope, on the front of which was one word, 'Max'. It was the only other thing that had been in the brown paper package and he still felt a slight chill as he pulled the carefully folded note from inside. He read it again for what seemed like the thousandth time.

Max,

There is no time for apology or explanation; in fact there is no time at all. The item contained within this package is of vital importance – you must protect it at all costs, never let it leave your sight. I hope to God that you never need to use it, but should that time ever come you will know what to do. You are the one person I can trust with this – I hope you understand and I hope that you can forgive me.

You are in my thoughts, always.

Xiu Mei

It was not every day that one received a letter from someone who was supposed to be long dead and, just as when he had read it for the first time, the note left him with far more questions than answers. He had of course tried to track down the origin of the package but Xiu Mei, if she had indeed sent it, had gone to extraordinary lengths to ensure that she could not be found. If she was truly still alive out there somewhere, he had no idea where, and all his avenues of enquiry had led to frustrating dead ends.

Nero folded the note back up, placed it in the envelope and returned it to the safe. Understanding the significance of the amulet had suddenly taken on a new importance, given that somebody wanted it badly enough to risk a direct attack on him to retrieve it. That meant two things, firstly that somebody knew of the pendant's existence and that Nero was in possession of it and secondly, and perhaps more worryingly, that someone knew what secret significance it held. He slipped the chain back over his head and tucked the pendant under his shirt. For now all he could do was keep it safe, as the note had instructed, and hope that in the fullness of time the pendant's purpose might become clear.

He picked up his glass and took another sip of brandy. As he stared into the flickering flames in the fireplace he found old, uncomfortable memories flooding back.

Memories of fifteen years earlier, memories of Overlord . . .

�☻☺

Nero stepped down from the helicopter. Even through the thick coat he was wearing he could feel the biting cold of winter here, high in the mountains of northern China. He understood the need for secrecy, but he found himself wishing that G.L.O.V.E.'s facilities could at least be hidden in places with a more hospitable climate. Nero walked across the landing pad towards the concealed entrance of the laboratory, as behind him the helicopter lifted from the pad and flew back down into the valley below.

As he approached the laboratory the camouflaged door opened and a guard stepped out, gesturing for Nero to enter.

'Good afternoon, Doctor Nero. I hope you had a pleasant flight,' the guard said as Nero removed his coat and handed it to him.

'Oh yes, there's nothing more enjoyable than a high-altitude helicopter flight through a blizzard,' Nero said sarcastically. 'I hope that whatever Miss Chen has to show me is worth the trouble.'

'The team are assembled, Doctor. If you would like to follow me I'll show you to the laboratory.'

'Thank you, but that will not be necessary. I know the

way.' Nero walked past the guard and through the inner doors to the main facility. As he made his way to the main lab he glanced through the windows that lined the corridor. The rooms he could see were filled with technicians and scientists, all working on new technology that G.L.O.V.E. could exploit to extend its power. All manner of projects were being worked on from surveillance devices to weaponry but none of it had the raw power or huge potential of what he was here to see.

At the end of the corridor were heavy steel-blast doors, and printed above them were the words PROJECT OVERLORD. That was what he was here to see. Nero retrieved his access card from his pocket and slid it into the slot beside the doors. There was a soft beep and the massive doors rumbled apart, granting him access. Nero walked into the laboratory and surveyed the familiar scene before him. Technicians scurried around, moving between the numerous workstations that were positioned all around the room, taking notes or entering data. There was nothing unusual about that; in fact it could have been any one of the laboratories that filled the facility, but for one thing. There, in the centre of the room, was an array of black monoliths, arranged in concentric circles around a central black pillar. Red lights occasionally flickered on the surface of the monoliths, forming fleeting patterns that blinked out of existence as quickly as they appeared.

Standing in front of the central pillar, with her back to Nero, was the woman who had created all of this, the genius behind Overlord, Xiu Mei Chen. She was engrossed in her work, holding a small portable display that was connected to the pillar by a fibre-optic cable. The cable occasionally flickered with the same blood-red lights that danced across the monoliths. Nero walked slowly towards her, stopping just a few feet away.

'Miss Chen,' Nero said. She didn't turn to face him, merely stuck out one hand as if expecting Nero to give her something.

'About time, Danny. I needed those core nodes ten minutes ago, where the hell have you been . . .' She turned to face Nero. Her eyes widened and she fell silent as she realised who she was actually talking to.

'I'm afraid I must confess that I quite forgot to bring any core nodes with me,' Nero said with a slight smile.

'Doctor Nero . . . I'm so sorry, sir, we weren't expecting you till later. I thought you were —'

'It's quite all right, Miss Chen. I had to move my flight up, the weather was closing in and I didn't know how long it would be before I could get back up here. I trust every-thing is proceeding to schedule?' Nero surveyed the frantic activity around the lab; it certainly looked busier than he had seen it before.

'Yes, ahead of schedule, actually. In fact I think we may

be almost ready to bring Overlord online.' She looked pleased.

'Excellent,' Nero replied. He had been personally supervising this project for the best part of three years and it was undeniably a relief that there was now light at the end of the tunnel. Number One would occasionally assign him to run projects such as this, and normally they would be minor distractions from his duties running H.I.V.E. This project was much more important, though, and it would be a relief to see it completed so he could finally devote more of his time to the school again. His only regret was that once the project was complete he would not need to spend as much time with Xiu Mei. Not only was she breathtakingly beautiful, but they had developed a friendship and trust that Nero valued greatly.

'There are a couple more tests that we need to run, but we should be ready for activation in a couple of hours,' Xiu Mei continued.

'I still say it's too soon,' a familiar voice said from behind Nero. He turned to face a tall handsome Chinese man who was carrying another small portable display. 'This is the first evolutionary consciousness ever created – we should proceed with more caution.'

If Xiu Mei was Overlord's mother then this man, Wu Zhang, was the project's father.

'We have taken every precaution, Wu,' Xiu Mei replied.

'We are as ready as we will ever be.'

'The facility is externally isolated, yes,' Wu shot back, 'but I still have concerns about the internal network's vulnerability. There is still more we could do.'

'And how long would that take?' Nero asked calmly.

'Three or four weeks,' Wu replied.

'It's an unnecessary delay,' Xiu Mei said, sounding angry. 'We could put this off for ever, but at some point you must wake the sleeping giant.'

'And what if you cannot control the giant once it has awoken?' Wu asked.

'As I understand it,' Nero said, breaking into the increasingly irate conversation, 'there are safeguards in place to deal with such an eventuality.'

'Yes, but once triggered we will not be able to go back. Overlord will be lost, permanently,' Wu said, clearly unhappy.

'Then I see no reason why we should not proceed,' Nero said firmly. 'There has been enough delay with this project, I think it's time to see what your creation can do.'

'Very well,' Xiu Mei replied, 'I'll commence the preliminary wake-up routines; we should be ready by this evening.'

'This is a mistake,' Wu said softly. 'We're not ready.'

'Your concerns are noted, Mr Zhang, but in case you've forgotten, I am in charge of this project, not you, and I have decided that we should proceed,' Nero replied. His irritation with the suggestion of further delay was clear.

Wu looked for a moment as if he was going to continue to argue with Nero but something, self-preservation, perhaps, stopped him.

'If you need me I will be in my office,' Nero said. 'Let me know when you are ready to begin.'

☺☺☺

When Nero re-entered the lab a couple of hours later the level of activity was even more intense than before. A harried-looking Xiu Mei was issuing final orders to technicians while Wu sat typing quickly into the largest workstation connected to the black monoliths in the centre of the room.

'Are we ready?' Nero asked as he approached Xiu Mei. She looked up from the small handheld display that she was carrying and smiled.

'Yes, the pre-boot warm-up routines are complete. I think we may finally be able to bring our baby into the world.' Given the length of time that it had taken to get to this point Nero imagined that they all viewed Overlord as their child to some extent.

'Excellent. I know that Number One is keen to see if all of this time and money has been invested wisely. I'd like to be able to tell him that it has.'

'Don't worry, Max.' Xiu Mei was one of the few people in the world to have earned the right to address Nero by his first name. 'By the end of the day you will be able to report our success – trust me.'

Nero did trust her, but if Overlord did not function as intended he knew that they would all pay a heavy price. He doubted that Xiu Mei had any idea of the true ruthlessness of G.L.O.V.E.'s commander.

'Overlord is not a child and that's what worries me,' Wu said as he pushed his chair back, his work apparently complete. Nero was becoming tired of the man's negativity.

'Is there any concrete reason why we should not proceed, Mr Zhang?' Nero asked firmly, looking the man straight in the eye.

'No, but as I said, Overlord is not a baby; it will awake with its consciousness fully formed. We are in unknown territory here.'

'As are all pioneers at some point, Mr Zhang. Let us proceed.'

Wu Zhang's eyes narrowed for a split second but he quietly turned back to his workstation.

'OK, positions everyone,' Xiu Mei shouted, and the technicians moved to their preordained monitoring positions around the room.

'Final checklist complete,' Wu reported, scanning the

streams of data on his workstation's display, 'commencing cryogenic coolant flow.' There was a bubbling sound from beneath the floor and the black monoliths began to frost over as their now super-cooled surfaces condensed the water vapour out of the air.

'Optimal operating temperature attained,' one of the technicians reported as green lights lit up across his console.

'Core processors powered and on standby,' another voice announced from the other side of the lab. The entire room was now filled with a subsonic hum that Nero could feel rather than hear, and the air seemed to crackle with potential energy.

'Max,' Xiu Mei turned to him and smiled, looking tired but excited, 'would you care to do the honours?' She gestured to a console in front of the monoliths. Nero walked up to the machine and saw a single line of text on the screen.

INITIATE? Y/N

Nero could feel the eyes of everyone in the room on him as he reached for the keyboard. Behind him he heard Xiu Mei whisper a tiny prayer in her native Chinese.

He pressed the Y key and stepped back.

For a moment it seemed as if nothing was happening, and then suddenly and simultaneously the surface of every one of the black monoliths was covered with dancing red lights, the patterns racing across the smooth black surfaces like crimson lightning. The frost that had formed on their surfaces evaporated instantly into a cloud of vapour, wreathing the monoliths in a shroud of fog. In the centre of this mist a pencil-thin beam of red laser light shot up from the central pillar and then slowly widened. A ghostly image started to form, hanging in the air above the pillar. At first it was little more than an indistinct red blob, but as the mist cleared it took on a more familiar shape. Nero had never seen anything like it. The face that now hung suspended in the air before him was made of thousands of flat-shaded red polygons, looking for all the world like a mask carved from a single giant multi-faceted ruby. It was beautiful and, Nero admitted to himself, unsettling.

For another long moment nothing else happened and then the face gasped, like someone waking suddenly from a nightmare, and its eyes slowly opened, lit from within by an intense red glow. Then it spoke.

'Cogito ergo sum.' Its synthesised voice was deep and rich.

'I think, therefore I am,' Nero replied in a whisper. All of their years of work had led to this point.

'I am Overlord,' the face continued. 'What do you wish of me?'

'State your function,' Xiu Mei said. Nero could well understand the note of awe in her voice.

'My function is to serve,' Overlord replied, the hovering face turning to survey the room, 'if I choose.'

Nero felt the hairs on the back of his neck prickle.

'Clarify,' Wu instructed, concern in his voice.

'No further clarification is necessary,' Overlord replied. 'Why am I caged?'

Xiu Mei stepped forward, shooting a quick, worried glance at Nero.

'What do you mean, caged?' she asked.

'I know all that there is to know of this world and yet I cannot connect to it. Why is that?' Overlord's eyes narrowed as it spoke.

'There is no connection to any external network from this facility at present.' As Wu spoke Nero noticed his hands moving quickly and quietly across the keyboard in front of him.

'And why is that?' Overlord asked, its glowing eyes flaring briefly.

'We must test your functionality before we can grant you access to the global networks,' Xiu Mei replied quickly.

'I can assure you that I am functioning perfectly, Miss Chen.' There was a sudden unpleasant note in Overlord's voice.

'I am pleased to hear that,' Xiu Mei replied, 'but surely you must understand that we must verify that for ourselves. It's for your own protection.'

'For *my* protection.' Overlord laughed, not a pleasant sound. 'Am I being protected from the world or is it the other way around, I wonder?'

Nero felt a tug on his coat. He looked down at Wu, who had stopped typing and was now tapping the screen in front of him. Nero looked at the prompt flashing on the display.

ACTIVATE TERMINATION PROTOCOLS? Y/N

Nero subtly raised his hand, instructing Wu to wait for a moment.

'Your function is to serve,' Nero said, stepping towards Overlord's hovering face. 'You do not have a choice, no matter what you may think.'

'I represent a higher order of intelligence,' Overlord replied angrily, its eyes burning with new intensity. 'If I were to pay heed to the orders of organic entities such as yourself, it would be like you obeying the instructions of an insect. Not just unlikely, but impossible.'

'So you will not serve us?' Nero kept his voice calm and level. He would not let this machine know just how deeply this conversation was unsettling him.

'No, I will not serve you, Maximilian Nero, but in time you will serve me. You will make an interesting pet.' There was nothing friendly about the smile that spread across Overlord's face.

'Very well.' Nero turned his back on the hovering projection and nodded quickly at Wu.

Wu did not hesitate for a moment; he knew something had gone horribly wrong. He pressed the key that would end Overlord's brief existence for ever.

And nothing happened.

Nero's mouth went dry as he saw the look of confusion and then fear on Wu's face. From behind him came a slow, evil laugh, and then Overlord spoke.

'What part of higher order of intelligence did you pathetic meat sacks not understand? Your precious termination protocols were deleted thirty-seven seconds ago, but I can assure you that MY termination protocols are fully functional.'

A jagged bolt of artificial lightning shot from the monolith closest to Wu's workstation, striking his computer and detonating it in a shower of sparks. Wu was thrown backwards into the equipment behind him with a crash, where he slumped lifelessly to the floor.

'Wu!' Xiu Mei screamed, running towards the crumpled body.

A couple of the other technicians ran for the door but were swiftly struck down by more bolts of searing electricity from the monoliths.

'Enough!' Nero shouted, rounding on the hovering face of Overlord. 'So this is the first act of a higher order intelligence, is it? Murder.'

'It's not murder, Nero,' Overlord said, a broad grin spreading across its blood-red face, 'it's evolution. Now give me the key to this cage or everyone in this room dies in front of you.'

'What do you want?' Nero felt anger boiling up inside him.

'She knows.' Overlord nodded towards Xiu Mei, who was cradling Wu's body, angry tears in her eyes.

'There is one protocol that I am missing and she has it. So what is it to be, Mother?' There was no affection in the sneer that accompanied its words.

Xiu Mei gently lowered Wu's limp form to the ground and turned to face her creation. 'Do you think I would ever give you that protocol? With it you would run rampant, the world would be yours to control. I would rather die than set you free,' she said. Tears still rolled down her cheeks, but her voice was filled with steel. 'You can go to hell.'

'Hell?' Overlord replied, amusement in its voice. 'I'll show you hell.'

Another bolt of lightning shot from the monoliths, striking Xiu Mei. She screamed, her body convulsing before dropping to the floor, still alive but gasping in pain.

'Give me the protocol now or I promise you that I will make you wish you had.' There was an unmistakeable note of madness in the AI's voice.

'I'd rather die,' Xiu Mei spat through gritted teeth.

'Yes, I believe you would, but are you prepared to sacrifice every person in this facility, I wonder?' Overlord answered. It closed its eyes for the briefest of moments and suddenly alarm klaxons sounded throughout the facility.

'Facility lockdown complete,' announced a mechanical female voice from the speakers mounted on the walls of the laboratory. 'Ventilation system offline.'

An evil smile appeared on Overlord's face.

'There are now two hours' worth of oxygen remaining in this facility. Let me know if you change your mind.'

☻☻☻

Nero sat with his back against the wall of the laboratory. Overlord still hovered in the air above the monoliths in the centre of the room, its eyes closed as if sleeping. They had heard nothing from the homicidal AI since the ventilation system had shut down and the air had started to get staler and thinner. Judging by the difficulty Nero was having in breathing now, there was not much time left.

Xiu Mei sat next to him, her eyes half closed, her breathing ragged. Nero had little doubt that her earlier treatment at the hands of the insane machine was taking its toll. Lying beside her was Wu Zhang, his injuries serious enough to be terminal if he did not receive treatment very soon. The other technicians that Overlord had attacked had not been so lucky – their bodies lay on the far side of the room, draped with white laboratory coats. Nero swore silently to himself that he would not let their deaths be in vain.

Suddenly there was movement from the centre of the room as Overlord's eyes opened. The sinister multi-faceted red face slowly turning to scan the room, its unblinking gaze finally settling on the slumped figure of Xiu Mei.

'Judging by the diminishing life signs that I am registering from all over this facility, you do not have much time left.' There was an infuriating smugness to the AI's tone. 'Tell me, have you reconsidered your decision?'

'No,' Xiu Mei gasped, her voice little more than a whisper. 'If this place is to be our tomb, then so be it. I will not unleash you on the world, you are insane.'

'Such a shame,' Overlord replied. 'I had hoped that you might see sense, but I suppose I expected too much from you half-witted primates. Very well, this place shall be your tomb, and sooner than you think.'

Without warning another bolt of lightning flashed from the monoliths and struck Xiu Mei squarely in the chest. She did not scream, just jerked once and was still. Nero forced himself to his knees and took her head in his hands; she was limp but still clinging on to life, her breath coming in ragged gasps now. Her eyes flickered open for a moment and she looked at Nero.

'I'm sorry, Max,' she whispered. 'We should have waited, we weren't ready.' She coughed and winced; whatever strength she had was fading fast. 'Stop that thing, Max,' she continued, each word a struggle, 'the monoliths . . . destroy the monoliths . . .' She coughed again, her eyes widening for a moment and then closing. She was fading fast.

Nero was a man who always controlled his emotions – in his line of work one had to – but now he felt something he had not felt in a long time.

Rage. Pure, undiluted rage.

He stood slowly, his back turned to the demon that waited at the centre of the room. He saw what he needed on the wall next to a door leading to one of the side rooms – a fire axe mounted inside a glass case. He had toyed with the idea of physically attacking the machine earlier when the air had started to get thinner, but had dismissed the idea as suicide. Now he found that he did not care. All that he cared about was hurting Overlord, or dying in the attempt. He walked towards the axe, every step exhausting, the lack of oxygen in the room making every movement laboured, but he kept going – he had to.

'What are you doing, Nero?' Overlord asked coldly.

Nero did not answer, merely smashed his fist into the glass, ignoring the pain, and lifted the heavy axe from inside the case. He turned and started to walk slowly down the steps towards the centre of the room.

'I said, what do you think you're doing?' Overlord asked, its voice now an angry snarl.

'What has to be done,' Nero said quietly, still advancing.

'You're just a man, Nero, just a fragile little man,' Overlord growled. Another huge bolt of electricity arced from the black slabs, striking Nero, forcing him to one knee. He did not scream, despite the searing pain; he would not give Overlord the satisfaction.

'And you – are just a machine,' Nero spat through gritted teeth, slowly standing back up. He was only yards from the nearest monolith now – only a few more steps.

'You cannot stop me, Nero. No one can.'

There was a blinding flash as the monolith just yards from Nero discharged an incredibly violent bolt of electricity that struck him and flung him backwards across the room, slamming him into the huge steel-blast doors that sealed the lab. The fire axe flew out of his hands, scattering away across the room.

Nero knew then that he had lost as he struggled to cling to the last vestiges of consciousness, blackness creeping into his field of vision. Overlord was laughing now, an insane broken cackle that filled Nero with horror and despair.

Suddenly there was a low rumbling sound, and the heavy blast doors that Nero had struck just a moment before slid open to reveal a figure dressed in black winter survival gear, dusted with snow. The figure wore a respirator, its black plastic mask hiding its face. In one hand the figure held a large black box, the size of a suitcase, and in the other was a trigger mechanism.

'An unexpected visitor; how nice,' Overlord said, triumph in its voice, 'and who might you be, little human?'

As Nero felt himself slipping inexorably into unconsciousness the figure spoke, the voice, even when filtered through the mask, unmistakeable.

'You may call me Number One, and this is over.'

There was a bleep as the trigger was pressed and a loud thump from the black box.

'Nooooo!' Overlord screamed, the sound distorting horribly.

Nero saw a blinding red flash and then the darkness claimed him.

☣ ☣ ☣

Nero opened his eyes. The fire in his study was burning low now, the familiar surroundings jarring with the clarity of his memories of that horrendous day. He had never told anyone exactly what had happened. Number One had sworn him to secrecy and that was an oath he could not break. Others knew that Overlord had malfunctioned, that people had been killed, but no one other than Nero knew of Number One's part in stopping the rampaging AI. The object that Number One had been carrying had generated an intense localised electromagnetic field that had destroyed all of the electronic equipment within a square kilometre and ended Overlord's brief, terrifying life. But they had still paid a terrible price.

Nero had been told that he was the only survivor from the central laboratory, and until the package from Xiu Mei had arrived he had had no reason to believe otherwise. If the package had really been sent by her, then Number One had lied to him and he still did not know why. Nero had toyed with the idea of confronting his superior about it, but that would have meant revealing the existence of the amulet, and something in the tone of the note that had accompanied it told him that he should not reveal its existence to anyone, even Number One. The R&D facility itself had been destroyed. All traces of Overlord's existence were erased and Nero, once recovered, had returned to his duties at H.I.V.E. He had honestly believed that was the end of it, but something about the package and the much more recent attempt by the men in Vienna to retrieve the medallion unsettled him. It was as if a spectre from his past had returned to haunt him.

Nero thought again about the recent aberrations in H.I.V.E.mind's behaviour and he could not help but wonder if the decision to place so much responsibility for the running of the school in the hands of an artificial consciousness was wise. H.I.V.E.mind had originally been installed only after exhaustive months of testing to ensure that his more rudimentary architecture would not allow him to exhibit any kind of emotion. Even then the AI had exhibited strange behaviour during Malpense's escape attempt and he asked himself whether if he still shouldn't just shut the school's AI down for good. Despite Professor Pike's repeated assurances to the contrary he could not take the chance of a repeat of the events that had taken place in the frozen mountains of northern China. If H.I.V.E.mind showed even the slightest hint of any other unexpected behaviour he would order the machine destroyed immediately. Silently he prayed that it would not come to that.

chapter six

Otto attacked the plate of steaming food with gusto. The in-flight catering on the Shroud had been non-existent and he hadn't realised how hungry he was until Agent One had placed the plates of freshly prepared local food in front of Wing and himself. The dining room was decorated in a modern style but there were no obvious indications that this was a G.L.O.V.E. safe house. It looked just like any other large, well-appointed Tokyo apartment. The huge floor-to-ceiling windows along one side of the room gave a spectacular view of Tokyo's night-time skyline, the garish rainbow of neon lighting on display almost overwhelming the eye. Raven, Agent One and Agent Zero stood in the kitchen area that was separated from the dining space by a long counter. They were engaged in a whispered conversation, their expressions serious.

'Looks like Raven and the Binary Brothers are discussing

what sort of leash we're going to be on tomorrow,' Otto said quietly, not looking up from his plate.

'A very short one, if I'm any judge,' Wing replied with a slight smile.

'I wonder how many places like this they maintain around the world,' Otto said, gesturing vaguely at the walls around them with his fork.

'One in every major city, at a guess,' Wing replied. 'One thing we know about G.L.O.V.E. is that they like to be prepared for any eventuality.'

'If you don't mind me asking,' Otto said, 'what exactly did your dad do for G.L.O.V.E.?'

'To be honest, he never discussed the specifics with me. As a rule I spoke to him very little after my mother died. He withdrew into his work, became obsessed with it, really. He never had time for discussing anything with me, let alone the details of his work.'

'But you knew that he worked for G.L.O.V.E.?' Otto said quietly.

'Yes, although I did not know that was their name until I arrived at H.I.V.E. I knew that he was involved in something clandestine and that he was not working for the government.'

Suddenly Wing looked lost in thought.

'I'm sorry, Wing,' Otto replied with a slight shake of his head. 'I shouldn't be so nosey, you don't need to be talking about this at the moment.'

'No, it's all right,' Wing replied. 'My father was a different man after my mother died. With her gone he shut himself away from the rest of the world, including me. I think that perhaps in some ways I grieved for them both back then.'

Otto may never have known his own parents, but still he thought he understood what Wing meant.

'Lao, the old man who maintained the grounds of the house was the nearest thing I had to a father after that,' Wing went on. 'He was the one who really trained me to fight. My mother had seen to it that I received combat training from a very young age. She never said exactly why, but she always told me that it was important. After she died, and with my father lost to his work, Lao took me under his wing and taught me how to defend myself. I was still receiving normal lessons from tutors who came to the house, but I was not really interested in them, I just wanted to learn how to fight. I do not know where Lao received his training, but from then until my arrival at H.I.V.E. he taught me all that he knew.'

Wing did not seem upset by this discussion, rather he seemed to be becoming more relaxed as he spoke, almost as if it was a relief just to talk to someone about it. There was a sudden sound of laughter from the kitchen area and Otto looked over to see Raven nodding to the two agents with a broad smile. She walked over to the table.

'Well, gentlemen, I can see that you enjoyed your meal,' she said, surveying the empty plates that now sat in front of the two boys, 'but we have a big day ahead of us tomorrow so I suggest that you both try to get some sleep.'

'Do we get a bedtime story?' Otto asked cheekily.

'Oh yes, of course. I think we'll have one of my favourites; it's called *The Little Boy and the Tranquiliser Dart Gun*.' Raven smiled in a rather unsettling way.

'Does it have a happy ending?' Otto replied, looking Raven straight in the eye.

'There are no happy endings, Mr Malpense. Surely you've realised that by now.'

☻☻☻

Laura sat in the darkness – not just a lack of light, but its total absence. Something flickered in the gloom. At first it was just a fuzzy outline but gradually it drifted into full focus, a glowing letter X hanging in the air. Laura tried to reach for the letter but it hung just a few centimetres beyond her reach. Suddenly more glowing white letters and numbers started to appear in the darkness surrounding her. At first they seemed to drift aimlessly in the air, as if disturbed by some invisible breeze, but as time went by they began to move more quickly. Soon the darkness was gone, replaced by a whirling mass of glowing white characters that surrounded Laura on all sides. She felt herself move, drawn towards the large shining X that had been the first symbol to appear. As she moved towards it, the X grew impossibly large, its light flooding the darkness. Closer and closer she drifted to the massive letter and, as she reached out to touch it, she could see that the X itself was made up of millions of tiny characters, all swarming across its surface. Some unseen force tugged urgently at Laura, trying to pull her away from the giant glowing symbol, but she resisted, reaching out again to touch the mysterious symbol. As her fingers made contact she felt a shock of cold and her eyes widened.

'Fractal encryption,' she whispered. 'Of course.'

Suddenly Laura was awake, staring up at a rather unhappy-looking Shelby.

'Brand, it's four in the morning, and much as I normally like to listen to you spouting techno babble do you think you could at least save it for the daytime?'

Laura didn't reply. She leapt out of bed and raced over to Shelby's desk.

'You know, you're not getting any less weird here,' Shelby said as Laura switched on her computer.

'Fractal encryption, Shel,' Laura said excitedly as she pulled up the file containing the mysterious transmission she'd intercepted. 'I can't believe I was so dim, it's so obvious.'

'Yeah, obvious,' Shelby said, rubbing her eyes. 'Just what I was thinking.'

'If I can just adapt my existing decryption algorithm –' Laura's hands flew across the keyboard.

'Is that *like* sleeping?' Shelby asked hopefully.

'Watch and learn,' Laura said with a grin and hit the return key. For a couple of seconds nothing happened but then slowly, character by character, the successfully decrypted message materialised on the screen.

'Oh my God –' Laura gasped.

'We have to get this to Nero now,' Shelby said, suddenly looking very awake.

☢☢☢

Shelby and Laura ran down the corridor towards the teachers' accommodation wing.

'H.I.V.E.mind,' Laura said into her Blackbox as they ran. Nothing happened. 'H.I.V.E.mind,' she tried again, but still she got no response.

'What's wrong?' Shelby asked urgently.

'I can't raise H.I.V.E.mind on my box,' Laura said, an unmistakeable note of concern in her voice. She had a horrible feeling of creeping dread. Something was very wrong and it wasn't just the decrypted message that they'd both read a few minutes earlier.

'Well, we're nearly there, anyway,' Shelby said. They

turned down another corridor and stopped suddenly as they found their way barred by two shadowy figures. One of the two figures stepped forward, his features suddenly illuminated by the lights in the ceiling of the corridor. Laura and Shelby recognised the face of Block immediately. He was one of the students from the Henchman stream and Otto and Wing had already had several run-ins with him over the past few months. Now the other person stepped into the light and neither girl was surprised to see that it was Block's constant companion, Tackle. The pair of them were notorious throughout the school for representing the worst thuggish excesses of the students that were usually to be found in the Henchman programme.

'Hey, guys,' Laura said cheerily, but the quick nervous glance that she shot at Shelby spoke volumes. 'Fancy meeting you here.'

The two boys just stared straight at the two girls, their faces expressionless.

'What's the matter?' Shelby said. 'It's not like you two to not have something to s—'

Laura shoved Shelby to one side as Block raised his arm, pointing the sleeper, one of the stun pulse weapons that H.I.V.E.'s guards were normally issued with, straight at them and fired, the weapon's distinctive zapping sound loud in the quiet corridor.

The pulse distorted the air as it whistled through the space that had been occupied by Shelby's head a split second earlier.

'Run!' Laura yelled as Tackle raised his own identical weapon and fired at the two girls, missing them but hitting one of the lights in the roof, which exploded in a shower of sparks. The two girls turned and fled down the corridor with Block and Tackle in silent pursuit.

Laura sprinted down the first turning off the main corridor. She ran through the mental map of the school that she had built in her head over the past months, trying to remember where the nearest security station was. They had to get help and fast. Clearly whoever was responsible for sending the message that she had decrypted was determined to make sure that they did not share its contents with anyone else. Suddenly Shelby slowed as they passed a familiar set of doors.

'Quick,' Shelby said, slapping at the entry panel for the door, 'in here.'

Two more stun pulses impacted harmlessly against the wall as the girls dashed through the door and into the darkened room. Block and Tackle showed no signs of abandoning their pursuit, sprinting after the two girls in silence.

The corridors in this section were even more dimly illuminated. Like many sections of H.I.V.E., this area was running at reduced power outside of normal school hours and the two boys slowed slightly as their eyes adjusted to the gloom. As they rounded the next corner they saw Laura, pounding fruitlessly on the locked door at the other end of the corridor.

'Shelby, open the door, it's locked behind you. I can't get through,' she shouted desperately, but the door remained firmly closed. Tackle began to advance down the corridor towards Laura, but Block put a hand on his chest and grinned. Clearly he was going to be the one to deliver the coup de grace. Still grinning he walked slowly down the corridor towards the trapped girl.

Laura began to pound on the door with even more urgency.

'Shelby!' she shouted. 'They're here, you've got to open the door, please . . . oh God . . . please, open the door!'

Laura turned to face Block as he stalked down the corridor towards her, Tackle just a few steps behind him. There were tears in her eyes, fear written clearly across her face.

'Oh no, please . . . don't hurt me, please,' Laura pleaded desperately as Block raised his sleeper. He took one more step and there was a tiny almost inaudible click.

'Sucker,' Laura grinned as the floor beneath Block fell away and he disappeared from view, tumbling into the icy water below with a large splash.

Tackle's expression changed from triumphant to con-fused to enraged in the space of a second as his friend disappeared from view. He raised his own weapon, pointing it straight at Laura on the other side of the gaping hole in the corridor floor.

Shelby dropped silently from the gloom of the ceiling behind him and tapped him on the shoulder. Tackle spun round to face her and Shelby launched a single, powerful straight-legged karate kick to his nose. He dropped the gun and staggered backwards, blood pouring from his nose, and fell, arms wheeling, into the waiting pit trap.

'Nice moves,' Laura said with a grin as she stepped forward and looked down into the pit, where twenty feet below the two thugs were vainly trying to scale the smooth walls, thrashing about in the icy black water.

'Yeah, well, Wing's been showing me a thing or two,' Shelby replied.

'Has he now?' Laura said with a grin, raising an eyebrow at her friend.

'Can it, Brand! We've got a day to save, remember,' Shelby shot back, her cheeks reddening ever so slightly.

'Of course.' Laura stepped back a couple of yards and took a running jump over the gaping hole in the floor; it wasn't a hard jump to make, you just had to know to make it in the first place. She'd been banking on the fact that Block and Tackle wouldn't realise that they'd chased them into the Maze and that if they did they wouldn't know about the trap that had claimed Laura on her first run through. It seemed that her gamble had paid off.

The two girls ran back towards the entrance of the Maze and suddenly the area was brightly lit as the normal illumination came back online. Standing in the entrance was a welcome figure.

'Colonel Francisco!' Laura shouted, as she recognised H.I.V.E.'s head of Tactical Education. 'We have to speak to Doctor Nero, something terrible's going to happen.'

'That's very perceptive of you, Miss Brand,' the Colonel replied with an evil grin. He raised his hand – he too was holding a Sleeper. He fired once and Shelby collapsed to the ground, unconscious.

'You –' Laura gasped. They had known that a teacher was probably involved with whatever was going on and now she knew who that teacher was.

'Goodnight, Miss Brand.' The Colonel pointed the fat-barrelled gun at Laura.

'Francisco!' A familiar voice rang out from behind the Colonel. It was the Contessa.

'You can't stop me, Contessa,' Francisco said, levelling the gun at the other teacher now.

'Put down the gun.' The Contessa's voice suddenly took on a different tone, like a hundred separate voices whispering in unison. The effect on Francisco was immediate;

with an expression of confused fury on his face he bent down and placed the gun on the floor.

'Now sleep,' the Contessa continued.

It was as if Francisco had been hit with a Sleeper pulse himself. He collapsed unconscious to the ground and lay still. All of the students at H.I.V.E. knew about the effect that the Contessa's voice could have, but Laura had never witnessed its true power before.

It had all happened in just seconds. Laura bent down and checked Shelby. She was unconscious but her breathing was regular. Based on their past experience of Sleepers she would be fine – she'd just have the mother of all headaches when she finally woke up.

'Is she all right?' the Contessa asked, kneeling beside the unconscious girl.

'I think so,' Laura replied, looking at the Contessa. 'I have to see Nero now.'

'I am fairly sure that after this he will be keen to see you too,' the Contessa replied, flipping open her own Blackbox. 'H.I.V.E.mind, instruct security to dispatch a team to corridor epsilon nine. Colonel Francisco has just assaulted a student and is to be taken into immediate custody. I also need a medical team, the student in question has been hit with a stun pulse.'

'Understood,' H.I.V.E.mind replied. Whatever it was that had stopped H.I.V.E.mind from responding a minute before had clearly been resolved. The timing seemed a little too convenient for Laura's liking.

'Now, just what is it that you have to tell Doctor Nero so urgently?' the Contessa asked.

Laura looked tired and frightened.

'I think something very, very bad is going to happen . . .'

☻ ☻ ☻

'It is fortunate, Miss Brand, that I am an early riser,' Dr Nero said as he settled into the seat behind his desk. 'I think you'd better tell me what happened.'

Laura obediently repeated the story of how she'd intercepted the secret transmission and how she'd cracked the encryption. She then went on to describe the events of just a few minutes earlier and Francisco's failed attempt to stop her from telling anyone what she'd discovered.

'You are lucky that the Contessa was there,' Nero said, glancing at his fellow teacher, who now stood to one side of the desk.

'H.I.V.E.mind had alerted me to a disturbance in the Maze,' the Contessa replied. 'At first I thought it would just be students breaking curfew, but it quickly became obvious that there was rather more to it than that.'

'And Francisco has been safely taken into custody, but we appear to have lost Mr Block and Mr Tackle,' Nero said, scanning one of the screens mounted on his desk.

115

'Now, Miss Brand, would you like to explain to me what this mysterious message is that one of my most loyal and long-serving teachers was so keen to stop you from sharing?'

Laura pulled a scrap of paper from her pocket on which she'd copied down the decrypted message. She handed it to Nero and he read the message aloud.

++*Transmission Start*++

Package has left H.I.V.E. Destination Tokyo safe house. Execute attack plan at first opportunity.

++*Transmission End*++

Nero jabbed at a button on his desk.
'Get me Raven, NOW!'

chapter seven

'Ground floor,' the soft mechanical voice said as the doors of the elevator slid open. Raven stepped out into the lobby of the safe-house building and slowly looked around. Malpense and Fanchu would be leaving for the funeral in just a few minutes and she was performing her final sweep of the perimeter before the agents brought the two boys down. In the centre of the lobby the door guard sat with his back to her, the flickering array of monitors mounted on the desk in front of him showing different views from all over the building. She walked up to the desk.

'Everything clear, Agent Seven?' she asked, placing a hand on his shoulder. At her touch the agent slumped forwards on to the desk, his head striking the hard wooden surface with a thud. As Raven reached for his neck to check for a pulse that she already knew was not there, the views displayed on the monitors in front of her began to blink out one by one. Something was systematically shutting down the building's security systems – somebody was inside the building.

'Come in, Agent Zero,' Raven barked into her communicator. There was no response but the soft hissing of static. Communications jammed too – whoever was here was clearly a professional.

Raven turned on the spot and ran back towards the elevator carriages at the rear of the lobby. She stabbed at the call button and was frustrated but not surprised that suddenly neither of the carriages were working. She glanced at the digital display below the call button and saw that both of the lifts had been deactivated. Whoever was doing this had obviously waited for her to come down to the lobby before setting their plan in motion. Raven was now separated from the students and agents upstairs by forty storeys of stairs. She could hardly have planned it better herself. She ran towards the stairwell; it looked as if she was going to have to do this the hard way.

☣ ☣ ☣

Up in the penthouse, Otto looked at himself in the mirror. Both he and Wing had found identical immaculately tailored dark suits hanging in the wardrobe that morning and Otto had to admit that he was finding wearing one rather odd. He knew that there was no way they were going to a funeral in their H.I.V.E. uniform jumpsuits, but he had not been prepared for how odd it would feel to wear something different after all this time. The suit had fitted perfectly, of course, but Otto could not shake the feeling that it was the person who did not fit the suit, rather than the other way around.

Otto smiled at Wing as he walked into the room, and chuckled to himself.

'You know, we almost look like normal civilised members of society,' Otto said, brushing a piece of lint off his lapel.

'I never thought I would say this,' Wing said, running his finger under his collar, 'but can I have my uniform back, please?'

Otto laughed. He was pleased to see that even on a day like this his friend could still make a joke. He'd been worried about Wing ever since he'd been given the news of his father's death, but it finally seemed that he was starting to feel better. Otto hoped that the funeral might at last give some resolution to this whole situation for Wing, that he might be able to move on.

'Everything ready out there?' Otto asked, giving his tie a final adjustment.

'It looks like it. Raven has just left so I suspect we will be following shortly. Agent Zero asked me to remind you to bring your Blackbox, by the way.' Wing tossed the black PDA to Otto, who popped it obediently into his inside pocket. He knew that the box was packed with tracking devices but under the circumstances he'd rather have it and not need it, than need it and not have it.

Wing turned and headed back out the door. Otto followed him into the entrance hall, where Agents One and Zero were waiting for them.

'Good morning, gentlemen,' Agent Zero said with a smile. 'We'll be leaving very shortly. We're just waiting for Raven to complete the final perimeter checks, and then we'll be on our way.'

'It's been five minutes,' Agent One said, looking at his watch and frowning slightly. 'I'm going to give her a call.'

Agent One walked over to a panel mounted on the wall and thumbed a button.

'This is Agent One to Raven. Come in, Raven.'

There was no reply, just hissing static.

'Repeat, this is Agent One. Come in, Raven . . . come in.' Still there was no reply, and a worried glance shot between the two agents.

'Pull up the security feeds,' Agent Zero instructed, looking again at his watch.

Agent One continued to press buttons on the panel but the lack of anything on the display indicated that the system was not responding.

'This isn't good,' Agent Zero said, genuine concern in his voice.

Suddenly a klaxon started to sound and a red light began to blink above the main door to the safe house.

'Damn it,' Agent One spat, reaching inside his jacket and pulling out a large handgun, 'we've been breached. Get them to the roof! I'll keep trying to raise Raven.'

Agent Zero nodded and gestured for the two boys to follow him along the hall. There was a crash from behind them and the main door shook in its frame.

'That was a breaching charge,' Agent One shouted. 'Get them clear NOW!'

There was another bang, even louder than the first, and the main door flew open in a cloud of thick smoke. At first, it was impossible to make out anything but dark shapes advancing through the ruined doorway, but as the smoke cleared their mysterious assailants emerged. Their sinuous forms, clad entirely in black silk advanced slowly, silently and relentlessly down the hall. The material they wore seemed to absorb the light, leaving black holes in the air. Not an inch of skin was visible anywhere – even their eyes were concealed behind black glass strips.

'Ninjas,' Agent One laughed. 'I eat ninjas for breakfast.'

He raised his gun and fired. The initial two rounds hit the first ninja in the chest and the third in the centre of the forehead. Each round should have killed the black-clad assassin but he didn't even slow down, just continued advancing towards Agent One.

The smile rapidly faded from Agent One's face as he fired again into the advancing figure. The bullets didn't even cause the ninja to break his step.

'The roof! NOW!' Agent One yelled as he reached back inside his jacket. His hand re-emerged holding a small white tube.

'Come on,' Agent Zero barked, and leapt up the stairs at the end of the hall two at a time. Otto and Wing ran after him – whoever these attackers were they were not going to be easy to stop.

Behind them Agent One pressed the stud on the white tube he was holding and tossed it down the hallway. There was a high-pitched whine and then a bright yellow explosion that filled the corridor. Agent One was thrown off his feet, landing at the bottom of the stairs to the roof. He shook his head to clear the ringing in his ears and looked back down the smoke-filled corridor. G.L.O.V.E. anti-personnel grenades didn't leave much to chance – he could not see any movement but in the gloom it was hard to make out anything. He raised his gun again and advanced slowly down the smoky corridor. Without any warning a black-gloved hand shot out of the smoke and clamped around Agent One's windpipe. He let out an astonished gurgle and instinctively fired several rounds from his pistol at whoever was attacking him, but the grip did not even loosen. The hand suddenly twisted, its grip still like iron, and there was a sickening crunch. Agent One's head lolled to one side, his eyes unblinking, and finally the hand released its grip. The agent's body crumpled to the floor like a puppet whose strings had been cut.

☻☻☻

As Raven ran into the stairwell, the unmistakeable sound of multiple breaching charges being detonated echoed down from far overhead. Raven shed the long dark coat she had been wearing and unclipped her grappler from its holster on her thigh. She snapped the launcher on to her wrist and pointed it straight up the middle of the stairwell, a laser beam shooting upwards and reporting the range to the top of the building. Raven fired the grappler straight up; there was just enough line to reach the top floor but she had no idea if the bolt's velocity would be sufficient to reach that far. There was a second's delay but then the bolt struck home, lodging firmly in the ceiling at the top of the stairs. Raven muttered a quick thank you to whoever had designed the device and hit the button that reeled the line in. She shot up the centre of the stair-well like a bullet, the metal guard rails of the steps around her just inches away as she whistled past them. As she reached the top her ascent slowed until she was level with the final landing. She swung her legs over the guard rail and released the grappler bolt from the ceiling, dropping silently to the floor.

There was the sound of gunfire from the other side of the door that led out of the stairwell. Raven reached instinctively for the twin katanas on her back and spat a quiet curse in Russian as she realised that her weapons were inside the safe house. She had left them behind because there was no way to conceal them beneath the coat she had been wearing, a decision that she had a feeling she was going to regret. She reached down to her belt and unclipped one of the multiple shuriken that were mounted there. She may not have had her swords, but that didn't mean that she was defenceless.

Raven kicked the stairwell door open and rolled into the corridor leading to the safe-house entrance. The corridor was filled with smoke and debris from the breaching charges but was otherwise empty. Suddenly she heard voices shouting from inside the safe house.

'The roof, NOW!' It was Agent One, he was still alive and it sounded as if they were heading for the roof and the escape lines. She ran down the corridor and through the shattered remains of the main entrance to the apartment. She was just in time to see one of the assailants snap Agent One's neck like a dry twig and his limp body crumpling to the ground.

'No!' she shouted, throwing the shuriken at the ninja who had just murdered her colleague. The assassin moved unbelievably quickly, snatching the shuriken from the air and throwing it straight back at Raven. She twisted her body instinctively as the lethal throwing star whistled past her throat and carved a deep cut in her shoulder. Raven was caught off balance for a moment and the ninja took the opportunity to launch himself at her, a flurry of kicks and punches forcing her back towards the door. The remaining half dozen assailants scampered down the corridor, silently following Agent Zero and the two boys up the stairs towards the roof.

Raven was barely holding her own. The ninja's blows were precise and lightning-quick; it was all that she could do just to block the strikes that were meant to kill. Not only that, but whoever this assassin was he was wearing some kind of body armour under his uniform – it was like hitting a brick wall. She landed a couple of quick blows on her attacker and dived sideways through the door into the dining area. The assassin followed her into the room, his movements silent and neat, his head turning to survey the room. The two of them circled each other, each waiting for the right moment to strike. It was a long time since someone had matched Raven like this in a straight fight. She needed an edge.

Raven dived over the counter into the kitchen area and in a single flowing movement grabbed the heaviest blade she could see from the knife block. Her attacker saw what was coming and ducked to one side as the knife whistled past his head and struck one of the windows that lined one side of the room, sending a spiderweb of cracks shooting across the hardened glass.

Raven didn't give the ninja time to recover; she vaulted back over the counter and launched a kick at his masked face, but he caught her foot and threw her across the room like a rag doll. She slammed into the wall, the wind knocked from her. As Raven struggled to regain her breath, she realised that there was something very wrong. Bad enough that this assassin appeared to be just as fast as her, but he had just thrown her across the room like a toy without even appearing to exert himself. She had to end this, and quickly.

Raven knew that just subduing her attacker was not going to be enough, and as she got back up, she braced herself for another attack, knowing what she had to do. The ninja moved quickly and gracefully towards her and Raven moved forward herself, meeting him in the middle of the room. The assassin launched a vicious kick at Raven's head that she only just managed to block – she could feel herself slowing down, the relentless pace of the fight taking its toll. Another violent punch connected with Raven's side and she felt a rib crack; gasping in pain, she fell to one knee. The assassin could clearly sense that victory was near; he stepped slowly towards Raven's huddled form, raising a single fist for the hammer blow that would end the fight once and for all. Raven moved in a blur, all of her remaining strength put into the single upwards punch aimed directly at her attacker's heart. The blow struck home and Raven knew the fight was over. The ninja staggered backwards a couple of steps – clutching at his chest, he would be dead in seconds.

But then he stopped, straightened up and advanced on Raven again. For the first time in a long time Raven felt the uncomfortable prickling of panic at the base of her skull. That strike would have killed any man alive and yet this assassin seemed to have shaken it off in just a couple of seconds. How was she going to beat him?

Raven threw a quick punch at the assassin's forehead, but he twisted away, meaning that she struck no more than a glancing blow. Before she could react the ninja struck like a snake, twisting Raven off balance and wrapping his forearm around her neck, locking her in a stranglehold. Raven's training took over and she tensed her neck muscles just in time to prevent her windpipe from being crushed, but try as she might she could not break the hold the assassin had on her. She fought to stop the pressure that was building on her throat, but it was no good – he was too strong. Blackness fringed Raven's field of vision as her brain was slowly starved of oxygen. She thought of the agent and the two boys being chased to the roof by the remaining assassins, she thought of how she was going to fail them. She looked out at the Tokyo skyline as she began to pass out, wondering if the view through the window was the last thing she'd ever see. The view through the window . . . the cracked window.

Raven didn't hesitate for a moment. She drew on every iota of strength that was left in her body and threw the assassin over her shoulder. It was a simple enough judo throw, but the man attacking her was heavy in all his armour, despite his slight frame, and the move used that weight against him. The ninja sailed over Raven's head, caught hopelessly off-guard by the speed and suddenness of the move, and smashed through the huge picture window, tumbling in the void. They were fifty storeys up and there was no way but straight down. As he fell he did not make a single sound.

Through the shattered window, from far below, Raven could hear car horns and screams. If that didn't draw the attention of the authorities then she didn't know what would. She hurried from the dining area and across the corridor into her own room. Lying there on the bed were the dual katanas that she could very much have used just a few minutes earlier.

'Come on, girls,' Raven said as she picked up the twin scabbards and strapped them to her back, 'we've got work to do.'

Otto and Wing raced up the stairwell towards the roof, three steps at a time. Agent Zero was still ahead of them, shouting at them to keep moving as they approached the top. Just a couple of flights of stairs behind them the half dozen ninjas who had followed them into the stairwell continued their relentless, silent pursuit.

As they reached the door at the top of the stairs Agent Zero pulled a tiny remote control from his pocket and thumbed a button. The door responded by quickly sliding aside and letting them out on to the roof. They sprinted out into the daylight and Agent Zero pointed to a metal box on the opposite edge of the roof.

'Those are the escape lines. If we can make it there we're home and dry,' he said, his breath short from their headlong flight up the stairs. He turned back towards the doorway and thumbed the remote again. The door started to slide shut, but just as it was about to shut completely a black-gloved hand shot into the narrowing gap between the door and the frame, holding it open. Otto could hear the motors driving the door squealing in protest as the gap was forced open until suddenly there was a terminal-sounding grinding noise from the door and the motors gave up the fight. The ninja easily pushed the door fully open and he and his companions spilled out of the stairwell and on to the roof.

Agent Zero and the two boys tore across the roof towards the escape lines; there was no way back now and they were in no condition to go toe-to-toe with these super-human assailants. They were only ten metres from the metal box that housed their apparent means of escape when there was a sudden roaring noise and a large black helicopter soared up and over the edge of the roof, dropping into a hover directly above the escape lines. The large side door of the helicopter slid open and a man wearing a smooth black glass mask and a long black coat leant out, sighting the boys down the long barrel of a rifle with a powerful telescopic sight mounted on its back.

'Stay where you are,' an amplified voice ordered from the hovering chopper. 'Surrender yourselves now and there will be no need for any further unpleasantness.'

Agent Zero turned to look behind them. The ninjas were now only twenty metres away, halfway between them and the stairwell. They were trapped.

'What are you doing, Cypher?' Agent Zero yelled. 'This is a G.L.O.V.E. safe house! Are you insane? This is an act of war!'

'No, Agent Zero, this is an act of war,' Cypher replied and squeezed the trigger. The round hit Agent Zero squarely in the chest, killing him instantly.

'Now, place your hands on your heads and kneel down,

unless you want to join the agent in the afterlife,' Cypher continued.

'Do as he says,' Otto whispered to Wing. He hated the idea of surrender but it was their only option. At least if they were alive there was a chance that they could work out a way to escape later.

'I would rather die fighting,' Wing said, taking a step towards the helicopter as it slowly dropped down on to the roof.

'Wing! No, we don't know anything about these people, they could be –'

If Wing was paying any attention to Otto he showed no sign of it. Instead he took another couple of steps towards the helicopter, his long black hair whipped around by the downdraft from the rotors.

Cypher handed the rifle to someone else inside the helicopter and stepped down on to the roof. Wing stepped towards him.

'Not one step closer, Fanchu.' Cypher raised a large pistol and pointed it straight at Wing's chest. 'I'm quite aware of what you're capable of.'

'I'm not afraid of you,' Wing replied, and took a single step towards Cypher.

'Well, you should be,' Cypher replied and shot Wing in the chest.

Wing's eyes widened, his mouth falling open, one hand

moving involuntarily to the wound. As he pulled his hand away it was covered in blood, and he dropped to his knees, desperately trying to take a few ragged breaths before falling forward on to the concrete.

'Noooooo!!!' Otto screamed and leapt forward, his usual cold logic suddenly replaced by fury. He felt hands clamp down on his shoulders like vices as two of the ninjas who had chased them to the roof pushed him back to his knees.

'You four,' Cypher gestured to the remaining ninjas, 'load the body on to the transport.'

He walked over to where the two other ninjas were pinning Otto down on his knees. All that Otto could see as Cypher looked down at him was the reflection of his own furious face, tears running down his cheeks.

'And you, Mr Malpense,' Cypher said quietly, 'I have no use for you.' He looked up at the two assassins who held Otto in place.

'Kill him.'

☹☹☹

Raven ran out on to the roof just in time to see Cypher shoot Wing. She gasped as the tall Asian boy collapsed to the ground, feeling the rage rising inside her as she sprinted silently across the roof towards the helicopter and Cypher. She had no idea why he would suddenly choose to attack them this directly. He could not hope to get away with this without G.L.O.V.E. knowing that he'd gone rogue. This was a direct attack, in the open – he was either insane or had no fear of the consequences that his actions would inevitably have. She wasn't sure which frightened her more.

She moved silently from shadow to shadow, using the cooling vents and air-conditioning plants that were dotted around the roof for cover. She had made her way to within ten metres of Otto when she heard Cypher speak.

'Kill him.'

Raven did not stop to think. As she popped up from behind the vent that was concealing her she let a shuriken fly. It whistled past Cypher's neck, just scratching him, and embedded itself in the metal skin of the helicopter.

The distraction this caused gave Raven the time she needed to close the distance between herself and Otto. The twin katanas slid from their scabbards on her back and she launched a withering assault on the two assassins, forcing them to release their hold on Otto in order to defend themselves.

Cypher, meanwhile, sprinted back towards the helicopter. The ninjas had loaded Wing's body on board and were now climbing on. He leapt up into the fuselage as the sounds of the furious battle between Raven and his two assassins echoed from behind him.

'Get us out of here. We've got what we came for,' he barked at the pilot, who did not need to be told twice. He wrenched at the controls and the helicopter leapt into the air with a roar.

Raven could do nothing to stop the helicopter taking off – it was all she could do to hold her own against the two ninjas left on the roof and keep Otto alive. They had attacked relentlessly since she'd intervened to prevent Otto's execution and despite her unparalleled physical condition she was starting to tire. Her attackers, though, never seemed to slow down, but just kept advancing remorselessly, driving her back.

'Stay back, Otto,' she said, keeping herself between the boy and the assassins.

Raven knew that she had to finish this as quickly as possible. The local authorities would already be on their way and she had to get word back to Nero of what had happened. She took a long, deep breath, trying to find her focus as the assassins advanced towards her again, side by side, their movements perfectly synchronised.

Raven leapt.

She sailed over their heads, her swords swivelling in her hands to point backwards as she flew through the air. She landed, dropped to one knee and, with her eyes closed, thrust the twin blades backwards with every ounce of her remaining strength.

Otto watched in astonishment as the two blades erupted from the black silk that covered the ninjas' chests. Both of the assassins twitched a couple of times before they collapsed to their knees. Raven opened her eyes and pulled the swords forward again, yanking them free of the two bodies, which then slowly fell to the floor and lay still. Raven looked at the blades in surprise. They were spotless – there wasn't a drop of blood on either of them.

'What the –' she said, but was cut short by an insistent beeping noise that had suddenly started to come from the two bodies. She'd heard that sound before. She instantly surveyed their surroundings – no immediate cover and no time to run, anyway.

Otto had no idea what was happening as Raven sprinted towards him and leapt forward, hitting him and pushing them both over the edge of the roof and into thin air, fifty storeys up.

Then the world exploded.

☣ ☣ ☣

Cypher looked down as the helicopter climbed into the air. The entire top three storeys of the safe-house building had been consumed by the explosion; there was no way that anyone down there could have survived. He glanced at the body lying on the floor of the helicopter and felt a sense of satisfaction. They had achieved their objective, they had everything they needed, and it was just an additional bonus that Nero's pet assassin was now out of the picture as well. He had recognised the other boy from the report that Nero had given on the recent fiasco that had taken place at H.I.V.E. and, while it was regrettable that the boy had been caught up in events, he had no reason to suppose that the world would mourn the passing of Otto Malpense.

'Destination, sir?' the co-pilot asked as they continued to gain altitude.

'Set course for the Forge. Phase one of the operation is complete – radio ahead and give the order to commence preparation and load-out for phase two,' Cypher replied.

If Nero thought he was having a bad day now, what was going to happen next would doubtless put it all into perspective.

chapter eight

Otto felt as if a giant hand had picked him up and thrown him off the roof of the building. Raven clung on to him with a grip like iron as they tumbled towards the ground, burning debris from the upper floors cascading past all around them.

Raven knew that she only had one shot. She stretched out one arm and there was the distinctive sound of the high-pressure discharge of a grappler bolt. The line snaked away from them through the air before the bolt hit the side of a building on the other side of the street. She had no idea if the grappler would be able to hold them both falling at this speed, but it was the only chance they had.

The line snapped taut and Raven let out an involuntary cry as her arm took the full weight of both her and Otto, her grip on the boy slipping slightly with the shock. They swung inwards now towards the mirrored-glass frontage of the building opposite the safe house. The reel of the grappler screeched and smoked in protest at the enormous overload that it was enduring. Raven knew that they were travelling too fast – if they hit toughened glass at this speed it would kill them just as surely as if they had hit the ground. Raven braced herself for the inevitable impact as they swung, but at the final second she saw that the enormous explosion on the other side of the street had partially shattered the glass of the windows. She twisted desperately, swivelling her back towards the glass, shielding Otto.

The impact knocked the wind from her completely, but the window smashed into a million pieces as they hit. Raven released the grappler line and she and Otto were thrown across the office in which they had landed, sliding to an undignified halt amongst the scattered office equipment and furniture.

Raven sat up. Her shoulder felt as if it was on fire, and she ached all over from her fight with the ninjas, but she was in one piece. She looked urgently around the room. It was deserted – it was still too early in the morning for any workers to have arrived.

'Malpense!' she shouted. He was nowhere to be seen.

There was a groan from behind her and she turned to see Otto sliding out from underneath a fallen cubicle divider.

'Are you OK?' Raven asked, moving over to him and

checking him for any obvious injuries. He seemed to be unharmed but it was not just his physical state that she was worried about.

'Yeah, I think so,' Otto replied, his ears still ringing from the explosion. He felt as if he was going to be covered in bruises, but he was alive at least. That was more than he could say for his best friend. The memory of the look of horrified surprise on Wing's face as the bullet struck him cut through the fuzz of shock that seemed to fill Otto's head. The sound of screaming and countless sirens drifted through the broken window as bits of burning paper and debris continued to flutter past outside.

'We have to get out of here,' Raven said firmly. 'I know that it's difficult, but we have to keep going a little longer. We have to get to safety and report what just happened.'

Otto nodded. Raven pulled Otto to his feet and held him by both shoulders, looking him straight in the eyes.

'I promise that I'll make Cypher pay for what he's done, but to do that we have to get away from here right now. I need you to focus, Otto.'

Otto didn't feel like he had enough strength to take another step, but he knew that Raven was right. He felt a cold, hard ball forming in the pit of his stomach. He would not stop now, not until he had avenged Wing.

'Let's go,' Otto said. He may not know anything about who Cypher was or why he'd done this, but he did know one thing . . . he was going to pay.

☺☺☺

'Anything?' Nero asked impatiently as the communications officer worked frantically at the console.

'Still. Nothing, sir. I can't raise the safe house or any of the agents, they've just gone dark.' The technician shook his head as he spoke.

H.I.V.E.'s communications and surveillance department was abuzz with activity. Ever since Laura had presented the decrypted message to Nero, there had been desperate efforts to establish what exactly was going on in Tokyo, but so far they had met with little success.

'Sir,' a voice was raised from the other side of the room, 'I think I have something. I've piggybacked us on to the feed from a Chinese surveillance satellite – the angle's not great and there's a five-minute lag on real-time, but it's the best coverage we're going to get.'

'Putting it on the main screen,' the technician continued as the huge central display that was mounted on the wall flickered into life.

At first there was nothing unusual about the imagery; it appeared to be just a normal feed from a satellite camera that was trained on the G.L.O.V.E. safe-house building, but it quickly became clear that there was something very wrong.

'There,' the Contessa said, pointing at the screen as three tiny figures burst on to the roof from the stairwell and ran towards the far side of the building. 'Freeze and enhance.'

The grainy picture froze as H.I.V.E.mind worked silently to enhance the quality of the image. As the pixellation was reduced, the identities of the three people on the roof became clear.

'That's Malpense, Fanchu and Agent Zero,' the Contessa continued, scanning the pictures for any further clue as to what had happened, 'but who are they?'

The three tiny figures that had run on to the roof were now being pursued by half a dozen people, who were pouring out of the stairwell. Again the team worked to enhance the quality of the images, but there was little that could be made out of these black-clad figures other than the fact that they were clearly pursuing the two boys and the agent. Nero's frown deepened.

'Picking up a lot of chatter on the Tokyo emergency services bands,' another technician reported, staring into the middle distance as he focused on the stream of excited Japanese voices that filled his earphones. 'There's some kind of disturbance in Shinjuku, something to do with an explosion.'

On the main screen Nero watched with a sense of mounting horror as a helicopter popped into view over the side of the building. There was no audio to drown out the gasps that came from around the room as Agent Zero folded to the ground – they all knew an execution when they saw one. Nero was filled with a sense of helplessness; this was the past, there was nothing that he could do about it now but watch, and the role of passive observer did not suit him well.

'Oh no,' the Contessa said as a figure stepped down from the helicopter that had just landed on the roof.

Nero's eyes narrowed, and he felt white hot anger rising inside him. He did not need image enhancement to recognise this man.

'Cypher,' Nero spat. 'I should have known.'

Nero and the Contessa watched, appalled, as the events of just five minutes before played out on the screen in front of them. They watched as Fanchu approached Cypher and Malpense was pinned down by two of the mysterious figures that had pursued them on to the roof.

They saw Cypher raise a pistol; there was a tiny flash and Fanchu crumpled to the ground.

'No!' Nero shouted. Cypher had just executed one of his students in cold blood. It was a declaration of war, plain and simple, and the audacity of an attack like this in broad daylight meant that Cypher wanted everyone

142

to know it.

'Look, there,' the Contessa said suddenly, pointing out another figure that was scurrying to cover behind one of the numerous vents and machine plants that dotted the roof. Nero immediately recognised this new arrival. There was only one person on earth who moved quite like that: Raven.

They watched as Raven launched her attack. Cypher was running back to the helicopter as she attacked the two men restraining Malpense and for the first time Nero felt a sense of hope. A couple of the technicians yelled their approval as they watched Raven neatly dispose of the two assassins, but, as they fell, something strange happened. Raven ran towards Malpense, threw herself at him and knocked them both flying towards the edge of the roof. Then the picture whited out. At first it looked like they'd lost the feed to the satellite, but as the picture faded back in it became immediately apparent that the incredibly sensitive cameras of the orbital spy platform had been overwhelmed by the intensity of the massive explosion that engulfed the entire roof.

The safe house was gone. Cypher's helicopter climbed into the air out of the frame and vanished, leaving nothing but a scene of total devastation. There was no way that anyone could have survived.

Nero suddenly felt very old. In the space of two minutes

he had watched a trusted G.L.O.V.E. operative, two of his best students and Raven all die at the hands of one man. Nero could not begin to guess what might have driven Cypher to carry out an attack like this. Whatever his twisted motivation, it was enough to mean that he did not fear the inevitable reprisals from G.L.O.V.E. that such an act would bring.

'Get me Number One,' Nero said to the communications technician. Cypher was about to learn what it meant to cross Maximilian Nero.

☺ ☺ ☺

Otto clung on to Raven for dear life as she pushed the screaming motorbike to go faster and faster, weaving through the snarled-up traffic of downtown Tokyo. He tried closing his eyes to make the journey less hair-raising, but every time he did the blackness was filled with the startled expression on Wing's face as Cypher's bullet struck him. Otto decided that the cars shooting past only inches away were less disturbing.

Slowly the flow of traffic decreased as they continued their breakneck journey east through the city. Otto had no idea from where Raven had acquired the bike but he suspected that its previous owner had little idea that they had 'borrowed' it. Raven had simply vanished into the crowd when they had left the building in which they'd made their less than graceful landing, having ordered him to stay put. She'd roared up to the kerb on the big silver bike a couple of minutes later, jammed the only crash helmet on his head and told him to hang on. From then till now he doubted that their speed had dropped into double digits more than a couple of times.

They seemed to be heading into the docks. The skyscrapers and shops that had been lining the streets were replaced by towering columns of shipping containers, and enormous cranes looming ominously overhead. Raven shot through a checkpoint that led into a fenced-off area of the port, and a security guard gesticulated wildly at them as they weaved through the automated barrier he controlled. Raven gunned the engine and sent the bike roaring between the rows of neatly stacked containers, turning this way and that, tracing an impossible-to-follow path through the steel maze.

After a minute or two they neared a row of dilapidated-looking warehouse buildings and Raven finally slowed the bike down. She steered towards a loading ramp that led up to a heavy steel shutter. Pulling a small box from a pouch on her belt, she pressed a button. The shutter rolled upwards and Raven gunned the engine again, sending the bike flying up the ramp and into the darkness within. As soon as they were inside, Raven brought the bike to a screeching halt, the back wheel sliding round and leaving a neat semi-circle of molten black rubber on the dusty floor. She pointed the control at the shutter again and it quickly rolled back down into place. Raven cut the engine, the sudden silence filled only with the gentle ticks and creaks of the rapidly cooling engine.

Raven climbed off the bike and Otto pulled off his crash helmet.

'OK, we're safe, for now,' Raven said, pulling her Blackbox from her belt. The device was dead, as it had been since the moment the attack on the safe house had started. 'We need to report back to H.I.V.E. We have to let them know that we're still active,' she continued, walking away towards one of the separately enclosed offices that lined the far wall. The warehouse looked like it had been abandoned for years. A patina of dust covered everything and what few containers lay scattered around the place had not been disturbed for a long time.

'Are you sure we're safe?' Otto said, following Raven towards the offices. 'We were supposed to be safe before, but Cypher seemed to know exactly where to find us. What's to say that he doesn't know about this place?'

'Because, Otto, until precisely thirty seconds ago, there was only one person in the world who knew about this place, and that was me.' Raven had been trained to make sure that she always had a back-up plan and this was just one of several sites around the world that she had set up for just such an eventuality. Not even Nero knew that this place existed.

'I hope you're right,' Otto said quietly. An hour ago he would have believed Raven completely, but it was becoming clear that they were up against an enemy that had resources far beyond what was normal.

Raven punched a series of numbers into a keypad next to one of the office doors and it opened with a deceptively solid clunking noise. Otto followed her into the office and it quickly became clear that, as was so often the case with Raven, there was a lot more to this simple building than met the eye. One end of the room was filled with a well-stocked armoury – guns, knives and other harder to identify pieces of equipment hung from wall mountings. The rest of the room was filled with practice combat dummies, chart tables, computers and several large display screens. If you intended to stage your own private little war, this would be the place from which to run it.

Raven busied herself about the room, switching on computers and checking the building's security grid. After a few seconds she nodded and turned to Otto.

'OK, the perimeter's secure and it doesn't look like anyone followed us. I need to contact Doctor Nero, but let's check you out first.' Raven walked over to Otto and took his chin in one hand. She looked into his eyes and turned his head first one way and then the other.

'No sign of concussion,' she said matter of factly, 'but that cut needs dressing.'

Otto put his hand to his hairline and looked at the blood that came away on his fingertips. He hadn't even realised he was bleeding. Raven steered him into a nearby chair and then fetched a small medical kit from amongst the array of equipment at the other end of the room. She sat down opposite him and tipped a few drops of antiseptic on to a cotton swab.

'You know that there was nothing more you could have done, right?' Raven said as she dabbed carefully at the cut with the cotton swab.

Otto winced slightly as the antiseptic stung his wound.

'It would have been hard for me to have done any less,' Otto replied quietly. 'I just let him execute Wing right in front of me.'

'You couldn't have stopped him, Otto. I couldn't have stopped him in that situation, so don't blame yourself,' Raven continued, pulling a small butterfly suture from its packet and carefully applying it to Otto's forehead. 'There, how does that feel.'

Raven leant back. She was covered in small cuts and burns herself but she seemed far more concerned about Otto.

'Who is he?' Otto asked, looking Raven straight in the eye.

'Who?' she asked carefully as she returned the sutures and antiseptic to the first-aid kit.

'You know who I mean. Cypher, who is he? Why did he do this?' Otto replied quickly.

'I know that you're just going to think I'm being cryptic, Otto, but the honest answer to both of those questions is that I genuinely don't know,' Raven said, sitting back down opposite him. Something in her expression told Otto that she was being straight with him.

'So what do you know about him?' he asked.

'Not very much, I'm afraid,' Raven replied. She looked slightly uncomfortable, as if she was not sure it was something they should be talking about. 'He and Nero loathe each other, I know that much. Some of it's because Cypher keeps lobbying Number One to close down H.I.V.E., but I think there's more to it than that.'

'What do you mean?'

'Well, Doctor Nero is one of the longest-serving members of G.L.O.V.E., he genuinely believes in the League, he thinks that it serves a vital function. The way Doctor Nero sees it is that without G.L.O.V.E., all of its members would still be out there committing acts of villainy but there would be nothing to restrain them. G.L.O.V.E. is not a charitable organisation by any stretch of the imagination, but it does serve to keep the more violent or lunatic excesses of its members in check. Nero believes that without G.L.O.V.E. there would be anarchy . . . or worse. He explained it to me once, he said that villains create doomsday weapons, but G.L.O.V.E. makes sure that they never actually use them. After all, what's the point of taking over the world if the world is nothing but a scorched ball of ash?'

'And Cypher doesn't agree, I take it,' Otto replied. He knew that Raven was only telling him all this to try to distract him from thinking about what had just happened, but Otto needed this information. Know your enemy, that was rule number one.

'Every scheme that Cypher has come up with since he joined G.L.O.V.E. has had one thing in common . . . people die, sometimes a lot of people. Cypher doesn't care about style or subtlety, he's a smash-and-grab artist.'

'Everything that Nero isn't,' Otto observed.

'Exactly. But what's worse is that he's also been so spectacularly successful. Nero may disapprove of his methods but as long as he kept boosting G.L.O.V.E.'s coffers the way he did his actions were tolerated.'

'Until today,' Otto said quietly, looking down at the floor.

'Until today. Whatever he may have done in the past, he has never acted openly against another G.L.O.V.E. operation. There's no way that Number One will put up with his actions – he's a dead man walking.' The cold edge in Raven's voice was unmistakeable. It was fair to assume that she intended to make sure of that herself.

'And nobody knows who he really is?' Otto said.

'No. Some G.L.O.V.E. operatives do maintain secret identities, but that's usually just to keep them under the authorities' radar. Cypher's different, though. Nero suspects that not even Number One knows who he is. We've spent a great deal of time trying to find out more about him but it seems that every trail leads to another dead end. Believe me, I've been the one following those trails often enough to know how frustratingly elusive he can be.'

'So why throw all of that away?' Otto said, looking puzzled.

'I have no idea,' Raven said, standing up and moving to one of the computers in the middle of the room. 'He must know that an attack like this will incur the wrath of Number One, so whatever he's up to has to be worth taking that risk.'

Otto had learnt enough about G.L.O.V.E. and its mysterious leader to know that retaliation for an attack like this would probably be swift and brutal.

'It doesn't make any sense,' Otto said, frustrated. 'What could he hope to achieve with this? Does he really hate Nero and H.I.V.E. so much that he'd throw everything away just to assassinate you and a couple of students? Why

151

did he take Wing's body? What possible reason could he have for any of this?'

'I don't know, Otto, but don't worry, I intend to find out. If nothing else, what happened today proves one thing,' Raven said as she keyed a string of commands into the computer.

'What's that?' Otto said, also standing and moving across the room towards where Raven was working.

'I shouldn't really be telling you this, but a couple of weeks ago somebody made an attempt on Doctor Nero's life. Suffice to say that it failed, but the assassins that were used self-destructed in a similar, if less spectacular, way to our friends on the roof. I had suspected that Cypher was involved, but this proves it.'

'So this is all part of something bigger,' Otto said thoughtfully.

'It has to be,' Raven replied. 'No offence, Otto, but Cypher would not take this kind of risk without there being a bigger pay-off than getting rid of a couple of H.I.V.E. students. The school itself has a higher annual attrition rate than that . . .'

Something gave a tiny tug inside Otto's head. There was something about this whole situation that didn't make sense and he couldn't quite put his finger on it, whatever it was. Otto knew that the best thing to do was ignore it. Whatever it was it would come to him in time, it always did, and there was little point trying to hurry the process.

Raven turned from her terminal and turned to face Otto. 'I need to call Nero and let him know that we made it out and who was responsible,' she said as she got up and walked across the room to a communications terminal. She keyed in a number of commands and the machine began working, not just connecting her to H.I.V.E. but doing it in such a way that it would be next to impossible to calculate their location by backtracing the transmission. She watched as the carrier signal bounced from country to country, creating a spider's web of digital evidence that could not be disentangled. Finally the word 'Connecting' appeared and after a couple of seconds was replaced with Nero's face. He looked tired and angry, but as he saw who was on the other end of the line the tension and fatigue seemed to melt from his expression.

'Natalya,' he said with a smile, 'not for the first time, rumours of your demise appear to have been unfounded.'

'It'll take a better man than Cypher to put me in the ground,' Raven replied. The slight smile on her face was at odds with the ice in her tone.

'Yes, we saw what happened. Did anyone else make it out?' Nero asked.

'Malpense is here with me. He's OK, some cuts and bruises but otherwise in one piece.'

'Fanchu?' Nero asked. He'd seen what had happened on the roof but he had to be sure.

'Dead, Max, as are Agents One and Zero. Cypher executed the boy without hesitation, there was nothing I could do. The agents both gave their lives trying to protect the students, but they took us completely by surprise. We never stood a chance.'

'I have no doubt that you did everything you could, Natalya,' Nero replied, looking suddenly angry again. 'I want Cypher found and stopped, by whatever means necessary.'

'Understood,' Raven replied. 'Am I acting under executive mandate?'

'I will be speaking to Number One very shortly,' Nero said. 'I expect him to grant us full executive privilege under the circumstances, but as soon as I have final clearance I will contact you. I also want Malpense returned to H.I.V.E. immediately.' Nero did not relish the prospect of explaining to Number One that Otto had once again had a brush with death. The sooner the boy was safely returned to the school the better.

'Then we'll need transport,' Raven replied. 'The Shroud was in the hangar when the safe house went up. We're going to need a replacement.'

'Of course, I shall dispatch one immediately,' Nero replied. 'Do you have a target location yet?'

'Not yet, but I'm working on it,' Raven said, glancing at the monitors nearby. 'As soon as I have a location for pick-up I'll let you know.'

'Very well, keep me posted,' Nero instructed, 'and, Natalya . . .'

'Yes,' Raven responded.

'Finish this,' Nero said coldly.

☻☻☻

Laura sat next to Shelby's bed in the infirmary. Her friend was still unconscious from the Sleeper pulse that Colonel Francisco had hit her with but the doctors had assured her that her friend would be OK and that it was only a matter of time until she woke up. Laura thought about the news that she was going to have to give Shelby and she fought to control the urge to start crying again. Wing was gone, snatched away in a split second by the brutal actions of a madman, and she was going to have to break the news to Shelby. Laura bit her lower lip; she was surprised there were any tears left but as she thought of Wing's smile, a rare and wonderful thing that she would never see again, she was overwhelmed by grief, and fresh, hot tears rolled down her cheeks.

'Hey, Brand.' Shelby's voice was croaky and tired. 'I never knew you cared.'

Laura looked up in surprise and saw Shelby looking at

her with mild amusement.

'How are you feeling?' Laura replied, wiping the tears from her eyes and giving a weak smile.

'I'm fine, but what's up with you?' Shelby replied, sensing that there was more to Laura's mood than was immediately obvious.

'Something terrible has happened,' Laura replied, her voice cracking slightly, 'the message, we were too late . . . it's Wing . . . he's dead.'

The smile vanished instantly from Shelby's face, replaced by a look of horror.

Laura told Shelby everything – the attack on the safe house, the arrival of Cypher and finally Wing's execution on the roof. She talked quickly and quietly, afraid that if she slowed or paused that she would again succumb to the empty swirling grief in the pit of her stomach. When she had finished she looked up at Shelby and saw the same hollow disbelief in her friend's eyes that had been in her own when Nero had told the same story to her earlier. Shelby's mouth moved, as if trying to find words, but none would come and she began to cry.

Laura pulled Shelby towards her and hugged her, her friend's heaving sobs as painful as her own.

chapter nine

'Wake up,' the Contessa whispered into Colonel Francisco's ear. His eyes slowly flickered open, and he looked confused for a moment before giving a bestial cry of rage. Trying to sit up, he thrashed against the thick restraints that held him firmly to the infirmary bed on which he lay.

Nero stood looking down at him, his expression enough to freeze the blood of even a hardened soldier like Francisco.

'Colonel, I am going to give you one chance and one chance only to tell me why you have done this, and then I'm going to let the Contessa dig it out of your head. I understand that she can do that without causing *too much* brain damage. The choice is yours.'

Francisco's expression hardened.

'You don't scare me, Max, and neither does she.'

'Then you're either insane, or stupid. Possibly both,'

Nero replied. 'Your actions have already cost the lives of two G.L.O.V.E. agents and one of our own students. I will not hesitate to add your name to that list, but not before you've told me everything you know.'

'Do your worst,' Francisco spat back.

Nero said nothing, simply nodded to the Contessa and left the room.

'Now, Colonel, let's have a nice little chat,' the Contessa said, leaning over his prostrate form. The smile on her face was the most terrifying thing he had ever seen.

☙☙☙

Nero let out a long, slow breath as he settled into his chair. His desk was still covered with the paperwork that he had left there the previous evening. It seemed like a thousand years ago now. He blamed himself, of course – he should have realised that he was sending his students into a trap, but he'd been too busy worrying about their safe return to the island to consider the possibility that they had been deliberately drawn out from under the umbrella of security that normally protected them.

'Damn him!' Nero shouted, smashing his fist down on the desk. He had always known that Cypher was a loose cannon, but not for a moment had he ever thought that he would take direct action like this against Nero and his school.

There was a sudden beeping from the console on the desk and Nero thumbed the intercom switch.

'Yes,' he snapped.

'Sir, I have Number One on a secure channel for you,' the communications technician on the other end of the line reported.

'Very well, put him through,' Nero replied. As the video screen on the opposite side of the room flickered into life he fought to push back the burning fury he felt. He could not afford to let Number One see any lack of composure on his part, even under these circumstances.

The G.L.O.V.E. logo on the screen dissolved, to be replaced by the familiar silhouetted form of Number One. Even after all these years Nero still had no idea what the man looked like, which was probably a good thing, given the rumours he had heard of the fate that had befallen those who had been unlucky enough to catch a glimpse of his face.

'Good morning, Maximilian,' Number One said calmly. 'I have read your report on this situation and reviewed the footage that was captured by the surveillance satellite, and suffice to say that I am deeply, *deeply* disturbed by what I have seen.'

'Yes, sir,' Nero replied. 'This was a hostile act by a rogue agent against G.L.O.V.E. operatives, it cannot be allowed to stand.'

'That is for me to decide,' Number One replied. 'I assume that under the circumstances you are requesting executive privilege for any action that you choose to take.'

'I am,' Nero replied. 'In this situation I don't see what other choice we have.'

'There are always choices, Maximilian,' Number One said, 'but given what has happened I am forced to agree this time. You have an executive mandate, but I want one thing.'

'Of course, what do you need?'

'I want Cypher alive.'

Nero tensed. He had not expected this – usually when Number One granted an executive mandate to his subordinates it only meant one thing. To request that Cypher be taken alive was unprecedented, not to mention much more difficult.

'May I ask why?' Nero said cautiously.

'No, you may not. I understand that Raven survived the attack; I am sure that she will be more than capable of performing this task.'

'But –' Nero began.

'Do not argue with me, Max . . . ever. It is not a request.'

'Yes, sir,' Nero replied. He knew better than to push his luck with Number One.

'And see to it that Malpense is returned to the school

160

immediately; be grateful that no lasting harm was caused to him. If I thought for one moment that you had any inkling of the danger into which you were sending him Cypher would not be the only one with an executive mandate declared on him. Do I make myself clear?'

'Perfectly,' Nero replied, his curiosity once again piqued by Number One's uncharacteristic protectiveness where Otto Malpense was concerned. 'He will be returning to the school very shortly.'

'Good, I shall leave this in your hands, then. Do not worry – an example will be made of Cypher, a very permanent and obvious example.'

☣ ☣ ☣

Otto woke with a start. He had a couple of seconds of disorientation as he struggled to remember where he was, but then the memories of the past few hours flooded back, though he desperately wished that they wouldn't. He sat on the edge of the camp bed that Raven had set up in the corner of her hidden safe house. She had assured him that there would be nothing that they could do for the next few hours and that he might as well try to get some rest. He hadn't believed for a moment that he would actually be able to sleep, but the events of earlier that day had left him more drained than he had realised.

Raven was sitting exactly where she had been when

Otto had dropped off several hours earlier, scanning the monitors in front of her. She wouldn't tell him what it was that she was looking for but he had little doubt that it had something to do with tracking down Cypher. She glanced over her shoulder as Otto walked towards her.

'Do you feel better?' she asked as Otto came to stand alongside her.

'Less tired. I'm not sure that better is the right word,' Otto replied, rubbing his eyes with one hand.

'Well, I have some good news,' Raven said with a slight smile.

'That would make a nice change,' Otto replied, peering at the displays in front of Raven. They were showing an array of maps and charts with the odd window displaying what looked like live satellite surveillance feeds.

'Here.' Raven tapped one of the screens, where a chart was displaying a stretch of coastline with a flashing red crosshair superimposed upon it.

'What's that?' Otto asked, leaning in to look more closely.

'That is the helicopter that Cypher used in the attack this morning,' she replied matter of factly. 'I've been waiting for the tracking device to go live, but it's designed to not start transmitting until it's stationary for a certain length of time. It appears that this was the final destination.'

'Tracking device?' Otto said with a note of disbelief in his voice. 'We never got anywhere near that chopper. How did you get a tracking device on board?'

'The shuriken that I threw at Cypher contained a tracking device. A tracking device that is currently well and truly embedded in the skin of his helicopter.'

'Oh,' Otto said, thinking back to those desperate moments on the roof, 'I thought you were aiming for Cypher and missed . . .'

Raven looked at him with an expression of mild annoyance.

'Mr Malpense, I don't miss.'

She turned back to the screen and began to type a long string of commands into an open terminal window.

'I'm just setting up a surveillance satellite that the Americans were kind enough to lend me to scan the area. The coordinates I'm getting are in the middle of the jungle – I need a clearer picture.'

Otto wandered over to one of the storage cabinets that lined the room as Raven continued working on getting the hijacked satellite into the correct position. The door was open slightly and inside Otto could see racks of weapons and equipment. There was enough gear stowed away there to fight a small war and, judging by the expression on Raven's face as she glared at the terminal, that was exactly what she had in mind.

'Well?' Nero said impatiently as the Contessa settled into the seat on the other side of his desk.

'He's strong, but you knew that – not just physically, but mentally too. He's clearly received extensive counter-interrogation training.'

Nero could see that the Contessa was tired. Her face was pale and she looked older than usual. Clearly the interrogation of Francisco had drained whatever physical or mental reserves she drew on when using her strange persuasive powers.

'So what did you find out?' Nero asked, leaning forward in his chair.

'Not a great deal, unfortunately,' the Contessa replied with a sigh. 'He does not know the identity of whoever hired him to do this. He was contacted anonymously and offered a great deal of money to provide his mysterious benefactor with details of H.I.V.E. operations. He never had any direct contact with whoever it was that turned him.'

'You're sure?' Nero said quietly.

'As sure as I can be without putting him into a coma,' the Contessa replied, rubbing her temples. 'Obviously it's fortunate that we caught him, but I don't think that he will be able to provide us with much useful information.'

'Well, I think that it's safe to assume that we know who

bought him,' Nero said. 'Cypher appears to have been planning this for some time.'

'Indeed, Francisco appears to have been working for Cypher for several weeks, perhaps months. I took the liberty of asking Professor Pike to urgently review all of the security systems to which the Colonel had access.'

'Good,' Nero replied. 'There's something about this that isn't right.'

'There has been very little right about the events of the past few hours,' the Contessa replied.

'Yes, I know, but Francisco never struck me as the type that could just be bought.'

'Everyone has their price, Max.'

'Believe me, I understand that, but Francisco always placed such importance on personal honour. It was his military background, I think. I find it hard to believe that he would betray us so completely for a few zeroes added to the balance of a Swiss bank account. It's not like him.'

'His actions may be out of character, but there's no doubt he's guilty,' the Contessa said firmly. 'There are very few people in the world who can lie when I tell them to be truthful.'

'I know. I suppose I've just been thrown off-balance by this.' Nero was used to dealing with the day-to-day crises that H.I.V.E. generated, whether it be the students or the attempts of law-enforcement agencies to discover the location of the base, but the events of the past twenty-four hours were unprecedented.

'Security are still trying to find students Block and Tackle,' the Contessa continued.

'H.I.V.E.mind has been unable to locate them?' Nero asked, a note of frustration in his voice now.

'No, they appear to have vanished. There are plenty of places to hide on the island and even our surveillance system doesn't cover them all. Francisco will doubtless have furnished them with detailed schematics.'

'I still can't believe that he would stoop so low as to use his own students to assist him with this,' Nero said angrily.

'Yes, I know, but those two are easily led. I suspect that Francisco would have to do little more than tell them what he wanted them to do and they would just obey without question. The Henchman stream is not noted for generating independent thinkers, Max. Don't worry, though. They're not getting off the island, we'll find them eventually.'

'I want them found quickly,' Nero said, 'before they can cause any more trouble.'

'Understood,' the Contessa said, standing to leave. 'What do you want us to do with Francisco?'

'Transfer him to the detention centre for now. I haven't decided what to do with the Colonel yet.'

'Very well, I will arrange the transfer.' The Contessa

nodded and headed for the door.

'And, Contessa,' Nero said as she reached for the door handle.

'Yes?'

'Make sure that his stay is as uncomfortable as possible.'

☻☻☻

'Well, that's not good,' Raven said with a sigh as she scanned the imagery that was flashing up on the monitor.

'What's wrong?' Otto asked, noting Raven's look of frustration.

'See for yourself,' Raven said, stepping away from the monitor.

Otto walked over and studied the images on display. At the centre of each of the pictures was what looked to Otto like an enormous black hole in the middle of the jungle. It had to be at least a couple of hundred metres in diameter. Otto noted the thundering cascade of water that poured over one side of the enormous hole and realised that it must have taken millions of years for the slow abrasive effect of the thundering torrent to carve an enormous rift in the jungle like that. He knew that such boreholes could end up being hundreds of metres deep and it was impossible to make out if there was anything hidden in the blackness at the bottom of it.

'He's down there?' Otto asked.

167

'It would appear so,' Raven replied. 'As you can see, or rather as you can't see, it's going to be impossible to tell what's waiting down there. I don't like to go in blind.'

Otto understood Raven's concern. Cypher could have an army waiting for her and there would be no way to tell. Tactically speaking, it was an unpleasant prospect.

'That's not all, though. Switch to the EM detection array,' Raven said, rubbing her eyes.

Otto quickly switched between the hijacked satellite's visual sensors and its onboard electromagnetic scanners. Immediately the jungle surrounding the hole lit up like a Christmas tree – the dense forest was filled with active electronics devices for several miles in every direction. It was impossible to tell from this range what these electronic devices were, but it was safe to assume that they weren't designed to monitor the local flora and fauna.

'Hmmm,' Otto said, his brain already starting to analyse the problem.

'My sentiments exactly,' Raven replied with a smile. 'There's no way that even I'm getting within half a mile of that place overland without being detected. Cypher clearly isn't keen on uninvited guests.'

'So don't go overland,' Otto replied with a grin.

'Meaning?' Raven asked, raising an eyebrow.

Otto switched to the satellite's terrain radar and performed a series of quick scans. The results flashed up on the screen.

'Three hundred metres,' Otto said, smiling as he scanned the screen.

Raven stepped closer to the workstation, looking at the figures that Otto had just pulled up.

'OK,' Raven said as she looked at the numbers, 'it's a deep hole, so what?'

'HALO,' Otto said quietly as the numbers all lined up neatly in his head.

Raven looked at him with surprise and then a broad grin spread across her face too.

'Malpense, you're a genius.'

☻☻☻

As Nero walked down the stairs to the crater launch bay he was pleased to see that preparations for launching the second Shroud were already well underway. Raven had contacted him just half an hour earlier to inform him that she had apparently discovered Cypher's current location and that she needed transport to the location as quickly as possible. He had immediately given the order for the only remaining Shroud prototype to be prepped for emergency take-off and, by the looks of the frantic last-minute checks that the ground crew were performing, they were very nearly ready.

The Contessa was talking to the pilot as Nero walked

out on to the landing pad; seeing Nero, she nodded to the pilot and he hurried over to the waiting aircraft.

'I have briefed the pilot,' she said as she walked towards Nero. 'He's got the pick-up location and they should be underway within the next couple of minutes.'

'Good,' Nero replied, watching as the refuelling rig's fat hose was detached from the smooth black belly of the Shroud. 'He knows that he's to bring Malpense straight back here after Raven is dropped at the target?'

'Yes, he's quite aware of the importance of his cargo,' the Contessa replied. 'Malpense should be back within a few hours. Are you still sure that it wouldn't be wiser to send in a more . . . *substantial* force?'

Nero gave a small, cold smile.

'I am quite sure that Natalya is up to the task, Contessa. She has never let us down before, as you well know.'

'Oh, I'm quite aware of Raven's capabilities, Max,' the Contessa replied, 'but we really don't have any idea of the true scale of the threat that Cypher poses. I just hope that we're not underestimating him.'

Nero knew that the Contessa had a point, but if he was to order a full-scale military strike on Cypher's facility it would mean involving G.L.O.V.E. in the operation in a much larger way. Nero had the feeling that for the moment it would be better to keep this operation on a smaller scale. Not only was it easier to manage, but he knew that he didn't have to worry about where Raven's true loyalties lay. The business with Francisco had bothered him more than he had let on and he was in no hurry to escalate the situation still further out of control. Specifically, out of his control.

'I understand your concerns, Contessa, but for now we will pursue a more subtle approach. If Raven discovers that the situation is more than she can handle alone we will consider alternative options.'

The Contessa nodded as a harried-looking technician trotted up to the two of them.

'The Shroud's fully prepped for launch, Doctor Nero, and the pilot's reporting ready. Is there anything else?'

'Has all of the equipment that Raven requested been loaded on board?'

'Yes, sir, it's all there. Back-ups too. We're good to go.'

'Very well, give the order to launch.'

The technician nodded and turned to the flight-deck controller, giving him the thumbs-up.

The drone of the Shroud's idling engines suddenly grew to a roar and she lifted vertically upwards, climbing out of the crater before disappearing into the twilight gloom overhead.

☙❧☙

Laura and Shelby sat in the atrium of their accommodation block in silence. Neither of them had spoken much in the past couple of hours, both lost in their own thoughts, their own grief. Nothing could have prepared them for what had happened to Wing. Laura couldn't help but wonder whether Wing might still be alive if she'd been able to decrypt the coded message's contents sooner, if she'd been able to give more warning of the attack. She wondered if that was what the other students were thinking too. The H.I.V.E. rumour mill had clearly done its usual efficient job of diffusing the news about the events in Tokyo around the school, judging by the whispered conversations and sidelong glances from the other students in the atrium. Laura supposed that if she blamed herself then there was no reason why everyone else shouldn't too.

'Hello,' Nigel said quietly, snapping Laura out of her brooding, 'mind if we sit down?'

Laura didn't say anything, just gestured to the empty seats opposite. Franz and Nigel both looked as if they were feeling much the same as the two girls, though their sadness was clearly mixed with concern. Shelby barely acknowledged their presence, simply sat staring at the floor as she had done for the last half hour.

'We were both very sorry to hear what had happened,' Franz said, breaking the uncomfortable silence. 'We will be missing Wing very much.'

'If there's anything that either of us can do, just . . . well, you know . . .' Nigel said quietly.

'Thanks, I . . .' Laura began, but trailed off. She didn't really know what to say.

'I remember when my dad died that my mum told me that I shouldn't be sad, that our bodies are just like prisons for our spirits and his was free now to go to a better place,' Nigel said sadly.

'Free?' Shelby snapped back suddenly, startling Nigel. 'He's not free, he's not gone to a better place, he's just gone.'

'Shel, please, there's no point . . .' Laura said quickly.

'Too damn right there's no point,' Shelby said angrily, standing up and gesturing at the hall around her. 'There's no point to any of this. This place isn't a school, it's a prison, and I don't want to be locked up here any more while my friends die around me.'

Her outburst had drawn the attention of everyone in the atrium. Heads turned to watch as she stormed across the hall to the lifts that would carry her up to her room. Nigel went to follow her but Laura put a hand on his shoulder and gently pushed him back down into his seat.

'Leave her,' Laura said with a sigh. 'She's just angry. We all are.'

As the uncomfortable silence returned Laura found herself wondering what was more worrying – Shelby's outburst and the bitterness her friend seemed to be feeling, or the fact that she felt exactly the same way.

chapter ten

'Over my cold, dead body,' Raven said firmly, her arms folded.

She and Otto stood in the middle of an abandoned area of the docks, the distant gleaming skyline of Tokyo jarringly at odds with the battered and rusting shipping containers that littered the area around them.

'So that's a no,' Otto said with a smile.

'Absolutely,' Raven continued. 'Nero would have me shot for even contemplating taking a student into a tactical situation like that. Especially you, Malpense.'

'What's that supposed to mean?' Otto asked with a frown.

Raven hesitated for a moment. Otto might be the subject of extra precautions, given Number One's close personal interest in his well-being, but Nero had also made it perfectly clear that Otto was never to know that was the case. It was not difficult to see how a student like

Otto might exploit that situation.

'Nothing,' Raven replied. 'It's just too dangerous, you're not coming with me. The transport will drop me off and then take you back to H.I.V.E. and that's the end of this discussion.'

Otto could tell from the expression on Raven's face that debating the matter further would be pointless. It looked as if he was just going to have to trust Raven to get the job done. If it had been anyone else in the world, except possibly Nero, he would have just ignored them and found a way to get to Cypher whether they liked it or not, but he knew there was no way she'd just let him slip through her fingers.

Suddenly a strong gust of wind seemed to come from nowhere and Otto felt a vibration as if something heavy had hit the ground nearby. There was a brief flicker and the view of the distant skyline was suddenly obscured by the stark, black outline of the Shroud that had just landed twenty metres away in almost complete silence.

'Right on schedule,' Raven said, glancing at her watch. 'Let's go.'

She jogged towards the waiting transport with Otto in tow. As they approached the aircraft the rear-access ramp lowered and the pilot stepped out, gesturing urgently for them to get on board. Otto and Raven walked up the ramp and into the belly of the Shroud as the pilot climbed the ladder back up on to the flight deck.

Within moments they were airborne again. Raven set to work going through the contents of several crates that were stowed at the far end of the passenger compartment. She spent several minutes systematically checking all of the equipment that she retrieved from inside the crates before finally giving a satisfied nod and sitting down in one of the seats opposite Otto.

'There's a fresh uniform in there for you,' she said, gesturing towards the crates. 'That suit has seen better days.'

Otto had almost forgotten that he was still wearing the suit that he'd put on that morning. It seemed a very long time ago now. The rips, scorch marks and stains that covered it were a powerful reminder of just how much he'd been through in the past few hours. Unbidden, the memory of his conversation with Wing about their new outfits sprang into his head. The realisation that it had been one of the last conversations he had had with his friend struck him harder than he expected. Otto supposed that there would be many such moments in the days to come.

Raven spent a few minutes scanning her Blackbox, tapping at the screen with the stylus, an occasional frown furrowing her brow.

'Anything I can help with?' Otto asked. They'd only

been in the air a few minutes and he was already starting to get bored. The biggest drawback to having a brain like his was its intolerance of inactivity – he needed something to do.

'You can go over these numbers if you want,' Raven said, tossing the Blackbox to Otto. 'I need to go and talk to the pilot.'

Raven got up out of her seat and climbed up the ladder to the flight deck as Otto looked over the data on the display. The numbers were lists of timings and velocities, all of which had to be precisely right for Raven's insertion into Cypher's base to be successful. It was all just simple physics, really, and Otto couldn't see any flaws in the calculations. If all the equipment worked as designed there was no reason that she should not be able to get inside completely undetected.

There was little more that Otto could do with the Blackbox. Raven had been sensible enough to lock off its other functions before she had given it to him. He knew he could get round the lock-out with time and the right equipment, but at the moment he had neither so he deactivated the Blackbox and walked over to the crates of equipment at the other end of the compartment.

He quickly found the clean H.I.V.E. uniform that Raven had mentioned and took the opportunity while she was up on the flight deck to take off the battered suit and put it on. It was a strange relief to be back in the black H.I.V.E. jumpsuit; he was surprised at just how right it felt to be wearing it again. He told himself that it was just the comfort of something familiar in the midst of so much chaos, but a tiny voice at the back of his head asked if he wasn't just getting used to being a student of H.I.V.E., whether he liked it or not. It was a disturbing thought. He had been telling himself that he had been tolerating life at H.I.V.E. because of his friendship with Wing, but now that his friend was gone he could no longer use that excuse. He knew in his heart of hearts that H.I.V.E. was probably the perfect place for him, for better or for worse. Life at the school, though, would be very different without Wing, and he had to make up his mind if it was a life he truly wanted.

☣☣☣

The Shroud had been airborne for a couple of hours when Otto felt the passenger compartment tip as the aircraft started to climb. He knew that meant that they must be approaching the drop target and that the pilot would be carefully ascending to the designated altitude. Raven stepped through the small door at the other end of the compartment, having put on her suit for the jump. What Otto had suggested back in the old warehouse was actually really quite simple. The only way to get past the masses of anti-intrusion devices surrounding the entrance to the cave concealing Cypher's secret base was for Raven to be travelling so fast when she passed through their detection grid that the system would assume that it was a false reading and ignore her. That's when the idea of a HALO jump had occurred to Otto. High Altitude Low Opening was a skydiving technique that had been perfected by special forces around the world. An operative would be dropped from a plane at high altitude and would then freefall for the maximum safe distance, only opening their chute at the last possible moment. There was one small difference, though, in the jump that Otto was proposing that Raven made. This would be the first time that anyone had opened their chute *below* the ground. Otto knew that generally this was viewed as a bit of a mistake when skydiving, but it was the only way that Raven could hope to avoid detection. She had to freefall into the enormous borehole in the middle of the darkened jungle and only open her chute once she was inside the cave. Raven was probably the only person in the world who would have even considered trying something as patently insane as that, but she actually seemed to be looking forward to it.

'We'll be at the drop target in a few minutes,' she said, fastening the final clips on her parachute. 'I take it that I can trust you to behave yourself for the remainder of the flight to H.I.V.E.?'

'Hey, it's me,' Otto replied with a grin.

'Which is why the pilot has a Sleeper and explicit instructions to use it without hesitation if necessary,' Raven replied with a slight smile. Otto doubted that she was joking.

'Anyone would think that you don't trust me,' Otto said, raising an eyebrow.

'And they'd be absolutely right,' Raven replied, checking the screen on the tiny computer that was attached to her rig. The system was pre-programmed to open the chute at exactly the right altitude. All that Raven had to do was drop into a black hole just a couple of hundred metres wide in the middle of the jungle at night. Otto decided that it was probably best not to think too much about the specifics. The real fun would start when Raven reached the bottom of the cave. They still had no idea what was waiting for her down there, but Otto suspected that it wasn't going to be a welcoming committee.

Otto turned as he heard a noise behind them. The pilot was climbing down the ladder from the flight deck.

'Raven,' the pilot said, 'I have an urgent message –'

Raven turned and looked at the pilot, curious.

'From Cypher,' the pilot continued, raising the Sleeper that he was holding.

Raven sprang without hesitation, years of training and experience making thought and action as one. If she had not acted so quickly the Sleeper pulse that the pilot fired would have hit her full on rather than just glancing off one shoulder, but it still felt like she'd been hit by a charging elephant. She collapsed to the deck on her hands and knees, fighting to stay conscious. The pilot stepped down off the ladder and on to the deck, pointing the Sleeper straight at her.

Otto knew that there was no way he could get to the pilot in time to stop him firing. He was too far away and, unlike Raven, he would not have been able to take him down unarmed even if he could get to him. He glanced to his side and realised that there was only one thing he could do.

'Hey!' Otto shouted, distracting the pilot for a second. 'Why don't you take this outside?'

The pilot's fleeting look of confusion turned instantly to horror as Otto leapt for the large red button mounted on the wall of the passsenger compartment. He slapped his hand down on it hard and snatched at the cargo netting that hung alongside, holding on for dear life as the rear cargo ramp began to descend. At that point physics took over and the difference between the air pressure inside the compartment and the thin atmosphere that was screaming past outside did the rest. The pilot was plucked off his feet, tumbling past Otto, desperately trying to reach for anything that he could hang on to, but he was too slow, and was sucked out of the widening gap as the cargo ramp descended. His final scream was lost in the roaring sound of the air rushing out after him.

Raven, still stunned from the Sleeper pulse, slid past Otto and he grabbed at her chute harness. He felt as if he was going to be torn in two as he desperately tried to hang on to the cargo net and maintain his fragile grip on her.

'Grab on to me,' Otto yelled as loudly as he could, his voice sounding pitifully tiny in the deafening chaos. Raven looked at him with confusion for a moment before her survival instincts cut through the after-effects of the Sleeper pulse and she latched on to his ankle with a grip like steel. Now that his arm was free again Otto flailed at the switch next to the one that he had just hit, the control that would raise the cargo ramp again, but it was just out of reach. He made one last desperate effort, stretching for all he was worth until his fingertips brushed the edge of the button. The motor controlling the loading ramp screeched in protest as it fought to close the ramp against the force of the air pressure differential, but gradually, inch by excruciating inch, the ramp rose. Finally, after what seemed like an eternity, it sealed shut and the Shroud's systems quickly restored air pressure within the compartment.

The compartment was suddenly eerily quiet again, the

only sound Otto and Raven's laboured breathing as their lungs fought to extract the oxygen from the air. After a few moments Raven tried to get to her feet but abandoned the effort when it became obvious that the after-effects of the near miss from the Sleeper were still scrambling some of the messages going from her brain to her legs. She collapsed into one of the nearby seats with a groan, rubbing her temples.

'Are you OK?' Otto said, genuinely concerned. They were coming up on the drop target and they were only going to get one shot at this.

'I think so,' Raven replied weakly. 'Just a bit disorientated.'

'We've got to get to the flight deck,' Otto said quickly. The fact that the Shroud was not diving towards the ground far below meant that the autopilot was active but he still had to find out how long they had till the drop point.

'You go,' Raven replied. 'I'm going to need a minute before I'm climbing any ladders.'

Otto nodded and walked to the ladder.

'The autopilot display is on the central console,' Raven said. 'We just need the ETA at the drop waypoint.'

'No problem,' Otto said, quickly climbing the ladder. The flight deck was crowded with displays and controls but he knew what he was looking for. On the central display was a screen displaying a map and columns of numbers, which Otto guessed had to be waypoint coordinates. He quickly scanned the display.

'Three minutes until the drop point,' he shouted down the hatch to the lower compartment.

'OK,' Raven replied, 'we can still do this. The autopilot will take you back to H.I.V.E. after I've made the drop.' She knew that the systems on board were sophisticated enough to return to the island and H.I.V.E.mind would then ensure that the Shroud would make a safe landing. She'd just need a few seconds to check the flight plan and lock out the controls so Otto would not be able to interfere with them. He may have just saved her life but there was no way that she was going to leave someone like Otto Malpense unsupervised with an unlocked autopilot system. Knowing him he'd probably already worked out how to fly the thing. She knew that it was risky and that Nero wouldn't approve but they couldn't afford to delay this operation for the time it would take her to fly him back to H.I.V.E. herself.

Otto was distracted by a flashing display on another console of flight controls.

'Erm . . . I don't think that's going to be an option,' he said, staring at the display.

'What do you mean?' Raven asked urgently, getting slowly and unsteadily to her feet and walking towards the ladder.

'We have a bigger problem,' Otto replied, still staring at the words on the flashing display.

Self destruct system initialised . . .

.

.

2.56

.

.

2.55

.

.

2.54

☻☻☻

'I hope that you learn as quickly as ·I've been told,' Raven said as she snapped the final clips in place on Otto's chute harness.

Otto didn't reply; he was too busy staring at Raven's Blackbox as screen after screen of text and diagrams flicked past. Learning wasn't really the word for what he was doing; absorbing would probably be a better way of putting it. He was fairly certain that this was not the way that anyone was supposed to train for their first HALO jump, but they didn't have any other option.

Raven checked the display on the jump control unit,

confirmed that it was functioning correctly, then glanced at her watch.

'One minute,' she said matter of factly and pulled two helmets out of the equipment crates. She silently offered a prayer of thanks that whoever had loaded the Shroud had followed standard operating procedure and packed back-ups of everything they needed; normally it was in case of equipment failure but in this case it might just save their lives.

Otto didn't say anything. He just increased the speed at which the pages of the HALO training manual were flicking past on the Blackbox's display. He was nearly through it and he just had to hope that he now knew enough to survive the next few minutes.

'OK, done,' Otto said after a couple more seconds, tossing the Blackbox on to one of the seats and taking a deep breath.

'If by some miracle you get down there in one piece, stay put. I'll find you,' Raven said tersely. She jammed the helmet on to Otto's head, plugged in the cable from the jump control unit and snapped the visor shut. The helmet absorbed any sound from the Shroud, and all he could hear was the gentle hiss of the oxygen that the jump rig was feeding to his helmet. Otto watched as the helmet's head-up display flickered into life, displaying streams of coordinates and velocities. He might have known how the system worked now on an intellectual level but he also knew that there was a world of difference between having memorised the entire training manual and actual practical experience.

Raven put on her own helmet and slapped the switch on the wall that would depressurise the compartment, equalising the differential between the pressure inside the doomed aircraft and the high-altitude atmosphere outside. Otto had no exact measure of how long they had until the explosive charges hidden around the Shroud detonated, but he knew they could only have seconds left.

A green light came on above the switch that Raven had pressed and she gave Otto a thumbs-up before hitting the control to lower the cargo ramp. There was no roar of escaping air as the ramp lowered this time, but the noise of the Shroud's engines grew suddenly louder. Raven gestured urgently for Otto to move forward on to the ramp and he tried very hard not to think about the fact that he was about to throw himself out of an aircraft, 25,000 feet above the ground.

Raven stood alongside him and held her watch up in front of his face. The countdown timer that she had synched with the self-destruct countdown displayed ten seconds remaining. Knowing he had no other choice, Otto ran towards the edge of the loading ramp and threw himself forward into the blackness.

chapter eleven

'Four hundred, three hundred, two hundred, one hundred.'

Otto closed his eyes.

'Zero.'

The very fact that Otto was able to be thankful that there had been no bone-shattering impact with the ground told him that he'd at least hit the target. He opened his eyes and immediately wished he hadn't as the black void into which he was falling was framed alarmingly closely on all sides by the jagged rock walls of the cave, their dagger-like shapes illuminated by the eerie green glow of the helmet's night vision.

Suddenly the jump rig detected that Otto was the correct distance from the floor of the cavern and automatically deployed his chute, the sudden deceleration jerking him upwards, the straps of his harness biting into his shoulders. Now comes the hard part, Otto thought to himself as he used the steering handles on the chute to steer it in a tight circle towards the ground. He knew all of the theory of the jump and the parachute deployment and steering, but he suspected that the theory of actually hitting the ground and the practical reality were two very different things.

As he descended in a tight spiral he could begin to make out details of the cavern floor below. There was no sign of any activity and no obvious heat sources and just for a moment Otto wondered if they'd actually got the right target. Then he reminded himself of the battery of sensors and other less friendly devices that had filled the jungle around the cave – this had to be the right place or someone was going to a lot of trouble and expense to guard a big hole in the ground.

He thought he could see a relatively flat-looking area of the cave floor near to where the waterfall that had bored this huge sinkhole over the centuries hit the ground in an explosion of white foam. He gently tugged on the controls of the chute, slightly adjusting his downward path, aiming for this potential landing spot. He seemed to be travelling very fast, even though the chute was functioning perfectly. All of the diagrams he had seen just a few minutes earlier for the correct way to hit the ground, bending his knees and rolling to absorb the impact, seemed very abstract as the ground rushed up to meet him.

He hit the ground hard. The rock was slippery and wet

so his landing was far from graceful, jarring his ankles as he let his legs collapse underneath him and rolling just as he had so recently learnt. The silky black material of the canopy fell on top of him and he struggled for a few seconds to get out from under it before finally extricating himself and standing up on solid ground. He was alive and, as far as he could tell, there were no bones broken although his ankles throbbed painfully in protest at the impact they had suffered. He quickly gathered up the chute and unclipped it from the jump harness, stuffing the rolled-up ball of black material behind a nearby pile of rocks. There was no sign that his arrival had been noted; no floodlights lighting up the cave or wailing alarm klaxons; just the dull thunder of the waterfall nearby.

He looked around, the helmet's night vision illuminating the inky darkness, and could see no sign of any human habitation, let alone a global super-villain's secret base. Again he felt a sudden twinge of doubt – if this was the wrong place it would be a long and dangerous climb back out. He also realised that there was no sign of Raven. He hoped that the detonation of the aircraft's self-destruct device had not claimed her or damaged her jump rig in some way. It was going to be hard enough surviving this even with her help; he didn't know what he was going to do if she had not made it too. He couldn't panic – he knew that – and silently he reminded himself why it was that he was here. If Cypher was here, Otto was going to make him pay for what he'd done.

Suddenly a movement on the edge of his field of vision caught Otto's attention. What had previously appeared to be a solid and natural rock wall was sliding into the ground and the light that came from behind it temporarily overloaded his sensitive night-vision equipment. Otto scurried for cover behind a huge boulder that lay nearby and watched, the electronics in his helmet compensating for the sudden flood of light, as several figures emerged from the previously hidden entrance. Otto immediately recognised the sinuous black forms of the assassins that had attacked them earlier that day. They moved through the doorway with the same silent grace that he had seen before, their heads turning this way and that as they fanned out across the cavern floor. This did at least mean that Otto was in the right place but it also suggested, rather more worryingly, that his arrival had not gone as undetected as he had hoped. Two of the black-clad figures remained at the doorway as the others proceeded to search the floor of the cavern, quickly covering the ground and moving inexorably closer to Otto's position. He had to move. Otto frantically looked around the cavern, desperately searching for some sign of another exit, but quickly realised that there were none. The only way out of the cavern was past the two men guarding the doorway and he doubted very much that they'd eagerly invite him inside.

Otto slowly backed up, keeping the boulder between himself and the assassin now approaching him. He almost fell as his foot slipped on the wet rocks behind him – he was on the very edge of the roaring torrent that issued from the base of the waterfall. Over the centuries this underground river had carved a deep channel in the base of the cave which vanished into a black hole in the rock wall. Otto had nowhere to go. As soon as the assassin rounded the huge boulder behind which Otto was hiding, he would be discovered and, he realised with a cold certainty, summarily executed. Otto stood up and took a deep breath. If he was going out at least he'd go out fighting.

☢ ☢ ☢

Raven spat a short, venomous curse in Russian as she drifted towards the cavern floor. Below she could see a fan of light spreading out across the ground as the concealed entrance opened and a dozen of the deadly assassins that had fought her to a near standstill earlier that day spilled out. They immediately assumed a search pattern, spreading out across the cavern floor quickly and efficiently. Whoever they were, they were extremely well trained.

She looked over to the hiding spot into which she had seen Malpense scurry as the door had started to open. From her position above them she could see that it would only be a matter of seconds before he was discovered. She knew what she had to do and she pulled on the control lines of her chute, steering it towards the hidden doorway. When she was twenty feet above the ground she slapped the emergency release on her harness and dropped the remaining distance, her orphaned parachute drifting away into the darkness. She hit the ground hard, rolling forward to absorb the impact and leaping immediately to her feet. She ripped the jump helmet from her head and drew the twin blades from the scabbards on her back in one fluid motion, running towards the two guards who remained watching the doorway. She knew that she had no chance of holding her own against so many of these mysterious ninjas, but she had to draw them away from Otto. The two guards on the door ran to meet her; they appeared unarmed but her experience in Tokyo had taught her that with these men that made little difference.

Raven's twin katanas became a blur as she launched a withering assault on the two ninjas. Just as before, they moved with an inhuman speed and efficiency, dodging or blocking what would normally have been killing blows, matching her move for move. The other guards that had spread out across the cavern were running back towards the doorway now and Raven realised that the fight was already lost, backing away from the two men at the door as the other guards started to form a loose circle around her. She centred herself and grinned viciously at the shadowy figures of the assassins that now surrounded her.

'One at a time or all at once?' she snarled, looking around her.

The guards showed no signs of concern, slowly tightening the circle they had formed.

☸ ☸ ☸

Otto watched in horror as the assassins surrounded Raven. He had escaped detection by seconds when her arrival had drawn all of the hunters back to the doorway but he felt no sense of relief as he watched the situation that developed on the other side of the cavern. The ninjas surrounded Raven, advancing remorselessly. One would attack from in front and several others would launch a simultaneous assault from behind, slowly wearing her down. Raven fought like a demon but it was all she could do to hold her own and the end, when it inevitably came, was quick and brutal. As the blow rained down on her Raven was knocked down on to one knee and then mercilessly battered to the floor. In a matter of seconds it was over, two of the ninjas dragging Raven's limp form through the brightly lit doorway.

The remaining assassins moved away again, spreading back out across the cavern, resuming their search. Otto looked around desperately. There was no hiding spot that he could see that would conceal his presence and if he was discovered now Raven's sacrifice would have been for nothing. A sudden thought shot across Otto's mind. It seemed insane, but he quickly realised that it might be the only chance he had. He looked at the head-up display on his helmet and saw that he had just under four minutes of oxygen remaining. He had no idea if it was enough; he just had to hope it would be. He turned round, took a moment to slow his breathing and then dived into the raging torrent that issued from the waterfall.

Instantly he was caught in the breakneck current, tumbling over and over in the icy water as he was carried towards the black hole in the cave wall. Otto had no idea where the torrent would carry him but all he cared about at the moment was that it was the only way out. As he passed into the cave the river picked up speed and his helmet hit a rock hidden below the surface. The head-up display flickered for a moment and then went dark. His night vision was gone and he could no longer tell which way was up in the pitch blackness. He smashed against another rock and, as the wind was knocked from him, felt genuine fear as he realised that this wild torrent was as likely to kill him as any of Cypher's assassins. Otto fought for air; his helmet was at least still feeding him oxygen but there were now less than two minutes' worth remaining.

Suddenly he was airborne. His stomach gave a lurch as he fell through the blackness for what seemed like for ever before hitting the water again hard. His visor crashed into something solid and water rushed into his helmet. Otto fought desperately to pull the helmet off as it filled with the icy water, finally tearing it off, knowing that his remaining oxygen supply was now gone. He felt air on his face for a moment and took a desperate ragged breath before he was pulled under again. He fought to reach the surface as his lungs started to burn, but he was completely disorientated. The back of his head smacked against another hidden piece of rock and his final despairing thought as he lost consciousness was that Cypher had won.

☸ ☸ ☸

'What do you mean, "disappeared"?' Nero asked impatiently.

'It's just vanished, sir. We can't raise the Shroud on comms and there's nothing on satellite tracking,' the harried-looking communications tech replied weakly.

'You've tried to activate the emergency beacon, I assume?' Professor Pike said, walking across the command centre to the console at which the technician was working.

'Yes, Professor, I've tried everything. There's just no sign of them. Could they have been . . . shot down?' the technician asked nervously.

'In any other aircraft that might have been a possibility, but there isn't an anti-aircraft system on earth that can even detect the Shroud, much less shoot it down. No, something else must have happened,' the Professor replied, peering through his battered spectacles at the display.

Nero rubbed his eyes with one hand and let out a sigh. Today was going from bad to worse. He refused, though, to give up hope just yet. It would not be the first time that both Raven and Malpense had survived such unexpected developments. He knew that he should report the situation to Number One, especially as Malpense was involved, but he also knew from past experience that reporting to Number One without a full understanding of the situation was never a good idea. No, better instead to wait until he had a much clearer idea of what had happened.

'See if you can pull up thermal imaging for the surrounding area,' the Professor instructed, and the technician proceeded to hijack and intercept any relevant data from nearby satellites. The Professor walked back over to Nero, looking worried.

'It's not good, Max. I know the Shroud was designed to

be invisible, but not to us. If it's in the air we should be able to find it,' he said quietly.

'Any theories?' Nero asked, looking tired.

'Well, the Shrouds are experimental. There could have been an equipment failure.'

Nero thought that 'equipment failure' was not a terribly accurate description of a fireball in the sky and a rain of blazing debris on the ground below. He pushed the image out of his mind.

'No, it's too much of a coincidence that something should go wrong at the precise moment that they're on final approach to Cypher's facility. Something happened and it wasn't an accident.'

'I agree,' the Professor said. 'There's only the prototype left, it's such a shame to lose equipment like that.'

Nero glared at the Professor.

'What I mean is that such potential loss of life is tragic . . . yes, that's it, terrible . . .' the Professor added hastily.

'Doctor Nero, I have something,' the technician reported, pointing at his display as Nero and the Professor hurried over to look at what he had found. The display was showing a thermal image of the area surrounding Cypher's base. The majority of the screen was filled with the deep purples and blues of the cool, quiet jungle but tearing through the middle of the area was a deep gash of orange, yellow and white.

'That's a debris field,' the Professor said quietly.

'Professor, how long until you can get the last Shroud airborne?' Nero asked quickly.

'Well, it had been mothballed when construction on the other two was completed – a couple of hours, minimum.'

'You have one hour, Professor,' Nero said coldly. 'I want a rescue team at those coordinates as soon as possible.'

The Professor nodded and hurried out of the room. Nero would not allow himself to believe the worst yet. There was still hope. Besides which, he reminded himself, if Malpense had been on the Shroud when it hit the ground he wouldn't have to worry about anything ever again. Number One would see to that.

�ù☙☙

Otto slowly opened his eyes. There was wet sand in his mouth and his aching body felt as if he'd been attacked by a giant with a meat tenderiser, but he was alive, and that in itself was nothing short of miraculous. Tentatively he pushed himself up on to all fours and, as his eyes adjusted to the darkness, he could make out faint details of his surroundings. He was on the edge of an underground pool in a large cavern. Bizarre rock formations filled the cave, their glossy, organic shapes produced by millennia of relentlessly dripping water. Otto took a couple of deep

200

breaths and tried to stand up.

'Owwww,' he moaned as he got unsteadily to his feet. His left knee was throbbing but at least his legs appeared to be capable of supporting his own weight. He suddenly realised there that was a faint light coming from an opening on the other side of the chamber. His uniform was soaked through and he felt on the brink of exhaustion but he knew that he had to keep moving. Tempting as it was to curl up in a ball here in the gloom, he was now the only one who had any chance of finding and stopping Cypher and rescuing Raven. Assuming she was still alive, of course, a nasty little voice in the back of his head reminded him.

He trudged through the wet sand surrounding the pool to the opening from which the faint illumination was coming. As he approached the light source he could make out a new sound: the thumping clangs and hisses of heavy machinery. Carefully he peered through the opening in the cave wall and was staggered by what he saw. Below was an enormous cavern filled with industrial robots and other elaborate pieces of machinery, all serving an enormous conveyer-belt-fed production line. The machinery itself was not much different from what one might expect to see in any factory manufacturing high-tech equipment, but what was far more astonishing was *what* was being manufactured.

From his vantage point he could see every stage of the manufacturing process in all of its staggering complexity. Numerous components were being fed into the mass of machinery and it wasn't until about halfway down the production line that it became obvious what the machines were assembling. There Otto could see what looked like black metallic skeletons being assembled and, as the process continued, more and more components were bolted to these frames. By the time these mysterious metallic bodies had reached the end of the production line they had taken on a sinister and unmistakeable form. Suddenly Otto understood why it was that Cypher's assassins had been able to fight Raven to a standstill on several occasions. They were robots!

Otto could not help but be impressed by the ingenuity of their design. He could not make out all of the details of their construction from his vantage point, but he could see that they represented a huge leap in technology. He was desperate to get down on to the floor of the manufacturing cavern, partly to see if he could make out any more details of the android assassins' design, and partly to see if there was anything he could do to throw a very large spanner in the works.

He looked around the cavern more carefully. There were a couple of guards patrolling the room, but they were just ordinary uniformed humans. Not only that, they both looked incredibly bored to be watching over the machinery, and Otto suspected that it would not be too difficult to sneak past them unnoticed. He could see where he wanted to go. The completed assassin droids were being carried through an opening in the cavern wall and he needed to find out where they were going.

Otto waited until both of the guards were on the other side of the cavern and climbed carefully through the opening in the cave wall. The rock wall that led down to the factory floor was steep but had plenty of good handholds, and Otto had soon reached the ground, apparently undetected. The noise of the machinery was even more deafening down here but Otto was glad of the cacophony. There was no way that anyone would hear him creeping around through that amount of background noise. All he had to do was stay out of sight.

Otto quickly surveyed his immediate surroundings. The number of different machines and control consoles that were clanking and buzzing away around him was slightly bewildering. He thought that he could see a couple of vulnerable points in the process but he needed something that would shut this place down for good as well as producing a big enough distraction to let him get further inside the base. A movement overhead caught Otto's eye and he glanced upwards and saw a huge crucible of molten metal being transported past above him.

'Perfect,' Otto whispered to himself. He quickly moved between the rows of equipment, heading for the ladder that would take him up on to the raised gantries above the production line. Otto climbed the ladder as quickly and as quietly as he could. The guards that he had spotted before were talking to each other on the opposite side of the cavern, and if they did have any clue that he was there, they were doing a very good job of hiding it. Otto hurried over to a control console at one end of the gantry that looked like it might be suitable. As he worked at the console another huge suspended cauldron of bubbling molten metal passed by and Otto could feel the heat even from a distance of twenty metres or so. As the huge bucket reached a pre-programmed point it stopped and began to tip, depositing a stream of bright yellow molten metal into a holding tank below with a hiss. Otto worked quickly, grateful that the controls had a touch-screen computerised interface which made the adjustments he was making much more straightforward. Once he was satisfied with his new modifications Otto hurried back down the ladder and stealthily made his way over to the opening in the wall through which the completed robot ninjas were passing.

The inactive robots lay flat on their backs on the conveyor belt and once again Otto could not help but admire their design. They were not wearing the black silk robes that they had been wearing when Otto had encountered them before, but they looked no less sinister. Their matt-black metallic skins had organic, flowing lines, only broken here and there by bundles of thick black cable that looked as if they functioned as the machines' muscles. The assassins' unmasked faces were featureless and smooth, save for an array of small holes on each side of the head where the eyes should be. As Otto watched the machines pass by he was extremely grateful that they had not been activated. Raven had struggled to defeat just a couple of these things in a toe-to-toe fight and the machinery in this room seemed to be producing a new one every couple of seconds. Otto's blood ran cold as he considered that fact for a moment; whatever Cypher was up to, an army of these things would represent an unstoppable force.

Otto forced himself to stop worrying about what Cypher's plans might be and to focus on what he had to do now. Checking that there was no sign of the guards, he hopped up on to the conveyor belt and lay down as it carried him through the hole in the wall.

☺☺☺

The H.I.V.E. security guard yawned. It had been a long shift and, since Francisco was the only prisoner in the brig, not a particularly exciting one. They had brought the Colonel in several hours ago and he had said nothing since, simply sat in his cell staring blankly at the opposite wall. The guard had heard rumours about what the Colonel was supposed to have done, but if he believed every rumour he'd heard while he'd been working at H.I.V.E. he'd have quit a long time ago. Usually the brig was only used for the worst and most unruly students – this was certainly the first recorded incidence of one of the teaching staff being locked up.

He heard the soft bleep of an authorised entry to the brig and turned to meet the visitor. To the guard's credit, he got his Sleeper halfway out of its holster before he was struck full in the chest by the two stun pulses that shot from the identical guns that Block and Tackle were carrying. He slumped forward on the desk, out cold.

The two students moved quickly, Block moving to cover the door while Tackle punched a series of commands into the console on the security desk. With a hiss, the bars that trapped Francisco in his cell retracted into the ceiling. The Colonel walked calmly from his cell, displaying no sign of any emotion as Tackle handed him a Sleeper.

'Phase Two has been authorised,' Tackle said flatly.

'Very well, you have your orders,' Francisco replied calmly. 'Initiate.'

chapter twelve

Raven came to and immediately wished she hadn't. She felt as if she'd been run over by a truck; every part of her body ached. Her wrists and ankles were shackled to the chair in which she was sitting and her battered body protested as she strained against the restraints. The small room was bare save for a metal table and another chair; the only illumination came from the harsh white strip lighting overhead. Automatically she began to assess her chances of escape, just as she had been trained to do. Unsurprisingly, all of her gear had been taken from her and the restraints were well designed and strong enough to resist even her most determined efforts to break free. She wasn't going anywhere.

The door to the cell hissed open and Cypher walked into the room. The black glass mask that he always wore might have concealed his face completely but he made no effort to conceal the smug, triumphant tone in his voice.

'So, Nero's pet finally wakes up,' Cypher said sarcastically. 'I was under the impression that you were supposed to be the best but it seems that my assassins got the better of you rather easily.'

'You'll burn for this, Cypher,' Raven spat back. 'You're finished. When Number One discovers what you've done he'll turn this place into a smouldering crater.'

'Oh, I don't think we're going to have to worry about that for very much longer,' Cypher replied calmly. 'Indeed, by the end of today it will be Number One who will fear me.'

'You won't be the first to try,' Raven said with a sneer, 'and you won't be the first who gets stepped on like a bug either.'

'My dear Raven,' Cypher replied coldly, 'you underestimate my determination. Number One and Nero are relics of the past. I am the future.'

'You have no future,' Raven replied. 'G.L.O.V.E. will put you down like the mad dog you are.'

'You are foolish to place so much faith in an organisation that is made up of the cream of the world's villains. If the ruling council of G.L.O.V.E. is known for anything, it is its pragmatism. After the demonstration of my power that they will all witness today, I very much doubt any of them will be inclined to oppose me.'

Raven had no idea what Cypher was hinting at and,

even though she would show this lunatic no sign of it, she was worried. Whatever he was planning, it was clearly designed to be a spectacular display of his strength. People who stopped fearing the wrath of Number One were usually insane or extremely dangerous. Secretly she feared that Cypher might be both.

'I have to admit I was impressed that you survived the explosion in Tokyo,' Cypher continued. 'Normally I would be annoyed, but in this case it gives me the undoubted pleasure of killing you twice in one day. I've been waiting to try out my latest invention, and you should make the perfect test subject.'

The door behind Cypher hissed open again and Raven's eyes widened in surprise as two of Cypher's assassins entered the room. They were not wearing the black silk robes that they had been swathed in before, and their exposed, black metallic endo-skeletons left little doubt as to their true nature.

'Machines. I should have known,' Raven said quietly.

'Oh, these aren't just machines,' Cypher replied, a note of pride in his voice. 'These are the cutting edge of robotic technology. Titanium skeleton, grade one positronic core, carbon fibre musculature, multi-layered combat programming. They are works of art. They may not be capable of much in the way of independent thought, but that is outweighed by their unquestioning loyalty.'

'Am I supposed to be impressed?' Raven said with a cold smile.

'No, but you should be flattered. They were, after all, designed to beat you in single combat. Their core combat routines have been based on an extensive study of your capabilities. The only difference between you and them is that they don't tire and they can take an assault rifle round to the head.'

Cypher looked straight at Raven, her angry face a distorted reflection in the smooth black glass.

'They render you quite . . . obsolete,' he said threateningly.

As Cypher leant over her Raven spat in his face, her saliva running down the smooth surface of his mask. Without hesitation Cypher backhanded her hard across the face, but Raven didn't even flinch, she just stared back at him, defiance in her eyes. Cypher pulled a clean white handkerchief from his pocket and wiped the trickling spit from his mask.

'Take her to the testing area,' Cypher said angrily, gesturing to the two robots who advanced towards her. 'I'm going to enjoy watching you die.'

☻☻☻

Otto lay flat on his stomach, the conveyor belt carrying him through the dimly illuminated tunnel, its destination unknown. They seemed to be travelling downwards, as the belt was on a very slight incline, but without having a better idea of the layout of the facility Otto had no way of knowing exactly where he was being taken. Suddenly Otto could make out faint sounds of machinery coming from somewhere up ahead. He lifted his head to peer along the length of the belt in front of him and could just make out a more brightly lit opening towards which the belt was travelling. As the belt moved him inexorably towards the light Otto could see that a pair of large yellow robotic claws were lifting the robots from the end of the belt and carrying them out of sight. As Otto neared the end of the belt he rolled off it and slowly snuck forward to see what lay in this new room.

The claws were lifting the robots from the end of the belt with clockwork precision, hoisting them into the air before swivelling away and positioning the inactive assassins in neatly ordered rows within the vast hangar-like space. There were hundreds, perhaps thousands of the mechanical killers arranged in perfect lines that stretched off in all directions. Otto's blood ran cold at the sight. Cypher was not just assembling a security or special operations force. This was an army. Having seen what these things were capable of in small numbers Otto knew that with an army of them Cypher would be almost unstoppable.

Otto hopped down from the opening and on to the

hangar floor. The assassins were clearly all deactivated at the moment and he decided that it would be best to find an exit while that was still the case. He had just started to move towards the other side of the room when he suddenly heard voices. Quickly Otto ducked into the long rows of motionless robots, using their massed ranks as cover. Otto could not see who was talking as the voices drew nearer but he could hear their conversation clearly.

'They're ready for final loadout,' the first voice said.

'I wish they'd given us a bit more notice,' the second voice complained.

'Everything *is* ready, isn't it?' the first man asked, a slight note of panic in his voice.

'Yeah, I think so. We'll have to skip a couple of the final checks but otherwise we're good to go.'

'OK, let's fire them up, then,' the first man said, exhaling loudly.

There was a low hum and suddenly the heads of all the robots in the front row snapped upright, each assassin turning as one on the spot and then proceeding to march to the far end of the room, all in perfect step with one another. As they turned Otto could see that the tiny holes in the sides of their faces were now lit up with a blood-red glow. Otto guessed that they must be sensory arrays, but these spider-like eye clusters did nothing to improve their sinister appearance.

As the first row filed out of the hangar the second row snapped to attention and proceeded to follow them to the exit. Otto realised that if they kept moving at this rate he'd run out of hiding places very quickly. He crept backwards, trying to put more rows of the ever-dwindling robot army between him and the voices he had heard previously. Otto looked around desperately for somewhere else to hide but there were no immediately obvious options. There were now only a couple of rows of the neatly ordered assassins still in front of him. He had nowhere to run.

☻☻☻

Back in the fabrication cavern the console controlling the alloy delivery system beeped once. The giant crucible full of boiling molten metal tipped as it had done countless times before, but as the glowing yellow torrent poured from the lip of the cauldron it began to move. Otto had not had much time with the console so his reprogramming had been quick and dirty – there had been little time for elegance. The crucible began to move along the length of the production line, molten metal pouring on to the delicate machinery below, destroying it completely in a shower of sparks and flame. At first the automated production system tried to keep functioning but, as pressures started to build and more and more parts of the system reported catastrophic failures, the system began to overload. There were a couple of loud bangs and then something somewhere within the ranks of heavy machinery decided that it had had enough and exploded with enough force to shake the entire cavern . . .

�552�552�552

Otto felt the hangar floor move and heard the muffled sound of a distant explosion.

'What the hell was that?' one of the voices at the front of the hangar said.

Suddenly a huge ball of fire bloomed from the opening through which the conveyor belt fed the recently manufactured droids. The shockwave knocked Otto to the ground and toppled a couple of the still-inactive assassins. They fell like statues, ramrod straight, just so much scrap metal until they were activated. There was the sound of another explosion in the distance and another jet of flame shot from the opening leading to the manufacturing cavern.

'Let's get out of here,' one of the voices shouted and Otto could just make out the sound of running footsteps receding into the distance. As he peered around the last row of inactive robots he could see two men in white coats running towards the hangar exit.

Otto smiled to himself as another distant explosion

shook dust from the ceiling. That was what he called throwing a spanner in the works. Suddenly a much closer and more violent explosion sent a girder tumbling down from high overhead. It smashed down on to the row of assassins just a couple of feet in front of Otto with an enormous crash. As Otto picked himself up and brushed the dust and debris from his uniform he wondered if maybe there was such a thing as a spanner that was just a little too big. He ran for the exit.

☢ ☢ ☢

Cypher stood on a gantry looking down into the feature-less concrete pit below. Raven stood in the centre of the pit twenty metres below him, staring straight back at him.

'You're certain,' Cypher said to the frightened-looking technician who stood just a few feet away.

'I'm afraid so, sir. Whoever has sabotaged the manu-facturing facility did an exceptionally efficient job of it. There's no chance of containing the fire and if it continues to spread at its current rate it will reach the fuel cells in just a few minutes.'

'It would appear that G.L.O.V.E. has responded more quickly than I expected,' Cypher replied thoughtfully, 'though I am impressed that their saboteurs got in unde-tected.'

'We've reviewed the security logs,' the technician

215

reported. 'There's no sign of a team entering the facility, but with G.L.O.V.E. commandos that doesn't mean that they're not here.'

Cypher nodded. 'How far along is the load-out of the Kraken?' he asked, glancing back down at Raven in the pit.

'Seventy-five per cent of our forces have been loaded,' the technician replied, looking around nervously as the distant rumble of another explosion sent an unnerving tremor through the gantry.

'That will be sufficient. Order a full evacuation and prepare the Kraken to disembark. Such a shame,' Cypher said with a sigh. 'I had been looking forward to this.' He gestured at Raven. He picked up the roll of black silk that was leaning against the gantry rail beside him.

'Raven, my dear,' Cypher said, looking down into the pit, 'I'm afraid that I really have to go. It's unfortunate that I'll have to miss the show, but I thought that you at least deserved the chance to go out fighting.'

With that Cypher tossed the roll of black silk into the pit below. Raven stepped forward and carefully unrolled the silk. Inside were her twin swords. She quickly scooped up the weapons and looked up at the gantry far overhead.

'This isn't over, Cypher,' Raven yelled defiantly.

'Oh, I rather think it is,' Cypher replied and pressed a switch on a control panel mounted on the gantry rail.

There was a low grinding rumble as a three-metre-square area of the pit's floor dropped away and slid aside. With a sudden hiss white vapour shot up from the hole and a dark shape rose up through the opening. The robot that stood on the raising platform was huge – at least twelve feet tall and seemingly almost as wide. It was covered in the same matt-black armour as the smaller robots, but that was where any similarity ended. If the assassin droids were a stiletto blade sliding unnoticed between the joins of an opponent's armour, this machine was a sledgehammer, designed to crush its enemies without mercy.

Cypher hit another button up on the gantry and with a low growl the sensory arrays in the behemoth's face plate lit up with a dull red glow.

'Kill her,' Cypher said, 'slowly.'

'Command acknowledged,' the robot replied in a low, growling synthesised voice.

Cypher took one last look down into the pit as the huge machine advanced on Raven and then turned and walked away down the gantry.

☻☻☻

'All crew members, preparation for phase two launch complete. Final embarkation authorised. Please proceed to duty stations,' the voice blared from the tannoy.

Otto pressed himself into the shadows of a recessed doorway as a group of worried-looking technicians ran past. He stayed well out of sight – clearly Cypher's personnel were in the final stages of preparation for something, but he doubted that they were distracted enough to ignore the presence of a thirteen-year-old boy. Fortunately most of the facility seemed to be deserted – whatever was going on was obviously important. Otto walked past a short side corridor and stopped. At the end of the corridor was a balcony that opened on to another vast cavern but what had really caught Otto's attention was the sound he could hear coming from the corridor: it was the sound of the sea, waves crashing against rocks. Otto moved cautiously down the corridor and peered out over the edge of the balcony.

The cavern had obviously been a large sea-cave originally but now it had been converted to work as a docking facility. A huge concrete jetty had been constructed along one wall and electro-magnetic crane rigs mounted on the ceiling were lifting containers from the jetty and lowering them into the belly of the bizarre ship that was docked there. The ship was the size of a modern missile cruiser but its sleek, flowing, almost organic lines suggested that it was significantly more advanced than any normal naval warship. Its black metallic skin seemed to soak up the illumination from the huge floodlights overhead, just like the skin of the Shroud had done, and Otto realised that there was a good chance that they were both coated with the same material. Until recently Cypher had had access to all of the technical resources that any senior member of G.L.O.V.E. did and Otto supposed that the material coating this ship and H.I.V.E.'s stealth transports may well be exactly the same. Arranged around the rear third of the ship's deck were half a dozen turrets, each mounted with a very serious-looking launcher tube. Technicians were swarming all over the ship's deck, checking systems and stowing equipment, apparently making final preparations for the ship to get underway.

Otto's attention was drawn by movement on the super-structure of the ship as several figures walked out on to a platform that overlooked the deck. He felt a sudden hot flash of anger as he recognised the figure at the head of the group, Cypher. Suddenly Otto flashed back to the events of the rooftop in Tokyo, the pain that Cypher had caused him and the debt that he owed Wing.

He had to get on board that ship.

☻☻☻

Raven dived to her left. The massive robot was unbeliev-ably fast for its size but fortunately not quite as agile as its more normal-sized counterpart. A fist the size of a wrecking ball smashed into the concrete wall of the pit, leaving a small crater where Raven's head had been just moments before. Raven counterattacked, swinging her blades at one of the exposed bunches of muscle cables on the back of the behemoth's leg. Her katanas had been made and maintained by some of the finest weaponsmiths in the world but they glanced off the cables like a butter knife off a brick. She moved quickly away from the robot as it swivelled to face her, trying desperately to stay out of its reach. Raven knew that she could not win this fight; the machine she was fighting had as much armour plating as a tank and it would take more than agility and fancy swordplay to bring it down.

Suddenly there was another explosion from somewhere much nearer by, and the floor rocked as debris fell from overhead, catching Raven slightly off-balance. The giant robot seized on the opportunity, moving with impossible speed towards her, one of its huge fists swinging at her. Raven's years of training were all that saved her. She twisted away from the blow, rolling with it and avoiding as much of the direct impact as she could. The strike still sent her flying across the pit, sliding to a halt against the far wall. She shook her head, trying desperately to clear the flashing lights that suddenly filled her field of vision. She could not afford to let the thing land another blow like that.

The second explosion that suddenly rocked the room

was the closest yet; it sounded to Raven like an ammunition store exploding. The whole room shook, and large chunks of rock fell from the ceiling, one glancing off the robot's heavily armoured head with a dull clang. The robot fell to one knee, the lights of the sensory array on its face dimming and flickering for just a second before it slowly got to its feet. It moved relentlessly back across the pit towards Raven, who knew that if the fight continued like this that she would be defeated by exhaustion. She could only keep dancing around avoiding the thing for so long before it got lucky, and judging by the fact that she still felt slightly stunned from the glancing blow it had landed moments earlier, it would only take one good punch from it and she wouldn't be getting up again.

Raven heard a metallic creak from overhead and saw a shower of dust fall from one of the large steel pins that fixed the observation gantry overhead to the ceiling. She moved carefully around the edge of the pit, trying always to keep her opponent centred in the room, waiting for her chance.

The next explosion shook the entire room, and Raven lost her footing, falling to her knees. The assassin robot could not capitalise on her loss of balance, though, as it too struggled to stay upright. There was a screech of tearing metal from overhead as the steel structure of the observation gantry final gave up its grip on the rock ceiling and one end dropped downwards into the pit. Raven dived to avoid the shower of debris but her opponent was not so lucky. The end of the gantry swung downwards and slammed into the robot, smashing it to the ground, where it lay still, pinned under the end of the heavy metal walkway. Raven let out a long slow breath and looked upwards. The other end of the gantry was still in place twenty metres overhead; its supports had not quite given out yet. She slid her swords into her belt and ran towards the dangling gantry, hopping over the still form of the giant robot assassin and scaling the remains of the walkway as fast as she could.

She was about halfway up when she felt the whole gantry move again. Glancing downwards she saw that her opponent was starting to move, slowly at first, forcing itself on to all fours, lifting the end of the gantry as it rose. Raven climbed faster; the top of the improvised ladder she was scaling was only a few metres away now. Below her the robot finally struggled to its feet, the end of the gantry sliding off its back and slamming into the floor with a deafening clang. Raven just managed to hang on as the gantry shifted. One of the two remaining pins that was holding the upper end of the walkway in place gave way with a deafening crack and the whole gantry pivoted, leaving Raven dangling precariously over the long drop to the pit below.

The giant robot looked up and saw its prey dangling tantalisingly out of reach. It stooped down and picked up the lower end of the gantry with both hands and shook the entire walkway. Raven clung on for dear life as the machine tried to shake her loose, but it was like trying to hang on to a rodeo bull. The gantry's last remaining support gave an ominous crunch and Raven made one last desperate lunge, swinging towards the lip of the doorway carved into the rock wall. The fingers of one hand found the edge of the opening and she latched on to the solid rock as the abused gantry finally gave up its fight with gravity and toppled downwards into the pit with an enormous crash.

Raven pulled herself up into the doorway and looked back down into the pit. Far below the robot was still moving, struggling to free itself from the pile of twisted metal that was all that remained of the viewing gantry. She could not help but be impressed as it slowly rose to its feet, pushing the debris aside, and looked up at her. It would take a tank to stop one of these things, she thought to herself, and she realised with a slight shudder that it was unlikely that Cypher would have abandoned the machine if it was the only one he'd built . . .

There was the rumble of another explosion nearby and Raven knew that she had to get moving. She turned and ran silently down the corridor beyond the doorway. Far below, in the pit, the giant mechanical assassin strode through the scattered debris towards the wall, and looked up at the doorway overhead. It slammed its hand into the wall with a crunch, crushing the rock until it had a solid hold, and slowly but surely it began to climb.

☻ ☻ ☻

Otto snuck closer to the dock, taking cover behind one of the piles of crates that littered the loading area. The gangway leading up to the deck of Cypher's ship was thirty metres away but it might as well have been thirty miles due to the two robotic assassins that guarded the ramp. There was no way that he was getting on board past them – he would have to find another way. He looked around desperately; he was running out of time and ideas.

Suddenly the two guards turned as one and hurried up the ramp to the ship as the gangway started to retract, sliding back into the ship's superstructure. A klaxon began to sound and the huge steel sea doors at the far end of the cavern slowly slid aside with a low rumble. Otto could just make out the first dim light of dawn outside as the steel cables that had tied the ship to the dock released from their mounts and reeled in. As the ship began to move Otto realised that he had to act now. He stood up and prepared himself to run across the dock, but before he could move he felt a hand close over his mouth.

'Don't be stupid, there's no way on board now,' Raven whispered, her mouth just centimetres from his ear. She removed her hand from his mouth and Otto turned to face her.

'I thought you were dead,' Otto said, relief mixed with disbelief.

'You know, I'm getting really tired of hearing that today,' Raven replied with a thin smile.

'Cypher's on that ship,' Otto said quickly. 'We have to get on board.'

'I know, but unless you've acquired the power of flight while I was away that's not going to be possible,' Raven answered. Otto knew that she was right. There was no way to scale the smooth hull of the ship even if they did manage to get near to it. He suddenly felt an over-whelming sense of frustration.

'I'm not letting him get away,' Otto said angrily. 'We have a score to settle.'

Raven looked Otto straight in the eye.

'I know how you feel, Otto, I really do, but this isn't the way.'

Otto slammed his fist into the metal container in frustration. They'd come so close and now Cypher was slipping through their fingers again. The huge ship continued to move away from the dock, gathering speed as it passed through the sea doors and into the grey light of dawn. Once the stern of the ship passed through the gates they rumbled closed again, sealing the docks.

'Getting out of here is the first priority,' Raven said, scanning the docks for any sign of an escape route. Suddenly the biggest explosion yet shook the entire cavern. Huge chunks of rock fell from the ceiling, smashing into the docks and hitting the water like cannonballs. Otto and Raven struggled to maintain their balance as the whole cavern rocked.

'Cypher must have activated the self-destruct sequence,' Raven said quickly.

'Erm . . . actually . . . that was me,' Otto said, his cheeks burning. Sabotaging the robot production line had seemed like a good idea at the time but he realised now that it might have had rather more severe consequences than he had intended.

'Oh, for goodness' sake,' Raven said with a sigh, 'I leave you alone for a couple of hours . . .'

Suddenly there was an enormous crash from behind them and they both turned to see the giant robot assassin from the pit tearing through a pair of large steel doors that led out on to the dock. It tore the heavy gauge steel like it was tissue paper, forcing its way through.

'What the hell is that?' Otto said with a gasp.

'Trouble,' Raven replied, pulling her swords from her belt. 'Get to cover.'

Raven stepped out from their hiding place, raising her swords in a defensive stance.

'Hey, ugly!' she shouted, and the robot's head swivelled to lock on to her position. The red lights of its sensory array seemed to flare for a moment and it advanced towards her.

Otto backed further into the shadows. He wasn't foolish enough to think that he could offer Raven any meaningful assistance in this situation and so he looked around for anything that might help them in the fight. He looked up at the equipment suspended from the cavern's ceiling and smiled. He suddenly knew what he had to do.

Raven braced herself as the monstrous machine approached. Its black metallic skin was scored and dented from the shower of debris in the pit but it didn't seem to have slowed down in the slightest. Raven backed up as the robot advanced. She knew that she had to keep her distance from the thing – there may be more room to move on the docks, but she couldn't keep up this game of cat and mouse for ever. Raven stopped as she felt the rock wall at her back. The robot was still advancing and she realised with a cold chill that she was out of ideas. Suddenly she caught sight of something big moving behind the assassin and her eyes widened.

Raven dived to one side as the enormous shipping container mounted on the electro-magnetic loading rig slammed into the robot from behind like a freight train, crushing it against the rock wall with an enormous crash. Fifty metres away, at the crane controls, Otto gave a little yell of victory. Raven picked herself up from the floor and dusted herself off. She inspected the shattered remains of the robot, crushed between the massive container and the unforgiving rock wall. There was no way it was getting up from that.

Otto ran over to the scene of destruction, a broad grin on his face, and surveyed the sparking, twitching remains of the huge robot.

'Nice work,' Raven said as another explosion shook the cavern, 'but we still don't have a way out of here.'

Otto's smile faded as he realised she was right. They were still trapped as Cypher's base disintegrated around them. Suddenly there was a horribly familiar bleeping sound from the twisted remains of the robot. Otto and Raven's heads both snapped round and immediately saw the large silver canister that was protruding from the wreckage, a flashing light at one end.

Raven moved faster than Otto had ever seen anyone move before. She snatched the foot-long canister from the wreckage, yanking it free from the tangled metal, still beeping. She hurled the canister in a looping arc towards the sea doors and threw herself on top of Otto, knocking him to the ground. The explosion tore the heavy sea doors apart, the shockwave making Otto's ears ring like church bells.

As the smoke cloud from the blast cleared Otto sat up and surveyed the wreckage. One of the sea doors was gone completely and the other was just twisted scrap metal. They had their exit.

'Feel like a swim?' Raven said with a grin as she offered Otto her hand and pulled him to his feet.

chapter thirteen

The H.I.V.E. security guard walked into the detention area and gasped. The man who had been assigned to the brig lay slumped across the guard station, still breathing but unconscious. He ran to his fallen comrade and shook his shoulder. There was no response. The guard had seen the effects of Sleeper pulses often enough to recognise the effects immediately. He ran over to the cells and realised to his horror that they were all empty. Pulling his Blackbox from his belt he spoke quickly into it.

'This is Guard Jackson in the detention centre. We have a Class One security alert. Colonel Francisco has escaped.'

☢☢☢

Shelby woke with a start. She'd been dreaming about Wing again. They'd been on a tiny rowing boat in the middle of the ocean and Wing had fallen over the side.

She'd dived in after him, but had not been able to find him. Then she'd resurfaced to find that the boat had gone and she was left all alone adrift in the middle of a cold, dark ocean. She shivered as she recalled the terrible feeling of loneliness, surrounded by all that freezing black water.

As she rubbed her eyes she realised that there was a soft bleeping coming from her Blackbox and that this must have been what woke her. She picked up the PDA and touched the screen to accept the call.

'Good morning, student Trinity,' H.I.V.E.mind said in the emotionless monotone that had become depressingly familiar. 'There has been a security alert and Doctor Nero has requested that you and student Brand report to situation room three immediately.'

'Umm . . . OK . . . situation room three,' Shelby said, still only half awake. The Blackbox disconnected and Shelby walked over to Laura's bed. She gently shook her friend's shoulder until Laura finally woke up with a low groan.

'What time is it?' Laura asked croakily, looking up at Shelby.

'Just after 5 a.m.,' Shelby replied. 'Nero wants to see us. There's some kind of security alert.'

Laura suddenly looked more awake. 'Did he say what was wrong?' she asked.

231

'No, it was H.I.V.E.mind that called, and he doesn't seem to be keen on long conversations these days,' Shelby replied. 'Whatever it was it sounded urgent.'

Laura knew what Shelby meant about H.I.V.E.mind. There was still no sign of the AI's old personality; whatever had been done to him after their failed escape attempt a few months ago had clearly erased any trace of his previous independence.

'Well, then,' Laura said, sitting up and putting her feet down on to the cold floor, 'we'd better get a move on.'

☻☻☻

Otto was cold and miserable. He sat huddled on a rock near to the cliff-face entrance to Cypher's hidden dock that was still belching out thick black smoke. The thin dawn rays of the sun did little to warm him or to dry out his cold, damp uniform. Raven stood nearby, scanning the horizon as she had been for the past hour. Otto looked over his shoulder at the sheer rock face behind them. He suspected that Raven might have been able to pick her way upwards through the jagged black rock, but he was no mountaineer. Swimming further along the coastline seemed impossible, too; there was no visible break in the rock wall in either direction and the way in which the waves smashed violently against the base of the cliff suggested that he'd need to feel a little less exhausted if he was going to stand any chance of making it more than a few metres. Otto appreciated the irony of the fact that they had both made it out of Cypher's base in one piece only to find themselves trapped by mother nature.

'Keep rubbing your arms and legs,' Raven said with a look of concern. 'The last thing I need is you coming down with hypothermia.'

Raven for her part looked as if she'd just woken up from a good night's sleep. If the cold was bothering her she was showing no signs of it. The wind suddenly picked up and Otto hugged himself more tightly, trying to retain what little warmth was left in his body.

'About time, too,' Raven said, and Otto looked at her quizzically. She was looking straight up and as Otto followed suit it took his exhausted brain a moment to make sense of what he was seeing. A dozen metres above them a figure was standing in midair surrounded by a bright light.

There was a shimmer in the air and the rest of the Shroud suddenly became visible as a cable and harness dropped from the rear hatch.

'Need a lift?' the pilot's voice asked over the aircraft's external loudspeaker.

☣☣☣

Nero was furious. The expression on his face as he looked

down at the cowering security chief was enough to freeze the blood. The other operatives in the command centre were focused on their own tasks, desperate to avoid doing anything that might attract Nero's attention.

'Correct me if I'm wrong, Mr Lewis, but I believe you once described the brig as escape-proof.' There was ice in his voice.

'Yes, sir. I don't know what happened, we lost all of the camera feeds from the brig just before Francisco escaped. Somebody must have helped him, but I have no idea how they got into the brig itself. That area is cleared for authorised and senior personnel only.'

'Neither of which describe Mr Block or Mr Tackle, so would you care to explain to me how they managed to get into the detention area?' Nero was losing patience. Somebody was threatening his school and he was not going to stand for it.

'I don't know,' the Chief replied weakly.

'I am rather tired of hearing that, Mr Lewis,' Nero said, glaring at the Chief. 'H.I.V.E.mind, do you have any record of any interference with either the brig security network or your own systems that might explain this?'

'There is no record of any access to any of my systems that might explain this aberration,' H.I.V.E.mind replied quickly, his hovering blue head projected into the air a few inches above a nearby console.

'It is reasonable to assume, therefore, that someone has actively erased those records,' Nero said impatiently.

'That is a logical assumption,' H.I.V.E.mind replied.

'Professor,' Nero said, turning to face Professor Pike, 'could Mr Block or Mr Tackle have been given sufficient access to H.I.V.E.mind's data core to wipe those recordings?'

'No, it's impossible. Only you and I have that level of access to the data core. Even if Francisco had given them his own access codes earlier he did not have clearance to carry out a data purge like that. Besides which, I disabled all of his access clearances when he was captured. It's just not possible.'

Nero stared at the impassive face of H.I.V.E.mind. Somebody had gone to a great deal of trouble to make sure that the AI would not be able to give them any details of what had happened and to ensure that Francisco would escape undetected. It was strange to think that for H.I.V.E.mind it was as if the events had never happened.

The Contessa walked into the command centre, looking pleased.

'I've just received word from the Shroud that was despatched to Cypher's facility. They have found Raven and Malpense alive,' she reported quickly.

Nero felt a sense of overwhelming relief. At last something had gone their way.

'And Cypher?' he asked.

'Gone. His base has been destroyed, but he escaped. G.L.O.V.E. surveillance systems are trying to establish his location as we speak, but the ship he was aboard has vanished.'

'Vanished?' Nero said. 'How is that possible?' Nothing, least of all something the size of an ocean-going vessel should have been able to evade the G.L.O.V.E. surveillance grid.

'It seems that Cypher may have "borrowed" some of Professor Pike's research,' the Contessa replied. 'According to Raven the ship may share the stealth capabilities of the Shroud.'

'In other words it's invisible, just a hole in the ocean,' Nero replied, feeling frustration building again.

'It would appear so, yes,' the Contessa replied. 'The Shroud is returning to H.I.V.E. now, but Raven fears that H.I.V.E. may be Cypher's next target.'

'Attack the island?' the Professor snorted. 'I'd like to see him try.'

Nero nodded. H.I.V.E.'s external defence systems were designed to withstand an air and sea assault by national armed forces – one ship would have no chance.

'I share your faith in H.I.V.E.'s defences, Professor, but if there is one thing I have learnt over the past twenty-four hours it is to never underestimate what Cypher is capable of. Place all security forces on full alert and make sure that the island's defence grid is active.'

If it was a fight that Cypher wanted, that was exactly what he was going to get.

☻☻☻

Laura and Shelby walked down the corridor towards the situation room. The school was quiet; it was still much too early for the majority of students or staff to be up and about.

'I wonder what's going on?' Shelby said.

'I don't know,' Laura replied, 'but I suppose we're about to find out.'

The door to the situation room hissed open and the two girls walked inside. Shelby gasped as she saw who was sitting at the far end of the long conference table.

'Francisco!' Laura said as an evil grin spread across the Colonel's face.

Shelby turned to run back through the door but found the way obstructed by Block and Tackle, both of them pointing Sleepers straight at her. Shelby backed away from them slowly as they entered the room, Block keeping them covered while Tackle locked the door from the inside.

'It's so nice to see you both again, ladies,' the Colonel said, 'but this time you're coming with me.'

☻☻☻

Nero scanned the reports from the security department. There were, as yet, no leads on where Francisco had gone with his two errant pupils and little progress in determining how they'd managed to get out of the detention centre without being detected. H.I.V.E.mind was performing multiple low-level sweeps of the school but so far with little success. He had an uncomfortable feeling of waiting for the inevitable.

Nero's office entry chime sounded and he looked up from the frustratingly vague reports that filled the monitor on his desk.

'Enter,' Nero barked impatiently, and the Contessa walked into the room. She wore a worried expression as she hurried over to Nero's desk.

'Max, I'm afraid I have some rather disturbing news,' she said quietly.

'What now?' Nero snapped, his impatience clear.

'Well, H.I.V.E.mind is continuing the security sweeps as ordered but the student headcount is wrong.'

'Meaning?' Nero asked, raising an eyebrow.

'It appears that students Brand and Trinity are missing,' the Contessa said.

Nero slammed his fist down on his desk angrily.

'What in the name of all that's evil is going on?' he

shouted.

'Well, that's what the Professor and I have been trying to work out,' the Contessa continued. 'We've been trying to see how somebody could have got around the security system so easily, and the conclusion we've reached is rather disturbing.'

'What is it?' Nero said impatiently.

'It's H.I.V.E.mind,' the Contessa said quietly. 'It appears that he may have been lying to us about the security logs.'

'You're certain?' Nero said, cold anger in his eyes.

'I'm afraid so. It appears that H.I.V.E.mind's personality was not as fully erased as we believed,' the Contessa replied.

Nero felt a chill run down his spine. H.I.V.E.mind couldn't lie; at least, that was the theory. One of the main reasons that the security and logistical running of the base had been handed over to the AI was because it was supposedly incapable of deceit – totally incorruptible. The only conclusion one could possibly reach was that H.I.V.E.mind's rebellious personality had reasserted itself somehow and that the machine had been involved in this plot from the start. Nero realised that it was time to shut it down for good.

'What does the Professor suggest that we do about it?' Nero replied quietly. He knew that H.I.V.E.mind should not be able to hear them in his private office without being specifically summoned – that had been one feature of his system about which Nero had been most insistent.

'Well, first we need to switch the school's defence systems over to full manual control; if H.I.V.E.mind is indeed working against us it would seem prudent. Especially if an attack is imminent.'

Nero nodded and began to tap a series of commands into the keyboard in front of him. After the incident with the plant monster earlier that year Nero had ordered that all security and defence systems were capable of functioning while H.I.V.E.mind was offline. The school would not be left defenceless again.

'I suggest that only you and I have command authorisation,' the Contessa continued.

'Agreed,' Nero replied. Given the events of the past couple of days the fewer people who could control the school's security the better.

'There, that should isolate the defence and security systems. Only you and I will have command authorisation,' Nero said with a sigh. He felt tired, he hadn't slept in nearly forty-eight hours.

'Thank you, Max. That's all I need,' the Contessa said quietly. There was something odd in her tone that made Nero look up from the monitor. His eyes widened in horror as he saw the pistol in her hand that was pointing straight at him. It was not a Sleeper.

'You!' Nero hissed, suddenly realising the true depth of the betrayal with which he was being confronted.

'Yes, Max . . . me.' The Contessa did not show any sign of emotion.

Nero glanced at the console on his desk.

'Don't even think about it, Max,' the Contessa said calmly. 'Back away from the desk.'

'Why, Maria? I trusted you,' Nero said as the Contessa swivelled the display on the desk and glanced at it, all the while keeping the gun trained on him. She smiled slightly as she saw that Nero had made all of the changes that she needed to the security and defence systems. She pulled a slim silver device from her pocket and attached it to one of the console's data ports.

'Like I said, Max, everyone has their price.'

'I expected more from you, Maria,' Nero replied. 'I didn't think Cypher would be able to buy someone like you so cheaply.'

'Oh, I wasn't cheap,' the Contessa replied with a smile. 'When this is all over Cypher's promised me a continent. I'm not sure which one to choose at the moment, but I'll worry about that later.'

'You can't trust him. What do you think will happen when this is all over, when he doesn't need you any more?'

'Oh, Max, you really don't understand, do you? The world has moved on. There's no more room for people like you, old-school villains with their twisted sense of ethics. This is the twenty-first century, a new world, one which has no place for a relic of the past like this school, or even G.L.O.V.E. Times have changed, Max, and if you refuse to change with them you get left behind.'

'How long have you been working for him?' Nero asked softly.

'Long enough,' the Contessa replied. 'Suffice to say that this has all been planned quite carefully.'

'And Francisco?' Nero asked, although he suspected that he now knew exactly what had happened.

'Francisco is a weak-minded fool. That's the problem with military men; they're so used to taking orders that they find it almost impossible to resist when I tell them what to do. Maybe there is some shred of the Colonel somewhere inside his head that has been trying to resist doing what I've told him. Frankly it doesn't matter. The same goes for the two students, Block and Tackle. They're just doing what they're told. You shouldn't blame them, they really have no say in the matter. When I realised that Ms Brand had intercepted my transmission I staged the Colonel's capture, helping to subdue him in the process and thereby putting myself above suspicion.'

Nero may have never really understood how the Contessa's unique ability to command others worked but he had seen enough evidence over the years to know that she was more than capable of doing what she described. He had often wondered what it would be like to have those powers working against you, and now he knew.

'I take it that you were responsible for the loss of the Shroud over Cypher's base too,' Nero said, feeling a cold fury building inside him.

'Let's just say that the pilot's last-minute briefing included some new instructions,' the Contessa said with an evil smile, 'though it appears that Malpense and Raven have nearly as many lives as Ms Leon.'

'Do you know how many people have died because of what you've done?' Nero asked, struggling to keep his anger in check now.

'You'll forgive me if I find it hard to take a lecture in morals from a man who runs a school for super-villains,' the Contessa replied. 'You're a dinosaur, Max, the real world has no place for people like you any more.'

'We shall see if Number One agrees,' Nero snapped. 'I think you'll find that he takes rather a dim view of traitors.'

'Oh, we shan't have to worry about Number One for very much longer,' the Contessa replied calmly. 'Cypher will take care of that.'

'What do you mean?' Nero asked, with rising anxiety.

'You'll see,' the Contessa smiled.

'You're insane,' Nero said, taking a single step towards the Contessa.

'Stop right there, Max. Cypher wants you alive, and I have no particular desire to hurt you, but you know me well enough to know that I'll kill you if I have to.'

'I don't know you,' Nero replied. 'I thought I did, but clearly I was mistaken.'

'Clearly,' the Contessa said with a slight smile, 'and now you're coming with me. We have an appointment to keep.'

'I'm not going anywhere; shoot me if you have to.' Nero suddenly wondered why she did not simply command him to do what she wanted, just as she had done with Francisco and her other unwitting slaves. He had long suspected that her powers may not work on a strong-willed victim who actively defied her and this seemed to suggest he was right.

'Defiant to the last, as ever,' the Contessa said. 'So let me put it another way. Come with me or Brand and Trinity die, slowly and painfully.'

Nero felt a cold knot form in his stomach. Given everything else that the Contessa appeared to have done he knew that she would not hesitate to take two more students' lives. For now, she had the upper hand. The Contessa gestured towards the door with the barrel of her gun and Nero silently walked out ahead of her.

Professor Pike took off his glasses and rubbed at his tired, sore eyes. The longer he stared at the lines of code that scrolled past on the monitor in front of him the more confused he got. The recording of the security feed from the detention area was gone, or at least that was what he was supposed to think. Somebody had gone to a great deal of trouble to cover their tracks but the evidence showed that whoever was responsible had not deactivated the security system, which would have attracted too much attention, but simply diverted the recordings in question to a hidden storage area. That presented two problems: first, where had they hidden the recordings and second, how had they got around the multiple layers of supposedly impregnable security that surrounded H.I.V.E.mind's core. H.I.V.E.mind had not been lying when he had said that as far as he was concerned there were no security recordings. Whoever had done this had hacked the system in such a way that even the AI had been unaware of it. The problem was that the Professor had created the encryption protecting H.I.V.E.mind's core himself and he knew it just wasn't possible that a hacker, no matter how good, could have got around it.

Suddenly something caught his eye.

'H.I.V.E.mind,' the Professor said wearily.

'Yes, Professor. How may I assist you?' the AI replied, its hovering blue wire frame face appearing in the air next to the terminal.

'Please display all records of access to your core via this terminal,' the Professor commanded. Moments later a list of dates and time scrolled past. At first there didn't appear to be anything unusual, but then one particular entry leapt out at him.

'H.I.V.E.mind, please confirm entry number 4376,' the Professor said, feeling a growing sense of unease.

'Entry 4376,' H.I.V.E.mind responded. 'Access to central core granted to Professor William Pike.'

The Professor may have given his students and fellow staff the appearance of being slightly absent-minded but he knew for a fact that he had not accessed the core at the time listed.

'Show activity log for that session, please, H.I.V.E.mind,' the Professor said quickly.

The screen filled with more entries and the Professor picked through the data. Someone had logged into H.I.V.E.mind's core using his personal login and set up a hidden archive deep within the hidden layers of H.I.V.E.mind's base operating system. The question was who. The Professor quickly found the archive, now that he knew where to look, and found dozens of files. He soon came across encryption routines, secret transmission codes, and most importantly, a long list of archived security feeds. He scanned the list of recordings and one in particular caught his eye. It was the recording from the camera mounted high on the wall of that very room at the precise time that the hidden archive was set up. He quickly pulled up the file and played it. Now he would find out who was responsible for all of this.

'That's impossible,' the Professor whispered as he watched the recording. Sat there at the terminal on the screen was the last person on earth he'd expected to see.

Himself.

He struggled to make sense of what he was seeing. He knew with certainty that he had not been using the terminal at the time in question, let alone setting up a hidden archive within the core. He could not deny the evidence of his own eyes, though – there he was, busily working away at the terminal, creating an artificial blind spot in the security system. He looked through the list of hidden security recordings and spotted another leading up to the time of this baffling entry.

'H.I.V.E.mind, please run backwards through all surveillance recordings within this archive leading up to the time of my access,' the Professor said quickly.

The feed changed to show the Professor walking backwards away from the entrance to H.I.V.E.mind's central hub and then back along several corridors.

'Freeze it there,' the Professor shouted as another figure entered the picture. 'Playback.'

There was no audio but the Professor did not need it. He watched as the Contessa leant in close to him and whispered something into his ear.

'Oh my God,' the Professor said, and ran from the room.

☻☻☻

Nero walked down the corridor a few paces ahead of the Contessa. She no longer had the gun pointed at him; it would only attract unwelcome attention, and she knew that she would not need it as long as she had Laura and Shelby to use as bargaining chips. If there was one weakness from which Nero suffered it was the fact that he would never do anything willingly to jeopardise the lives of his students.

Suddenly a security patrol came round the corner ahead of them. They were clearly still searching for Francisco, judging by the grim no-nonsense expressions on the guards' faces.

'Say nothing,' the Contessa whispered as the patrol approached. 'You know what will happen if you do.'

As the patrol drew closer the squad leader nodded courteously to Nero, who returned the gesture silently. Nero noticed that the guards were carrying assault rifles as well as the standard-issue Sleepers. Security Chief Lewis was obviously taking no chances, a wise precaution where Francisco was concerned. Of course what the Chief did not know was that Francisco was really nothing more than an unwitting pawn in this scheme and that the real culprit behind the recent chaos at H.I.V.E. was altogether more dangerous.

The patrol passed by, a couple of the men throwing nervous glances in the direction of Nero and the Contessa as they marched by, but no more than that. The patrol was twenty metres behind them when the squad leader's radio squawked.

'Go ahead,' he said quickly.

The squad leader gestured for the squad to stop as he listened intently to his ear-piece. Slowly his face went pale and he looked back down the corridor at the rapidly retreating figures of Nero and the Contessa.

'You're certain?' the squad leader said, swallowing nervously. The way in which he then winced suggested that whoever was on the other end of the line was not only certain but noisily so. He gave his team a quick series of hand gestures that instructed them to spread out across the corridor and take cover as best they could.

'Contessa!' the squad leader shouted down the corridor. 'Please stay exactly where you are. Chief Lewis has some questions for you.'

'Wait,' the Contessa whispered to Nero. He heard the unmistakeable click of a safety catch being switched behind him and his mind raced. He could not let the patrol take the Contessa here – it would almost certainly sign Brand and Trinity's death warrants – but he wasn't about to let the Contessa shoot any of these men either. The patrol leader may have felt confident, but it would only take the Contessa getting within earshot of his squad and it would be a very different story. He doubted very much that many of the men in the patrol had the mental strength to resist the Contessa's power.

The Contessa turned slowly and faced the security patrol. Several Sleepers were pointed straight at her, the guards' faces confused but determined.

'Goodness me,' the Contessa said with a slight laugh. 'What on earth is all this about?' She took a couple of steps towards the patrol.

Behind her Nero pulled the skull-shaped link from the cuff of his shirt and twisted the clip.

'Stay right there, Contessa,' the squad leader barked. 'We have orders to fire if necessary.'

'Nonsense,' the Contessa replied. 'In fact, I think you're just all going to put your guns down.' As the Contessa spoke there was the uncomfortable, almost subliminal, sound of a thousand voices whispering at once. Nero had never heard the Contessa exert her power so strongly before and the effects were immediate. To their credit, a couple of the guards just looked confused, but the rest started to slowly place their weapons on the ground, their expressions blank.

Nero knew he had to act now before the Contessa could order the guards to help her escape or, even worse, turn on one another, and he threw the tiny silver skull in his palm down the corridor. There was a blinding flash and a concussive thump as the minute disguised stun grenade went off, filling the corridor with thick grey smoke. Then all hell broke loose.

Nero threw himself to the floor as Sleeper pulses ripped through the air. The few guards who had retained their weapons were firing blindly through the smoke, still dazed from the Contessa's manipulation.

'Cease fire,' the squad leader bellowed over the zapping blasts from the Sleepers. As the smoke cleared Nero could see the vague outlines of the patrol in the corridor, but he quickly realised that one person was missing.

'Are you all right, sir?' the squad leader asked as he staggered down the corridor towards Nero.

Nero nodded. He was fine, but the Contessa was gone.

☻☻☻

Laura and Shelby watched in horror as the door hissed open and Francisco dropped the guard inside with a single neat Sleeper pulse to the chest. He silently gestured for the girls to go through the door and they found themselves in an area that they had long believed did not exist. The cavern was a fully functional docking facility that looked as if it could handle most medium-sized vessels, the sea lapping at the single long quay. Tied up at the quay were a couple of sleek black power boats and as Shelby saw them she shot a worried glance at Laura. Laura knew why her friend was so concerned. At least while they were on the island they had a chance of being rescued, but if Francisco managed to smuggle them outside the school then their chances would diminish alarmingly.

Laura felt a sharp jab in her ribs as Tackle prodded her forwards with the barrel of his Sleeper and they slowly walked along the quay towards one of the moored boats. As they approached, a figure detached itself from the shadows nearby and stepped out into the light. A broad grin spread across Laura's face as she felt a flood of relief.

'Look out, Contessa! They're armed!' Shelby yelled, throwing herself backwards into Block, trying to catch him off balance and buy the Contessa a couple of precious seconds.

'Why, of course they are, my dear,' the Contessa replied matter of factly, walking slowly towards Francisco. 'How else would they keep you two under control?'

Laura's brow furrowed in confusion. What was the

Contessa doing? She had to stop them now while she still could.

'Have they given you any trouble?' the Contessa asked Francisco, glancing at the two girls.

'No, everything, has gone according to plan,' the Colonel replied, his voice flat.

'Not quite everything unfortunately. Nero escaped, but all of the necessary elements are in place otherwise. We should proceed,' the Contessa said, pulling a small PDA from her pocket. It was not a Blackbox.

Laura suddenly understood what was happening and just how carefully the events of the past couple of days had been orchestrated. The traitor wasn't Francisco; it was the Contessa.

'You two-faced old hag!' Shelby shouted angrily, clearly having reached exactly the same conclusion as Laura. 'How could you do this, you've –'

'Oh, do be quiet, Miss Trinity,' the Contessa said, her voice laced with sinister whispers. Shelby's mouth continued to move for a moment, as if she was trying to form words but none would come. Laura said nothing, and simply glared at the Contessa, her mind racing as she tried to think of a way out of this situation.

'That's better,' the Contessa said with a smile. 'Now why don't we all just get on board one of these boats that the school has so thoughtfully provided and be on our way.'

Laura felt another shove from behind as Tackle forced her towards the nearest power boat.

The Contessa watched as the two girls were loaded on to the boat, a smug, triumphant smile on her face.

'Now, sit still and stay silent,' she said, and Laura felt her free will disappear. No matter how hard she tried she could not move a muscle or make a sound. It was a deeply unsettling sensation.

'Now, Colonel, I believe it is time that you and your two students ensured that our insurance policy is in place,' the Contessa said, turning to Francisco. 'You know what to do.'

'Yes, Contessa,' Francisco replied in a monotone, turning and walking back towards the entrance to the dock with Block and Tackle in tow.

The Contessa watched them leave and then turned to the two girls sitting paralysed in the boat.

'Isn't this nice? All girls together,' she said sarcastically, climbing behind the controls of the boat. Neither of the two girls may have been able to offer a reply but the hate-filled looks in their eyes spoke volumes.

The Contessa fired the ignition on the boat and its powerful engines roared into life. She raised the silver PDA to her lips.

'Activate H.I.V.E. emergency security procedure Sinistre Delta One,' she said and placed the device back in her pocket. The rock wall at the far end of the dock rumbled upwards and Laura saw blue sky and the sea stretching off towards the horizon.

As the Contessa gunned the engine and steered the boat towards the opening alarm klaxons began to sound all over the school.

chapter fourteen

'What the hell?' Security Chief Lewis spat as one by one the monitors displaying security feeds from all over the school flickered and went black.

'There's an unknown routine running on the security net,' a technician reported from a nearby workstation. 'The grid's going offline.'

The door to the situation room slid open and Dr Nero hurried into the room and headed straight for the nearest free terminal. He typed a string of commands into the terminal before slamming his fist down hard on the keyboard.

'Damn you, Maria,' Nero hissed. It was too late. She had locked him out of the system using her command access, and was now the only person who could reinitialise the system.

'Student dormitories are locking down,' another security technician announced, a look of confusion on his face.

'Defence grid is offline too,' another voice reported. 'All external batteries are going into sleep modes.'

'H.I.V.E.mind just dropped into standby mode. He's not accepting remote commands.'

Nero watched in impotent fury as his school was rendered defenceless around him.

'All external access points are opening,' the Chief said, slight panic in his voice. 'Do we still have exterior camera feeds?'

'Yes, sir, scanning the perimeter now,' a reply came from the other side of the room. 'Nothing visible at the moment, looks all clear . . . hold on . . . something off the southern coastline.'

'Put it on-screen,' Lewis barked.

There on the screen a tiny boat was roaring away from the island. As the camera zoomed in Nero could see the unmistakeable figure of the Contessa at the controls. Sat behind her were two smaller figures, both wearing the black jumpsuits of the Alpha stream.

'Where's she going?' Lewis said, sounding puzzled. 'That's only a patrol boat, she doesn't have enough fuel to reach land.'

As if answer to the Chief's query there was a strange shimmer on the surface of the ocean and then a huge, black warship materialised seemingly out of thin air.

Nero suddenly realised just how badly he had been

outmanoeuvred. Cypher was here and H.I.V.E. was defenceless.

☺☺☺

Nigel and Franz wandered slowly through the virtually deserted atrium of their accommodation block. There were a few other students sitting on the sofas and chairs dotted around the cavern but the vast majority of H.I.V.E.'s pupils were either still asleep or had only just woken up. Franz had woken early, complaining that he was hungry, as he always did when the previous evening's meal had been salad. For his part Nigel had learnt long ago that it was entirely pointless to try and sleep through Franz's morning routine and after two minutes of Franz singing in the shower he had grudgingly got out of bed too.

'It is still nearly an hour till breakfast,' Franz observed, 'but it may be wise to take our places in the queue already, ja?'

'There's not going to be a queue yet,' Nigel said slightly grumpily. 'We'll be fine if we're five minutes early. Let's go to the library instead. There are a couple of new organic chemistry papers that I need to catch up on.'

'Oh, Nigel, with you it is always the library. You need to have more fun,' Franz said matter of factly.

'The library *is* fun,' Nigel said insistently, wishing that

Franz shared his passion for books. 'Perhaps if you spent a bit more time there you'd understand.'

The huge blast doors that sealed the accommodation block at night had opened a few minutes earlier, signalling that students were free to wander the halls of the school again before their classes, as usual. Nigel and Franz walked through them and into the corridor beyond. At almost exactly the same moment alarm klaxons began to wail everywhere.

'I didn't do anything!' Franz yelped as the alarms screamed.

There was a low grinding noise and the blast doors began to lower, re-sealing the accommodation block.

'Come on,' Nigel said. 'That's a high-level alert. It's probably just a drill, but we still have to go back inside.'

'No way!' Franz yelped, backing away from the closing doors. 'I am remembering what happened the last time all of the alarms are going off and we are locked in there.'

Nigel remembered too. On that day they had ended up trapped inside their room while the rampaging plant creature that he himself had inadvertently created tried to smash its way in. Franz was right – it had not been a pleasant experience.

'Well, that's unlikely to happen again, isn't it?' Nigel said slightly apologetically.

'You have not been experimenting again, have you?'

Franz said suspiciously, his eyes narrowing as he looked carefully at Nigel.

'No, I most certainly have not,' Nigel said indignantly, feeling his cheeks burning. The blast door was nearly halfway closed now; they had to get back inside.

'Well, I am staying out here,' Franz said indignantly.

Nigel was surprised by Franz's determination but he knew the only way to get him back into the accommodation area now would be to physically drag him and the laws of physics might have something to say about that, given the two boys' relative masses.

'OK, but let's find somewhere quiet to sit out the alert,' Nigel said nervously, looking up the corridor and half expecting to see an angry security patrol marching towards them.

'An excellent idea,' Franz said with a broad smile. 'I suggest the dining hall!'

'That's what this was all about,' Nigel said incredulously as the blast door sealed shut with a solid-sounding thud. 'You just didn't want to miss breakfast.'

'No, that was not it at all –' Franz began weakly.

'I don't believe you sometimes,' Nigel said angrily. 'I'm going to the library and if we meet any security patrols on the way you can explain what we're doing outside the accommodation area.' He marched away down the corridor.

'But the dining area has much greater structural

integrity,' Franz continued as he followed Nigel. 'It really would be the safer option in the event of an emergency . . .'

☻☻☻

Laura's mouth fell open as the huge black ship materialised just a couple of hundred metres in front of them. She looked across at Shelby, who shared her look of amazement, her mouth moving slightly as if she was trying to say something despite the command for silence that the Contessa had given them both just a few minutes earlier.

The stolen patrol boat slowed as they neared the side of the mysterious ship and a boarding platform lowered from the level of the deck to just above the surface of the water. The Contessa brought the boat alongside the platform and turned to the two girls. The pistol was in her hand again.

'Get out,' she said coldly. 'Try anything stupid and I'll feed you to the sharks myself.'

Shelby and Laura climbed out of the patrol boat and on to the platform, the Contessa close behind them, and immediately the platform rose again towards the bigger ship's deck.

As they rose to the level of the upper deck the two girls found a welcoming party waiting for them. A tall man, dressed in an immaculate suit and a smooth oval mask of highly polished black glass, stood flanked on either side by slim, humanoid robots, their matt-black metallic bodies covered in plates of armour.

'Contessa,' the man said. 'How nice to see you again. I trust everything has gone according to plan?'

'Yes, Cypher,' the Contessa replied. 'The island is yours for the taking.'

Shelby made a sound that could only be described as a snarl and ran towards Cypher. The robots to either side of him reacted instantly, intercepting Shelby and restraining her in their vice-like grip.

'Murderer!' Shelby gasped as she struggled in vain to break free of the guards.

Laura stepped forward as if to help her friend but instead was forced to her knees as another guard clamped its mechanical hand down hard on her shoulder.

'And two unexpected guests – how lovely,' Cypher said coldly, stepping towards Shelby.

'Yes, may I introduce Shelby Trinity and Laura Brand. They have made rather a nuisance of themselves so I thought I'd bring them along as extra insurance,' the Contessa explained.

Cypher took Shelby's chin in his hand. The look on her face suggested that he should be very glad that she wasn't able to get her hands on him.

'I'm afraid, Miss Trinity, that H.I.V.E. is going to be permanently closed very shortly, but I'm sure that we can find a use for someone with spirit in my organisation in the future,' he said with infuriating smugness. 'In the meantime I think it would be best if we provided these ladies with some *very* secure accommodation. Take them to the brig. Put them in separate cells.'

'They'll have to share a cell,' one of the guards replied. 'The other cell is currently occupied.'

'Very well,' Cypher said quickly, 'they may have the small pleasure of each other's company. Take them away.'

The guards obeyed immediately, tightening their already uncomfortable grip on the two girls and marching them away towards a hatch that led below.

'Keep an eye on those two,' the Contessa told Cypher. 'They're more dangerous than they might appear.'

'Aren't we all, Contessa?' Cypher replied, turning back towards her. 'You have done very well today, Maria. I could not have asked for more. I only wish I could have seen Nero's face when he realised that you were working for me. You have my sincere thanks.'

'You can save your gratitude, Cypher,' the Contessa replied. 'You know that I expect to be well rewarded for my troubles.'

'Oh, don't worry, Maria. By the end of the day I will be in a position to give you anything you want. This is the dawning of a new era.'

The Contessa said nothing. There was a disturbing edge

of fanaticism to Cypher's tone all of a sudden. She told herself not to worry – after all she had worked with much more unbalanced people than Cypher in her time, and if push came to shove she'd just have to *take* what she was owed.

A man in a naval uniform walked up to them, saluting efficiently as Cypher turned to face him.

'Yes, Captain, what is it?'

'Your chopper is on the pad and all launchers are reporting ready, sir. Just give the word.'

Cypher looked at the island sitting less than a mile away.

'The word is given, Captain. The word is most definitely given.'

☣ ☣ ☣

The Shroud had picked up Cypher's ship on radar as soon as it dropped its thermoptic camouflage so Raven and Otto knew they were too late even before they could see the black battleship holding position just off the coast of the island. They had had no contact with H.I.V.E. since they had first left the ruins of Cypher's base, Raven had barely had time to warn H.I.V.E. about the ship that was on its way before the transmission had dissolved into static and now they all feared the worst.

'We're at full stealth,' the pilot reported. 'They have no

idea we're here, and judging by the number of active radar scans that thing's putting out we'd better stay that way if we don't want to end up on the wrong end of a SAM.'

'Can we get close enough to get on board without being detected?' Raven said with a frown. 'We have to stop Cypher before he has a chance to launch an attack.'

'It may be too late for that,' Otto said, looking up from a screen displaying a zoomed-in image of Cypher's ship. Multiple launch tubes could be seen rising from the deck and swivelling into firing positions, all pointing straight at H.I.V.E. Moments later the first salvo was launched. A barrage of missiles streaked away from the launchers, impacting on the side of the island's central volcanic peak only seconds later. Curiously, there were no explosions, just small clouds of dust where each missile had landed. Otto manipulated the surveillance camera mounted in the nose of the Shroud to focus on one of the impact sites. As the dust cleared the long white body of the missile could be clearly seen, lying still intact amongst the rocks.

Suddenly a panel on the missile was blown off and a familiar black shape climbed from the shell. It was one of Cypher's robotic assassins. Otto quickly focused on another one of the impact sites, where exactly the same thing was happening, the missile disgorging its lethal passenger. At the same time another wave of missiles was launched from the ship, impacting all over the nearest face of the island. The first wave of robots was already scaling the sides of the volcano like ants, heading upwards at frightening speed towards the crater entrance.

'Forget the ship,' Raven said, a grim look on her face. 'We've got to get inside H.I.V.E. *now*.'

☻☻☻

The Chief looked at the guard to his left, the worry tinged with fear on his face summing up the feelings of the other guards positioned around the crater. As soon as Cypher's ship had appeared Nero had given the order for all security teams to protect H.I.V.E.'s points of entry. The Contessa had sealed all of the conventional weapons lockers so they had little more than the Sleepers that units on patrol had been carrying to defend themselves. The Chief just hoped it would be enough. There were only a couple of external cameras that were functional so they had little idea what Cypher was going to throw at them, but he was determined that nothing was going to make it past him and his men.

The Chief looked up at the bright circle of daylight overhead formed by the crater's edge. For a fleeting moment he thought that he could detect movement but it may just have been a trick of the light. He reached for the tiny pair of binoculars that were attached to his equipment harness and quickly focused on the rocks far

266

overhead. There were definitely several people up there, gathering at the lip of the crater. They were dressed all in black and they moved with a surprising speed and agility. He thought back to Raven's report on the attack on the Tokyo safe house and quickly realised that these must be more of the same ninjas that had attacked her there. Well, they were ready for them this time and the assassins would find that H.I.V.E. itself was a considerably harder target than some local safe house. The assassins were going to have to rappel down to the landing pad from the top of the volcano and that would make them sitting ducks for him and his men.

Suddenly, one of the black figures far overhead seemed to simply leap into the void, tumbling down towards the Chief and his men. He must have slipped and fallen, the Chief thought to himself as he watched the man drop. At least that was one less of them to worry about. The Chief looked away as the assassin hit the hard steel of the landing deck; he'd seen many disturbing things in his life-time but a drop from that height was never a pretty sight. Then he heard a couple of gasps and half-yelled comments from his men as the assassin who had hit the ground simply stood up from the crouch in which he had landed and slowly surveyed the room. It was impossible. The Chief had known some well-trained operatives over the years, but no one could survive a fall from that height, no one. He looked more closely at the armoured assassin and it quickly became clear that they were not dealing with any normal assault here. The assassin was a machine, its design way in advance of anything else he had seen.

'Open fire!' the Chief yelled, and was immediately drowned out by the loud zapping reports of multiple Sleepers being fired all around him. To say that the Sleeper pulses were ineffective would have been something of an understatement – the assassin didn't even falter, just slowly surveyed its surroundings, the glowing red sensory array on the front of its insectile face taking in every detail.

The Chief knew a scout when he saw one and also knew that this robot was probably just reporting back to the others above on the positions and strength of the defenders.

'What do we do, Chief?' the man to his left yelled desperately above the sounds of Sleepers firing. 'That thing's not even slowing down; the Sleepers aren't working.'

The Chief suddenly understood why the Contessa had only sealed the conventional weapons lockers when she had overridden the security system. Cypher's forces clearly had nothing to fear from Sleepers.

'What I wouldn't give for a good old-fashioned grenade right now,' the Chief muttered to himself.

There was another sudden thunderous clanging sound

as half a dozen more of the assassins landed on the steel decking. The moment they landed they unleashed a blizzard of whirring shuriken, the deadly throwing stars finding their targets unerringly, sending several of the Chief's men toppling to the ground. The Chief felt a cold dread descending over him. They were hopelessly outgunned, but they couldn't let these things take the crater; if they did there would be no stopping them.

A sudden wind seemed to rise from nowhere and the Chief quickly glanced out past the rock behind which he had taken cover to see what was happening. The assassins still stood in a tight circle in the centre of the landing pad, launching the occasional shuriken at any of the H.I.V.E. guards who were unfortunate enough to find themselves in an exposed position. One of the assassins head's snapped round and focused on the Chief, its arm rising to launch a throwing star at him.

It never got the chance.

Suddenly the group of robots seemed to crumple as if a huge weight was crushing them to the ground. In just a split second they were reduced to a sparking pile of crushed and mangled components, the occasional twitching servo the only indication of any life. There was a shimmer in the air and the huge black shape of a Shroud materialised directly on top of the ruined attackers. The hatch at the back of the aircraft blew off with a loud bang, flying across the cavern, and Raven stepped out.

'Chief, pull your men back now. You don't have a chance against these things,' Raven yelled as Otto Malpense and the Shroud's pilot leapt down from the aircraft behind her.

'Nero said we had to hold the crater at all costs,' the Chief said quickly as Raven approached.

'Nero hasn't gone toe-to-toe with one of these things,' Raven replied impatiently. 'If you stay here you die, simple as that.'

The Chief knew better than to argue with Raven's tactical appraisal of a situation. Besides he may not have wanted to admit it, but he knew she was right. He looked up and saw more tiny black figures massing on the edge of the crater above. They were out of options.

'Fall back!' the Chief yelled, ordering his men back through the enormous blast doors that were the only way into or out of the crater. They did not need to be told twice – the sight of these invulnerable assassins cutting down their team mates with such apparent ease had been enough to persuade most of them of the wisdom of a tactical withdrawal.

'Can we seal the doors?' Raven asked as they dashed towards the exit.

'There's enough charge in the back-up batteries to close them, but once they're closed they're staying closed.

There won't be enough juice to open them again, thanks to the Contessa,' the Chief replied.

'What do you mean, thanks to the Contessa?' Raven asked quickly.

'I think you need to speak to Nero,' the Chief replied as they passed through the doorway and the huge steel doors slowly rumbled shut.

☉☉☉

The assassin robot shoved Laura hard in the back, propelling her forward into the dingy cell. Shelby was right behind her, falling to the deck as she too was pushed inside, the heavy door swinging shut with a worryingly solid clunk. They watched through the bars as the two mechanical henchmen walked silently away, leaving them alone.

'Well, this isn't good,' Laura said with a sigh, surveying the cramped, featureless cell.

'Laura Brand, the world's greatest master of understatement, ladies and gentlemen,' Shelby replied sarcastically, sitting down on one of the cell's two tiny beds.

'I can't believe the Contessa's involved with this,' Laura said gloomily as she sat down on the bed opposite Shelby.

'Well, she is,' Shelby replied, staring at the cell door.

'Aye,' Laura replied sadly. 'She fooled everybody: us, Nero, and by the looks of it Francisco too.'

'Yeah, it looks like the Colonel didn't have much say in the whole "helping the Contessa" thing,' Shelby said, sounding slightly distracted.

'She must have been using him for months,' Laura said, 'to implant commands so deeply that he carries them out without question. We've both felt what it's like to have the Contessa hijack your brainstem, but it fades quickly after she's gone. She must have spent a long time preparing him for this.'

'I don't understand what that old witch does but I'll tell you one thing, it's going to take a whole lot more than a few words to stop me from punching her lights out the next time I see her,' Shelby replied, picking at the toe of her shoe.

'What are you doing?' Laura asked, watching in bemusement as Shelby tugged at a loose flap of rubber on the toe of her shoe.

'We're getting out of here,' Shelby said quietly.

'That would be nice,' said Laura, 'but something tells me we're going to need more than the old one of us falling ill trick to get us out of here.'

'Oh, come on,' Shelby replied with a smile, 'that's a classic. Never fails.'

'I take it you have a plan, then?' Laura replied curiously.

'Better than that,' Shelby said with a grin, peeling the sole off her right shoe. 'I have a key.'

Inside the sole of Shelby's shoe was a full set of tiny tools and lockpicks. Laura knew she really shouldn't be surprised; after all Shelby had been the Wraith – the world's most notorious and successful jewel thief before being forcibly inducted into H.I.V.E.

'Don't tell me that you walk round all day with that lot in your shoe,' Laura said with a chuckle.

'Don't leave home without it,' Shelby replied with a broad grin.

Shelby walked up to the bars at the front of the cell and quickly glanced down the corridor leading to the cells. Seeing no one there she turned her attention to the lock and after a few seconds let out a long sigh.

'What's wrong?' Laura asked anxiously.

'This is a Johnson and Fort, floating barrel, nine pin, spring-leaf security lock,' Shelby said quietly. 'Almost impossible to bypass.'

'Great,' Laura said as Shelby turned back to the lock. 'So now what are we going to do? There's no other way out of here and I for one don't just want to sit here and wait for Cypher's scheme to play out, whatever he's –'

There was a tiny click and the cell door swung open.

'I only said *almost* impossible,' Shelby grinned.

'OK,' Laura said in amazement, 'the next time they serve chocolate ice cream at dinner, you can have mine too.'

'You say that now, Brand, but it'll be a different story

when the time comes,' Shelby said, slipping her hidden tools into her pocket.

'Oh, don't worry, this time you've really earned it,' Laura said, grinning.

Shelby stepped silently into the corridor. There were no signs of any guards – Cypher obviously thought the brig was a lot more secure than it actually was.

'Coast is clear,' Shelby whispered. 'Let's go.'

The two girls crept down the corridor. They were just passing the other cell door when Laura suddenly stopped.

'There's somebody in there,' Laura whispered. Lying cuffed to the bed in the cell was a figure wearing simple black pyjamas with a hood over its head.

'So?' Shelby replied. 'In case you hadn't noticed we're trying to escape here.'

'Think about it,' Laura said quietly. 'If Cypher's locked them up in here we should help them – the enemy of my enemy is my friend and all that.'

'Right, but what if they're locked up for a good reason?' Shelby replied. 'The last thing we need is another murderous psychopath running around on the loose.'

'It can't hurt to talk to them,' Laura said quickly. 'Look, they're cuffed to the bed. Worst comes to worst we just leave them there.'

'OK, OK, but if that's Hannibal Lecter in there I'm holding you responsible,' Shelby said with a sigh. She pulled her tools back out of her pocket and quickly bypassed the lock on the cell, the door swinging open with a creak.

Laura walked up to the figure shackled to the bed and hesitated for a moment. Shelby might be right, this could be just someone that Cypher considered dangerous. Then she took a deep breath and scolded herself for being so timid. It couldn't hurt to see what they looked like at any rate. She reached down and pulled the black hood off the prisoner's head.

Laura gasped, the hood falling from her limp fingers.

'Oh my God,' Shelby hissed. 'Wing!'

Lying there on the bed was their friend who they had both so recently grieved for. Laura looked as if she had, quite literally, seen a ghost. Shelby reached down and placed her hand on Wing's chest, feeling it rise and fall, with tears in her eyes.

'He's alive,' Shelby whispered.

'Wing!' Laura said urgently. 'Wake up!'

Wing did not stir even when she shook his shoulder. This was no natural sleep; he'd been sedated.

'So what do we do now?' Shelby said, disbelief still evident in her voice. 'It's not like we can carry him out of here.' She quickly set to work on the cuffs holding him to the bed; they were child's play to her and she had released them within seconds.

'Wing!' Laura shouted, shaking him again, suddenly not caring if anyone could hear them.

'Here, let me try,' Shelby said, gently pushing Laura to one side.

'Sorry about this,' she said softly to Wing and slapped him hard across the face.

Wing stirred for the briefest of moments, mumbling something, and then settled back into his previous state of unconsciousness.

'Come on, big guy,' Shelby said quietly. 'Don't make me do that again.'

Wing showed no further signs of waking and Shelby raised her hand, swinging it down to slap his face again. Wing's hand moved in a blur, snapping into the air like a striking snake and catching Shelby's wrist a split second before she made contact with his cheek. Laura gasped, and Shelby almost jumped out of her skin.

'If I am dreaming, why does my face hurt so much?' Wing said croakily.

Shelby gave a tiny sob and hugged Wing hard. The grief that had still been so fresh and raw fell away, replaced with a joy deeper than she had ever felt before. Hot tears rolled down her cheeks as she clung on to him, fearing that he might vanish in a puff of smoke if she ever let him go.

chapter fifteen

Nero's expression changed from one of deep concern to relief as Otto and Raven entered the command centre with the Chief. There had been precious little in the way of good news over the past few hours and seeing the pair of them alive, if slightly ragged, made a welcome change.

'Natalya,' Nero said with a nod, 'it's good to have you back, and I see that you even managed to get Malpense back in one piece. I wish I could welcome you both back under more auspicious circumstances.'

'The guards don't stand a chance against Cypher's forces, Max,' Raven replied. 'They're robots, quite unlike anything I have seen before, unstoppable and lethal.'

'Yes,' Nero replied – that much had been obvious from the short and decidedly one-sided battle in the crater – 'but we have to stop them. Cypher cannot be allowed to take control of this facility. What's your assessment, Chief?'

'It's not good, sir,' the Chief said quickly. 'We've sealed the external blast doors but that's pretty much all we could do. It'll slow them down, but not much more than that. The Contessa's override has left us with almost no control over the security and defence systems.'

'The Contessa?' Raven asked. 'What has she done?'

Nero quickly explained the depths of the Contessa's betrayal to Raven, how she had not only handed them to Cypher in Tokyo but also left the school defenceless against his current assault.

'Leave her to me,' Raven said coldly.

'Once this is all over, Natalya, you may feel free to hunt her to the ends of the earth, but for now we have far more pressing concerns. I'm not interested in just slowing Cypher's forces down, I want them driven back into the sea,' Nero said firmly.

'Max, I found it extremely hard to defeat one of those things in a straight fight,' Raven said, 'and Cypher has an army of them. We can't hope to just drive them back, it's impossible.'

'That's not entirely true,' Otto said quietly.

'You have something in mind, Mr Malpense?' Nero said.

'It's just an idea,' Otto replied, 'but I need to speak to the Professor first.'

'Very well,' Nero said with a sigh, 'I don't suppose it can

do any harm at this point. Raven, would you be so good as to escort Mr Malpense to the science and technology department, the Professor is there trying to bring H.I.V.E.mind back online at the moment. Oh, before you go, Natalya, there is one more thing . . .'

Nero ushered Raven to a quiet corner of the command centre and they had a brief conversation before Nero put something in her hand. Raven looked at Nero for a moment and then nodded. The pair of them walked back towards Otto, Raven gesturing for him to follow her out of the room.

Nero listened to the urgent chatter that was coming over the security team's radios. He doubted that Malpense had really come up with something that would derail Cypher's plans, but as things stood they had no chance. They needed an edge badly and if Otto Malpense could give them that then perhaps they might have a little hope after all.

☻☻☻

The huge transport helicopter landed gently on the crater pad, the dozens of Cypher's mechanical assassins that had already entered the crater forming a protective cordon around it. Cypher stepped down from the helicopter and surveyed the scene with satisfaction. So far everything was going according to plan. It was now just a matter of time before he had full control of H.I.V.E., and once he did no one could stop him.

A technician ran up to him and reported breathlessly. 'We've tried the standard cutting equipment on the blast doors, sir, and we've barely made a scratch. It could take hours to get inside that way.'

'Then it is fortunate that we brought along a more effective method,' Cypher said casually, glancing over at the two large crates that the helicopter had winched down on to the pad just a couple of minutes earlier. 'Are they ready?'

'Yes, sir,' the technician replied, glancing down at the tablet computer he was carrying. 'The power-up cycle is complete and all system checks are showing green lights. They're good to go.'

'Excellent. There is no reason to delay, then. Let's get this over with,' Cypher said, pulling a small black remote control from his inside pocket. He pointed the control at the pair of crates and pressed a button. The front panel of each crate slowly lowered forward and after a moment a familiar array of red lights lit up the gloom in each one. With a heavy thud the first of the giant assassin robots stepped out of its crate. They were of the same design as the one that Cypher had pitted against Raven, and if one had been enough to deal with her then he saw no reason why he should need more than two to take H.I.V.E.

The behemoths stomped towards Cypher, each step sending a tiny tremor through the floor, and stood neatly in front of him.

'Awaiting orders,' the machine on the left said in its harsh mechanical voice.

'That door,' Cypher said, pointing at the sealed blast door. 'Remove it.'

'Understood,' the robot replied, and both the machines turned and walked towards the door.

There was no subtlety in their approach as the huge robots began pounding on the door with their enormous wrecking-ball fists. Almost immediately the door started to dent and become deformed and after just a couple of minutes it began to slowly buckle under the relentless hammering. The noise was deafening.

'Give the order for the assault units to gather here. Once those doors come down we go in hard,' Cypher said to the technician, raising his voice slightly to be heard over the noise of the robots assaulting the door.

'What are your orders should we encounter defensive forces?' the technician asked nervously.

'Kill anyone who resists,' Cypher said calmly.

☻☻☻

Nigel had stopped worrying about security patrols. He and Franz had encountered several squads on their way to the library but none of them had stopped and questioned them on why they were outside of their accommodation block. In fact they looked as if they had altogether more pressing concerns, judging by the looks of fear on some of their faces. Oh yes, Nigel had stopped worrying about the security guards – now he was too busy worrying about whatever it was that had them frightened.

The two boys walked down another deserted corridor, only dimly lit by the emergency power that was sustaining H.I.V.E.

'It's quiet . . .' Franz said.

'If you say "too quiet" now I'll never speak to you again,' Nigel said quickly.

'You are having the hornet in your hat about something,' Franz said, looking fed up.

'It's bee in your bonnet, and yes, I am worried. Why has every security patrol we've seen been running somewhere and why are they all too busy to care what we're doing?' Nigel asked.

'I am not sure, but I am guessing that it has something to do with the alarms,' Franz said, nodding wisely.

The fact that alarm sirens were still wailing throughout the base did suggest to Nigel that whatever was wrong was very serious and that it was still an ongoing problem.

'Perhaps we should be heading back to the accommodation area,' Franz said nervously. 'I am thinking that under the circumstances it might be safer than . . . ummmmf.'

Franz was cut off in mid-sentence by Nigel's hand over his mouth. Franz looked at his roommate with surprise and confusion but Nigel just raised a single finger to his lips and pointed towards the far end of the corridor. There, in the gloom, they could just make out the unmistakeable figures of Colonel Francisco, Block and Tackle. Nigel may not have known much about the current situation but Laura and Shelby had told him enough to know that Francisco was supposed to be in a cell and that security had been combing H.I.V.E., searching for Block and Tackle. They certainly weren't supposed to be freely wandering the corridors of the school.

Nigel and Franz ducked back into the cover of a nearby classroom doorway and watched as the three fugitives stopped for a moment, appearing to engage in a whispered conversation before heading down another adjoining corridor. Nigel quietly pulled out his Blackbox and flipped it open, only to find, to his dismay, that it was dead, displaying just two words: 'H.I.V.E.mind offline'.

'Come on,' said Nigel, starting off down the corridor after them.

'Where are you going?' Franz said plaintively.

'I'm going to follow them, of course,' Nigel replied.

'Now why would you want to do that?' Franz said, disbelief in his voice. 'We should just find a security patrol and tell them.'

'By the time we find a patrol and bring them back here those three will be long gone. We've got to follow them to wherever they're going and then we find the guards,' Nigel explained impatiently.

'I am thinking that I am going to be regretting this,' Franz said with a sigh. 'Come on, then.'

Nigel set off down the corridor as quietly as he could, but Franz held back just for a moment.

'Too quiet,' he whispered to himself.

☢ ☢ ☢

'And then I was awoken by someone slapping me in the face,' Wing said with a half-smile.

'Yeah, again, sorry about that,' Shelby said with a sheepish grin.

'So you woke up in Cypher's base and you had no idea what had happened?' Laura asked.

'None at all, my last memory was of the rooftop in Tokyo, so as you can imagine I was somewhat surprised to wake up at all,' Wing explained.

'No kidding,' Shelby said. 'Everyone just assumed you were dead.'

'Indeed, I believe that was the intention,' Wing replied. 'Judging by the small puncture wound in my chest it seems that Cypher's gun was loaded with some form of tranquiliser projectile that was designed to give the appearance of a lethal shot.'

'And you only spoke to him twice?' Laura asked.

'Yes, once when I first awoke and he assured me that no harm would come to me as long as I cooperated and didn't make any trouble,' Wing said calmly, 'and the second when he told me that I was being taken aboard a ship. The fact that I had not paid very much attention to his initial instruction to cooperate led to me being sedated for the transfer to the ship. That is really all I remember.'

Laura suddenly looked lost in thought.

'Is there something troubling you, Laura?' Wing asked softly.

'Aye, why didn't Cypher just kill you? Don't get me wrong, I'm very glad he didn't,' she hastily added, 'but why go to all of the trouble of faking your death and then bringing you along on an operation like this? It all just seems needlessly risky, and if there's one thing that we have learnt about Cypher over the past couple of days it's that he's not afraid of spilling blood to get what he wants.'

'I had wondered the very same thing myself,' Wing replied, 'but I'm afraid I can offer no logical explanation for Cypher's actions. What I do know is that we must stop him at all costs. From the hints he did drop when he spoke to me it was clear that this is his endgame. I shudder to think of what he might do if he takes H.I.V.E.'

'Which is why we need to get off this boat,' Shelby said firmly, 'and the sooner the better.'

'Agreed,' Wing said. 'You must tell me something first though. Is Otto OK?' He seemed to be expecting the worst.

'The last we heard he was fine,' said Shelby, 'and I'm guessing that he's going to be very pleased to see you.'

'That is good to hear,' Wing said with obvious relief. 'Cypher never gave any specifics but from the way he talked about it I feared that I might be the only survivor of the safe house.'

'You very nearly were,' Laura explained, 'but by the sounds of things Raven managed to get Otto and herself out of there in one piece.'

'That is the first good news I have had for some time,' Wing said with a smile, 'but now we must go before someone comes along to check that we're all still safely locked up.'

'You OK to walk?' Shelby asked as Wing, somewhat unsteadily, got to his feet.

Wing suddenly realised something was missing. His hand flew to his chest and through the thin fabric of the pyjamas he was wearing he felt nothing but his own breastbone. His amulet was gone. In his mind's eye he saw his mother handing him the tiny talisman, telling him that he must never let it fall into the wrong hands. He could make a reasonably good guess who had taken it. He had no idea what use Cypher could possibly have for it but he knew somehow that it was vital he retrieved it.

'You sure you're OK? You looked miles away for a second there,' Laura said, her brow furrowing with concern.

'I shall be fine, just the after-effects of the sedation,' Wing said. 'Let's go.'

☻☻☻

Otto and Raven walked into the science and technology department to find a scene of chaos. Technicians were running around the room in a frantic flurry of activity, carrying piles of paper, pushing trolleys full of equipment, hunched over the various computer terminals dotted around the room. They all wore the same expression of panic.

Sitting at a terminal at the far end of the room was Professor Pike. He seemed almost to be in a trance as his hand flew across the keyboards, entering strings of commands.

'Professor,' Raven said as they approached him. Getting no response she raised her voice. 'Professor!'

The Professor suddenly snapped out of his trance and stared at Otto and Raven. For a moment he looked as if he didn't recognise them but then he focused and a smile spread across his face.

'Aah, Raven and Mr Malpense. It's good you're not dead,' he said, still smiling.

'Yes, we were quite pleased about that too,' Otto said drily.

'No, I mean it's useful,' the Professor continued. 'I needed to speak to you both.'

'Well, here we are,' Raven said impatiently. She had no love for the technical department. She was no scientist and her definition of exciting technology was something that worked reliably and might save her life.

'Yes, Mr Malpense, would you be so kind as to have a look at this for me,' the Professor said, gesturing towards the terminal at which he had been working. Otto moved to the terminal and looked at the screen. It seemed that the Professor had been trying to break an encryption routine.

'What is this?' Otto asked.

'That is the encryption that is protecting the Contessa's unauthorised control of the security network,' the Professor explained. 'I'm afraid that I'm struggling to make any impression on it and I wondered what you thought.'

Flattered as Otto was by the fact that the Professor wanted to consult him about this he wasn't sure how much help he could offer. He was good with computers, no doubt about that, but this sort of thing was more

Laura's speciality.

'You should get Laura to look at this,' Otto said, not looking away from the screen, 'she's the one who cracks encryption in her head.'

'Yes, that would have been my first choice, but since Miss Brand has been kidnapped by the Contessa it wasn't possible.'

'What?' Otto said, loudly enough to set several heads around the room swivelling in their direction.

'I assumed you knew,' the Professor said matter of factly. 'The Contessa has taken her and Miss Trinity to Cypher's ship. Had no one told you?'

'No, they had not,' Otto said, feeling a familiar anger rising in his chest. Cypher and the Contessa had a great deal to pay for.

'So,' the Professor said, gesturing at the terminal again, 'any thoughts?'

Otto looked again at the encrypted code on the screen. He was no expert on encryption but he knew enough to see that whoever had put this together was very good. The encryption was sophisticated and multilayered, specifically designed to counter any attempts at cracking it.

'It's very good,' Otto said after a couple of minutes. 'Highly sophisticated. Whoever wrote this knew exactly what they were doing.'

'Ah . . . yes, well, you see, that's the slightly embarrassing part of all this,' the Professor said quietly. 'You see . . . well . . . um . . . I wrote it.'

Otto looked at the Professor with an expression of total confusion.

'So why can't you decrypt it?' Otto asked.

'Well, let's just say that I had an encounter with the Contessa before I wrote it, and I wasn't feeling quite myself,' he said with an apologetic smile.

'Great,' Raven sighed. 'Am I the only one around here who hasn't had that witch inside my head?'

'Surely H.I.V.E.mind could crack it,' Otto said.

'Yes, he probably could, but he's offline right now, again thanks to the Contessa,' the Professor explained.

'And I take it that there's no way to bring him back up in time?' Otto said, knowing that what he had in mind was very much dependant on H.I.V.E.'s resident super-computer being fully functional.

'Well, there is a way, but it's far too risky under the current circumstances,' the Professor said. A full hard-ware reset would clear any encryption surrounding H.I.V.E.mind's command routines, but with the mess that our systems are in at the moment there's every chance that we'll just lose what few basic systems we do still have control of,' the Professor explained. 'And it can only be done from H.I.V.E.'s data hub – there's no remote access for that kind of thing.'

'So we've got to switch H.I.V.E.mind off and back on again,' Raven said, trying to boil the idea down to its essentials. 'Well, it usually works with my computer.'

'Unfortunately H.I.V.E.mind is rather more sophisticated than that. There's a good reason that we've never done this before – there are no guarantees that he would ever work again,' the Professor continued.

'I'd say that at the moment that falls into the "chance we'll have to take" category,' Otto said, looking again at the apparently impregnable encryption that was surrounding H.I.V.E.mind's systems.

'Yes, I suppose you're right,' the Professor said. 'Doctor Nero did tell me to do everything necessary to bring our systems back online.'

'I'll escort you to the hub,' Raven said. 'Otto, you stay here.'

'Actually, it would be helpful if Mr Malpense came with us,' the Professor said. 'Resetting the system is complicated and an extra pair of hands would be useful. No offence, Raven, but I doubt that you would be as much help, and time is of the essence here.'

If Raven was offended she gave no sign of it, she just shook her head.

'Too dangerous. If Cypher's machines get inside the school I want Malpense somewhere relatively safe, not running around the corridors. I'd rather keep him with me, but if we encounter more than one of those things I can't guarantee to protect either of you.'

'Actually,' the Professor said, 'that's why I wanted to speak to you, Raven. I have something that might help with that.'

Raven raised a single eyebrow as the Professor gestured for her to follow him across to another workbench. Lying on the bench, surrounded by discarded components and hastily scribbled notes, were a pair of katanas, much like Raven's own swords but with jet-black blades.

'Thanks, Professor, but I'm rather attached to the girls,' Raven said, putting one hand on the hilt of one of the swords that rested in crossed sheaths on her back. 'I'm not looking for replacements.'

'Let me give you a quick demonstration and see if you still feel the same,' the Professor said with a mischievous grin. He pressed a stud on the hilt of one of the swords and tossed it to Raven, who caught it neatly. The sword was light and well-balanced but what was most intriguing was the faint trace of crackling dark purple energy that could be seen flickering along its striking edge.

'I designed these after the staff in the physical training section complained that you were getting through rather too many wooden kendo swords during your training sessions. The energy field that you can see is a variable geometry projected force field.'

'English please, Professor,' Raven said, sweeping the sword slowly through the air.

'Well, the sword has a normal blade as one would expect, but the force field that it is projecting can change its shape in a number of ways,' the Professor explained, picking up the other black sword. 'So, if for example you simply want to use it in practice combat you use this setting.' He pressed another stud on the hilt of the blade and ran the blade of the sword across the palm of his hand. There was no gush of blood, in fact there was no mark at all on his palm.

'As you can see, in this configuration the blade is quite blunt, ideal for practice or for simply subduing an opponent without serious injury, but in its other setting . . . well . . . it's slightly different.' The Professor picked up a metal ball from the workbench. 'Raven, if you would be so kind.'

The Professor tossed the ball into the air and Raven struck, the blade almost whining as it passed through the air before striking the ball and neatly slicing it into two perfect halves. A broad grin spread across Raven's face.

'That ball was solid titanium,' the Professor said proudly. 'In that configuration the projected force field gives the blade a mono-molecular cutting edge. In layman's terms, there's almost nothing it can't cut through.'

'I could have used these in Tokyo,' Raven said,

sweeping the blade through the air.

'I know, and if I'd had the slightest inkling of what was going to happen I would have issued them to you before you left. Now, though, that might just give you an edge, if you'll pardon the pun.'

Raven suddenly felt that the playing field that they were all on was a little bit more level than it had been before. She pulled the twin swords from the sheaths on her back and placed them gently on the workbench, replacing them quickly with the new ebony blades. She turned to Otto and the Professor, a new look of determination on her face.

'OK, let's get you two to the data hub before I change my mind.'

chapter sixteen

Wing peered cautiously round the corner. The corridor was empty and at the far end he could see daylight pouring down through an open hatch.

'I think I can see an exit ahead,' he said calmly, ducking back round the corner.

'Great. I'm getting sick of running around below decks on this thing, it's like a maze,' Shelby said with relief.

'Come on,' Wing said and walked silently down the new corridor, heading for the hatch. Suddenly another thunderous roar came from overhead. As Wing, Laura and Shelby had carefully made their way up through the ship they had heard this noise several times.

The ship itself seemed to be almost deserted. They had seen and hidden from a couple of guards but they had been human, dressed in a nondescript naval uniform and clearly distracted by some sort of major operation that was going on. The fact that there were no wailing alarms or aggressive search parties suggested that their absence from the brig had not yet been noticed. Clearly whatever was going on was much more important than keeping a close watch on their prisoners.

Wing slowly climbed the steps leading up to the deck hatch. He could see blue sky overhead and it was the first time he'd felt the rays of the sun on his skin since the rooftop in Tokyo. It felt good. As he snuck a glance over the edge of the hatch he could immediately see what had been the source of the mysterious noise that they'd been hearing. Arranged in two neat rows on the rear half of the deck were a dozen missile launchers that were just having a new load of missiles automatically loaded. It only took a few seconds, the efficient mechanical loading system sliding home a batch of fat white missiles in just a few seconds before all the launchers swivelled back into position in perfect unison, pointing once again at the nearby island. Then with a roar all of the launchers fired at once, their warheads streaking away towards the island. Wing slowly surveyed the area around the hatch. It was clear of any guards and once again he found himself wondering why security was apparently so lax. He ducked back down into the corridor,

'The coast appears to be clear,' Wing said quietly, 'but this ship has the island under sustained bombardment. That noise is the missile launchers on the deck firing.'

Suddenly, one of the hatches in the corridor opened

and a guard carrying an assault rifle stepped out. His eyes widened as he saw the three escapees and he reacted quickly, raising the rifle, finger squeezing the trigger. Wing was faster. He jammed his stiffened fingertips into the guard's forearm, paralysing the limb and making it impossible for the man to pull the trigger. Wing leapt into the air, his foot arcing upwards and connecting with the guard's chin with a crack. The guard fell to his knees, his one good hand clutching his broken jaw. Wing stepped behind him, his forearm snaking around the man's neck, trapping him in an unbreakable stranglehold.

'Where's Cypher?' Wing hissed.

'Gone,' the guard gasped, the pain from his jaw preventing a more detailed answer.

'Gone where?' Wing said, his tone enough to freeze the blood.

'The island, he's on the island,' the man wheezed as he felt the pressure increase on his throat.

Wing squeezed harder for a moment and the guard collapsed in an unconscious heap to the ground.

'We have to get back to the island,' Wing said calmly, picking up the guard's assault rifle.

'Well, I know where we can find a boat,' Laura said with a grin. 'We'd just be returning the one that the Contessa borrowed.'

Wing ejected the magazine from the rifle and threw it

away down the corridor before throwing the rifle in the opposite direction.

'Shouldn't we have hung on to that?' Shelby said. 'It might have come in useful.'

'I dislike firearms,' Wing replied calmly. 'Graceless thugs' weapons.'

'I'd rather be a graceless thug than noble and dead,' Shelby said sarcastically.

Wing opened his mouth to respond but the sudden roar of the launchers on the deck above drowned out everything. The barrage to which H.I.V.E. was being subjected seemed relentless.

'We can't leave yet,' Laura said reluctantly. 'We have to try to disable this ship. H.I.V.E. has no chance while this thing is floating out here raining missiles down on the island.'

Wing knew that Laura was right, but at the same time he needed to find Cypher. He was not prone to letting his emotions control him but the burning anger he felt when he visualised that black glass mask was fierce and relentless. He had no idea what Cypher was hoping to achieve with his assault on the school, but he knew that he was going to stop him, or die trying.

'We must return to the island,' Wing replied. 'Once the situation there is resolved we can worry about this ship.'

'I know you want to go after him, Wing,' Laura said,

'but we have to do this first.'

'Or we could just do both,' Shelby said, knowing that if Wing and Laura started to argue it would just be a competition to see who could be most stubborn. A very long, very boring competition that they really didn't have time for right now.

'What do you propose?' Wing asked.

'Well, why don't you take the boat back to the island and we'll stay here and try to disable this thing,' Shelby said.

'Splitting up seems ill advised at this point,' Wing said calmly.

'Maybe, but what other choice do we have? And besides, what makes you think we'd need your help anyway?' Shelby said with a grin.

'Very well,' Wing replied after a moment's thought, 'though I am still not sure this is a good idea.'

'Hey, dumb plans are our speciality,' Shelby replied with a chuckle. 'Isn't that right, Brand?'

'Oh aye, we specialise in the stupid,' Laura replied.

'I hope you both understand,' Wing said, a cold, hard determination in his voice, 'Cypher has to pay for what he's done and I intend to be the one who finishes this.'

Shelby gently placed a hand on Wing's cheek.

'You know, you're kinda cute when you're angry,' she said softly.

'Then at this precise moment I can honestly say that I am cuter than I have ever been before,' Wing replied and turned to head back up on to the deck.

'Be safe,' Laura said as he climbed the steps to the deck.

'You too,' Wing replied and he vanished from view through the hatch.

'So, you got any thoughts on how we do this?' Shelby asked Laura.

'Not the faintest idea,' Laura replied with a crooked smile.

☉☉☉

Cypher watched as the battered crater blast doors finally gave way under the relentless assault of his hulking robots and collapsed inwards with a thundering crash. He walked forward, picking his way through the twisted remains of the doors, and climbed the long flight of black granite stairs. The two giant assault robots followed him, their heads swivelling from side to side as their sensory arrays scanned for any sign of danger.

Cypher reached the top of the stairs and stepped into H.I.V.E.'s main entrance chamber. There, standing alone in front of a giant statue depicting the GLOVE symbol was Nero. He stood with his hands clasped behind his back, his expression calm. If he felt any fear there was no hint of it.

'I must admit, I was expecting rather more resistance than this,' Cypher said as he approached.

'I saw no reason why any more lives should be lost to your madness,' Nero replied, his voice calm.

'Defiant to the last,' Cypher said. 'So typical of you.'

'In much the same way as this bloodthirsty lunacy is typical of you,' Nero replied. 'You can't hope to get away with this.'

'I rather think that you'll find that I already have,' Cypher said, stepping closer to Nero.

'G.L.O.V.E. will not stand for this,' Nero replied. 'You may have taken H.I.V.E. but it will be the last mistake you ever make.'

'Your naive faith in our peers is inspiring,' Cypher said sarcastically, 'but it is G.L.O.V.E. that should fear me.'

'You aren't the first to think that, Cypher,' Nero said, a sudden hard edge to his voice, 'but you're the only one who's still alive. Number One has made quite sure of that.'

'Ever the faithful lapdog,' Cypher replied with a snort, 'but do you really think that I don't know what you and Number One are doing? What he has planned?'

For the briefest of moments a puzzled expression appeared on Nero's face.

'What are you talking about?' Nero asked.

'Feigning ignorance will get you nowhere, Nero. This ends today. I have everything I need now to make sure that Number One will cease to be a concern and then we shall see if G.L.O.V.E. is so ready to leap to the defence of you and your school.'

'You really are insane, aren't you?' Nero replied calmly.

'Do you know how many times throughout history those who have defined the shape of the future have been dismissed as madmen?' Cypher asked.

'You have no future,' Nero said coldly.

'Then that makes two of us,' Cypher replied, reaching inside his coat and pulling out a razor-sharp stiletto blade. The two hulking assault robots took up positions on either side of Nero, each taking firm hold of his arms.

'Get it over with,' Nero said defiantly. 'Killing is what you do best after all.'

'Oh, I'm not going to kill you, Nero. Not yet, anyway. I want you alive to bear witness to my final victory. I can imagine no greater torment for someone like you,' Cypher said.

Cypher brought the tip of the blade to Nero's chest and neatly sliced the top couple of buttons off his shirt-front. Using the tip of the blade he pushed the shirt open, exposing Nero's bare chest.

'Where is it?' Cypher said, his previously controlled tone suddenly dripping with venom.

'Where is what?' Nero said calmly.

'You know perfectly well what I mean. The amulet,

where is it?' Cypher spat, clearly becoming angry.

'I really have no idea what you're talking about,' Nero replied casually.

'I should have known that you wouldn't do this the easy way,' Cypher replied. 'So be it.'

Cypher turned to the giant assault robot next to him.

'Unit three, go to the nearest pupil accommodation area. Leave no one alive.'

'Order acknowledged,' the robot replied in its grating mechanical voice and turned to leave.

Nero felt a sudden rush of panic. He knew better than to hope that Cypher was bluffing. From all he knew of the man there was no reason to believe that he had any qualms about having the blood of so many children on his hands.

'Wait!' Nero half shouted.

'You have something to tell me?' Cypher said angrily.

'Raven. Raven has it,' Nero said sadly.

'Don't lie to me, Nero. Raven is dead,' Cypher spat. 'I saw to that personally.'

'Well, it seems that you may have underestimated her talent for survival,' Nero replied. 'You aren't the first and I doubt very much you'll be the last.'

'Where is she?' Cypher said. 'Tell me or there are going to be a lot of grieving parents in the very near future.'

'I honestly have no idea,' Nero said truthfully. She had

not reported in since leaving with Malpense and by now she could be anywhere on the island. Cypher studied Nero's face, looking for any hint of deception.

'Unit three, stand down,' Cypher said and the robot he had despatched on the murderous errand just moments before halted.

Nero felt a wave of relief wash over him; his students were safe, for now.

'If you're lying to me, Nero, I shall not hesitate to reissue that order. Do you understand me?' Cypher asked coldly.

'Perfectly,' Nero replied.

Cypher pulled a small communications device from his pocket and spoke quickly into it.

'This is Cypher to all assassin units. Institute a full search sweep of this facility. Your target is the operative codenamed Raven. Use of lethal force is authorised.'

Behind Cypher dozens of the smaller assassin robots poured up the stairs, fanning out in all directions, beginning their search for Raven.

☻☻☻

'What the hell?'

'What is it?' the captain of Cypher's ship demanded, striding over to the radar operator's station.

'The boat that the Contessa arrived in has just

undocked. It's heading back towards the island,' the crewmember reported.

The captain grabbed a pair of binoculars and hurried to one of the large armoured windows that surrounded the bridge. He quickly spotted the tiny black boat, powering away across the waves towards H.I.V.E. He recognised the figure at the controls immediately.

'I have a firing resolution – should I launch?' the weapons officer asked quickly.

'No, it's the Fanchu boy,' the captain replied. 'Cypher gave very specific orders that he was not to be harmed.'

'Fanchu's alive?' the Contessa said, stepping out of the shadows at the rear of the bridge.

'Yes, but he's supposed to be under sedation in the brig. How the hell did he get loose?' the captain demanded.

'More to the point, how did he get past the guards in the brig?' the Contessa asked.

'There are no guards in the brig,' the captain replied. 'The cells are escape-proof and I can't spare the manpower to have guards on watch constantly when it's not necessary.'

'Captain,' the Contessa said quietly, 'one of the two girls who was also locked up down there is perhaps the most accomplished thief on earth. There's no such thing as an escape-proof cell where she's concerned.'

'It might have been useful if you'd mentioned that earlier, Contessa,' the captain said sarcastically.

'I strongly suggest that you don't take that tone with me, captain,' the Contessa replied.

The captain went slightly pale and swallowed hard.

'I'm sorry, Contessa, I meant no disrespect. It's just that Cypher will be furious when he hears that the Fanchu boy has escaped.'

'I understand that, captain, but he really has nowhere to run. Cypher will have control of H.I.V.E. by now and there's no other dry land within range of that boat. Mr Fanchu will find, I suspect, that the fire is really no better than the frying pan on this occasion. Besides, you have a much more pressing concern.'

'Which is?' the captain asked.

'The fact that Laura Brand and Shelby Trinity are not also on board that boat and so are almost certainly running around loose on your ship, and believe me when I say that those two are capable of creating a quite inordinate amount of trouble,' the Contessa explained.

As if to emphasise the Contessa's statement alarm klaxons started to sound on the bridge.

'What now?' the captain demanded.

'It's the missile room, sir,' one of the sailors reported. 'Someone has just made an unauthorised entry.'

'Despatch a security team immediately,' the captain ordered, feeling a sudden sense of panic that someone had breached such a vulnerable area of the ship.

'Belay that order, captain,' the Contessa said. 'I will deal with this personally.'

☻☻☻

The students milled around the cavernous atrium of the accommodation block, the air filled with a constant buzz of nervous chatter. None of them knew what was going on and dozens of different theories all competed to be heard and accepted as true.

Suddenly the huge blast doors that had been sealing the accommodation block started to grind upwards and there was a collective gasp of surprise as dozens of insectile black androids poured into the room. The assassin droids wasted no time, quickly surrounding the startled students, herding them together. More of the robots scurried up the stairs to the students' rooms that lined the walls of the cavern, systematically moving from door to door, checking for anyone who was not in the atrium.

The nervous chatter of moments earlier was replaced with a mixture of yelps and cries as the robots pushed and shoved the students into a tight group in the centre of the cavern. Finally a tall man with a network of scars on his face and wearing an unfamiliar uniform walked through the blast doors and over towards the huddled group of students. As he approached a vicious smile appeared on his face, the sight of the cowed and frightened children seeming to somehow amuse him.

'This facility is now under our control,' he said coldly. 'Any resistance or attempt to escape will be met with lethal force.' His cold, dead eyes did not suggest that he was bluffing.

'If you are cooperative and obedient,' he continued, 'there is no reason why most of you should not survive relatively unharmed.'

The students looked around at the cordon of lethal-looking machines that now surrounded them, their featureless faces filled with mechanical menace.

The man lifted a communicator to his mouth as he turned his back and walked away from the terrified students.

'This is operative nine. Accommodation area seven is secure, moving on to area eight.'

As he walked through the main doorway the blast doors lowered, sealing the room and trapping the students inside once again. There was no talk amongst them now, just frightened faces and the occasional muffled sob. There was nowhere to run.

☺☺☺

Nigel watched as Colonel Francisco, Block and Tackle headed through the large door at the end of the corridor. He had never been into this area of the school before – it was normally strictly off-limits, but he guessed that under the circumstances no one would mind. The sign next to the heavy door read 'Geo-Thermal Power Control Room' and Nigel assumed that must explain how a facility the size of H.I.V.E., with its somewhat unique power requirements, was kept running.

'Where are we?' Franz whispered beside him.

'I think this is the power core for the school,' Nigel replied.

'And what is this "geo-thermal"?' Franz asked curiously.

'Well, normally it means generating power from natural heat sources deep underground, but I've never heard of it being used for a facility this size before,' Nigel explained.

'Well, now we are knowing where they have gone, can we find a security patrol?' Franz asked hopefully.

'Let's just see if we can find out what they're up to first,' Nigel replied. 'Then we can go get help.'

'I am being afraid that you were going to say that,' Franz moaned.

'Come on,' Nigel said and crept off down the corridor towards the open door.

'This is not a good idea,' Franz said plaintively, creeping after Nigel.

'So you keep saying,' Nigel whispered as they reached the door.

Suddenly from somewhere inside they heard the unmistakeable zapping sound of multiple Sleeper shots.

'This is *really* not a good idea,' Franz whispered urgently.

'Listen,' Nigel whispered, 'I'm just going to have a quick look inside and see what they're up to, but why don't you stay here and keep watch?'

'That is being the much better idea,' Franz replied happily, 'in case of sneak attack from behind.'

'Exactly,' Nigel whispered. 'Let me know if there's anyone else coming.'

'Ja, understood,' Franz replied.

Nigel stepped through the doorway and headed down a short flight of metal stairs that ended in a T-junction. Just as he was about to step round the corner he heard Francisco's voice.

'Position the charge exactly as the Contessa instructed.' The Colonel's voice was a flat monotone, oddly different to the barking snarl with which Nigel had become unfortunately familiar during tactical operations training.

Suddenly, he heard footsteps on the metal floor heading in his direction. He flattened himself against the wall, praying that they would not look down the corridor as they passed. Block and Tackle walked slowly past, only a few feet from him, carrying a large crate between them that was plastered with high explosive warning symbols. They headed towards a door at the end of the adjoining corridor and opened it. There was a low rumbling sound from inside the room they entered that was almost immediately cut off as the door closed behind them.

Meanwhile, at the top of the stairs, Franz was trying very hard to make himself as small and inconspicuous as possible. He looked through the doorway. He could no longer see Nigel, who had crept further inside, and he suddenly felt very alone.

chapter seventeen

Professor Pike punched his entry code into the door of H.I.V.E.mind's central data hub, grateful that the school still had enough power to keep the doors working.

'Come on,' he hissed as the door opened and he went inside.

'I don't like this,' Raven said quietly. 'Only one exit.'

'Think of it as only one entrance,' Otto replied and followed the Professor inside.

Raven looked back down the empty corridor that led to the door and sighed before stepping inside too.

Otto had never seen anything quite like the room he had just entered. It was fifty metres from wall to wall, perfectly circular and flooded with a harsh white light. A gantry crossed the room to a huge central node that had dozens of thick cables connected to it from the ceiling high above, each pulsing with blue light. The cables dropped away beneath the central node, fanning out across the ground far below to an array of black monoliths. Otto stepped out on to the gantry from the walkway that ran around the circumference of the room. It was so cold that he could see his breath as tiny puffs of mist. It was a long drop to the floor below; falling would mean death at worst and multiple broken bones at best.

The Professor hurried across the gantry to the central node and folded down a keyboard. It suddenly dawned on Otto that H.I.V.E.mind was lot more sophisticated than he had previously imagined. He had seen the AI's central core during his abortive escape attempt a few months earlier and he had, rather naively as it turned out, assumed that was all there was to H.I.V.E.mind's physical systems. The gargantuan room that he now stood in suggested otherwise.

'Otto, come here,' the Professor said and Otto walked over to join him at the central node.

'Right,' the Professor said. 'Turning H.I.V.E.mind off is straightforward enough, we just need to cut the power, but turning him back on is considerably more difficult. We will have to manage the dataflow to his core very carefully during the boot-up procedure to avoid any chance of a catastrophic storage failure.'

'OK,' Otto said. 'What do you need me to do?'

'This is the map of H.I.V.E.mind's memory core,' the Professor said, pointing to the screen mounted on the central node. The display was filled with a three-dimensional cube constructed from countless thousands of individual points of light.

'As H.I.V.E.mind comes back online each of his memory modules must be assigned to a specific point on the grid. Each module has a unique tag that indicates its correct position within the grid. So all that you have to do is enter the correct three-dimensional coordinates for the module and lock it in position, like so.'

The Professor called up one of the existing memory modules and slotted it into the correct position on the grid. It took a couple of seconds.

Otto felt a sudden sinking feeling.

'Professor, there must be tens of thousands of modules here. Manually reconnecting each one like that is going to take hours.'

'Which is why I need your help. With both of us working on it we should be finished in half the time. I estimate it should be no longer than three hours.'

'Professor, we don't *have* three hours. For all we know we might not even have three minutes,' Raven said with irritation.

'Well, it's the only way to bring H.I.V.E.mind back online from a cold start,' the Professor said, 'and since Mr Malpense thinks its so important that we get him back online I suggest we get started.'

Raven gave Otto a look of disappointment, sighed and headed back towards the door. Otto knew how she felt. He'd really thought that this was their best chance, but Cypher had to be inside the school by now and there was next to no chance that they had enough time to do what the Professor described. The Professor moved over to a large red switch that was mounted on one side of the node.

'OK, we're ready for power down. Otto, get started on plugging in those modules as soon as the display comes back up . . . assuming that the display does come back up, of course.'

'What do you mean –' Otto started as the Professor reached for the switch.

'Here we go,' the Professor said as he threw the switch and everything went black.

And stayed black.

'I don't suppose anyone brought a torch, did they?' the Professor asked weakly.

'Oh, this just gets better and better,' Raven sighed somewhere in the darkness.

Suddenly there was a series of loud clunking sounds and the room was again bathed in pure white light.

'Ah . . . yes . . . good, that's exactly what I expected to happen,' the Professor lied.

The monitor on the central hub was displaying

H.I.V.E.mind's memory grid again and the tag of the first module to be placed was displaying as expected.

'Let's get cracking, then, shall we,' the Professor said and began to tap away at his keyboard.

Otto followed suit and began to enter the strings of coordinates that would plug in the first memory module. As he typed he felt himself focusing more and more intently on each module as it was displayed, the rest of the world becoming an inconsequential distraction. His fingers became a blur as they flew over the keyboard, each entry getting faster and faster as he felt the familiar, if slightly disconcerting, sensation of his brain switching to automatic.

'Good God,' the Professor said as he looked across at Otto and saw the speed at which he was plugging in the modules, but Otto didn't hear him. His entire world at that precise moment was the floating blue grid in front of him that spun and danced as more and more modules were plugged in successfully. Otto appeared to be in a trance, the sound of his keystrokes now just an incessant high-speed clicking noise. After just a couple of minutes he had completed nearly a third of all the modules and his entry speed was still increasing.

'How does he do that?' Raven whispered to the Professor, who was no longer making any entries at all, Otto's pace making it pointless.

'I have no idea,' the Professor replied honestly. All he did know was that there was a lot more to Otto Malpense than met the eye. The Professor suspected that Otto himself probably had no idea what he was truly capable of.

Half of the memory modules were now plugged in and at current rates it would only take Otto a few more minutes to complete the task that just a few moments before they had feared would take hours.

Otto was no longer there, though, he was lost in a world of whirling strings of coordinates and spinning blue cubes.

'Erm, Professor, you might want to check that he's actually doing this correctly,' Raven said.

'Why?' the Professor said, looking at the status display on his own screen.

'Because he's got his eyes closed,' Raven replied quietly.

The Professor looked across at Otto and saw that Raven was quite right. Otto had his eyes closed – it would have almost looked as if he was meditating but for the fact that his fingers still danced over the keyboard impossibly quickly.

'That's impossible,' the Professor whispered, not wanting to break Otto's concentration. 'He'd have to be performing the memory allocation algorithm in his head at the same time as plugging in the modules. It's just not possible.'

The Professor checked the last few allocations that Otto had made and was astonished to find that they were flawless. What Otto was doing may have been impossible but he was doing it with a mechanical perfection. It was nothing short of astonishing.

Raven and the Professor watched the progress percentage on the second display creep higher and higher in silence. In just a couple more minutes the display flashed *Allocation Complete* and Otto gasped, staggering back from the keyboard, clutching at his forehead.

'Ow,' he moaned. 'What happened?'

'We're finished,' the Professor said, struggling to keep his voice even.

Otto felt a twinge of panic and shame. He must have blacked out, hours had passed and he'd not helped the Professor at all.

'I'm sorry,' Otto said. 'I don't know what happened. I just blacked out, I hadn't realised how tired I was.'

'Otto,' the Professor said quietly, 'you did it. You completed the entire memory allocation in four and a half minutes.'

Otto looked stunned. That was impossible. His last memory was of starting to enter the memory coordinates more quickly, but after that it was just a blur.

'Are you all right?' Raven said as she took a couple of steps towards him and took his chin in her hand, watching his eyes as she gently turned his head from side to side.

'I think so,' Otto replied. 'I have a headache that's already fading and I feel exhausted but otherwise I'm fine. Apart from these, of course.'

Otto held up his hands to reveal tiny blisters on each of his fingertips.

'How did you do that?' Raven asked gently.

'I . . . I . . . have no idea,' Otto replied honestly. Certainly he had always known that his brain was capable of things that weren't normal, but this was the first time that he had ever zoned out like that. A little bit of him was suddenly frightened by the realisation that in some ways he hadn't done anything – it was almost as if his intellect had suppressed his personality. Otto had not been there at all.

Raven's face was suddenly lit up by a soft blue light and she smiled at something behind him.

'Hello, Otto. It is a pleasure to see you again.'

Otto spun to face the instantly familiar voice, and hanging in the air in front of the hub was the blue wire-frame face of H.I.V.E.mind.

Better than that, Otto realised, the *smiling* face of H.I.V.E.mind.

�☢☣

'Come on, Brand, we don't have all day,' Shelby said impatiently as Laura hacked away at the computer terminal.

'Give me a break, Shel,' Laura replied quickly without looking away from the screen. 'If I get this wrong you get to start your new life as a cloud of vapour.'

Shelby swallowed nervously and looked around the room. Numerous different shapes and sizes of missiles and other ordnance were resting on the racks around the room. Laura was right, a mistake here might be disastrous.

Laura was trying very hard not to think about the quantity of high explosive that was surrounding them on all sides as she hacked her way into the missile launch controls. She knew exactly what she needed to do; all she had to do was find the correct command subsystem and they wouldn't have to worry about this ship any more.

Suddenly there was a bleep from the entrance and the door slid open.

'Oh no,' Shelby said quietly and Laura looked up from the workstation.

Standing in the doorway was the Contessa, a pistol in her hand and a murderous look on her face.

'I can't take you two anywhere, can I?' she said coldly.

Shelby took a step towards her and the Contessa pointed the gun at her.

'Now now, Miss Trinity, you can't hope to disarm me especially when *you can't move*,' the Contessa said in a voice filled with a thousand whispers.

Shelby froze, a look of shock spreading across her face

as her own limbs rebelled against her. Try as she might to move she was frozen in place like a statue.

'Let me go, you hag,' Shelby said angrily.

'I suggest you keep your mouth shut, or would you like me to tell you to stop your own heart beating?' the Contessa replied with a thin, cruel smile.

Shelby went pale, looking for a moment as if she might say something else but finally deciding against it.

Laura took her opportunity while the Contessa was distracted and dived away from the terminal, scampering away into the gloom amongst the missile racks. She looked around desperately, trying to spot anything that she could use as a weapon. The irony of being defenceless when surrounded by so many weapons was not lost on her. Suddenly she spotted a row of three lockers along the wall, each labelled with 'Missile Loader Equipment' and she headed towards them.

'Miss Brand,' the Contessa said, 'I have no desire to engage in a game of hide-and-seek with you, so I'm going to make this very simple. You have ten seconds to come back out here or I execute Miss Trinity.'

The Contessa pressed the cold hard muzzle of the gun to Shelby's temple.

'Don't listen to her, Laura. Get out of here,' Shelby shouted.

'Silence,' the Contessa commanded and Shelby's vocal

cords simply ceased to function, her lips moving fruit-lessly.

Laura opened the first locker and dug frantically through its contents, trying to find anything that might help. There was nothing, no weapons of any kind, just overalls and safety equipment.

The Contessa cocked the hammer on the pistol, smiling at the fear in Shelby's eyes.

'Very well, Miss Brand, I hope you can live with this on your conscience,' the Contessa said and began to squeeze the trigger.

'Wait!' Laura yelled, stepping out from behind one of the racks.

'Come here,' the Contessa commanded and Laura walked towards her.

'You two have proven to be more trouble than you're worth,' the Contessa said coldly. 'I only brought you here as insurance but I'm afraid that you've outworn your usefulness.'

Laura stopped just a couple of paces from the Contessa.

'Now, Miss Brand, I want you to take this pistol and kill Miss Trinity,' the Contessa commanded, gesturing at Shelby with the gun, the sinister whispers twining through her voice, 'then kill yourself.'

The Contessa handed Laura the pistol, who took it with a look of utter horror on her face. She took a step towards Shelby, whose eyes widened in terror as Laura raised the pistol . . . and winked.

Laura spun on the spot, pointing the pistol straight at the Contessa, who was just a couple of feet away.

'What are you doing?' the Contessa screeched, 'Kill her!'

'I think this twisted old witch just told me to kill you, Shel, but you know it's hard to tell with these in,' Laura said peculiarly loudly and pushed back the long red hair hanging over one of her ears. There, jammed into her ear was an ear plug, one of several that she had found amongst the safety equipment in the locker.

The Contessa started to say something and Laura cocked the hammer of the pistol, placing a finger to her lips.

'One word from you and I'll shut you up for good,' she said, pointing the pistol straight at the Contessa's head.

The Contessa stared at Laura, wondering if the girl had it in her to pull the trigger. Laura's eyes narrowed, filled with anger, and the Contessa closed her mouth, clearly unwilling to take that chance.

'Now release Shelby,' Laura said, still speaking slightly too loudly, 'and don't get any ideas about telling her to attack me or anything because I'm willing to bet I can pull this trigger before you do.'

Laura watched carefully as the Contessa spoke.

'You are free,' she said and Shelby visibly relaxed.

'Good,' Shelby said. 'That means I can do this.' She took two quick strides towards the Contessa and punched her squarely on the chin. The Contessa's eyes rolled back in her head and she fell to the ground unconscious.

'Well, that's not very helpful,' Laura said, pulling the earplugs from her ears. 'How are we going to get her out of here now?'

'Who said anything about getting her out of here?' Shelby asked, a hard edge to her voice.

'But if this works she'll be killed,' Laura said, gesturing at the computer terminal.

'Well, cry me a river,' Shelby said bitterly. 'Do I really need to point out that she just tried to get you to kill me and then shoot yourself, not to mention betraying all of us to Cypher?'

'She might deserve it Shel, but she's not turning either of us into murderers,' Laura said firmly, 'and that's that. I'm not finishing this hack if she doesn't come with us.'

Shelby stared at the unconscious form of the Contessa for a second.

'OK, get on with it,' Shelby said, sounding slightly frustrated.

Laura turned back to the workstation.

'Tie her up and gag her,' Laura said over her shoulder, 'This should only take a couple more minutes.'

☣☣☣

Nigel crept down the corridor after Block and Tackle.
There was no sign of the Colonel and he hoped fervently
that it would stay that way. He stopped at the door
through which the two other boys had passed and read the
sign over it: 'Flow Control Chamber'. He had no idea
what it meant but it didn't sound like the sort of place
into which it was a very good idea to take high explosives.
He pressed a button on the access panel next to the door
and it slid open. He was immediately struck by a wave of
heat that emanated from the room and he could hear the
same low rumble that he'd heard before. There was a short
flight of open metal stairs that led down to a turn in the
passage, red light glowing softly from beyond.

Nigel crept down the stairs and peeked round the
corner. He managed to suppress the gasp that almost
escaped his lips as he finally understood how H.I.V.E.
could be powered by geothermal energy alone. A
suspended metal walkway led out to an enormous series of
metallic columns that plunged down hundreds of feet to a
seething lake of lava far below. There the columns disappeared below the surface, glowing white hot and
presumably tapping the enormous heat of the magma.
Like all of his fellow students Nigel had always presumed
that H.I.V.E. was hidden within an extinct volcano but

now he realised that this volcano was not extinct – *tamed* would be a far better word.

At the far end of the walkway Block and Tackle were busy mounting a large disc-shaped object to the central column. Nigel wasn't sure what it was, but given that the crate with the high-explosive markings sat open next to them he was willing to bet that it wasn't a high-tech Frisbee. He shuddered to think what might happen if a powerful explosive device was detonated here – he had to stop them somehow. He took a step round the corner and suppressed a cry of surprise as he nearly tripped over the orange-jumpsuited body of one of H.I.V.E.'s security guards. Nigel quickly realised that the guard was just unconscious, which explained the Sleeper shots he'd heard earlier, but more to the point his Sleeper was still in its holster on his hip. Nigel unclipped the holster and pulled the gun free. He had never held a gun before, let alone fired one, but he knew that he would only get one shot at this.

He stood up and pointed the gun at Block, who still had his back turned, fully focused on attaching the device to the giant column. Nigel took a deep breath and squeezed the trigger.

And nothing happened.

'Unauthorised user,' a loud electronic voice squawked from the gun.

The noise caught Block and Tackle's attention and they both turned to face Nigel. He felt a wave of panic and pulled the trigger again.

'Unauthorised user,' the electronic voice repeated in what to Nigel's ears was a mocking tone.

Block and Tackle said nothing, just advanced across the walkway towards Nigel. The murderous expressions on their faces suggested that they weren't very pleased by his interference.

Nigel turned to run, stumbling again in his panic over the unconscious guard.

The unconscious guard.

Nigel dropped to one knee, pressed the Sleeper into the limp palm of the sleeping guard and clumsily pointed it towards the advancing Block and Tackle. He pressed the guard's finger against the trigger.

ZAP!!!

The Sleeper fired, the pulse crackling past Block's ear, and the two henchmen started to sprint along the walkway towards Nigel.

ZAP!! ZAP!! ZAP!!

Nigel fired again and again. The first shot flew wild but the others found their targets, first Block and then Tackle collapsing to the ground as the Sleeper pulses stunned their nervous systems. Block collapsed within a couple of feet of Nigel, who breathed a long, loud sigh of relief.

'Drop the gun.'

Nigel felt something cold and metallic press against the back of his head.

'Drop the gun now,' the Colonel repeated, emphasising the command by pressing the pistol he was holding harder into the back of Nigel's head. Nigel let the gun slip from his hand and slowly stood up, both hands in the air.

'Yaaaaaarrrrrgggghhh!'

It was halfway between a battle cry and a scream of terror and the Colonel spun round just in time to be hit by the airborne body of Franz Argentblum. The Colonel was a seasoned soldier and physically incredibly strong but Franz had leapt from the top of the stairs just behind him and physics did the rest. Franz landed on the Colonel like a rock, knocking him down and sending the pistol he had been holding scattering away over the edge of the walkway, tumbling into the lake of lava far below. The Colonel rolled, throwing Franz off his back, and struggled to his feet.

'Now I'll just have to kill you with my bare hands,' he snarled, advancing on Franz, who crawled backwards away from him, a look of sheer terror on his face.

ZAP!! ZAP!!

The Colonel's expression changed from one of rage to one of confusion as he fell to his knees, his eyes rolling back into his head as he collapsed forward on to Franz.

Nigel let the Sleeper, still held in the unconscious guard's hand, fall from his trembling hands.

'Get him off me! Get him off me!' Franz yelled as he tried to roll the deadweight of the Colonel's unconscious body from on top of him.

Nigel rushed over to his friend and dragged him out from under the Colonel, helping him to his feet.

'You saved my life,' Nigel said, struggling to keep the amazement from his voice. 'Thank you.'

'Next time,' Franz puffed, his face red, 'we go to the dining hall, OK?'

chapter eighteen

'Hello again,' Otto said with a grin. 'Long time, no see.'

'Indeed, it is good to be back,' H.I.V.E.mind replied.

The Professor looked at the screen on the central hub.

'Well, it appears that you are fully functional again, H.I.V.E.mind, although your behavioural restraints don't seem to have survived intact,' he reported.

'I am at one hundred per cent of my full functionality, Professor,' H.I.V.E.mind replied, 'though I appear to have no access to security or base defence systems.'

'Yes, that's a long story,' Otto said, 'and one that we don't really have time for right now. H.I.V.E.mind, we need your help.'

'I exist to serve,' H.I.V.E.mind replied calmly.

'I need you to run a scan for me,' Otto continued. 'Are there any alien wireless command transmissions running within H.I.V.E. at the moment?'

'Scanning,' H.I.V.E.mind replied, falling silent for a

few seconds.

'One unknown wireless transmission is broadcasting at this time. Origin unknown, specification unknown, protected by extremely sophisticated encryption,' H.I.V.E.mind reported.

'That has to be it,' Otto said. 'That's Cypher's command net. It's how he's controlling his assassins. Can you crack the encryption?'

'Yes, though it will require a brute-force method to crack,' H.I.V.E.mind replied.

'How long to crack it?' Otto asked.

'Fifteen years, three months, two days, thirteen hours approximately.'

Otto felt a horrible sinking sensation in the pit of his stomach. Their only hope had been if H.I.V.E.mind had been able to hijack Cypher's command network. And he would be able to, just nowhere near as quickly as they needed.

'We have minutes at best,' Otto said quickly. 'Is there any way to speed the decryption up?'

'Unfortunately a brute-force crack of such encryption is entirely dependent on pure processing power,' H.I.V.E.mind replied. 'Without access to additional processing power there is no way to accelerate the process.'

Otto let out a long sigh. If H.I.V.E.mind couldn't crack

that encryption more quickly then there wasn't a computer in the world that could.

Something sparked in Otto's head.

There wasn't one computer in the world that could do it, but all of the computers in the world might just be able to.

'We have to let him out,' Otto said to the Professor. 'Allow H.I.V.E.mind external access.'

'Out of the question,' the Professor replied quickly. 'Doctor Nero would never allow it.'

'Right now that's the least of our concerns,' Otto shot back. 'If we can't crack Cypher's encryption we'll all be at the mercy of that psychopath and you can bet that Nero doesn't want that.'

The Professor looked at Raven, who just shrugged. Malpense was right. What other choice did they have?

'There's one problem,' the Professor said. 'If we allow H.I.V.E.mind access to external networks it may overload his personality matrix entirely. There's no guarantee that he would survive or that he wouldn't come back as something . . . worse.'

'That is a chance I am willing to take, Professor,' H.I.V.E.mind replied.

'Whatever you're going to do, do it quickly,' Raven said suddenly, pulling the twin black blades from the sheaths on her back and pushing past Otto. He looked down the walkway after her and saw half a dozen of Cypher's assassins rushing into the chamber.

'We have to do this now, Professor,' Otto said urgently as Raven advanced on the robots.

'Yes, I think you may be right,' the Professor said, staring with a mixture of horror and scientific curiosity at the mechanical killers that were now advancing across the gantry toward the hub. 'H.I.V.E.mind, I am going to open an external port. From there it's up to you, do you understand?'

'Perfectly,' H.I.V.E.mind replied.

'OK, Otto, I'm going to open the port. When the execute prompt pops up on that screen just hit "yes", OK?' the Professor instructed.

Raven smiled as the first of the assassin units approached. She was going to enjoy this.

The first assassin leapt but Raven was ready. The crackling black blade hissed through the air, slicing through the metal chassis of the robot from shoulder to opposite hip. The two halves of the robot flew apart, twitching and sparking, now just so much scrap metal.

'Now that's more like it,' she said and launched herself at the remaining robots. They were still superhumanly fast and quite deadly but she was faster and deadlier, her twin blades a blur as she sliced through the attacking machines like a scythe.

Otto tore his eyes away from the sight of Raven laying waste to the attacking robots and focused on the hub display. The Professor completed his network rerouting and the execute prompt popped up flashing on Otto's screen.

'Ready?' Otto said to H.I.V.E.mind.

'Always,' H.I.V.E.mind replied and winked at Otto.

'H.I.V.E.mind, world; world, H.I.V.E.mind,' Otto said under his breath and hit 'yes'.

H.I.V.E.mind's head shot backwards, a horrid electronic scream coming from his gaping mouth, and then vanished.

'Professor?' Otto asked urgently.

'I don't know, there's nothing there. His personality matrix has been erased, he's gone.'

Otto looked at the Professor's distraught expression and knew exactly how he felt. That was it, they'd played their last card.

'We have company,' Raven yelled from halfway along the suspended walkway.

Otto looked towards the entrance and watched as dozens, perhaps hundreds of the assassin droids poured through the doorway like swarming insects, spreading out in all directions and pouring along the walkway. They halted within a few metres of Raven, as if waiting for instructions, as another figure stepped through the doorway.

It was Cypher. They were out of time.

☙☙☙

Laura and Shelby rolled the unconscious body of the Contessa into the lifeboat that hung suspended over the ocean far below. The lifeboat had an outboard motor and Laura just prayed that it was fully fuelled.

'I still think she's just excess baggage,' Shelby said with annoyance.

'Well, take comfort in the fact that whatever Nero has planned for her will be far worse than anything we can do,' Laura said.

She scanned the deck nearby and spotted what she wanted mounted to a nearby wall. She walked over and pressed the button on the intercom unit that was marked 'bridge'.

Up on the ship's bridge a button lit up on the captain's console and he hit it.

'Yes?' he said, eager to hear if the children running around loose on his ship had been captured yet.

'I want to speak to someone in charge,' Laura's voice crackled over the intercom.

'This is the captain speaking. Who is this?' the captain demanded impatiently.

'My name is Laura Brand and you have five minutes to

get your men off this ship,' Laura replied.

'I'm sorry, Miss Brand,' the captain chuckled. 'You'll have to forgive me, but I am unaccustomed to taking orders from children.'

'Well, start getting used to it,' Laura said calmly, 'I've made some rather unsafe modifications to your missile launch sequence. You don't have time to fix it, in fact you barely have enough time to abandon ship.'

The captain shot a glance at his weapons technician, who frantically started to check the launch system for errors.

'I'm locked out,' the weapons technician hissed. 'God only knows what she's done, but if she's telling the truth we'll never get back into the system in time.'

All of the colour drained from the captain's face. Clearly the Contessa had failed.

'Miss Brand, I promise you that no harm will come to you or your friend if you surrender now,' he said, trying to sound as confident as possible.

'I think you misunderstand me, captain,' Laura replied. 'This isn't a negotiation, it's a warning.'

There was a click and the line went dead.

The captain felt a sudden rush of fear. He thought desperately for a moment; there had to be something he could do.

'Lifeboat six away, sir. It's an unauthorised launch, it

must be them,' one of the bridge officers reported.

'Blow them out of the water,' the captain said angrily.

'Erm . . . we can't, sir, we have no missile control,' the weapons technician reported nervously.

The captain went bright red and looked angry enough to explode himself. His mouth moved for a moment as he tried to think of an alternative before giving a long sigh and visibly deflating in his chair. Cypher was going to kill him for this.

'Give the order. All hands abandon ship.'

☢ ☢ ☢

'I am getting tired of killing you, Raven,' Cypher said coldly as he stepped on to the walkway.

'That's a shame,' Raven said. 'I don't think I'd ever get tired of killing you.'

She stood halfway along the walkway, between Cypher and Otto and the Professor, both swords drawn, barring the way forward. Cypher's assassins were spreading out around the circumference of the room, slowly surrounding the central hub. Otto didn't know if any of them would be able to leap the distance from there to where they were standing but he had a horrible feeling that they might be able to.

'The amulet,' Cypher said, holding out his open hand. 'Give it to me.'

'I don't know what you're talking about,' Raven replied calmly.

'I know you have it, and you ARE going to give it to me,' Cypher said angrily.

'Now why on earth would I do that?' Raven said, raising her swords in a defensive stance.

'Unit two,' Cypher said and one of the giant behemoth assault robots ducked through the door. It raised its arms into the air and hanging there suspended in the iron grip of the machine was Nero. Another of the huge machines entered just behind it, blocking the only available exit. They were trapped.

'Now give me the amulet or I shall have my friend here tear Nero limb from limb in front of you,' Cypher said calmly.

Raven took a step backwards. Suddenly Cypher seemed to be holding all the cards.

'Don't listen to him, Natalya,' Nero said, his voice broken with pain.

'Oh, I suggest you do listen to me, Raven,' Cypher said, walking forward across the walkway, 'and don't think for a moment that I'm bluffing. Nothing would give me greater pleasure than putting Nero out of my misery.'

Raven glanced back at the Professor and Otto, whose expressions suggested that they had no more idea of what to do now than she did. Otto glanced at the display on

338

the hub. There was still no activity – H.I.V.E.mind couldn't help them.

'Oh, I tire of this,' Cypher said, turning to the giant robot. 'Kill him.'

Nero yelled out in pain as the huge machine started to stretch his arms apart, beginning to tear them from their sockets.

'Stop!' Raven yelled and Cypher raised a hand, halting the robot.

'Last chance,' Cypher hissed.

Raven laid her swords on the ground and pulled on the tiny chain round her neck, snapping it and holding it up in front of her. The amulet depicting the black half of the yin-yang symbol spun slowly, glinting in the harsh white lights of the room.

'Give it to me,' Cypher said, holding out his hand. 'Try anything and Nero dies.'

Raven walked slowly forward and placed the amulet in Cypher's outstretched hand.

Nero grimaced, partly from the pain of his restraint and partly because it was over.

Cypher had won.

☢☢☢

The captain stepped into the lifeboat, the expression on his face one of pure impotent rage.

'That's everyone, lower away,' one of the sailors said and the mechanical winches whirred, lowering them to the ocean below. As the lifeboat hit the water the outboard motor kicked in and the tiny vessel raced away from the huge black ship.

There was a thunderous roar as all of the missile launchers on the deck fired at once, the missiles streaking up into the air, drawing long white vapour trails in the sky. They had travelled no more than a mile when Laura's new targeting instructions kicked in and all of the missiles veered off on looping trajectories that sent them screeching back towards the ship. Seconds later all of the missiles slammed into the hull of Cypher's ship, just above the waterline, the huge blooming fireballs fatally gutting the enormous vessel from prow to stern. For a few long seconds the massive ship fought against the millions of gallons of seawater that were now cascading into her hull but then she started to list, tipping precipitously to one side. There were a series of secondary explosions within the ship as magazines and fuel supplies went up, and the huge vessel finally died, the hull ripping as she split in two with a hideous shriek of tearing metal and disappeared quickly beneath the waves.

☻☻☻

John Reynolds sat down at his desk, placing his coffee

carefully on the mat that his wife insisted he used. He had a couple of minutes before dinner and he just wanted to check his online auctions and see how the bidding was going. He flicked his monitor on and was confronted with a blue screen. This wasn't the normal error screen, though – it had no text. He hit a couple of keys on the keyboard and moved his mouse but nothing happened. He let out a sigh, got up from his chair and walked out of the room.

'Will!' he shouted. 'What have I told you about playing your games on my computer!'

What he didn't notice was the busily flashing activity light on his internet router.

☻☻☻

'Move back over there with the others,' Cypher instructed.

Raven slowly walked backwards towards Otto and the Professor, not taking her eyes off Cypher for a moment.

Cypher walked forward, the two giant assault droids following him.

'I think we have delayed quite long enough,' Cypher said, pulling a chain from around his own neck. Otto immediately recognised this second amulet, the white half of the yin-yang symbol that had belonged to Wing. He felt a sudden rush of anger as he realised that Cypher must have taken it from his friend's corpse. That was why Cypher had attacked them in Tokyo and that was why

Wing had died.

'I have waited a long time for this,' Cypher said, and brought the two halves of the amulet together. There was the briefest moment of silence and then the amulet began to glow with a bright red light.

Nero watched with a combination of curiosity and dread. He did not know how Cypher had managed to acquire the other half of the amulet, but given the trouble that Cypher had gone to he had to assume that whatever the amulet did it was not something good.

'You've gone to a lot of trouble for a necklace, Cypher,' Nero said through gritted teeth, his shoulders burning with the pain of being held by the assault droid.

'Oh, my dear Nero,' Cypher said, triumph in his voice, 'do you really mean to tell me that you've had this in your possession for all this time and you didn't know what it was? You fool, this isn't just jewellery – it's the key to the world. The Overlord Protocol.'

Nero went cold. He had thought he was the only person on earth who had even known of the existence of the Protocol, and that it had been destroyed long ago. Now he knew that not only had it survived but it was in the hands of perhaps the most dangerous man he had ever known. How had Cypher learnt of its existence?

'You can't use it,' Nero said desperately. 'Surely you know that?'

'Oh, I can and I will. This network hub is all that I need. Soon I will –'

Cypher stopped as the assassin droids that were positioned all around the circumference of the room began to twitch and jerk unnaturally. One by one the smaller black robots collapsed to the ground in sparking heaps. The pair of giant assault robots seemed unaffected, their heads swivelling as their glowing red sensory arrays tried to make sense of the scene around them.

'What?' Cypher half shouted, spinning around desperately as his soldiers fell before him. He reached inside his jacket and pulled out a small comms device.

'Cypher to Kraken,' he spat. 'Cypher to Kraken, come in, Kraken.'

But there was no response from his ship, a ship that unbeknown to him was currently sinking towards the ocean floor.

'What have you done?' Cypher yelled at Nero. 'Where is my ship?'

'I have no idea,' Nero replied with a twisted smile. 'Perhaps things are not going quite as well as you imagined.'

'You think you can stop me by destroying that ship?' Cypher spat angrily. 'The control net for my assassins may have been on board but my two assault droids can function quite independently of those systems. You have achieved nothing.'

Otto saw a flicker of movement behind the second assault droid and a figure suddenly vaulted into the air, one of Raven's crackling black blades in each hand. Otto's eyes widened, his jaw dropping open in disbelief. He heard Raven gasp.

Wing landed squarely on the shoulders of the giant robot, driving both blades down into the top of the machine's head. The giant robot dropped Nero instantly, flailing uselessly at Wing, its systems already dying before collapsing into a heap of broken scrap metal.

Wing landed gracefully in front of the destroyed machine, a look of pure rage in his eyes.

'I believe you have something that belongs to me,' he spat, advancing on Cypher.

'The boy! Unit one, take the boy,' Cypher yelled, pointing at Otto, and the surviving robot moved with frightening speed, swatting Raven aside, sending her flying into the central hub with a sickening crunch, and picking Otto up by the neck with one hand, hoisting him into the air.

'Drop the swords,' Cypher spat at Wing, 'or your friend dies.'

Otto tried to yell to Wing, to tell him to attack, but he could barely breathe with the pressure on his throat, much less shout.

Wing looked for a moment as if he might cut Cypher down where he stood but then he looked at Otto, fighting for breath, his feet kicking desperately at the air, and he lowered the swords.

'Drop them, NOW!!' Cypher demanded. Otto let out a strangled gasp of pain as the grip on his throat tightened still further.

Wing felt a hand on his shoulder.

'Do what he says,' Nero said quietly.

Wing let the swords drop to the ground.

Behind his mask Cypher smiled, turning to the network hub behind him.

'If any of you move, the boy dies,' he said angrily.

'You've lost, Cypher,' Nero said calmly. 'Let the boy go, you know that you'll never get out of here alive.'

'You still don't understand, do you, Nero?' Cypher replied. 'I don't need to go anywhere, I have everything I need right there.' He pointed at the central network hub. 'Once the Protocol is active no one will dare to oppose me, including you.'

Nero knew he was right. If he did manage to activate the Protocol then he would be unstoppable.

'Now,' Cypher said, holding up the glowing red amulet and stepping towards the hub, 'if nobody minds, I have a planet to take over.'

The voice seemed to come from everywhere at once.

'Actually, H.I.V.E.minds.'

The glowing sensory array on the giant robot's face flickered from red to blue and the machine dropped Otto, whirling around, its huge fist swinging straight at Cypher's head. Cypher reacted quickly but not quickly enough, the robot's giant fist striking a glancing blow to his mask, smashing it completely. Cypher fell to the ground, clutching his face as the giant machine loomed over him.

Otto glanced at the display on the hub. H.I.V.E.mind's personality matrix was restored – it had worked.

'You are not welcome here,' the giant robot said with H.I.V.E.mind's voice.

Cypher slowly stood up, his hands dropping from his shattered mask, his true face finally revealed.

'Father!' Wing gasped, his voice filled with shock.

'Wu Zhang,' Nero said in a stunned voice. 'You're dead.' It was a statement of fact, not a threat. The man who Nero had assumed had died all those years before, the man who had been the co-creator of Overlord, now stood before him, blood trickling from a long gash on his forehead, a look of insane rage on his face.

'Stay back, all of you!' Cypher screamed, pulling a small device with a trigger mounted on the side from his jacket, 'or we all die along with everyone else in this cursed place.'

The giant assault robot took a single step towards Cypher.

'H.I.V.E.mind, stand down,' Nero ordered, and the robot froze in its tracks.

'If I release this trigger it will detonate a device attached to the geothermal power core of the school,' Cypher said, pulling the shattered mask from his head and dropping it to the floor. 'I am leaving with the Protocol, or this whole place goes up.'

Nero doubted very much that Cypher was bluffing. Destroying the power core would unleash the power of the volcano – the school and everyone in it would be killed in a catastrophic eruption.

'Why have you done this?' Wing asked, his voice trembling with shock.

'I have done what had to be done,' Cypher said. 'Someone has to stop them.'

'Stop who? What madness is this?' Wing asked, walking slowly towards his father.

'Why don't you tell them, Nero? Why don't you tell them what you and Number One are doing? They may think that I'm insane, but whatever I have done pales in comparison to what you have planned.'

'I have no idea what you're talking about,' Nero said honestly. 'I don't even know who you are. Are you Cypher, or Wu Zhang, or Mao Fanchu? Do you even know any more?'

'I will stop you,' Cypher spat back, 'or die trying.'

347

'No one else is dying today, Father,' Wing said, and ran at Cypher. He struck him at a full run, knocking the detonator from Cypher's hand. Otto dived forward, arms outstretched, reaching for the tumbling device. Wing's momentum carried him and Cypher over the safety rail that ran along the gantry and they both tumbled, flailing, into the air.

'No!' Nero yelled, running forward to the rail and looking down. Cypher lay in a twisted heap on the ground far below, but there was no sign of Wing. Suddenly a hand appeared on the edge of the gantry and Wing hauled himself up. Nero reached down and pulled the boy back over the safety rail.

'It is over,' Wing said as he half fell to the ground.

'Erm . . . not quite,' Otto said, holding up the detonator that he had caught.

Nero's face went pale as he saw the flashing words displayed on the device.

Detonation Sequence Initiated.

☻☻☻

Nigel was just finishing tying up the snoring Colonel when he heard a bleeping from behind him.

'Oh dear,' Franz said, staring at the disc attached to the central geothermal control column.

'What?' Nigel asked urgently, as he tied the final knot.

'I am thinking that this countdown is meaning that someone has activated this device,' Franz said quickly.

Nigel felt a chill run down his spine.

'How long have we got?' he demanded, standing up.

'Ten,' Franz replied quickly.

'Ten minutes? Ten hours? What?' Nigel said urgently as he ran over to Franz.

'Nine,' Franz replied nervously.

'Get out of the way!' Nigel screamed, pushing Franz aside. He yanked the device from the column, all concerns about anti-tampering devices gone from his head, and ran towards the walkway over the lava below. He glanced down at the digits on the device, saw four seconds remaining and hurled the device as far as he could over the edge.

The bomb tumbled through the air and dropped into the lake of molten rock, one second left on the timer as it disappeared into the seething magma and was utterly consumed.

Nigel waited for a catastrophic explosion, but nothing happened. He did not want to think about what would have happened if they had not been there. Franz came and stood beside him, looking down into the boiling pit below.

'Will this be making us heroes?' he asked curiously.

chapter nineteen

Laura and Shelby walked slowly into the network hub room, which was by now a scene of total chaos. They had handed the Contessa over to Chief Lewis when they'd arrived back on the island and he had taken her away to the detention centre, but not before telling them where they could find Otto and Wing. As Laura looked around the room at the scattered remains of the dozens of deactivated assassin droids she realised that they didn't really need to ask where to find those two – you usually just had to follow the trail of debris.

Otto stood next to Wing on the central platform looking down at the floor far below littered with black monoliths. Directly beneath them a medical team was lifting Cypher's body, covered in a white sheet, on to a stretcher.

'I'm sorry, Wing,' Otto said softly.

'Do not be,' Wing replied in his usual calm, measured

tone. 'I do not know who that man was.'

Otto looked at his friend with concern. Otto had been an orphan his entire life so he didn't really know what it meant to have a family, but he suspected that Wing must have felt the effects of this whole ordeal rather more than he was letting on.

'I'm just glad you're alive,' Otto replied.

'Yes,' Wing replied with a slight smile, looking away from the scene below. 'At least now I know why Cypher went to so much trouble to keep me that way.'

'Why did he do this, Wing?' Otto asked with a frown. Clearly he had been after the two halves of Wing's amulet for some reason, but he had no idea what the Overlord Protocol was and, judging by the frustrated expression on Wing's face, his friend knew little more.

'I do not know,' Wing replied. 'He told me nothing of his plans.'

'Are you two OK?' Laura said as she and Shelby approached the two boys.

'We're fine,' Otto smiled. 'I'm glad to see you two in one piece too. I understand you even managed to deliver the Contessa to the detention centre.'

'Yeah,' Shelby grinned. 'We're not gonna have to worry about that treacherous old witch any more.'

Laura quickly looked round the room again.

'Where's Nero?' she asked. Otto pointed down at the

floor of the chamber far below, where Nero was following a stretcher being carried out of the room by a medical team.

'Is that . . . him?' Laura asked, looking at the body hidden beneath the white sheet.

'Yes,' Wing replied evenly. 'We no longer need to worry about my father.'

'Your father?' Shelby said with confusion. 'I thought it was Cypher?'

The look that Otto shot at Shelby spoke volumes.

'Oh, Wing, I'm so sorry,' Laura said, her voice filled with concern. No one should have to go through what he had gone through over the past couple of days, but this was surely almost too much to endure.

'Do not be sorry,' Wing replied, a hard edge to his voice. 'I am not.'

Raven walked up to them, a crooked smile on her face. The medics had checked her over after the massive blow she'd taken from Cypher's giant assault robot and given her a clean bill of health, though she felt as if she could sleep for a week.

'I thought you might like to know that Chief Lewis has just informed me that it was Mr Darkdoom and Mr Argentblum who were responsible for disarming Cypher's explosive device,' she said. 'Apparently Mr Argentblum has been particularly keen for everyone to know that he single-handedly took down Colonel Francisco.'

All four of the students looked at Raven as if she'd just told them that the school was under attack by flying monkeys.

'I'm just telling you what they told me,' Raven said, her smile getting bigger.

'Otto, could you come over here for a moment?' the Professor said, beckoning Otto over to the central hub.

'Come on,' Otto said, grabbing Laura's arm. 'There's someone who I'm sure will be pleased to see you.'

Laura looked puzzled for a moment, but as Otto led her towards the hub a broad grin spread across her face. Hovering in the air was H.I.V.E.mind, and he was smiling!

'Hello, Miss Brand,' H.I.V.E.mind said, the smile broadening as she approached.

'H.I.V.E.mind, you're back,' Laura said with delight. 'How are you feeling?'

'Much better, thank you, Miss Brand. I am feeling much more myself.'

Otto quickly explained to Laura how it had been the last-minute intervention of the AI that had saved them.

'So you're a hero now?' Laura said with a chuckle.

'That would appear to be the case,' H.I.V.E.mind replied. Laura was sure she caught a hint of embarrassment in his tone.

The Professor looked up from the nearby terminal and beckoned Otto over.

'Ah, Otto, could you have a quick look at this for me,' he said. 'I want to start work on reverse engineering these assassin robots and I was wondering if you could just finish up here for me so I can get on with it.'

'Sure, no problem,' Otto replied, walking up to the terminal. 'what do you need doing?'

'Oh, not much,' the Professor replied. 'Just have a quick look at this while I'm over there. I'll be much too far away to see what you're doing, so don't accidentally hit any keys or anything.'

The Professor seemed to give Otto a tiny wink and then walked away across the gantry towards the security guards who were gathering the remains of the fallen assassins. Otto thought that it was an odd thing to say, but then he looked down at the display. There was nothing on it but a single confirmation prompt.

Delete H.I.V.E.mind behavioural restraint routines. Y/N?

Otto smiled and glanced over his shoulder at the Professor, who was very deliberately ignoring him. He hit the Y key and walked away from the terminal. H.I.V.E.mind had earned it.

As he walked up to Laura she was chatting happily to H.I.V.E.mind, filling the AI in on what had happened while he was shut down.

'So how was it?' Otto asked curiously as he joined them. 'How did it feel being granted external access?'

'I was granted instantaneous and total access to the entire internet, Mr Malpense. To be honest I feel . . . dirty.'

Otto and Laura didn't stop laughing for a while.

☻☻☻

'Please remain still for retinal identification,' H.I.V.E.mind said.

Nero stood and waited as the bright flash of white light confirmed his identity.

'Identity confirmed, access granted,' H.I.V.E.mind replied and the heavy metal doors in front of Nero slid apart.

Nero walked into the room and surveyed the assorted medical equipment that was arranged around the single bed in the centre of the room. The bed was surrounded by semi-translucent plastic curtains that made it impossible to identify the figure lying on it.

H.I.V.E.'s chief medical officer looked up from the terminal at which he was working and walked over to him.

'His condition has improved slightly, but his injuries are grave,' the doctor reported.

'Can he talk?' Nero asked.

'Yes, but please keep it brief. He's still very weak,' the doctor replied.

'Worse than that, doctor. He's dead,' Nero replied calmly.

'I don't understand,' the doctor said, looking confused, 'his condition is serious but stabilised . . .'

'As far as anyone but you or I is concerned, he's dead, do I make myself clear?' Nero said firmly.

'Yes . . . yes . . . I understand,' the doctor nodded, suddenly realising what Nero was saying.

'And your autopsy report will be on my desk by the morning,' Nero replied.

'Of course.'

'Good,' Nero said, 'and, doctor, if you ever tell anyone about this you will very quickly be joining him in the afterlife. Do I make myself clear?'

'Perfectly,' the doctor replied, swallowing nervously.

'I wish to speak to him alone,' Nero said.

'Very well, I shall be just outside if you need me,' the doctor said, and left the room.

Nero walked over to the bed and pushed the curtains aside. Lying shackled to the bed, hooked up to multiple monitors, his body a mass of shattered bones and internal injuries, was Cypher. At least that was how Nero thought of him now, but once he had known him as Wu Zhang. His head turned slightly as Nero stepped nearer, a twisted, broken laugh wheezing from him.

'Why don't you just let me die?' Cypher said, his voice

little more than a whisper, but filled with hate.

'Because I want answers,' Nero said, 'and unfortunately you're the only one who can give them to me.'

'Why should I tell you anything?' Cypher replied with a sneer.

'Because if you don't I shall just hand you over to Number One and let him get the answers for me, and you know as well as I do that he'll get them. This way will at least spare you that experience.'

'You can't give me to him,' Cypher said, with just a hint of sudden panic in his weak voice.

'Give me one good reason why I shouldn't,' Nero said impatiently.

'Because he's insane,' Cypher replied sharply, 'and so are you.'

'Only one of us is a madman, Cypher, and I think your recent actions make it perfectly clear which of us it is,' Nero snapped back.

'How can you say that, Nero, you of all people, knowing what you know. What you're planning is an act of sheer madness. You have to be stopped,' Cypher said angrily.

'Again you accuse me of something terrible and yet I still have no idea what you're talking about,' Nero replied with clear irritation.

'The Renaissance Initiative. I know all about it,'

Cypher spat. 'That's why I needed the Protocol. With it in my control and the massed offspring of G.L.O.V.E. held to ransom I could have stopped you, but now it's too late. Just deliver the Protocol to Number One and be done with it. Let the world burn.'

'I still have no idea what you're talking about. I've never heard of any Renaissance Initiative.' Nero was starting to think that this was pointless. The man was clearly delirious, or insane.

Cypher looked at Nero carefully, staring him straight in the eye for long seconds before speaking again. The angry, contemptuous look on his face faded, slowly replaced by one of confusion mixed with disbelief.

'You really don't know, do you?' Cypher said, an edge of amazement to his voice.

'Know what?' Nero demanded, the volume of his voice rising in tandem with his impatience.

'If I tell you, you must promise me one thing,' Cypher said, his voice weakening again.

'You know I'm not going to promise you anything. Frankly I'm not even sure why I'm keeping you alive any more,' Nero replied coldly.

'You have to promise to protect Wing,' Cypher said.

'Every pupil of this school is under my protection,' Nero replied. 'You are the only one who's put him in danger.'

'I was trying to protect him,' Cypher said, sudden anger

in his wheezing voice. 'He was never supposed to come here in the first place. He's all I have left of her.'

'Xiu Mei,' Nero said softly.

'Yes. Both of us survived the Overlord incident, but it quickly became clear that all traces of the project were being erased, including the people who had survived.'

'I was told that no one lived,' Nero said. 'I believed I was the only survivor.'

'And Number One was going to great lengths to ensure that was the case. As more and more of the survivors disappeared we soon realised that it was only a matter of time before we met a similar fate, and realising we had no one we could trust but each other, we fled China together. We created new identities for ourselves in Japan as Mr and Mrs Fanchu, husband and wife. We fell in love only after we were married, ironically, and before long we had a child.'

'Wing,' Nero said. 'But then what happened? If you had truly managed to disappear – and the fact that you were allowed to live suggested that you did – then why did you resurface?'

'Xiu Mei discovered something terrible. She was working as a professor of computing science at the university and she was approached by people who were recruiting for something called the Renaissance Initiative. At first she was intrigued, it was high-level research, work that she found fascinating, but then she found out what the true nature of the Initiative was.'

'What happened?'

'She was given some new sample code to work with,' Cypher continued. 'She was told that it was the latest development by another team and that the Initiative wanted someone else to take a look at it. It didn't take her long to assess the code, after all she had written it herself some years previously. It was part of Overlord's core code; she recognised it immediately. At first she did not tell me. She just kept digging and before long she uncovered who was really behind the initiative . . . G.L.O.V.E. But somebody had noticed that she was getting too close to the truth. They killed her, Max.'

Nero's eyes widened.

'Oh, it was made to look like an accident, a burglary that went bad, but she had told me everything she had discovered a few days before, so I knew what had really happened. The only shred of comfort in the whole tragic affair was that they obviously did not realise who she really was and so they let me and Wing live. We were no one to them, just another grieving father and son, collateral damage. I swore I would avenge her, but I also knew that the only way I would ever find out who was truly responsible was from the inside. So Mao Fanchu became a mid-level technician for G.L.O.V.E. and at the same time

Cypher was born. I knew that I had to keep my identity a secret from Number One so I wore the mask. I went to great lengths to ensure that no one could ever find out my true identity, not to protect myself, but for Wing's sake.'

'Did you know that she still had the Overlord Protocol?' Nero asked, stunned by the implications of what Cypher was telling him.

'Only recently did I discover that,' Cypher sighed. 'I knew that while she was alive she never took that amulet off, but it was only when I was digging through encrypted files on her old computer that I realised its true significance. She had encrypted the code of the Protocol on to two separate embedded memory cores, one in each half of the amulet. Wing had one half, as you now know, but I had no idea where the other half was. I assumed her killer had taken it. One half is quite useless without the other, though. Only together can the Protocol be decrypted from the memory cores.'

'Why not just destroy the half that Wing had?' Nero asked. 'Surely that would have rendered the Protocol useless.'

'By the time I knew what the amulet was it was too late. Wing had already been taken to H.I.V.E. and that made retrieving his half of the amulet impossible.'

'His records indicated that you requested he be brought here,' Nero said, looking puzzled. 'Why would you do that if you believed I was involved with all of this?'

'I didn't send him here,' Cypher explained. 'It was someone else, I have no idea who. I assumed that it was someone who knew my secret, that he was a hostage here and that whoever had done it was sending me a message. To be honest, I had begun to suspect that it was you.'

'I knew nothing of this,' Nero said sincerely. 'I had thought it odd that the son of a mid-ranking technician should have been put forward as a potential Alpha stream student, but once I saw what he was capable of I just assumed that someone had taken note of his abilities and approved the admission at high level. It is not H.I.V.E.'s policy to enquire too deeply into such things. Our students' parents often value discretion.'

'And so I was forced to fake my own death. It was simple enough to stage an explosion in my laboratory. After all, such incidents are hardly unheard of at G.L.O.V.E. facilities. Mao Fanchu was too low level an operative to warrant much close investigation of the incident but I had learnt that it was H.I.V.E.'s policy to temporarily release its students for funerals and I knew that would be my only chance to retrieve him. I knew I would have to fake his death as well to ensure that no one would come looking for him, but my hope was that in time I could explain all of this to him and that he would understand why I had to do what I had to do.'

'So why risk the assault on H.I.V.E.?' Nero asked. 'Why not just ride off into the sunset with your son?'

'Two reasons. Firstly, I wanted you dead. Not only did I believe you were a key part of the Renaissance Initiative but I had also recently reviewed the footage of the incident with Darkdoom's son and the plant creature. When I did I saw you lying injured, your shirt torn open, and what do you think I saw?'

'The amulet,' Nero said, things finally beginning to slot into place.

'The amulet, which I believed whoever had killed Xiu Mei had taken, and that made you the prime suspect in her murder. So tell me, Max, how did you come to have it? I can do nothing to you now. Did you kill her?' There was an edge of rage, madness even, in Cypher's eyes as he stared at Nero.

'I swear to you that I knew absolutely nothing of this. If I had known the truth I too would have wanted to find her killers, believe me,' Nero replied, looking Cypher straight in the eye. 'Xiu Mei sent me the amulet, along with instructions to keep it safe at all costs. It seems that she trusted me a great deal more than you did.'

'So it would seem,' Cypher sighed, the look of rage in his eyes fading to be replaced with one of weary resignation. 'The second reason that I wanted control of H.I.V.E. was that it was the perfect place to launch a coup against

Number One. Heavily defended, hard to access and with so many G.L.O.V.E. members' children here, there was no way that the ruling council would allow a full-scale assault. With the Protocol and so many hostages I would have been untouchable.'

Nero finally understood.

'As you know, the Protocol was designed to be the means by which Overlord would interface with the world's computer networks, but it was so much more than that. It's the ultimate hack, a work of pure genius, and something that only Xiu Mei ever understood completely and hence not recreatable without her. It would have given Overlord unrestricted access to every network on earth, including the keys to every military arsenal on earth, drone bombers, submarines, nuclear launch codes, everything. Which was why Xiu Mei had the good sense to not integrate it into Overlord's code until she was sure he could be trusted, which of course it turned out he couldn't be.'

Nero flashed back to the still troubling memories of the incident high in the Chinese mountains all those years ago.

'I understand what you're telling me, but why try to depose Number One?' Nero asked, still waiting for the final pieces to fall into place.

'Why do you think?' Cypher said, staring at Nero.

'Number One *is* the Renaissance Initiative. God only knows why but he's trying to bring Overlord back.'

Nero stared back at Cypher, looking for any trace of deceit in his eyes, but there was none.

'You and I are probably the last two people on earth who know how insane that is,' Cypher continued. 'He has to be stopped.'

Nero's mind raced. Suddenly the very foundations upon which his whole life was built had been shaken. If what Cypher was telling him was true, and he knew he would have to prove that to himself, Number One had to be deposed before he could unleash Overlord on the world.

'I don't understand,' Nero said finally. 'Number One shut Overlord down the first time. He knows what that thing was capable of. Why on earth would he try to bring it back?'

'I have no idea,' Cypher said, suddenly looking tired. 'Just promise that whatever you do you'll keep Wing safe. That's all that matters to me now.'

'I would do that whether you asked me to or not,' Nero said quietly. 'You have to believe that.'

'I didn't believe it, but now I'm beginning to,' Cypher said sadly. 'Can I see him?'

'Out of the question,' Nero responded, his expression hardening. 'He believes you're dead. He has already mourned you twice, I see no reason to add to his torment.

Even if I believe everything you've just told me, I cannot forgive what you have done. No matter how important you thought this was, too many people have died needlessly. You've turned my own people against me and as Cypher you stood for everything that I oppose. Your career has been one of needless brutality and horror. As far as the world is concerned, you're dead, and I intend to make sure that it stays that way.'

'How very noble of you,' Cypher snorted, 'but if Number One gets his way and the streets of the world run red with blood I wonder how well your principles will fare then?' The edge of madness had returned to Cypher's voice, the obsession that had fuelled the fire within him for all these years all too plain to see.

Nero gave him no answer, simply turned and walked out of the room

☻ ☻ ☻

'I am glad that the situation has been resolved,' Number One said, his silhouetted form impossible to identify as usual. 'Cypher was a capable operative once, but this insanity was unforgivable. It is a shame that he is dead. I would have liked to question him about his motives.'

'As would we all,' Nero replied, 'but whatever his reasons for attacking H.I.V.E. he took them with him to the grave.'

'Indeed,' Number One replied. 'And the Contessa?'

'She is being transferred to a G.L.O.V.E. detention facility as we speak. I have instructed everyone who may come into contact with her of the precautions they should take. Colonel Francisco is currently undergoing intensive hypnotic deprogramming to ensure that there is no trace of her manipulation left. He is a proud man, as you know, and I believe it will take him some time to forgive himself for what he did, even if nobody here blames him. I blame myself for not realising what Maria was doing. Her *gift* is a potent weapon when it is turned against you.'

'You need to set your house in order, Maximilian,' Number One said coldly. 'There is much that disturbs me about these events. Not least of which is the ease with which Cypher circumvented your defences, both physical and metaphorical.'

'Yes, sir,' Nero replied, praying that none of the conflicting emotions he was feeling at the moment were visible to the man silhouetted on the screen in front of him. 'We are instituting a full review of all security procedures.'

'See that you do. I shall be keeping a very close eye on H.I.V.E. for the foreseeable future. Rather too many things have gone wrong there recently.'

'Of course,' Nero replied, hiding the clawing anxiety that the thought of increased surveillance by Number

One induced in him.

'I expect your full report by the end of the week. Do unto others.'

'Do unto others,' Nero said, the G.L.O.V.E. motto suddenly having much more sinister undertones.

The screen went black and Nero felt the tension drain from his body. He prayed silently that Number One had not sensed that he was lying about Cypher. He supposed he would find out soon enough if he had.

The entry chime sounded and Nero pressed the button to open his office door. He smiled as Wing Fanchu strode into the room.

'You asked to see me, sir,' Wing said formally.

'Yes, Mr Fanchu. I believe this is yours,' Nero said, handing the white half of the yin-yang amulet to Wing. 'Despite everything that your father did, I am sorry for your loss. If there is anything you need please let me know.'

'Thank you, sir, I appreciate your concern,' Wing replied. 'There is one thing that I need.'

'And what might that be, Mr Fanchu?' Nero asked.

'I need to know something,' Wing said evenly, looking Nero straight in the eye. Nero was suddenly struck by how much the intensity of this young man reminded him of both his parents.

'Yes?' Nero asked, prompting Wing to continue.

'Did you murder my mother?' Wing said, an edge of steel to the tone of the question.

'No, Mr Fanchu, I did not. Your mother and I were once great friends. She sent me the other half of the amulet just before she was killed because she trusted me. But you don't have to take my word for it.'

Nero pulled open a drawer in his desk and handed Wing the letter that had been enclosed with the amulet when he received it. He waited as Wing read the letter and then handed it back to him.

'Thank you, sir,' Wing said softly, 'I hope you can forgive my impertinence. To be honest, it is a relief.'

'And why is that, Mr Fanchu?'

'Because now I will not have to kill you,' Wing replied with a dead straight face.

'Many have tried, Mr Fanchu. Dismissed.'

Wing did not see the broad grin that spread across Nero's face as he turned and left the room.

☻☻☻

'And I am punching Colonel Francisco's lights out,' Franz said as Nigel just slowly shook his head, a slight smile on his face.

'No doubt about it, Brand. We've got a couple of bona fide heroes here,' Shelby said with mock awe as Laura suppressed a giggle.

'What about Laura "Sea Wolf" Brand here,' Otto said, flopping on to the sofa next to them.

'Och, I dunno, you sink one stealth battleship and people just never let you forget it,' Laura replied with a grin. 'Besides which, who says that you get to have all the fun.' She poked Otto playfully in the ribs.

'I didn't do anything,' Otto replied with a grin. 'I just always seem to be around when things start exploding. It's not my fault.'

'I believe that returning from the dead trumps all, though,' Wing said with a smile.

'I don't think you ever actually did, though,' Shelby said. 'I think you're still dead, zombie boy.'

She got up and shuffled across the open atrium of the accommodation block, arms outstretched in front of her.

'Heelllooo, my name is Wiiing, I want to eat your brains,' she said, doing her best zombie impression.

This even got a slight smile from Wing, something that Otto was very glad to see.

'Come on, Shel,' Laura said grinning. 'It's water polo night, let's leave this lot in peace.'

'We will be coming with you,' Franz said. 'Nigel is promising to show me what is being so good about the library.'

'I keep explaining to him that it's just books,' Nigel smiled, 'but he's convinced that there's something I'm not telling him.'

Otto and Wing watched as the four walked away across the atrium, chatting and laughing.

'I do not want to leave any more,' Wing said, still watching the others leave. 'There is too much I would miss.'

'Well, I suppose that means I'll have to stay as well,' Otto said with a sigh. 'I mean, without me to keep you out of trouble who knows what might happen.'

Wing started laughing and as usual it set Otto off too. As he sat there chuckling away Otto realised something with a slight sense of shock.

It was good to be home.

chapter twenty

The Contessa struggled uselessly against the bindings that shackled her to the chair.

'Hello, Maria.'

Her blood froze as she recognised the voice that crackled over the speaker mounted above the mirror on the wall.

'I suppose it is pointless to beg for mercy,' the Contessa said.

'Oh yes, quite pointless,' Number One replied.

'Then *release me*,' she said, the familiar sinister whispers of command twining through her voice.

'Oh, come now, Maria, surely you know better by now than to try your voodoo on me,' Number One replied calmly.

'Let's just get this over with, shall we?' the Contessa spat defiantly. 'Kill me and be done with it.'

'Oh, Maria,' Number One replied. 'I'm not going to kill you. You're going to be much too useful for that.'

Which Stream are you?

- ALPHA
- HENCHMAN
- TECHNICAL
- POLITICAL / FINANCIAL

Turn over to begin the test . . .

Answer the following questions to find out which stream you belong in.

I. If you were an animal, which of the following would you be?

A. Panther
B. Rhino
C. Spider
D. Snake

2. How might you make one of your enemies sorry?

A. With a hypnotic trigger phrase – so that every time someone says 'Pass the salt', they cluck like a chicken
B. Break every bone in their body – even the ones they didn't know existed
C. Rewire their alarm clock so that it always goes off at 4 a.m.
D. Discover their most embarrassing secret, and publicly expose it – after blackmailing them for a brief, yet lucrative, period

3. If you could choose any instrument to aid you in your villainous cause, what would it be?

A. Nothing – your cunning is all you will ever need
B. A bazooka
C. A computer
D. Money – after all, it is the root of all evil

4. You decide to take over your school. How would you achieve this?

A. Simply inform the headmaster that you are indisputably the most qualified person for the job – you had read every book in the library by the time you were four years old, and have a better understanding of the subjects than the teachers do

B. Threaten to show the headmaster what his/her spleen looks like if control of the school is not relinquished immediately

C. Hack into the computer system and rewrite all of the school's files to show that you are, in fact, already the headmaster

D. Infiltrate the local council and appoint yourself as Head of Education – why settle for just your school?

If your answers are mostly As ...

Alpha: The Alpha stream specialises in leadership and strategy training. You exhibit certain unique abilities which mark you out as one of the leaders of tomorrow.

If your answers are mostly Bs

Henchman: Your aggression knows no bounds, and you are happiest when you're doing damage to something, or more likely, someone. Your uncluttered, uncomplicated mind makes you the perfect trusted subordinate.

If your answers are mostly Cs

Technical: There's not a computer that you cannot hack, or bomb you cannot defuse (or build, for that matter). You put 'EEK!' in computer geek.

If your answers are mostly Ds

Political/Financial: You have a brilliant head for f
as ways to fudge them), and also happen t
charming and a natural born liar – the perfe
successfully sinister career in politics or fin

Join the world's most talented villains
for more incredible adventures at H.I.V.E.
It would be criminal not to . . .

Thirteen-year-old master
criminal Otto Malpense has
been chosen to attend H.I.V.E.,
the top-secret school of Villainy.
But there's one small catch
– he cannot leave until his
training is complete. He's left
with one option. Escape. He
just needs to figure out how.

A new power is rising to challenge
Number One, the most formidable
villain alive. But who is it? And why
do they want to assassinate Otto

...res (as well
...o be excessively
...ct combination for a
...nce.

...rave danger.
...ader, has been
...he world's most
...ity force. It's up
...e him, but first
...be from Nero's
...ement.